POLAR DAY 9

Public reaction proceeded at first with chaos then with the coherence of an unstoppable tragedy... Switchboards jammed; anxious crowds began to gather in front of city halls, churches and temples, and in government centers. And people accustomed to blizzards and hurricanes wasted no time. By 9:00 P.M. they had cleaned out the few open drugstores of their supply of insulin, vitamins, first aid kits; the overnight supermarkets of their canned goods, baby food, pasta...

On the following day, the National Guard was called out as a crowd control force.

Praise for Kyle Donner
and *Polar Day 9*:

"Kyle Donner has launched a new breed [of thriller]: the environmental techno-thriller... and a damned exciting one it is. Taut... absorbing."

—Earl W. Foell,
World Monitor magazine

"Just as Jules Verne brilliantly used fiction to anticipate that which later became reality, so Kyle Donner paints with imagination and authority a vivid environmental scenario which governments and international agencies will soon be hastening to catch up with."

—Professor Lincoln Bloomfield,
Former White House Global
Issues Director

WORLD OF BOOKS
WE BUY & SELL
140 HURONTARIO ST.
COLLINGWOOD, ONT.
PHONE 445-6101

POLAR DAY 9

KYLE DONNER

DIAMOND BOOKS, NEW YORK

This book is a Diamond original edition,
and has never been previously published.

POLAR DAY 9

A Diamond Book/published by arrangement with
the author

PRINTING HISTORY
Diamond edition/May 1993

ISBN: 1-55773-894-7

Diamond Books are published by The Berkley Publishing Group,
200 Madison Avenue, New York, NY 10016.
The name "DIAMOND" and its logo
are trademarks belonging to Charter Communications, Inc.

PRINTED IN THE UNITED STATES OF AMERICA

10 9 8 7 6 5 4 3 2 1

This novel is dedicated to three special people: Delia, my wife; Michael Rybarski, my literary agent; Andrew Zack, my editor.

ACKNOWLEDGMENTS

A novel is like a cathedral. It requires the cooperation of many. The list of names of those who have contributed to the writing of *Polar Day 9* would make up a book of its own. Nevertheless, I must express my gratitude to the following:

Pamela Painter, Department of Creative Writing and Journalism, Harvard University School of Continuing Education; Dr. William Daniels, Department of English, Southwestern University; Rick Frankusty of Digital Corporation; the engineers and the public relations staff of the Pilgrim Nuclear Power Plant, Plymouth, Massachusetts; Professor Thomas Sheridan, Center for Information-Driven Mechanical Systems, M.I.T.; John Kean of Kean Incorporated, Boston, Massachusetts; Anthony Nesto, of Sanders Electronics; Richard Chandler, coordinator of the *Alvin,* Woods Hole Oceanographic Institution; Captain Richard Edwards, Skipper of the *Knorr,* Woods Hole Oceanographic Institution; Matthew Abbate and Melissa Vaughn of M.I.T. Press; Creon Levit, Ames Research Center, NASA; Eric Howlett and Greg Rivera, of LEEP Virtual Reality Systems, Waltham, Massachusetts; the staff of South Shore Skin Divers, Inc., of Weymouth, Massachusetts.

The source of man's unhappiness is his ignorance of Nature . . . one that will doom him to continual error.

—PAUL HENRY THIRY D'HOLBACH

1

George Dunlap, only seven years away from full retirement, could still remember the day the men from the Army Corps of Engineers turned over operation of the Locke Dam to the county water authority. For eight years, the dam had provided the local men with hard work and the best wages that could be earned in Idaho.

With the wonderment of a small boy, Dunlap had stood with his father at the commemoration of the new dam. The governor had come to speak. He told the people how the dam meant a better way of life for Locke County, how it would provide for improved irrigation of farmlands and increased crops. And the people had been pleased; they were proud of their new dam.

Dunlap often thought of that day as he completed his rounds on Locke Dam. For thirty years he'd been a security guard, guarding access to the dam's floodgate control systems and scaring off the few high schoolers with the artistic inclination to mar the dam's high walls with neon-colored spray paint. George Dunlap was as at home walking the Locke Dam as he was walking through his own living room.

Of course it didn't rain in his living room.

God, will it ever end? thought Dunlap as he toured the base of the dam for the third time in his shift. For days, the rain had fallen heavily and without pause, at first bringing welcome relief to the parched, drought-plagued county, but quickly bringing the many dry streambeds back to life and beyond, flooding roadways and basements, and leaving the state engineers more than a bit concerned about the old Locke Dam's ability to restrain the floodwaters that had filled Locke Reservoir nearly to capacity for the first time in a decade.

Dunlap ran his hand along the smooth concrete, as familiar to him as the curve of his wife's hip, though for a moment he thought something seemed different. *Just all this rain,* he thought, *washing all the dust off the old girl.* He was nearly halfway across the base when it began.

A religious man, Dunlap couldn't help but think of Jericho as the Locke Dam crumbled. Dunlap was spared the torment of drowning in the cold water; the pressure of thousands of cubic feet of water being suddenly released crushed him before he took his next breath.

Looming well over twenty feet high, and laden with massive chunks of concrete from the broken dam, a surging wall of water flowed into the Locke River channel.

From the river channel, it entered Spring Mountain valley, already supersaturated with torrential rain, and banked sharply left and over the Route 28 bridge, swallowing it whole. It then tore up a mile-long strip of evergreens before reaching Knutson's Farm. Six horses, eighteen cows, and two John Deere tractors were carried away like children's toys.

Gathering momentum, the whirling mass of water rose to the height of a tidal wave, engulfing Anaconda Industrial Park and the Pioneer Lumber Mill and releasing hundreds of gallons of PVCs and other toxic chemicals. Raw logs and finished lumber floated like matchsticks in the torrent.

Approaching thirty feet in height and carrying tons of debris, the wave swallowed Red Rock Road and headed in the direction of the Osgood County Junior High School, some five hundred yards away.

At Osgood, young cheerleaders in blue-and-white uniforms faced a crowd of nearly two hundred families watching their team break the school record for wins in a season.

"Give me an—"

A dusty charge of compressed air, like that preceding a locomotive barreling through a tunnel, struck the north side of Osgood's gymnasium. Few took notice as the building groaned and the brick wall bowed nearly two full inches. When the wave of water slammed against it full force, the wall imploded. Shattered brick and mortar flew in all directions like shrapnel. Darkness fell as the electrical systems shorted out in a blazing flash of bluish light, filling the air with the stench of ozone.

The cries of many rose in one single scream. Then there was nothing. In only ten seconds the seething rush of water and debris filled the gym, carrying parents and children from the bleachers as the building around them collapsed. Without pause, the water continued to carve its path through Spring Mountain valley, rolling school buses over and toppling Eggar Farm's corn silos.

Still towering, but with a white cap of spray frothing at its top, the wave bulldozed its way through Idaho Light and Power's substation, throwing all of Locke County into darkness.

Nearly an hour after George Dunlap died, the reservoir itself began to move as its base of silt and sediment, accumulated over decades, started to flow over the remnants of the broken dam. Gray as clay and soft as quicksand, the mud flowed over the valley like mindless lava from an erupting volcano.

Shortly before sunrise, the onlookers—survivors—who had reached safety in the hills overlooking the valley began to realize what had befallen Locke County. A swath of death and destruction more than a half mile wide had been cut through the valley beneath them. Bright yellow school buses lay buried; trees, bleachers, and farm animals were far more discernible amid the carnage than the smaller bodies of the hundreds of parents and children who died in the flood.

"Oh, my God!" a woman wailed. "They're not moving. *None* of them are moving!"

For three days, rescue helicopters overflew the area, searching for survivors. The mud, up to six feet deep in places, had been contaminated with toxic chemicals and tons of raw sewage, preventing rescue crews from wading in with shovels. Fire fighters from all over the state and beyond answered the call for help, donning sealed fire-fighting suits and retrieving the dead.

It fell on the Thirty-ninth Signal Battalion of the Idaho National Guard to do graves registration work, an unpleasant task made all the more difficult by the length of time the bodies lay buried. Hundreds of wriggling, yellowish maggots welled up from inside many of the torn bodies.

The Thirty-ninth had only fifty government-issue body bags in its stores, so garment bags donated by a local merchant had to be used for some smaller children. Many of the dead were simply rolled into plastic tarpaulins until more body bags were available.

Choking, gagging, their gloves long since torn on debris and discarded, many guardsmen cursed their duty, their luck, the awful stench, and, most of all, the mud. Others just did their job with their eyes closed, taking shallow breaths only after long intervals.

The Thirty-ninth's armory was converted into a make-shift morgue, which soon came to resemble a sea of mud, decorated with little white caskets and brightly colored garment bags, many torn, exposing small, swollen limbs. Vague figures in plastic sheets and dull black body bags formed line after line. The powerful exhaust fans did little to improve the air fouled by the putrid odor of rotting meat.

A strange silence—a sort of paralyzed horror and suppressed anger—hung over the armory. No screams of "Why,

God?" or "How, Jesus?" came from the mourners. After all, everyone knew the answers to those questions. The rain that had broken the back of the Locke Dam had been artificially induced as part of a weather-modification plan to end the long drought. Huge C-135 transport planes had dumped tons of silver iodide pellets on the clouds as local television and radio stations aired programs dealing with weather modifications.

As dusk fell over Locke County, a tall figure—obviously an outsider, for his trench coat and dark wool slacks were all too clean of mud—stood with a bedraggled state trooper at the armory's entrance. He could go no further. The foul odor overwhelmed and nauseated him.

Cliff Lorenz stood there stunned, shaken, and numb. Even though he had toured the devastated area and had known what he could expect to find at the armory, the scene caught him off guard. So powerful was the shock of the sight that Cliff found himself unable to comprehend what had been wrought. "Oh, my God," he murmured, pressing a handkerchief over his nose and swallowing the bile rising in his throat.

A raw, primitive feeling of guilt overwhelmed him. A few years away from his fortieth birthday, with the build of a health-club regular, brown hair, and wide, bright blue eyes, Cliff Lorenz loved a challenge. An oceanographer by training, he now worked for the under secretary of the Department of the Interior, specializing in weather modification and geoengineering research. The project to seed the skies above Locke County had been his department's responsibility.

Hundreds jammed the steamy armory, some praying, some reading identification tags, and some simply staring blankly. Few showed signs of hysteria, most sobbed quietly. *Like a child having a bad dream,* thought Cliff. Sometimes complete strangers with nothing in common but the shared experience of losing a loved one embraced silently, knowing words could never express the feelings each experienced. Reporters and television crews moved quietly about, taking notes and shooting video. National Guardsmen, exhausted and numb, compared missing-persons reports with unidentified bodies. And there were flowers everywhere. Flowers, but no fragrance. A metaphor expressing the lifeless bodies surrounding him, Cliff recognized.

A loud shouting captured his attention. "Go puke outside. That's your sister, you know!"

Cliff saw a young couple carrying a soggy pom-pom leave and felt the need to tell them how sorry he was, or that he could relate to their sorrow because he had a young son. *Butch! What if he were inside one of those bags?!* Cliff thought it unwise, though, or even dangerous, to talk to the young couple. *Nobody wants to see a man from Washington today,* he thought. *Or any other day after this disaster. After all, we caused this, didn't we?*

A minister kneeled a few feet away beside a body bag and intoned, "May the Lord forgive the sins of Jennifer Egan and accept her to His . . ."

Cliff barely heard him. By now he was filled with disgust and fear of what his science had done, and shame at his own involvement with climate modifiers. When he had joined the elitist community of "brilliant" scientists in the challenge of controlling nature, he had never imagined anything like what he was seeing this day.

A reporter, notebook in hand, approached Cliff. "Kollingwood of the *Washington Post.* I covered the hearing on offshore drilling last year and your stance against it. Remember?"

Cliff forced a smile. "Yes, sure." A hint of displeasure crept into his tone. He cared little for what the *Washington Post* or any of the other news agencies reported. Half of what he had said at last year's hearings had been misquoted or taken out of context.

A news crew turned its cameras on Cliff as the *Post* reporter asked him, "Are you the official representative here, on behalf of the president?"

"No," Cliff replied, "I'm not."

"But you are still with the Department of the Interior?"

Another news camera focused in on Cliff, and he found himself surrounded by onlookers attracted by the bright spotlights mounted on the video cameras.

"Yes," he answered. "I'm still with the Department of the Interior."

The reporter pressed closer, the lights burned hot.

"With the WMS, the Weather Modification Section, I mean."

Cliff nodded and a woman grabbed one of the microphones being held by a local news reporter. Bringing it close to her mouth, she nearly shrieked, "You ought to be ashamed of yourself."

Cliff fought to maintain his composure. Only the repeated clenching of his jaw gave any indication of the anger and frustration he felt at being so boldly—and rightly—chastised. "Ma'am," he replied, "I would be less than human if I wasn't. These poor children"—he gestured toward the rear of the armory—"whose future has been—"

"You leave that to Reverend Gibson," the woman interrupted brusquely. "We trusted you. You said you were going to make it rain, end the drought. You didn't say you were going to destroy the town. How could you do this to us? How could you let this happen?"

Cliff was a scientist. He knew better than to speculate on the disaster without researching it in detail. He answered, "I don't know." He knew, though, that he could have relied on "logicons" or fundamental premises about climate modifiers—CLIMODs, as he called them—to answer the woman and would have been close to the right answer. One held that the weather remained unpredictable despite weather satellites and Doppler radar; another said that CLIMODs disturbed the balance and interplay of such factors as solar flares, the behavior of the jet stream, movements of air masses, cloud cover, cyclical periods of solar radiation, and the amount of man-made gas trapped in the atmosphere. But he only repeated his first answer, "I'm sorry. I just don't know."

The woman released her hold on the microphone, allowing the television reporter to regain control. Cliff turned back to the *Washington Post* reporter. "Is there anything else?"

"You must have some idea of what happened. Give it to us."

Cliff stood silent.

"How 'bout just a statement then?" the reporter pressed.

"I think any comment on behalf of the Department of the Interior would be premature at this time."

"How 'bout your opinion, then, as a scientist? What do you think personally about what's happened here?"

Cliff's jaw ached as he ground his teeth in concentration. "What do *I* think?" Cliff exploded. "Okay, I'll tell you. But you had better get this down right. I know where you guys hang out in D.C., and if you misquote me, I'm going to come looking for you." He paused.

"Climate modification isn't an exact science yet. I got into researching CLIMODs because it presented me with new challenges, new possibilities. But nature isn't willing to be controlled by man, and we can't make it obey our rules." He made a sweeping motion with his arm. "The proof is in front of us. We played with fire and we got burned, and the cost was way too high. I'll recommend that further research into climate modification be halted. And I know that regardless of the official position, I'll never work on another modification."

The cameras rolled on into the silence that followed Cliff's statement.

"Thank you, Dr. Lorenz," the *Post* reporter finally said. "It sounds to me like you've learned something here."

"Yes, I certainly have." Cliff paused, then spoke again, "One final comment: whether it be through the power of the atom or the power of nature, we've got to realize that it isn't power that's in our control. In the end, we've got to realize that *man cannot play God.*"

• • •

It took a thirty-man team of scientists and climatologists, working twenty-hour days under direct pressure from the Oval Office, to determine what had caused the disaster in Idaho.

The five-day advance forecast issued by the National Oceanic and Atmospheric Administration (NOAA) had predicted that a band of clouds a thousand miles long would move from the Aleutian Islands into the state of Washington and proceed over the Rockies. The forecast also indicated that the southern edge of the cloud bank would pass over Locke County, presenting a 30 percent chance of rain. Ideal conditions for cloud seeding, reported the climatologists assigned to the Weather Modification Section, and the only way to end the drought that had turned Locke County into a dust bowl.

The plan called for planes to begin seeding the cloud bank as it entered Idaho. According to the WMS experts, as the bank moved over Locke County, it would clash with a cold front moving east across southern Idaho and produce rain.

The gargantuan C-135 transports released tons of pellets through a system most accurately described as a giant crop duster. But as the planes completed their mission over northeast Idaho, the cold front began losing its easterly momentum and became stationary. When the clouds, heavy with iodide pellets, reached Locke County, the stationary cold front brought them to a halt. Rain fell, as predicted. But not for a day or two. Because the stationary front refused to give way, torrents of rain fell for nine days, often at the incredible rate of one inch per hour, much too quickly for the Locke County Water Authority to control as it brought the reservoir to capacity and overwhelmed the Locke Dam.

The following week, the team presented its finding to a panel of political figures, including two congressmen from Idaho, the head of the NOAA, the commanding general of the Army Corps of Engineers, and the president's science adviser. The final report itself was personally presented by the science adviser to the president. It stated the scientific reasons for the disaster, and in response to both the public outcry and pressure from the president's policy-making chief of staff, it also called for a ban on the use of modifiers for anything but controlled research purposes. The president, happy to have had the decision made for him, immediately called for the suggested ban.

In response to the president's call, the U.S. ambassador to the United Nations introduced a resolution calling for an international ban on climate modifiers, arguing that the chance was at hand to put the genie back in the bottle, before climate modifiers became as dangerous in their possibilities as nuclear weapons.

Representatives from fifteen non-industrialized nations, including several plagued by long droughts, opposed the resolution. They argued that a ban on modifiers would take away a chance for their countries to "ameliorate economic conditions with limited financial resources." An astute columnist from *U.S. News and World Report* noted that each of the opposing countries had also never signed the Nuclear Nonproliferation Treaty.

Following extended debate, an amended resolution earned the approval of the General Assembly, prohibiting only the use of modifiers for military purposes. "I am encouraged," the ambassador said in a press conference following passage of the resolution, "by this united action on the part of so many nations."

George Dunlap's grandson stood beside his widowed father, whose wife had perished like so many others when the Locke Dam collapsed. The little boy smiled, unaware of his father's dark mood, as the governor of Idaho stood with a party of local county officials and praised the federal government for its help in funding the rebuilding of the dam and the Army Corps of Engineers for its untiring efforts that had led to the completion of the new dam in only five years. Then, with great solemnity, for the governor could not forget how many lives had been lost in the past, he dedicated the new dam to the memories of all those who had perished.

Tears streaked from down George Jr.'s face as he turned to his own young son. "Timmy. C'mere, son. Let me zip up your jacket. It's mighty cold out here. Can't be much more'n freezing."

Damn cold, George Dunlap, Jr., thought, *for April.*

Jane Garson couldn't believe her luck. *Every geology major I know would kill for this job.* But that didn't do much to alleviate the boredom she endured while wading through foot after foot of seismic readouts showing continued activity along the San Andreas Fault. Since January, a series of quakes had led a number of Californians to seriously rethink their need for year-round sunshine and state-approved self-esteem counseling programs. Most would be happy if the ground would only stop shaking.

Three months earlier, in January, a quake measuring 5.8 on the Richter scale had cleaved open the crack running along the fault for eighty-two miles south of San Jose. Because there were fewer injuries than might have been expected, most Californians hardly gave it a second thought, except when the a new tremor struck. But it wasn't the tremors that had seismologists worrying. As subterranean gases escaped from the widened crack, thousands of cubic tons of invisible crystalline dust particles rose into the atmosphere. The free-floating particles, like ash from erupting volcanoes, formed large clouds that presented an immediate hazard to aircraft and a potential threat to the environment about which most scientists feared to speculate.

While most of the United States seemed to be experiencing a late spring, the effects of dust loading in the atmosphere had already become noticeable at the United States polar research station on Ellesmere Island. There, and at the station's Russian counterpart on New Siberia Island, temperatures had been dropping steadily since mid-March, and winds were gusting up to fifty miles per hour. Most, however, attributed the falling temperatures to a normal "seasonal reversal" of the sort that often took place in early spring, a temporary climatic setback that would last one or two weeks at most.

This reversal, however, had a new component: solar output meters at both the U.S. and Russian stations recorded lower-than-normal solar energy readings, lower than could be accounted for by the cyclical drops in solar energy called Maunder Minima.

Scientists at NASA's Satellite Imaging Center in Orlando, Florida, were alarmed by the color images coming back to them from the *Nimbus 7* satellite. They confirmed suspicions that particles from the San Andreas Fault were responsible for an atmospheric dust layer that was to blame for the low solar energy readings. The reflective particles acted like millions, perhaps really billions, of tiny mirrors, bouncing the sun's rays back into space. In a report to the president's science adviser, the director of NASA/SIC wrote: *The decrease in solar radiation must be attributed to the crystalline haze (from 220 parts per million to 375 just this week). This, unfortunately, comes at the beginning of the Maunder cycle. Continued loading of the atmosphere could lead to a prolonged seasonal reversal whose climatic characteristics could well approximate those of an ice age. Since there has been no discernible decrease of dust loading from the San Andreas Fault—and none is foreseen in the near future— it is safe to assume that the seasonal reversal now taking place in the polar regions is an incipient deep freeze.*

At the Center for Climatic Studies in Moscow, scientists had reached a similar conclusion. They too had studied the digital images of temperature gradients, measurements of solar intensity, and air quality readings. But for the center's director, nothing could be as convincing as seeing the situation for himself.

A thin man with pale skin and surprisingly bright eyes, forever caught in a swirl of pipe smoke, Dr. Andrei Konlikov worried most about the signature, or structure, of the crystals forming the increasing polar ice masses. Ice that cracked or formed crevasses easily presented an immediate danger to all those in the polar regions.

Upon arriving at polar station Kinsky on March 19, Konlikov ordered the immediate cessation of all current research projects, and set the scientists and researchers to work on a two-part examination of the polar ice: first, a microscopic analysis of surface ice; and second, an analysis of core ice from the Cretaceous period, buried 3,600 feet below.

The Russian scientist wanted to see if the Cretaceous ice revealed structures similar to the surface ice. During the Cretaceous period, an asteroid five miles in diameter hit the Yucatan Peninsula, near the town of Chicxulub, forming a crater 112 miles wide. Some 400 cubic miles of dust loaded the atmosphere and blocked solar energy to such a degree that it triggered an ice age severe enough to wipe out much of the life on Earth, including the dinosaurs. In 60 million years of geologic history, only the asteroid and the ongoing destabilization of the San Andreas Fault had sent so much dust into the atmosphere.

While a crew used a radio ice sounder, similar to sonar, to pinpoint the precise depth of the Cretaceous ice layer, Konlikov and his assistant prepared a study of the surface ice at the molecular level. Their principal instrument was a Leica optical microanalyzer capable of magnifying objects as small as one-hundredth of a millimeter in diameter. Set up at the center of the science compound, it stood surrounded by a cluster of prefabricated housing units that were interconnected by a series of underground tunnels.

Konlikov put his pipe down and uncapped a thermal-insulated bottle containing a mixture of distilled water and methanol, the latter serving to lower the freezing point and slow gelation. He placed a drop of the mixture on the polished mirror of the analyzer and then focused a narrow beam of light upon it. As the water began to freeze, Konlikov peered through the eyepiece. "I don't believe it," he muttered. He took a second sample, watching it lose its fluidity, quickly transforming into thin, sharp crystals of ice. Some were bright and beautiful, others darker and misshapen, each very different from the others.

Konlikov shook his head, puzzled. Could the methanol have influenced the irregularity? He took a pure sample and examined it. No, it didn't seem to have an effect. He took a sample of pure water and placed it under the analyzer. Peering through the eyepiece, he shook his head in continued astonishment.

"What's the matter?" his assistant asked.

Konlikov ignored him and increased the magnification on the analyzer. The result caused him to flinch back from the eyepiece. Five-sided crystals. Asymmetrical crystals! Not the symmetrical beauties normally found in examining snow and ice. And not favorable toward the formation of good ice.

The asymmetrical crystals were rough edged, like badly cut diamonds. As Konlikov added more water, needle-shaped crystals grew longer and spread. But instead of forming one solid wall, the flawed crystals remained loose, obviously because of the difference in structural symmetry.

Increasing the magnification again, Konlikov saw that the crystals had serrated edges that didn't interlock with normal symmetrical crystals. And they were larger, too. The combination of the two types, symmetrical and asymmetrical, both different shapes and sizes, created tiny spaces in the overall ice formation, making it more voluminous and more likely to crack and crevasse. "This ice is dangerous," he muttered.

When the core crew finished drilling for a sample of the 60-million-year-old Cretaceous ice, Konlikov compared it with the surface sample. His worst fears were immediately confirmed, for there, in the Cretaceous ice, were the same irregular, asymmetrical crystals that were now consuming the surface ice like cancer cells.

Konlikov pondered the implications. *A long seasonal reversal? Certainly. But how long? Two, three years?*

Longer? He tried to imagine life in the struggling states of the former Soviet Union during a long deep freeze.

Konlikov stood up. Thirty-five men and women lived at Kinsky, and he knew he had to have them airlifted before crevassing made the ski strip inaccessible to aircraft. He ordered the immediate evacuation of the research station. *Moscow be damned,* he thought, knowing they would object to his taking action without approval. And then he thought, *It already is.*

The following day, as the first of the evacuation aircraft left the still-smooth ski strip, Konlikov walked to the radio shack and told the operator to set the transmitter for continuous broadcast. "I don't want the Americans to think that we are, as they say"—he smiled, revealing a shiny gold tooth—"chickening out."

2

At the United States polar research station NP/5, meteorologist Ned Gray predicted a "polar day nine." The prediction referred to a scale Gray had developed during an extended polar blizzard in Antarctica. Running from one to ten, one being normal conditions and ten being weather conditions unsuited to human life, the scale became an everyday measure of just how bad circumstances at the station had become. According to Gray, polar day nine was only two weeks away.

As the sun finally dissipated the darkness of another nineteen-hour-long night, geologist Jane Lane began to believe in Ned Gray's prediction. A hissing wind tossed a stinging swirl of dry snow as fine as glass that penetrated zippers and scarves, leaving Lane wishing for the warmth of her hut. But first she and her assistant needed to finish installing the new recording drums on the temperature meters. A pointless task, Lane observed, since the drums weren't designed to handle weather this cold.

Lane and her assistant, shapeless, undistinguishable twins in their arctic anoraks, stomped their feet and used sign language in the bitter cold; their mouths were completely obscured by the Thinsulate face masks they wore. At minus forty degrees Fahrenheit, uncovered flesh froze almost instantly. The job of changing the recording drums should have taken minutes, but they had been outside for nearly half an hour working on just one drum. Already they were exhausted from the effort; fighting the cold sapped their energy.

The hut whose comfort Jane Lane so craved was one of sixteen buildings resembling oversized trailers that stood in rows of four, forming the heart of the compound. From the north side, they looked like ski moguls, buried by the snowdrifts. To the northwest and 500 feet away from the huts stood the station's nuclear power plant. Steam billowed from the single cooling tower next to it.

Fumbling with the drum, Lane finally gave in to her frustration and removed her down mitten. Grabbing the drum, she let out a little yelp as the skin-bonding film of frost crystals on the metal drum forced her to tear her skin to finish her task. Cursing her own stupidity, she pulled her mitten back up to her cuff.

"Screw this," she said. "Let's get back inside. The damn drums won't work in this cold anyway." Nodding his agreement, her assistant followed her into the station mess hall, where hot soup and coffee awaited them.

The mess hall buzzed with news of the worsening weather. At lunch, during coffee breaks, in the tunnels connecting the camp buildings, even in their sleep, the inhabitants of NP/5 talked about the increasing cold. Ned Gray found celebrity in his status as station meteorologist. In the trying times facing the station, scientists and researchers turned not to the interfaith minister or the station psychologist but to the station weatherman for comfort and guidance.

John Van Muren, director of NP/5, a balding, bony, forty-five-year-old specialist in climatology and the atmosphere, sat drinking coffee and staring at the nervous crew around him. The mess hall resembled a high school cafeteria the day before the big prom. A sign over the food counter read: To Strive, to Seek, to Find, and Not to Yield—

Admiral Byrd, but the crew at NP/5 seemed dangerously close to cracking. Van Muren had expected a lot of things when he agreed to take on the directorship of the station, intending to pursue ground-breaking research in the destruction of the ozone layer, but he hadn't planned on anything like this.

At a nearby table, a bearded scientist researching the effect of extreme cold temperatures on reaction time voiced a common opinion: "We should call an emergency meeting and plan on getting out of here. Nowhere in my contract does it say that I can't quit my job whenever—"

"True," a young M.D. with flaming red hair interrupted, "but since you can't take the bus to Juneau, you'll have to wait until the Air Force decides to come and get you." A specialist in the psychology of small groups in hardship situations, she considered the current situation a research bonanza. Few of her associates shared her enthusiasm.

"You're goddamn right," the bearded researcher said, "and I bet you anything that Van Muren's not going to call them to pick us up. He's too concerned he'll lose the funding for his big ozone project if he closes up shop here."

A pale, sandy-haired specialist in magnetic anomalies jumped in. "This isn't a penal colony. It's a research station. If Van Muren won't call them, we can. They'll come. I could be home writing my book before Gray's big polar day nine comes."

"Yeah," the M.D. asked, "and what will the title of the book be, *Mutiny on the Pole*?"

There were some smiles but no laughter.

Van Muren bore it all with little reaction. Fortunately for him, he could still claim that the lack of warming temperatures reflected a seasonal reversal—though longer than usual. In 1974, a seasonal reversal had forced the cancellation of all research activities at NP/5 and its Soviet counterpart, Kinsky. And as far as anyone knew, Kinsky remained operational. The station's call sign could be heard even on a portable radio at 5.533 mhz, Kinsky's beacon frequency. It gave the NP/5 researchers a sense of security. They weren't the only nuts out there.

Of course, regardless of the Russians' stalwart behavior, Van Muren could order the evacuation of NP/5 anytime he chose. As director of the station, he bore responsibility for the welfare of forty-five men and twenty-nine women. Except what would he do about Little Bertha?

"Little Bertha," NP/5's nuclear plant, generated vital electricity and distilled fresh water for countless uses, especially steam for the heating system. Twelve people worked in shifts to keep Little Bertha going, but many more would be needed to shut it down. And the station couldn't be evacuated until the crew decommissioned Little Bertha.

As Van Muren pondered the dilemma of the reactor, a rushing figure startled him from his thoughts. Breathing hard, Peter Hall, one of the four station glaciologists, came over as soon as he spotted Van Muren in the crowded mess hall.

"Come see, quickly, please," Hall urged.

Van Muren managed to stay calm. "Sure," he said, but he could sense the fear in Hall's voice. "What's up?" he asked.

"The creep meter in the service tunnel," the glaciologist said, tripping over the words, "is way out of line. This goddamn ice is growing like yeast."

In the service tunnel, the Bendix creep meter, an instrument that could also be used to measure the motion of tectonic plates along a geological fault line, showed an unusual dislocation of the floor due to upward stress.

"Well, Pete, what do you expect?" Van Muren said to the glaciologist, "aren't we having a seasonal reversal?"

"Reversal? Bullshit. Tell that to the cooks, not to me. I know what the fuck is going on. I'm here to study ice, not how many times a polar bear shits in a day, you know."

"Relax, Pete. Sure this reversal is a little more severe, but I don't see a real threat to anything here. Let's talk later." Turning away before the glaciologist could explode again, Van Muren headed down the service tunnel toward the nuclear plant. Approaching the final turn in the tunnel, he heard a loud cracking noise from around the bend. Coming around the corner he saw that a small crevasse had opened on top of a bulge in the ice just to the right of the wooden walkway.

Van Muren stood at the crevasse and a warning voice whispered in his head. *What next?* Yes, he had stalled the evacuation of NP/5, acceding to the wishes of Washington. His crew would create panic back home, where they would reveal the truth of the seasonal reversal. But the politicians in Washington weren't sitting on a noisy and active floor of ice. Van Muren had to get his crew out. Perhaps the NP/5 crew could be quarantined at an Alaskan Air Force base under some pretext until the Washington spin doctors could get a handle on the situation. But he had to move to get the evacuation under way.

Van Muren wasted no time. He called an emergency meeting of his section leaders in the cryogenics hut. A row of small refrigerators lined the gray walls of the long and rectangular building. Under the dim incandescent lights, one could read the labels on the refrigerators, indicating the file number and extraction dates for the long cores of ice they housed. Instruments of all kinds rested on counters lining the opposite wall. Coffee-colored leaks stained the low ceiling. The odor of stale perspiration hung in the air.

Shivering violently after just the brief run across the compound, Van Muren hurried to start the meeting.

"I'm worried about the condition of the ice in the service tunnel," he said, as he began the discussion on shutting down Little Bertha.

"No doubt about it," a black glaciologist agreed, "there is a definite deterioration of bonding that's going to wreak havoc in the tunnels." According to him, the temperature plunge had been too rapid for the ice to retain its molecular structure. Activity in the subsurface ice would be more pronounced. One could, therefore, expect more pressure surges, like the one that had heaved up in the tunnel. "If the trend continues," he concluded, "we can expect the surges to affect the base ice beneath the reactor."

For a moment, they were silent, and then Van Muren began to nod, agreeing quietly with the glaciologist. He told his section leaders to begin preparations for decommissioning the plant. If the ice surged beneath the plant, it would crack the containment vessel and turn NP/5 into an arctic Chernobyl.

He ordered a transfer to battery power and the discontinuation of all nonessential power usage. He said he would contact Washington and request the evacuation of all nonessential personnel, but he warned that given the conditions they faced, nearly everyone was essential.

As the section leaders left to begin their preparations, Ned Gray approached Van Muren. "Have I been your friend all these months?" he asked, speaking in a low, conspiratorial voice.

Van Muren answered warily, "Sure, Ned."

"Have I supported you in all your decisions? Didn't I go along with your seasonal reversal story even though I knew it was hogwash?"

Van Muren nodded, and Gray drew closer.

"Then get me the hell out of here," he growled, barely restraining his emotion.

"Ned," Van Muren began, as he put a calming hand on Gray's trembling shoulder, "all of us will get out of here as long as we work together as a team."

"John, I lived through a polar day seven in Antarctica, and I don't want to see an eight, let alone the nine we'll be facing in a couple of weeks."

"You won't," Van Muren lied.

Outside the cryogenics hut, a miniature arctic mountain range—a long, jagged cliff of icy splinters—speared skyward. It rose three feet above the surface ice and ran for thirty feet, ending only four hundred feet from the power and steam tunnel connecting the reactor and the utility hut. As he exited the hut, Van Muren looked left and saw crevasses formed by the surging ice. The largest, forty feet long and five feet wide, glowed blue-black in its depth. Beyond them stretched the arctic flat, a white and formless expanse of desolation. Van Muren shook his head, wondering just how much time NP/5 had left.

3

For over a week, an unaccountable interference had disrupted communications with NP/5, time enough for rumors of trouble at the station to begin circulating at the Institute for Global Climate Studies in Washington. Internal IGCS memoranda attributed the lack of communication to a change in solar activity that disturbed the ionosphere—the electrically charged layer that reflects radio waves on Earth—and caused the interference. After all, the Maunder Minima was in progress.

Not surprisingly, when radio reception improved, many assumed that atmospheric and climatic patterns were returning to normal. They were wrong.

Professor Peter Kronin showed no surprise when he received the coded dispatch from NP/5. A stocky, short man with a garland of gray hair framing a shiny bald head, and sporting a Vandyke beard that did little to camouflage a growing second chin, Kronin had taken leave of his position as chairman of the Department of Geophysics at M.I.T. to assume the leadership of the IGCS, the independent government agency created to study the effects of pollution on the climate and to monitor the academic research on climate modifiers still allowed by the ban imposed after the Locke County disaster.

The coded message read:

NNNN
NORTH POLAR/5—2 MAY, 09:30 ZULU
KRONIN IGCS, ROUTE COMSAT—NWS
SEASONAL REVERSAL CONTINUES. VERTICAL EXPANSION OF ICE MOST PRONOUNCED IN REACTOR SERVICE TUNNEL. REACTOR THREATENED. KATABATIC WINDS HAVE REAPPEARED. MORALE SLIPPING. REQUEST EVACUATION OF NONESSENTIAL PERSONNEL. REQUEST IMMEDIATE EVACUATION OF FREDERICKS, SAMUEL, DR. FOR MEDICAL REASONS. VAN MUREN.
　END MESSAGE.

An additional page of meteorological data followed.

Kronin read the message through twice and then took off his reading glasses. "I knew it. I just knew it," he said, hurrying toward the plotting room.

A large map of the North American continent, peppered with colored push pins and round tags, dominated the room. White pins, forming a wavy line and running east to west, showed the southern movement of the polar ice sheet; blue tags indicated the areas with temperatures below freezing; orange, those above.

Kronin handed the data page that had accompanied Van Muren's message to a technician standing nearby. The technician studied the page, added it to a growing pile of incoming reports from various satellites and research stations, and pointed at the northernmost orange tag. Kronin nodded, exhaling in defeat. "Go ahead," he said.

The technician nodded, climbed a stepladder, removed the orange tag, and put a blue one in its place. For the next five minutes, as Kronin watched, the technician completed the update of the map, using the information from all of the accumulated reports.

Kronin shook his head. Colder temperatures were spreading south, completely out of season. The rapid shift in temperature stunned him.

Kronin motioned for the technician to step down. He jabbed a finger in the direction of the phone. "Call Secretary—*Acting* Secretary Roscoe, or whatever the hell he is," he ordered as he lumbered back toward his office. "Tell him to come here immediately. It's time he started taking this seriously."

His words echoing down the corridor, Kronin reached his office. Though he had only been in Washington a few weeks, his office already appeared to be an exact replica of his office at M.I.T.—bookcases overflowed with large volumes, stacks of journals and manila folders containing research fought for floor space, and a pile of unopened mail threatened to consume his in-box.

Kronin took off his jacket and unbuttoned his shirt collar. A dirty ring of perspiration marked his collar. Kronin then settled himself into his cushioned, high-backed chair and swiveled to stare out of his office window.

A promising spring sun shone, yet failed to push the thermometer into the sixties. The grass along the Mall remained the brown thatch of winter, rather than the lush green of spring. A red Miata zipped along Connecticut Avenue with the top down, but the police officers directing traffic around the Washington Monument wore lined nylon jackets.

Kronin's eyes saw none of it. Consumed by the new information from NP/5, his mind sought the solution to the unyielding seasonal reversal. Only the week before he'd announced that if dust from the San Andreas Fault continued to load the atmosphere, the seasonal reversal reported by NP/5 would be but the tip of the iceberg. It presaged a threat that would soon affect most of the world. He called it "glaciation."

At 10:15 A.M., a robust man whose dark beard required him to shave twice each day, marched briskly down the corridor to Professor Kronin's office, the man's Eighty-second Airborne tie clasp glinting under the overhead lights. Brant W. Roscoe, sixty years old, acting secretary of the interior, touched his forehead in salute to a guard's nod of recognition, wished him good morning in the harsh, parade-ground voice he used to make up for his five-eight height, and moved on. His polished shoes struck the tile floor in concert with a silent cadence. With his tight mouth, his slicked-back, thinning hair, and wearing an expensive blue suit, Roscoe remained every bit the soldier he'd once been, but with a Brooks Brothers propriety. Yet he seemed unused to civilian clothes, like a defrocked priest. Running behind him was an aide carrying Roscoe's shiny briefcase.

Roscoe had done well in the Army, leaving the service with a record of combat decorations, field promotions, and special citations. He had done even better at the Department of the Interior: head of land reclamation, chief of personnel, budget director, under secretary, and, during administration changeovers, acting secretary. But he'd been passed over twice for a permanent cabinet post, and was determined to make up for it.

Despite the number of times they had met at social functions and professional events, Roscoe and Kronin were not friends. Roscoe was a soldier turned politician, enjoying his second marriage to a Washington widow who complemented his role in politics. Kronin was a scholar and scientist who preferred real facts and research. And his wife didn't like "the little social-climbing bitch" Roscoe had married.

Kronin didn't even let Roscoe sit down. He simply shook his hand quickly and turned him toward the door.

"Come, come," Kronin said, moving off. "We're in it now. What I have to show you confirms my worst fears." He stormed into the plotting room and heaved himself up the stepladder.

"Look at this," Kronin said. "Glaciation in full force." He pointed at the line of blue tags. "Look at those temperature drops. The crew at NP/Five is only days away from freezing to death. And they've got that damned reactor to handle. Do you have any idea what will happen if the ice surges or crevasses beneath the containment vessel? And do you have any idea how many more reactors are in line after that?

"Brant, we have to mobilize all our resources into immediate countermeasures. This is the beginning of May. We have four, maybe five months. That's all."

Roscoe nodded, his face impassive. "By all means, Professor. What do you suggest?"

"Climate modifiers."

Roscoe's poker face slipped. After the tragedy in Idaho, a tragedy Kronin had to be all too aware of, how could he propose climate modifiers? CLIMODs spelled disaster. He looked up at Kronin, still perched on the ladder. "You're joking, right?"

"Joking?" Kronin pounded down the ladder, nearly falling. He stood directly in front of Roscoe. "How can I be joking? The world is freezing. Modifiers are the only option. How else are we going to forestall wholesale panic and the need to evacuate all of Canada and the northern United States?"

Roscoe didn't answer. He was still thinking of his last experience with modifiers, the broken dam, the hundreds killed, and the others left homeless. Turning away from Kronin's puffy red face, he said, "Modifiers are merely research projects, nothing more. They were banned after Idaho. They're too unpredictable and impossible to control."

Kronin sighed with exasperation. "As a natural disaster, glaciation becomes your headache. It will bring about destruction that will make Idaho look like a spring shower.

"My advice to you is that you act now. Once this becomes public—and it *must* become public to give people the time to evacuate—every eye in Washington will be watching to see what kind of leadership you provide. Line officers are tested under fire, aren't they?" Kronin turned and left the room, heading back toward his office.

Several minutes passed before Roscoe followed along. He walked into Kronin's office. Kronin turned from the window to face him. "We have to act, yes. But after Idaho how can you propose modifiers?" Roscoe asked.

"Brant," Kronin began, raising his hands palms up, "what other alternative is there? We need a modification to change the weather because the weather isn't going to change for us. There's really no other choice."

After a long pause, Roscoe surrendered. "All right," he said, "I'll brief the president on our discussion. But it shouldn't be interpreted as an endorsement of modifiers."

"Hold it." Kronin jabbed a finger in Roscoe's direction. "If by tomorrow you haven't recommended to the president that we use modifiers, I will. I can get in with one phone call to his science adviser. Either you tell him or I'll do it."

Roscoe recognized blackmail when he heard it. Kronin had all the right credentials; his name was synonymous with nuclear winter, climatology, and geophysics. If he said the world would freeze, the president would believe him.

"What kind of modifier do we need?" Roscoe asked, caving in.

Kronin pondered the question for a moment and then spoke. "Something with ocean currents, I believe. They really control our climate as it is.

"A friend of mine, Dr. Marshall at UCLA, has been working on one for nearly twenty years. And there's another oceanographer, a young man who used to be Marshall's research assistant, a Dr. Cliff—"

"Lorenz," Roscoe interrupted. "But they had a falling out. I brought him to D.C. several years ago. He works for me."

"What do you know about his modification? Did he continue his research?"

Roscoe frowned. "No," he said. "He quit working on it after about five years; after Idaho, he decided it was more important to understand how the ocean is, not how it could be. He had this plan to reroute the Gulf Stream so that it would become more useful—to the United States, I mean— but he never took it beyond theory."

Kronin nodded. "Good. At least it can serve as a backup to Marshall's plan. Tell Lorenz to get back on it. I'll need to see his proposal as soon as possible."

Roscoe nodded, wondering all the while how he would convince Lorenz to get back into climate modification research knowing the potential for disaster. As he drifted out of Kronin's office, picking up his assistant down the hall, he doubted Lorenz could be convinced.

Kronin already had Marshall on the phone before Roscoe had reached street level.

"What's the problem?" Marshall asked.

"I must talk to you at once. Here in Washington."

"If it's your golf, forget it."

"It's your Gulf Stream."

There was a brief silence. "In that case, make it Tuesday.

"Monday," Kronin said, hanging up.

At NP/5, tensions ran high.

"I'm getting out of here," Ned Gray told Jeff Robertson, the nuclear engineer who had dropped by the meteorological lab for an update.

Robertson looked doubtful. "How?" he asked.

"I'm not sure yet," Gray replied as he continued to stuff warm clothing and several maps into a large backpack. "You don't think we're doomed, do you?" he finally said, looking up at Robertson.

"I don't know, but I doubt Van Muren would deceive us."

Gray shrugged. "Think what you like," he said, checking the shoulder straps on the pack. He walked over to a chart-covered wall. "Look at this," he said, pointing at a graph showing the vertical expansions of the ice. "I took this off the creep meter after lunch. It shows another half inch of movement since this morning. That's enough for me. I'm getting out."

Robertson shook his head. "Even if you did manage to hitch a ride on the mail plane or reach Eureka by Snow-Cat, you'd just be arrested when you get there. This may not be the Army, but Uncle Sam signs the paychecks and he doesn't like it when you go AWOL at the North Pole."

"I'd rather sweat it out in jail than freeze to death at the bottom of a crevasse."

With that, Gray hefted the pack onto his back and strode out of the hut. Robertson followed close behind, but veered toward the radio shack instead of following Gray to the motor pool.

I wonder what the sentence is for grand theft Snow-Cat, Robertson thought, entering the radio shack. About the size of a walk-in closet, the radio shack housed all primary communications gear for the station. Most station members had their own shortwave receivers, but the only outgoing traffic came from here.

"Any news?" Robertson asked the operator.

"Nope, not a peep." He flipped a switch and tapped a dial with his finger. "But for two days now, I've been getting chirps on the Russians' signal. And it's off frequency by two KCs." The operator shook his head. "Either the operator is too stupid to know that he can't screw with the d.c. voltages on the oscillator during keying or . . . the bastard is in Moscow drinking vodka."

It was a good guess. Kinsky was deserted except for its ghosts.

4

Cliff Lorenz drove through the early Thursday-morning traffic looking for a clear stretch to pick up some speed. With a glance at his radar detector, Cliff stepped on the gas. The Porsche 3.5-liter, duel-carb engine responded with a quick surge of horsepower. As Cliff cruised smoothly down Route 50, he opened the sunroof, shivering a little as the cold morning air rushed into the car.

He punched the eject button on the compact disc player and the radio kicked on. *"This is Morning Edition, and I'm Bob Edwards. The number one item in the news this cool spring morning will bring sadness to many.*

"Over thirty pilot whales beached themselves last night. While the beaching of whales remains a mystery, some scientists suggest that disease may affect the whales' sense of direction. Others say pollution from offshore dumping poisons the whales, forcing them to beach themselves when they can no longer feed themselves in the sea.

"This is the first time—"

Cliff turned the radio off. The broadcaster had little to add to the story Cliff had heard earlier.

It isn't a disease, Cliff thought. *And it's not the pollution or electromagnetic interference, either.* Cliff believed that whales beached themselves for really only one reason: exhaustion. Like cattle, whales travel in herds—schools, actually—and like any herd, they tended to stampede when frightened. They then beached themselves to keep from drowning. After all, they are air-breathing mammals. Rather than sink, whales seek shallow water in order to breathe and regain their strength. Cliff felt that most whales beached themselves after something—most probably strange sounds—frightened them into a rushed swim for safe harbor that left them exhausted and forced to beach themselves.

Mekonhoe Beach/22 Miles, a sign read. Cliff turned right on Route 424 and headed southeast.

There really isn't a more valid theory, Cliff told himself. Of course, a theory without documentation was no better than any other. Yet he based his own on some observations made during the week of the earthquake that had cracked wide the San Andreas Fault.

Three days before the quake of last January 6, seismometers had picked up vibrations caused by rock fracturing under the stress of rising magma. Those vibrations resonated through the shifting and grinding tectonic plates in the form of low-frequency waves. In part, such waves explained why animals, more sensitive to them than humans, always seemed to sense an oncoming earthquake before humans.

And on the third of January, Cliff's friend, Captain Evan Wilson, skipper of the salvage and research ship *Glomar,* had reported seeing "hundreds of whales swimming westward like a school of frightened mackerel."

It seemed clear to Cliff. Because of their acute hearing, he reasoned, the whales had picked up the vibrations that had preceded the 5.8 quake in the form of low-frequency sound waves. Sound waves, like those generated by the spinning shaft of a ship's propeller, traveled well in water, for hundreds of miles. That might explain what had caused the Mekonhoe whales to beach themselves. But as far as he knew there had been no reports of tremors occurring anywhere along the geologically stable East Coast. And, technically, the generator would have to be east of the shore, and probably north in order to drive the whales onto the beaches here. *That puts us in the Arctic Circle, though,* Cliff thought. Unless Nova Scotia had gone the way of Atlantis. He needed more data.

On Route 424, the traffic grew heavier, cars moved slower, and Cliff enjoyed the warmth of the sun on his face. The chill of the rushing wind left him.

As an experienced oceanographer, Cliff knew that he could do little for the beached whales. Unless the tide could lift their great mass, most would die a slow death in the sand, their own weight crushing their internal organs as they baked in the sun.

Still, he remained an optimist. The trip to the beach had been a last-minute idea, a suggestion of his best friend, with whom he would spend the next several days working on an investigation into offshore dumping of toxic wastes. Fritz Hoffmeister had remained true to his calling by staying on at Woods Hole while Cliff left for Washington. The two remained close friends, and Cliff secretly hoped that his resourceful friend might have a trick or two up his sleeve that could help the whales.

Mekonhoe Beach—Breeze Point to many—had once been a favored place for summer homes built by wealthy Washingtonians in the late nineteenth century. Now only a massive brick bathhouse covered with graffiti, an echoing bandstand, and a rotting section of a once brightly colored pavilion were all that remained.

Cliff slowed and looked for a place to park. A hand-lettered parking sign stood at the entrance to an Exxon station and Cliff pulled in. After paying the attendant, he grabbed his binoculars and strapped his "fanny pack," a long, narrow pouch filled with a notebook, a couple of pens, and a chart of the bay, around his waist. The neon green pack clashed badly with his yellow Polo shirt and red Patagonia shorts.

Jogging toward the beach, his view of the water was

obscured by the seawall. A foul wind blew onshore, reminding him of the stench of a low tide near a busy harbor.

A silent crowd of about fifty people had gathered along the seawall.

Cliff moved through the crowd and stood atop the wall. Black pilot whales lay everywhere. Some twitched their dorsal fins; others waved their flukes. A few, somehow beached on their backs, moved side to side with convulsive jerks—pathetic turtles unable to right themselves. Four or five seemed to be trying to breathe through their mouths, their fibrous tongues wedged between the baleen plates.

Cliff looked around. Individuals and groups moved up and down the beach. In some places, children offered food to the large beasts, but only the sea gulls fed. Many of the onlookers stood about rubbernecking, wondering aloud what would be done with all the whales after they died.

A Park Services officer assigned to beach patrol sat in his Chevy Blazer watching the scene indifferently. Cliff approached him.

"Tell me, how many of them are still alive?"

"Quite a few here," the officer replied, then tilted his chin up the beach, "and several more over there."

"They'll be towed out to sea, of course."

The officer shrugged. "Maybe. Maybe not." He went on to say that he didn't know what would happen or who was even responsible to take action. He had been on the beach all morning, mostly to make sure that the whales were allowed to die unmolested, and he hadn't heard anything about saving them.

"Look," Cliff began, "you're the man in charge here, right?"

The officer shrugged again. "Looks that way."

"Well then, I suggest you organize a bucket brigade right away. These whales are suffering—they're dying of heat."

"So why prolong the agony, eh?" the officer said.

Cliff hesitated, then spoke. "Because there may be a way

to save them; a team from Woods Hole should be here shortly." He turned his back on him and started walking away.

"Great," the officer called after him. "Where do you suppose I get the buckets for this brigade you want?"

Cliff turned back toward the man, his anger evident in his stride. He walked right up to the window of the Blazer and looked the officer square in the eye.

"Look, *Officer,* I'm with the Department of the Interior. You know, the place your paycheck comes from. Now, get on your goddamn radio and have your boss call a couple of supermarkets. I want fifty buckets, pails, or whatever can carry water on this beach in twenty minutes. Understood?"

The officer nodded; Cliff nodded back and headed toward the water line. He stopped when the water began lapping at his feet. Looking at his watch, he wondered what could be holding up Fritz.

Moving away from the water, Cliff joined a group of people standing by one of the young whales. He had seen plenty of whales before, yet never failed to be awed by their colossal size.

The whale was about thirteen feet long, dark, and wrinkled like a prune. Its blowhole was wide open and twitching, and the left fluke, which had been moving, was now still. Its clicks, the unbreakable Morse code of the sea, sounded like a slow, creaky door. The eyes were the worst, crying out in a mute appeal. *Anyone who doesn't believe that whales are intelligent creatures that have to be protected from the harpoons of whale hunters should be made to stand here and look into these eyes,* Cliff thought.

The buckets appeared, free of charge from a generous hardware store owner, and Cliff joined in helping to pour water over the dying creatures.

"Make way, please," called out a man in jeans, a sweatshirt, and a baseball cap, carrying a black bag. The cap bore the letters A.S.P.C.A. and Cliff smiled at the irony. The man dedicated to the protection of animals had come to inject the whale with phenobarbital sodium, to put the whales out of their misery.

"It won't be long," the man whispered as he spread a towel over the whale's flipper, took out a frighteningly long syringe, and placed it under the towel. The crowd watched in silence as the whale's soulful eyes closed and the twitching stopped. A young boy looked up with an unspoken question. The father nodded, and the boy passed a hand over the whale's side a few times. A young girl brushed tears away. *Some whale watching,* Cliff told himself.

Cliff stood by the seawall and looked through his binoculars at the southern horizon. Fritz should have been there by now, and Cliff searched the skies for the familiar sight of a Woods Hole chopper. As he paced the beach, the mossy odor of seaweed reminded him of his years spent in hands-on ocean research. His job as director of the Bureau of Marine Affairs within the Department of the Interior kept him landlocked in his Washington office. He looked forward to working with Fritz over the next few days, and had to grudgingly admit that he owed his boss, Brant Roscoe, a favor for letting him take the time to participate personally in this project. With his son, Butch, away at school, and himself widowed barely more than a year, Cliff knew he'd become a hermit, working like a dog and not socializing much. Sure, he occasionally visited with a few friends who shared his interests, but he'd ignored opportunities to start dating again, much to Fritz's annoyance. The good-natured East German–born researcher fancied himself something of a ladies' man, and thought Cliff should get out more.

The rotor wash of a swiftly descending helicopter pulled Cliff from his thoughts, blinding him with blowing sand. Bearing the blue and white colors of the Woods Hole Oceanographic Institution, the helicopter landed at the southern end of the beach.

Cliff smiled broadly as he and Fritz greeted each other with a bear hug, like brothers who hadn't seen each other for a long time.

Handsome, muscular, his face burnished from years of sea winds and ocean spray, and wearing the bright WHOI flight suit with its blue-and-gold patch, Fritz looked more like a recruiting poster than a scientist. Holding his blue baseball cap tightly against the rotor wash, he yelled to Cliff, "I have bad news. There are more beached whales all along Locust Grove Beach."

The news surprised Cliff. "How many?" he asked.

Fritz hesitated. "A lot, maybe a hundred. Something is not right."

As the helicopter's rotor spun down, Cliff lowered his voice. "What have you heard from the biologists on board?" Fritz had flown in from the *Knorr*, a WHOI research vessel he had been working on since before Cliff had come to Washington. Owned by the Navy, the ship had been leased by WHOI, and was equipped with state-of-the-art oceanographic equipment.

Fritz drove the heel of his boot into the sand as he formulated his response. While fluent in English, having left East Germany long before the Wall came down, he nonetheless took the time to construct his answer carefully.

"They speak of the same old theories. I believe it could be cyclical, related to the seasonal shift, a natural culling out of the weak that forces them ashore." *Weak* came out like *veek, them* like *zem*. The accent remained.

"No," Cliff said, "I don't think so." He went into his theory on low-frequency vibrations. Fritz's Nordic blue eyes widened. "Now, that is a theory I haven't heard before." He paused. "I will have to think about it more. But now, we should try and do something for these poor whales." He didn't sound optimistic.

With Cliff walking beside him, Fritz dragged his feet through the sand and measured off distances. "The sand is too soft, we cannot use trucks to move them."

"That's it, then?" Cliff asked.

Fritz nodded.

Half an hour later, after meeting with the local Park Services chief and the director of the National Aquarium, who had driven out to survey the situation also, no solutions had been found. The carcasses of the dead whales would have to be removed with bulldozers and Caterpillar tractors. The larger whales would have to be cut up with chainsaws before they could be removed.

Cliff and Fritz sat on the helicopter's pontoon, dejected and helpless. Nearby, a golden retriever, oblivious to the death around him, rolled playfully in the sand.

"How long can we stay here?" Cliff asked.

Fritz looked distracted. "As long as you like," he said. "But we must return to Norfolk by four o'clock if we want to make it out to *Atlantis II* before dark." The *Atlantis II,* anchored offshore, would serve as the launching platform for *Alvin,* a deep-sea submersible—famous for its role in the discovery of the sunken *Titanic*—that would allow them to search the ocean floor for the barrels of toxic waste they feared had been dumped.

"Well, there seems little—" Cliff stopped speaking as Fritz stood up quickly, looking at the dog and muttering in German.

"What?" Cliff asked.

"We can roll them," Fritz shouted suddenly.

"Roll what?"

"The whales, what else?"

"You're crazy."

"No, I am not," Fritz insisted. "We can just roll them as if they were . . . oil drums."

Cliff looked doubtful.

"Cliff," Fritz said, "they are dying now. Surely we should try and save them if we can?"

Cliff hesitated. Who ever thought of rolling whales? And, for the smaller ones, it did seem possible. He stood up. "Okay, let's try it."

While Fritz ran to halt the A.S.P.C.A. vet from injecting another small whale, Cliff found the Park Services officer.

"Do you have a bullhorn?" he asked.

Cliff took the bullhorn and put it to his mouth.

"Listen up, everyone," he called. The people on the

beach turned to see Cliff waving them over. "Over here, please!"

The crowd drew near and Cliff went on. "There's a way we can help save some of these whales." He pointed at a medium-sized whale still waving her flukes. "I'm an oceanographer. If we can get this whale back into the water, it will live."

Fritz took the bullhorn. "We can do this by rolling the whale down the beach, back into the water. We just need to roll it like an oil drum."

Several of the crowd expressed disbelief. But Fritz looked authoritative in his Woods Hole flight suit. He went on, "High tide will be here at nine-thirty. See how the bow of that sail boat is pointing toward shore, it means the tide is coming." Several turned to look. "If we can roll these whales beyond the sandbank," he urged, "the slope of the beach and the undertow will do the rest. Okay? Any volunteers?"

A few hands went up. Fritz picked out the strongest-looking volunteers and directed them toward the whale.

The young whale lay—like most of the others—parallel to the seawall and about twenty-five feet from the sandbank.

As Cliff watched, Fritz lined up his team of volunteers along the side of the whale. Then he placed himself in the middle of them and, bending his knees, slipped his hands under the whale, instructing the others to follow his example.

Fritz turned his head left and right, a quarterback checking his offensive line before the snap. "Ready . . . Roll! Roll!" he barked.

Suddenly, the whale shuddered. The volunteers recoiled, frightened of the whale's crushing weight.

"Don't be afraid. She's helping you," Fritz shouted, his voice hoarse.

More volunteers joined in.

"Roll!"

Grunts of exertion filled the air as the whale clicked excitedly.

Halfway. They hadn't been able to roll the whale even one full turn. The volunteers began backing off. For a moment, they had hoped . . . but it was simply too difficult.

A thought came to Cliff. "Wait," he shouted. "Let's try this." He said the whale was like a car stuck in the snow. You had to use its own momentum to help. Rock it first, then roll it. "Back and forth," he said, demonstrating, "back and forth and then roll."

"Of course!" Fritz shouted, resuming command.

Cliff joined the line. He knelt and placed his hands under the whale. Now he could feel the massive roundness of the whale, the rubbery quality of its skin. How strange that it had no smell of its own. But the faint odor of fish came from its blowhole. As they began to rock the whale, Cliff had the sensation of lifting a huge, wet inner tube filled with jelly. He lost his footing, falling forward as the rocking succeeded and the whale completed a full roll.

The crowd cheered, as Fritz yelled, "We are not finished yet. Another time. Ready?"

And the whale rolled, two, three, four times, ever closer to the water line.

The crowd now numbered about sixty eager volunteers, all wet and sandy, and Fritz began breaking it up into teams to work on other whales. "You," he told a woman in a red Windbreaker, "Go and start rolling that baby whale over there." He looked around. "And you, sir, see if you can get some people to roll that whale by the bathhouse. Hurry."

Cliff turned to a teenager. "Here's some change. Go call the local radio station and tell them we need help out here to save these whales."

Within an hour, hundreds crowded the beach and the first whale rolled sat in four feet of water; one more had reached the water line and another was nearly there.

A wave washed over the first whale, nudging it slightly. Ten minutes passed as waves continued to lap at the whale.

Time seemed to slow as people, standing ankle deep in the cold water, watched for movement.

Another ten minutes passed. The volunteers continued to move whales toward the water, but morale was slipping as the first whale sat immobile. The cold water now kissed Cliff's knees with every wave.

Larger waves began to crest over the whale as the tide rushed in; like mysterious hands working to free her, each wave and the following undertow created a long channel beneath the whale, baring her white belly. The crowd watched expectantly as the whale wriggled in its channel, waiting for the wave that would set her free. Finally, a powerful undertow pulled her from the sand and she slipped underwater.

Suddenly, the whale appeared on the surface, floating freely, and blasted a mist of seawater and air from her blowhole. "She made it!" Cliff shouted, as the whale flipped her flukes at the crowd.

The crowd cheered and pitched in to float more whales off the beach. Cliff and Fritz helped until midafternoon, when it was time to leave for Norfolk. Cliff jogged quickly back to the Exxon station and slipped the attendant several bills. "Keep an eye on it for me, will ya? I'll be back in a couple of days."

Then, overnight bag in hand, he headed back to the helicopter on the beach. He sat on the pontoon and scraped wet sand off his bare feet, pulling on socks and sneakers and taking a moment to catch his breath.

Too many whales had died. It could have been worse, though. If only they had a way to rescue the bigger whales. It was as though Fritz had found the cure for cancer, but only for people under five feet tall.

Most of the crowd had left. Only a few police officers and Park Services people still roamed around. Gray clouds filled the sky, and a cool breeze blew. The receding tide had erased the footprints of the hundreds who had swarmed over the beach. Looking at it now, one would never realize the struggle that had taken place on the beach that day. But the flock of sea gulls circling near the pavilion signaled that the disposal of the dead whales had begun. He imagined a similar picture over Locust Grove Beach.

Cliff tied his sneakers and looked at the overcast sky, tracking the altocumulus clouds now scuttling from the west. It wouldn't make for good diving weather, he knew.

Standing, he called to Fritz, "Let's get going."

The rotor wash swept the beach smooth as the helicopter lifted off.

5

From a distance, the *Atlantis II* looked more like a passenger cruise ship than a research vessel fitted to launch, retrieve, and maintain a minisub.

Darkness had fallen during the time it took the Coast Guard boat with Cliff and Fritz aboard to reach its destination. The boat slowed down and moved to dock along *AII*'s port side. Floodlights along the decks and catwalks turned night into day.

Resting high in its cradle on the aft deck, the white-painted *Alvin* looked to Cliff like an egg from the Loch Ness monster.

A noisy crowd of divers, scientists, and handymen wearing red berets piped Cliff aboard as if he were a visiting admiral. In addition to welcoming a friend and one who helped raise the "Water Baby"—the *Alvin*—the group wanted to celebrate the successful rescue at Mekonhoe. Thanks to the helicopter pilot, the crew from Woods Hole had received whale-by-whale radio reports throughout the day.

Cliff joked about getting piped aboard, but he was moved. "You bastards," he said, raising a plastic glass filled with champagne and drinking to their friendship.

Yet he wished they had skipped the ceremony reserved for former members of the *Alvin* group. It made him feel old.

The formalities over, Cliff dropped his carry-on bag in the guest cabin, then glanced at his watch. He had twenty minutes before the pre-dive briefing began. He decided to go to the library, sure he would be able to find the reference book he wanted among the three hundred titles available.

The library, a small room with crammed bookshelves running from deck to ceiling, was empty, but like any other place on the *AII*, loaded with diesel oil fumes. Cliff sat at the small table by the porthole and quickly thumbed through the index of Richard Carpenter's *A History of Cetacean Whales*, then opened it to page ninety-six and read: . . . *the use of whale oil appears to be of ancient, if not of prehistoric, origin. It was doubtless first obtained from whales accidentally stranded on the shores—a frequent occurrence at the onset of the last ice age. In 1886, the discovery of abundant whale bones along the Virginia and North Carolina coast led marine archeologist Peter Michaud to theorize that the stranded whales, moving away from the advancing ice sheet, were also moving away from the food chain that kept them alive.* Cliff closed the book. "Jesus," he muttered, and felt his knees go weak.

"Dive number two thousand fifty-one is on behalf of the Department of the Interior and the Environmental Protection Agency. The three-man crew will consist of pilot Bill Bates, chief scientist Cliff Lorenz, and our nuts-and-volts master mechanic Fritz Hoffmeister," coordinator Chris Chambers said at the start of the briefing. A blond, strong-profiled Texan in his early thirties, he spoke in a business-like tone, conducting the pre-dive briefing as though addressing a board meeting.

First he reviewed the reason for the dive: the Coast Guard had received an anonymous letter dated April 26, informing them that in violation of the Ocean Dumping

Act, a number of steel casks filled with toxic waste had been dumped off Newport News on January 22. The author of the letter had given coordinates 38° 49.2′ north and 76° 12.6′ west, obtained with a Magnavox SATNAV and therefore an accurate fix. The data placed the casks 55.2 miles southeast of Newport News. If found, a Navy DOWB (deep-ocean workboat) would try to recover the casks to prevent further contamination of area fishing grounds.

Chambers then went on to spell out the mission: a survey of the ocean floor to determine whether recovery was possible; a study of the condition of the casks; the depositing of transponders and sonar reflectors to make it possible for the DOWB to find the casks; and scientific observations of the toxins' immediate effects, if possible.

The condition of the ocean floor came next, and Chris spent considerable time discussing it. According to echo sounder images, the bottom sloped considerably, leading him to assume that the casks had rolled down into an "active" volcanic trench that ran along the ridge. "If that's the case, the search could be a tricky one due to the presence of hot vents, chimneys, black smokers, the works. Of course, I don't have to remind you that even the new Plexiglas of the view ports has a melting point of one hundred and fifty degrees." He turned to Cliff and added, "So it's up to you when and where to pull the plug and surface. By the way, bottom is eighty-six hundred and forty."

Cliff nodded and Chris went on to remind the diving trio to triple-check their photo gear. "The pictures will be the only evidence the government will have to convict the fuckin' bastards—excuse me—and recover some of the money lost by fishermen and merchants."

The rest of the briefing focused on the outline of procedural changes and new equipment installations, most notably the Xenix, a computer system with a time-sharing operating program that allowed simultaneous multiple data-processing functions. It also interfaced with the precision clock used for acoustic navigation, the gyrocompass, the altimeter, a battery of other instruments, and the outboard Benthos camera. "We tried to have the Xenix interface with the espresso machine, but we had no luck," Chris said, and closed the briefing book. They all smiled.

Rather than go to the galley with Fritz, where the cook had left a light supper, Cliff went to his cabin to do his homework. Once settled in the small guest cabin, an eight-by-five room that reminded him of a modest sleeping-car compartment, he put his head between his hands and began reading. He spent almost an hour going over the regulation pre-dive checklist the maintenance chief had prepared for the pilot, which Cliff wanted to double-check for his own peace of mind. He paid particular attention to the work done on the air circulation system, for he knew that an oxygen imbalance could be the most serious of the potential problems they might face. With the silent, odorless addition of just 5 percent more oxygen to the 20 percent concentration needed, a tiny spark from a relay could ignite a fire as bright and as quick as the one inside a flashbulb. How well he remembered that three astronauts burned to death because of an oxygen leak.

Cliff allowed himself a break when Fritz came by with a tray of food, then went back to work on the two-inch-high pile of charts, echo sounder images, and sonar photos all relating to the ocean floor and the water above it. He would be providing the pilot with navigational instructions once they reached bottom, and Cliff spent a lot of time studying its features to get a sense of the flow of a cold current that meandered in that area. If it moved faster than the *Alvin* at full speed, it could present a real threat to the minisub, possibly driving the *Alvin* against a dangerous underwater obstruction.

Deck lights were on when Cliff finally felt prepared for the dive and went to bed. They were still on when Fritz knocked at the door to wake him up.

After more than two thousand dives, the launching of the *Alvin* no longer resembled the circus of confusion it once had. Years of experience and automation had reduced the launch crew to six line handlers, two escort swimmers, and one winch operator.

The day had dawned peaceful and fogless. The sun cast rippling yellow reflections on the calm Atlantic. Some isolated patches of nimbus clouds lingered high on the northeast sky. A brisk breeze blew. The temperature was fifty-one degrees and expected to reach the upper sixties by the time the *Alvin* would surface in the afternoon. Ideal conditions.

It had been a lot colder when the crew chief rousted his people out of bed, and most had donned baseball caps and Windbreakers to battle the morning chill. They were nothing compared to what Cliff now wore: woolen underwear, lined ski pants, a heavy flannel shirt, an old Irish sweater over it, and a woolen watch cap. Even on the hottest days it was terribly cold inside the *Alvin*—and damp.

Bill Bates was already inside the *Alvin,* now hooked on the ship's large A-frame crane by a hoisting bit, ready to be lowered into the water. As tall as Cliff and just as old, but without Cliff's distinguishing good looks, Bates had been there since five A.M., checking and double-checking. Everything that could be tested, he tested. Yet he could not predict a power failure, or a friendly whale bumping into the craft.

While Fritz made his inspection of the minisub and talked with the launch chief, Cliff took a good look at the newly redesigned *Alvin. Some things never change,* he told himself, smiling. Little *Alvin* was still the same fat and short, pug-nosed offspring of a Trident submarine that it always had been. Ugly, but totally functional. In 1966, it found the H-bomb that had rolled out of the wreckage of a downed B-52 off Palomares, on the east coast of Spain. And it had been indispensable in locating the *Titanic* and, just last year, the hulk of a Spanish galleon filled with gold. The idea that he was to dive in it as chief oceanographer filled him with a certain pride and sense of purpose he had begun to lose in D.C.

Getting inside the minisub was tricky—up a ladder that straddled the distance between the *Alvin* and the *AII*'s fantail, down a very narrow ladder through a twenty-inch hatch. Cliff went up the first like a fireman, but needed help on the second. "A bit out of practice, wouldn't you say?" he quipped to Bill, then halted as he took in the updated interior of the minisub. New monitors, a new tracking system, new ballast controls, a new gyrocompass . . . "Oh, this is a dream," he exclaimed.

Yet the sphere had remained basically familiar—a control room resembling the inside of an Apollo capsule with "natural mapping," all the controls arranged so that they matched the things they controlled in natural sequence. The three view ports were still very small, offering poor visibility, and getting up close to them seemed more difficult because of the extra gear. TV and sonar were the *Alvin*'s real windows.

A seven-foot, one-and-a-half-inch-thick titanium ball with barely room enough for three people with short legs, the sphere was the business end of the *Alvin*. The remaining sixteen feet of the vehicle housed batteries for the propulsion system, ballast tanks, and weights, and provided a structure for mounting antennas, lights, cameras, mechanical arms, and other remote-controlled tools.

The *Alvin*'s weaknesses went beyond poor visibility. Space, obviously, came at a price the Navy hadn't been willing to pay; and an NFL locker room compared favorably to the magnified sounds and intense odors of the sphere. A handwritten note taped over the sonar screen read: The Important Thing Is to Keep Your Wits About You at All Times, and More Important Than That Is Not to Go to the Bathroom. Normal dive duration was six to ten hours.

Fritz entered the sphere last, and with him came the order from Chambers to prepare to launch. But nothing could really prepare them for a journey to the bottom of a black ocean in a free-floating minisub.

Five minutes later, the A-frame operator put the *Alvin* gently on the water, and escort swimmers quickly made their final check. Then, after clearing with Chambers at surface control, Bill Bates flipped a number of switches, salt water rushed into the ballast tanks, and the *Alvin* began its descent.

For Cliff, the first 150 feet were always the best because of the color metamorphoses taking place outside his view port. First the warm shafts of sunlight shone bright and disappeared—the red, the orange, the yellow; then the cool colors of light changed from green, to purple, to blue, to black. It gave him the sensation of dropping through a rainbow.

After that, the world became dark and monochromatic, made more monotonous by the unchanging hum of the gyro and the hiss of the radio. At a speed of only a foot per second and with the outside lights turned off and those inside dimmed to conserve battery power, the *Alvin*'s interior seemed more like that of an elevator stuck halfway down a coal-mine shaft.

Dark and silent as each crew member concentrated on his job, the *Alvin* descended past fifteen hundred feet. Cliff concentrated on the *Alvin*'s trouble indicators: the panel meters and the warning lights. Then his eyes traveled professionally along the row of penetrators, the cigar-size devices through which cables and wires from the sphere passed to the equipment outside. He noticed tiny beads of water forming on one of them. Penetrators were always a problem on minisubs and one that prompted the image of a high-pressure water knife used by stone cutters.

Forty-five hundred feet.

His ears didn't pop, and he wasn't getting the old squeeze on the sinuses. That was good news. It told him that the inside pressure system was holding steady at one atmosphere. Not the outside one. It continued to build at incredible speed: two thousand, twenty-five hundred, three thousand pounds per square inch. It would almost double at bottom.

If Cliff had any sensation at all, it was a slight nausea caused by the strong odor of Old Spice. Like most

Europeans, Fritz practically bathed in it. It was over-powering, and worse, there was no way of removing it. It even went continuously through the CO_2 scrubber without losing any scent. Perhaps it was a blessing, Cliff mused. It masked the smell of the HERE (Human Element Range Extenders), the jury-rigged flasks used for urinating that somebody hadn't cleaned well.

The elapsed-time clock indicated that the *Alvin* had been descending for an hour and fifteen minutes. It would take almost as long to surface from that depth. If anything went wrong, it would seem like days.

Negative thoughts were like unnecessary oxygen, so Cliff busied himself observing Bill Bates and Fritz at work. Fritz, stretching to flip toggles and punch numbers on an illuminated keypad, then bending down to put liquid soap around the fittings of the oxygen line to check for gas leaks, had an air of energy and resourcefulness. The pilot, working the variable ballast system, appeared competent and calm amid fireworks of alphanumeric LED displays, the changes of patterns on the sonar screen, the fading chorus from the snapping shrimps with their crackling and sizzling sounds now mixing with the whistles and squeaks of mammals picked up by the hydrophone. Of the two, Fritz was the real techno-natural. He looked as if he were born with push-button ability encoded in his DNA. Cliff wondered in how many seconds Fritz could program a show on a VCR. Certainly not the twenty minutes it had taken Cliff last time.

"Alvin, *this is* AII. *How's everything?*" The voice of the surface control officer came through a bit distorted by the speaker of the underwater telephone.

"Fine," Bill Bates answered into the mike. "No problems at . . . sixty-four eighty."

A minute later, like a B-17 pilot turning the plane over to the bombardier, Bates turned to Cliff on his left and said, "It's all yours."

"Thanks, Bill, I've been waiting for this moment a long time," he said. But the words came hesitantly, as if he didn't mean them.

Alternately watching the sonar screen and the readings reported by the temperature probe, Cliff told Bates to reduce the rate of descent and start the directional thruster. "Temperature has dropped almost a degree. We are entering the current's outer edge," Cliff said, and turned to Fritz. "How are the batteries, Fritz?"

"Power supply steady at twenty-six volts. No fluctuations on the ammeter," Fritz replied.

Cliff passed a hand over his Irish sweater, wiping cold sweat from his palm.

The *Alvin* descended slowly, firing small bursts from the thrusters, now directing water jets upward: 8,100 . . . 8,200 . . . 8,300. . . . All eyes were focused on the display reporting velocity from the current meter, a device resembling a squirrel cage that was mounted on top of the sail, the *Alvin*'s minuscule conning tower. Its maximum reading was 0.4 knots, strong for the ocean floor.

Yet it hinted something to Cliff, who called surface control to request permission to go down to fifty feet. "I want to see just how strong the damn thing is," he said.

The reading climbed to 0.9 knots.

"Damn. That's too fast," Cliff shouted, shaking his head. "Bill, up seven zero and hold it there."

Cliff reported the news to the surface control officer, and then, checking his position in relation to the target coordinates, radioed his intent to begin the search relying on sonar.

Battery life had been Cliff's primary consideration when he designed the *Alvin*'s search pattern.

The *Alvin* would travel along an elliptical course two miles long, a half mile wide. This at an altitude of 120 feet would not only stay out of the current but would also give the Continuous Transmission Frequency Modulated sonar a good sweeping angle. An invaluable instrument for rough bottom navigation, CTFM could detect gallon-size objects at a 100- to 200-meter range.

Cliff could have conducted the search from a lower depth but he knew that to counter the current, the thrusters would have to operate at maximum speed. That would exhaust the batteries rapidly, reducing bottom time. And Cliff needed all he could get to carry out his mission.

The *Alvin* searched without success. Cliff was now faced with a dilemma. Surface, or probe the same area from a lower altitude? While that would reduce the size of the area covered, it would improve the angle of attack.

As the *Alvin* dropped to thirty feet and with thrusters at maximum output, Fritz turned on six powerful thallium iodide floodlights.

Suddenly, the view ports came alive, like TV screens flashing on. Marine snow, tiny globs of particulate matter, small gelatinous fish, limpets, snails, mucus, and thumb-sized zooplankton floated by the view ports.

"Alvin, *this is* AII. *Your bearing is three four four and looking good,*" the surface control officer said. He was tracking the *Alvin* on an Ore Trackpoint II Acoustic System. It made use of synchronized precision clocks (one on the *Alvin* the other on the *AII*) for measuring the time of emission of acoustic pulses from the minisub and the time of their arrival to the *AII* in order to calculate slant range, bearing, and altitude.

"*AII,* this is *Alvin.* Confirm three four four on gyro. Going for a good look-see."

All three passengers peered through their view port.

After a few seconds, faint features began to emerge. Cliff motioned Bates to go down more. Now the bottom came into view. Cliff looked at it carefully—granitic, sloping steeply down to a dense, gloomy blue-green void and littered with smooth, oil-drum-size boulders sloughed off from the ridge above. His eyes strained to see. Eyeless shrimp swam above stones deposited by melting icebergs; crabs swarmed around thatches of "spaghetti," eerie clusters of long, thin wax-colored worms pointing in the direction of the current.

"Alvin, *this is* AII, *we're tracking you fine. Anything for science?*"

"Yeah, that"—Cliff got very close to the Plexiglas of the view port—"fecal matter, detritus, and mucus survive toxic waste rather well," he said.

Suddenly Fritz shouted, "What's the matter with you guys? Can't you see that track?"

"Where?" Cliff and Bill asked in unison.

"Spin right hard and you'll see it."

From a distance of ten feet it looked like the tracks left on snow by the plastic saucers children use to slide in, but this was thirty inches wide, with narrow depressions running across it at regular intervals.

"*All*, this is *Alvin*. Have sighted one track . . . make it two . . . three. If we search, we'll probably see one caught between chimneys." He was referring to the rock structures resembling stalagmites formed by thermal spouts. Some rose to a height of one hundred feet. "Plenty of them around."

"Alvin, *this is* AII. *What's next?*"

Cliff looked at Fritz and Bill. "The trench. By the way, what's the new bottom?"

"Eleven thousand and two hundred forty feet," Bates answered.

With the track now providing a clear direction, the *Alvin* began to descend to the new bottom. Soon the clear surface of something man-made appeared on sonar. Bates steered toward it until it was visible to the naked eye. The cask was only a few yards from the point where the steep granitic slope cut almost abruptly into the sediment eroded from the land, which typified for Cliff the edge of the marginal ocean basin. He had seen dozens of them along volcanic faults, especially in the Sea of Japan. Marginal ocean basins had very unstable sediment, and a good look at it from an altitude of ten feet confirmed what he knew. The surface of the basin, like all the others he had seen, was a grayish, gluey, almost viscous mud soft enough to cover the landing skids of the 37,000-pound *Alvin*.

The cask resembled a beer keg, only it was larger. Long, shiny rusticles and hydroids partially covered the surface, which was dented in several places. A dark area in the center of the cask showed that it had split along the weld seam.

Cliff reported the observation to surface control and asked permission to probe the area to see how many casks were still intact, if any.

"Alvin, *this is* AII . . ." After a few seconds of hiss, the same voice came in. "*We can leave that for another dive, now that we know where the hell they are. Pull the plug and come up.*"

"*AII*, that's a—" Cliff broke off his transmission as Fritz yelled.

"*Gott in Himmel!*"

A pinpoint stream of water, forced into the minisub by the cubic pressure of their greater-than-ten-thousand-foot depth, cut across the sphere.

"Look out!" yelled Bates. "Don't cross it. At this depth it'll cut you in half."

"It is the *verdammt* temperature gauge cable. The gasket has separated," Fritz said, fumbling through a toolbox near his position.

"Alvin, *this is* AII. *Do you have a problem?*" the surface controller radioed.

Cliff squeezed the transmission key on his microphone. "You're damn right, we have a problem, *AII*. We have a gasket failure on the temperature gauge cable. We're trying to get a handle on it. Wait one."

"*Roger,* Alvin."

As Cliff spoke with surface control, Fritz put a hose clamp around the cable, which was filled with oil in order to compensate for water pressure. He moved the clamp an inch away from the penetrator and tightened the screws as hard as he could. "*Diese verdammte Abdichtung muss jetzt halten*" (this contraption had better work), he said, swearing in between words.

With the clamp choking off any flow, and five thousand pounds of pressure squeezing the cable from the outside, extra oil was forced into that portion of the cable that passed through the penetrator. As the rubber covering of the cable expanded, it tightened the fit against the gasket. The water stopped leaking.

Cliff sighed in relief that the crisis had been averted. As he reached for the microphone to notify the *AII*, he looked up and saw an obstinate digital display glowering at him with higher and higher numbers. "Jesus!" he cried out, feeling a shiver of panic.

"Up, Bill, up," he shouted, trying to keep his control from one crisis to the next. "We're picking up a jet from a vent."

With all the thrusters in a vertical position, the *Alvin* began to ascend. Fritz immediately passed a hand over his view port's Plexiglas. Cliff did the same, not knowing if the water he felt in the palm of his hand came from the view port or was left from the leak. From the latter, Fritz quickly reassured him. Cliff let out a long breath and patted Fritz on the shoulder.

Slowly the temperature readings began to drop: 48.09, 47.05, 46.03 . . .

Drying his hand on the sleeve of his sweater, Cliff peered through his view port. Below the *Alvin,* a billowing, sulfide-colored cloud moved parallel to the bottom, then rose up and dissolved into a shimmering vortex hot enough to melt lead.

The search continued, with Fritz and Cliff now working the Benthos 372, a thirty-five millimeter camera.

The casks were within a quarter-mile area. Many had dents but looked intact; a few had split cleanly·in half along the weld seam.

Cliff took a tally and reported that of the eighty-four casks he had seen, fifteen were empty. "But we haven't anything incriminating except pictures."

"Alvin, *this is* AII. *It would be nice if you could find something. But you had better move it.*"

Cliff frowned, shaking his head. Suddenly he found his mission vaguely disturbing. There was something special about diving for science, with danger ennobling the effort. What was noble about finding a piece of evidence?

"Alvin, *this is* AII. *Well?*"

Cliff put the mike close to his mouth. Perhaps man had entered an age when ennobling acts were not limited to risking a man's life in search of knowledge but extended to the prevention of crime against the environment. He pressed the button and said, "Yes, it would be nice."

The search continued for another twenty minutes, while the crew released transponders and sonar targets.

Then the trio hit the jackpot. As they hovered slowly over the casks, Bill Bates noticed that there was something shiny dangling from the hexagonal screw-on cap of one of the casks.

Hovering at neutral buoyancy so that the *Alvin*'s skids were barely touching the mud, Bates positioned the minisub in order to let Fritz use the TV camera lens to zoom on the object.

Almost at once the shape of something similar to a padlock appeared on the colored screen. While Cliff kept the camera aimed at the target, Fritz put his hands on the feedback master/slave mechanism, a small replica of the port mechanical arm, and extended the port arm until it was inches from the casks. Then he gingerly worked its wrist pitch and pincers to grasp the shiny brass object and turn it around.

On the TV screen appeared the words UNITED STATES GOVERNMENT. ENVIRONMENTAL PROTECTION AGENCY SEAL NUMBER 152.

"Bingo," Fritz shouted. "OK, Bill, pull the plug!"

He did, and the long trip to the surface began.

All outside lights were quickly turned off; those inside dimmed, and now digital LED displays began washing the sphere with a rainbow of their own—amber from the clock, aquamarine blue from the frequency counter, yellow ocher from panel meters, emerald green from the depth gauge: 10,110 . . . 9,360 . . . 4,233. . . .

It was quiet now inside the sphere and Cliff began thinking about the casks. . . .

Obviously sealed by the EPA for burial in a steel plug deep in rock, he reasoned, the casks were dumped in the ocean to save storage money. Before that, the seals were cut off. More than an oversight, leaving one of them was intentional. Perhaps the guy that sent the note to the Coast Guard made sure of that. It made sense. It would make sense to a jury.

At 5:10 P.M. that afternoon, a red flare marked the spot where the *Alvin* surfaced.

6

It may have been only May 19, but the demons of arctic winter were already back at NP/5.

The wind came like an angry god to punish them. It forced everybody to walk with their backs to it across icy sheets that creeped like miniature glaciers.

After hours of a hypnotic shimmering caused by the northern lights, night had once again lingered without dawn. The sun, an orange wash of light at ten A.M., hung in the sky like a Japanese lantern, radiating nothing. The only sign of spring was the cover of an L. L. Bean catalog promoting camping goods.

Yet NP/5 still functioned, though all research activities had been canceled. Just keeping warm had become a full-time job.

Trouble came in the afternoon by coded message. All personnel were to remain on-station to assist in decommissioning the reactor.

According to the message Van Muren received, "no radiation—even the smallest amount—should be allowed to be carried into Canada and the United States by Arctic air masses in their normal southeasterly route."

So Van Muren now faced the task of having to cool down the reactor, dismantle its core components, heat exchangers, and piping by remote controlled equipment, then remove "scrud" from radioactive surfaces and structural material by chemical cleaning and hand scraping.

Dangerous and time consuming as decommissioning was, Van Muren knew he had to do what was best for his people as well as the millions of others downwind. If he began cooling down the reactor, there would not be enough electricity and steam to keep his people warm.

The tension at NP/5 stretched to the breaking point.

"In a nutshell, we have no choice," said Duncan Garner, the self-appointed spokesman during a meeting in the mess hall. As head of the Health Physics Department, he was in charge of radiation control. "We either die of hypothermia or glow before we die of radiation exposure. Is that it? Well, Mr. Van Muren," he continued, "I want you to promise us that you will not start cooling down that fuckin' thing out there until we get the emergency generators and the kerosene stoves you requested." He picked up a knife from the table and pointed it at him. "We want you to promise that *now*!"

Fearing a mutiny and chaos, Van Muren agreed to the demand. "You have my word and be reassured that—"

"Good," Sarah Woodridge interrupted, "and stop giving us that bullshit about the seasonal reversal. I know what's going on. I haven't heard the Khabanikhovs for days. No one has."

Woodridge had been in charge of Project AI, a study prompted by the greenhouse effect. It focused on glacial deterioration and the rate of ice melt so that estimates of the rise of the sea level could be predicted. She knew ice. She was on her second tour at NP/5 and had studied glaciers in the Swiss Alps before this.

Yesterday afternoon, as she was walking back to the compound after securing her files, an acoustic illusion tipped her off that Van Muren had been lying about the seasonal reversal.

She stopped walking and listened. No sound came from the ice under her feet. *Strange*, she thought.

Again she walked, stopped, listened, then squatted, cupped her hands around her ears, and listened. Again no sound, not one "voice in the snow."

As she stood with her back to the wind, Woodridge realized that there was something wrong with the ice.

If it was spring, she reasoned, the structure of the ice should be looser. It would pack easily under her one hundred plus pounds weight, she thought, and make a sound, one that the Soviet scientist Khabanikhov fancifully described as a "distant voice calling for help." She walked a few feet and heard no "Khabanikhovs." It sent shivers coursing through her body.

The next day, at a meeting held after lunch, Van Muren convinced his people that reducing reactor output was a necessary and immediate step if they hoped to leave NP/5 within a reasonable time period. He made it clear that since there were no volunteers waiting to decommission the plant, they would have to do it. "No decommissioning, no aircraft. It's that simple," he said. He spoke with quiet, but desperate, firmness. But he assured everyone that temperatures in the compound would remain around fifty degrees provided they accepted a self-imposed energy conservation program.

That afternoon, as nuclear engineers worked out a timetable for reducing power, half of the high-wattage light bulbs were removed; electric shavers, radios, stereos, and personal ceramic heaters were turned in. But in the mess hall the jukebox played all selections free. Regular emergency kerosene heaters helped to keep the temperature above fifty-one degrees in ten of the sixteen arctic huts normally kept sixty-five degrees year round.

But the evacuation of personnel remained a problem. Because crevasses had restricted the use of the ski strip to small planes, the Air Force had to rely on long-range helicopters. Two were already in Juneau, and they were being refitted with wall insulation and special navigation and communication gear. However, pilots with Arctic weather experience were rare. Thule Air Force Base had one, but he was needed at the base. A worldwide search was ordered by the Air Force chief of staff.

The only aircraft able to land was a two-engine Cessna owned by Transarctic Express, a Canadian company, the same plane NP/5 and Eureka chartered to carry mail and spare parts. But Katabatic winds had kept the small plane grounded for days.

NP/5's Boiling Water Reactor (BWR) was a steel enclosure or pressure vessel twelve feet high and five feet wide. Shaped like an oxygen tank, it was housed by a concrete structure and connected to the control room by a tunnel ten feet under the surface of the ice. Built by General Electric, the BWR was of the same type installed in the first nuclear submarines.

In the reactor's central core fifty-four fuel rods shot off trillions of neutrons per second, striking the nucleus of U-235–enriched atoms and splitting them apart. The splitting— nuclear fission—generated vast amounts of energy in the form of heat. Water circulated through the core to slow down fission and produce the steam piped to the turbine.

Van Muren was in the control room when Rip Nelson, the senior reactor operator (SRO), and his assistant, Jeff Robertson, the reactor operator (RO), completed the first series of procedural steps that prepared the reactor for lower output.

"Well, that went off smoothly. The rest shouldn't be too bad either, if metal fatigue is what's bugging this gauge," Nelson said, and tapped one labeled CONDENSER COOLING WATER FLOW RATE. Then Nelson shook his head.

Van Muren noticed it. "You seem concerned."

"I am," Nelson replied, and without further prodding he added, "We have a problem with the water going into the condenser."

Van Muren creased his brow questioningly. "What do you suspect?"

The answer came quickly. "A, a faulty armature in the meter; B, a malfunctioning pump; C, something wrong with the pipe."

C was what Van Muren feared most. "A kink?" he asked with half his voice.

"Maybe, but where? The coil is half a mile long and buried ten feet under the ice."

Van Muren didn't say anything. He just kept looking at Nelson, his brow creased in concentration.

"So," Nelson said, "Larson can check the pump, Jeff here could fly to Juneau and get a new meter, and we pray that's all it is."

Van Muren managed to keep his features deceptively composed. "I'll see that Jeff makes the next flight."

Robertson, who had been listening, nodded. "These gauges are old. They should've been replaced long ago," he added, and closed a large three-ring notebook.

Robertson, a dark figure of a man, tall and athletic, was seated in the RO swivel chair and faced the control panel. Fifty-four red pilot lights, one for each of the fuel rods, glowed brightly, indicating steady operation. To his left, trace recorders marked levels on revolving drums: temperature 850 degrees Fahrenheit; pressure 900 psi; water level fluctuating in the green zone between 8.3 and 9.2 feet. Voltage, wattage, and turbine speed meters were to the right of the lights. Each read normal.

Nelson stood behind Robertson, his eyes riveted on the symptom-based chart mounted to the right of the control panel. Known as the "Ten Commandments of the Nuclear Plant," it dictated the key list of operations in the given order.

A thin, almost anorexic man who blinked like an owl, Nelson passed a hand over his chin, as if smoothing a beard. His only choice was to replace the gauge and check the pump. *How safer it would be,* he thought, *if Little Bertha had a reactor with a negative void coefficient instead of a positive one.* But Washington had never approved his request. So now he faced the possibility of a surge in heat output with a reduction in cooling water. "Cooling down a plant isn't that simple. Ask the guys at Chernobyl or Three Mile Island," he said to Van Muren.

Van Muren didn't say anything. If Nelson was trying to build himself up, he was succeeding. But what if he wasn't?

May 21. Dr. Fredericks, long designated as the number one evacuee to fly out of NP/5 because of a broken and infected leg, finally got his break with diminishing winds opening the first weather window in days. The other scheduled passenger was Jeff Robertson who was going to Juneau to see if he could find a new condenser meter and choose the shipping canisters for the fuel rods.

Some off-duty personnel accompanied them to the plane, acting as if just another NP/5er were going home at the completion of his or her tour.

Against the sputter of the plane's engines turning over, Van Muren asked Robertson to go and talk with the commander of the Air Force base at Juneau and explain NP/5's situation to him. "Tell him to send helicopters even without insulation, tell him to send vertical-takeoff jets, tell him to send anything that flies. He has to get us out of here fast. Ned Gray says we're already doomed." He squeezed his arm. "Come back, won't you?" Robertson nodded, turning his face away from a swirl of ice crystals.

Van Muren watched the plane take off, climb, turn around, and buzz the station, tipping the plane's wings. It was the pilot's traditional way of saying "see you tomorrow."

Van Muren waved at the departing plane and then continued his inspection of the reported signs of ice expansion, stopping first at his office to pick up a Geiger counter, which he put inside a gym bag.

Passing by the entrance to Hut 4, Van Muren stuck his head inside the photo lab where Canal, a journalist from *National Geographic* magazine, stood loading a thirty-five-millimeter camera. "Do you think you have enough for a story?" Van Muren asked.

The journalist looked up. "I'd say a book."

"Good! By the way," asked Van Muren casually, "how did that picture of me waving the flag on top of the pole come out?"

Canal opened an aluminum box and gave him a photograph. Van Muren thanked him and, leaving, told him that according to his schedule, Canal would be in Eureka in four days. Seconds later, Canal caught up with him. "A favor," he said.

Van Muren nodded, and Canal gave him a plastic pouch with cans of thirty-five-millimeter film. "Just in case I . . ." he said, and shook his head. "I mean, so they don't get spoiled in the next four days."

Van Muren smiled at him, grateful for his restraint. "They'll be on the next flight," he said.

In the tunnel, he suddenly stopped walking, took out a pen, and on the back of the photograph he wrote: *That's the day I stood where all time zones converge; I did an about-face and walked around the world. The kids will get a big kick out of that, someday. Lovingly . . .*

He then put the photograph inside the envelope, together with a letter he'd written that morning, but he didn't seal it.

Next, Van Muren stopped to see head mechanic Ed Larson, a man with the frame of a running back. "How're we doing?" asked Van Muren, shutting the door of the shop against the freezing wind.

Ed looked up. "All right, I guess."

"Anything to report?"

"The ridge, sir, the one by the service tunnel . . ." There was a catch in his voice. "If it grows . . ."

"It won't grow," Van Muren interrupted, and pulled out a handkerchief to blow his nose. "A seasonal reversal doesn't last long."

But it did.

Cold, strong winds gusted to fifty-five miles per hour during the night, covering NP/5 with drifts of ice crystals. The wind-chill factor dropped to minus seventy-five degrees. Subsurface ice expanded; more and more crevasses formed.

But the most alarming sign was found in the tunnel to the emergency generator. Three more sections of its wooden walkway had come loose.

"Is that all?" said Van Muren to the middle-aged head carpenter who had worked hours to fix it.

Next morning, Van Muren joined a group of scientists and technicians for breakfast. He told them that with the sudden drop in temperature, it was natural that the much colder subsurface ice would expand at a faster rate, causing surges and cracks. "We're out of the woods," he said. "I've experienced worse polar days." As he got up to leave, he asked one of them, a cryogenicist named James Mills, to follow him. In the tunnel to the radio shack, Mills stopped Van Muren. Before the director could say anything Mills said, "You were lying back there, weren't you?"

Van Muren glanced quickly around, then back to the cryogenicist. His eyes were tired. "Yes, I was, and that's why I need to talk to you. Get your gear and be ready to fly out of here with the next flight. I'm charging you with an important mission." Speaking softly, he explained that at the rate the decommissioning was going, it would be two weeks before he left NP/5, another three to four weeks before he reached Washington. By then, irreversible decisions would be made at the White House. "You know and I know this is no freak reversal—"

"And so does everybody else in here," Mills said, cutting in. "And they're scared."

Van Muren nodded. "I know that, too." He looked straight into the cryogenicist's eyes and added, "It may be too late for us here but—"

"Don't say that," Mills interrupted.

"I know what I'm talking about. Listen."

Mills closed his eyes, nodding, and Van Muren continued. "It may be too late for us here, but one thing can save the others back home—climate modifiers—and you heard me talk about them a while ago."

Mills said nothing; Van Muren went on, "Obviously, I can't push for them here with communications the way they are." He spoke faster now. "They're just as bad in Eureka. So you'll have to do the pushing for me." He told Mills to get in touch with Peter Kronin, the head of the IGCS. "Tell him that what you saw here is what most Americans will see in a few months, and that climate modifiers are the only means of stopping the deep freeze. Climate modifiers, remember that."

Mills who had been listening, blinking with bafflement, just nodded. He was so shocked by Van Muren's plea that he seemed to have lost his voice.

"Climate modifiers. Repeat."

"Climate modifiers . . . Yes, I know what they are."

"Good. It looks as though we may get another weather window. Go get ready."

Mills didn't move. "What will the others say?"

"They'll wish you Godspeed, after I tell them everything."

Just before three in the afternoon, the little Cessna stood ready for takeoff.

Van Muren accompanied Mills to the Cessna. They ran to the strip without saying a word. As Mills boarded the plane, Van Muren pulled out an envelope and gave it to him. "It's for my wife," he said. "It's unsealed. Don't mail it."

Mills nodded.

The pilot started the engines.

Mills reached for the safety belt, then turned to Van Muren and said slowly so that Van Muren could read his lips "Cli-mate mo-di . . ."

At this point, from the south side of the strip came a claxon blast.

They turned. A Snow-Cat moved full speed toward the plane. Quickly Van Muren pointed a finger up and moved it in circles. The pilot revved the engines. A louder claxon blast. Van Muren turned again and saw the driver of the Snow-Cat, signaling him to wait. But Van Muren opened the door, stuck his head inside the cockpit and said, "Don't forget us, will you, Mills?" He shut the door then pounded on it shouting, "*Go . . . go!*"

The pilot eased momentarily on the throttle and pointed at a person running toward the plane.

"*Go!*" Van Muren ordered.

A gust of wind shook the plane, kicking up eddies of dry snow.

Mills opened the cockpit door. "It's Ned Gray," he said.

Van Muren ignored him. "You've got a mission, god-damn it," he yelled, and slammed the door shut. He cupped his hands around his mouth and yelled to Gray, "Next flight!"

"Why not this one?" Ned Gray snapped, shielding his face from the knifing swirl of ice crystals whipped up by the propeller.

"Why not?" Gray pointed at Mills, anger in his eyes. "How come he can?" He was nearly hysterical.

Van Muren knelt down and and removed snow from under one of the skis. He reached for the plane's window and pounded on it. "Go, goddamn it!"

But the pilot shook his head and pointed to Gray, who had moved in front of the plane, legs wide apart, arms raised.

Just then there was another long gust of wind. It drove drift snow under the plane's skis.

The pilot pushed the side window open. "She'll never go," he shouted.

Angrily Van Muren motioned Gray to make way, but the latter refused to move. "You promised," he cried out. "You promised."

Suddenly Van Muren ripped his anorak open and reached for the pistol he'd started carrying. *It's already come to this*, he thought. "I order you to move," he said.

Ned Gray raised his chin defiantly. "No!"

"Move, Ned," he said, raising the pistol. He aimed it at him and held it there with both hands wrapped around the grip, the barrel glistening in the swirl of snow. Deliberately he pulled the slide back, then released it. "Move, you fool," his voice cracked.

Mills opened the window. "Hold it, hold it, for God's sake," he shouted.

"Shut up," Van Muren growled as he moved two steps closer to Ned Gray, who gaped at him trembling, eyes wide and glasslike.

Seconds passed.

Van Muren released the safety catch. "You're interfering with official United States operations," he said, waited, then fired a shot in the air. Gray gasped and moved aside. He then dropped to his knees, his head cradled in his arms.

Waving his gun at the pilot, Van Muren fired again in the air. "Hurry," he urged. "Hurry!"

The plane shook, then started moving in a cloud of snow. Van Muren walked a few steps along Mills's side shouting "Good luck!" He stood waving as the plane taxied and took off, then went to Ned Gray, put an arm around him, and helped him get on the Snow-Cat.

Those watching the plane take off noticed that it buzzed over the station without tipping its wings.

And so did Dr. Mills, who asked the pilot why he had forgotten to signal those below.

"Why?" he shouted. "Because I ain't going back. Next time, there could be fifty guys trying to board this plane and one might have a shotgun. Things are bad enough without that shit."

They would be a lot worse at NP/5.

7

Cliff Lorenz parked in the lot behind the Department of the Interior's offices and sat for a moment gathering his thoughts before climbing out of his Porsche.

A message from Brant Roscoe had reached him aboard the *Atlantis II* immediately after the *Alvin* had been winched aboard. Tired, wet, and still shaking with adrenaline, Cliff had read the message with apprehension. Roscoe, not knowing whether or not the *Alvin*'s mission had been completed, had ordered Cliff back to Washington immediately. And now, sitting in the car, Cliff still could not figure out what could have prompted such an order. And while Roscoe didn't put much effort into keeping his subordinates informed, the complete lack of information in the message was unlike him. He never called a meeting without a set agenda.

Cliff got out of the car and pulled his raincoat closed, tying the belt in a knot at the front, but not buttoning it up. *Another winter in Washington that'll end just in time for summer,* he thought. He missed the New England springs that seemed to last a year in comparison to D.C.'s.

The Department of the Interior was situated diagonally

opposite the White House, between E and C streets. A symmetrical five-story structure, the building reminded Cliff of a late Italian Renaissance palace.

As Cliff walked across the lot toward his office building, he heard someone calling him. He stopped, recognizing Phil Jackson, the head of security for the DOI and a good friend. They shook hands.

"The old man is pissed," Jackson said, pointing a thumb over his shoulder toward the building. "Roscoe called all the division directors in and kicked their asses. Told them they'd better all clear their desks and cut out any bullshit projects they're working on."

Cliff told him of Roscoe's mysterious order to make an appearance.

"Better watch out, buddy," Jackson warned. "He's taking no prisoners. He's been over to see the Man twice this week and it seems to have put the fear of God into him."

Cliff thanked Jackson and headed into the building, wondering all the while what could have prompted Roscoe to visit the White House twice in one week. Usually only a national disaster of biblical proportions brought such attention, but Cliff hadn't seen anything on the news, and Jackson would have known if that were the case.

He sprinted up the marble steps, then took the elevator up to the fourth floor.

Maybe Pam knows what's up, he thought.

Dr. Pamela Wycoff was Cliff's closest friend and associate at the DOI. She specialized in environmental-impact studies, often working closely with the EPA, but more often clearing the way for the government to issue licenses to corporations interested in mining, harvesting, or drilling for natural resources on government land. That hadn't been her original goal when she came to the DOI, and her underlying environmental protectionist feelings had resulted in Roscoe's lecturing her more than once about separating personal opinion from government policy.

As much of a health club regular as Cliff, Pamela could

pass for much younger than her thirty-four years. With her auburn hair and wholesome good looks, she looked less like a researcher and administrator and more like a model for L. L. Bean or J. Crew. She came out from behind her desk and gave Cliff a welcome-home hug. Cliff responded, wishing still that it was more than a friendly gesture.

Cliff and Pamela had met during the debate on allowing oil companies to drill on Georges Bank. Though the Republican administration, and therefore Roscoe, had favored granting permission, both Cliff and Pamela opposed it. Their opposition gave environmental groups more than just a leg to stand on as they brought enormous pressure to bear on the government. The license to drill was never issued.

The pressure of the situation brought out a mutual attraction neither one could deny. But Cliff was happily married to Marla, a beautiful art historian, and Pamela was deeply engrossed in her career. Neither was willing to risk the personal or professional consequences of becoming involved in an affair. And gossip flowed quicker than the Potomac through Washington.

Still, their friendship was real, and even stronger than their attraction to each other. Pamela became Cliff's best friend at work, and a good friend to both him and Marla outside of the office. He never could have made it through the grieving process after Marla's death without Pamela.

Following Marla's death in a head-on collision with a drunk driver, Pamela kept after Cliff to remain involved. Even as they collaborated on new projects, she refused to allow him to become buried in his work. She made sure he didn't abandon Butch at his boarding school, often organizing father-and-son outings that allowed all of them to celebrate life instead of mourning death.

Only a little more than a year had passed when Cliff realized he was in love with her. And, more important, he *liked* her. He liked her organized way of doing things; she was always making lists. He liked her knowledge of virgin and extra-virgin olive oil, her recipe for goulash, her print collection . . . her eyes, her legs, the way her breasts moved as she jogged along the beach. . . .

Pamela loved Cliff, too, but not in the same way. She loved his imagination and creativity. She couldn't ask for more in a project partner. She liked his sense of humor. Butch was as much her pride and joy as he was Cliff's. But even as she cared so deeply for him, she made it clear that there was no romance here, just the deep bond of two friends. But he hadn't given up.

As their embrace ended, Cliff spoke. "Do you know what's going on? Roscoe sent me a cryptic message to get my tail back here, and Phil Jackson just told me he's been on the warpath and over to see the president twice."

Pamela sat down at her desk and, palms up, gestured at the piles of paperwork covering it. "Well, Phil's not kidding. He called us in and killed every proposed project and license request with one wave of his hand. He told us to stonewall anything new. Also, he canceled everyone's vacations and told us to leave a contact number whenever we go out. When we asked why, he said it was all 'need to know' and that we'd find out soon enough. Half the staff are updating their resumes and the rest are planning for World War Three."

"Sounds serious, all right," Cliff said. "I guess I'd better go see Roscoe and find out what I can."

"Let me know," Pamela said, a feeling of frustration evident on her face.

Cliff left the office and headed down the hall. Glass doors separated Roscoe's carpeted reception area from the tiled hallway. A temporary secretary—Roscoe couldn't seem to hold on to a permanent one—held him up while she buzzed Roscoe. He told her to send Cliff in.

Roscoe sat behind his massive desk, filling the chair, his thin lips hinting at the strict discipline that had made him feared by his troops. His office furniture was all heavy mahogany, and memorabilia of his military service decorated the space. A plaque on the wall read: If You Aim at Nothing, You'll Hit It Every Time.

Roscoe pointed at one of the three chairs in front of his desk and Cliff sat down. "We have a serious problem," Roscoe opened. "One of our responsibilities is dealing with the effects of national disasters. And we now face the greatest ever."

Cliff recoiled. "What are you talking about?" he asked.

"You know Peter Kronin, right?"

Cliff thought a moment. "The new head of the IGCS? The geophysicist from M.I.T.?"

"Right," Roscoe said. "He's been tracking the effects of dust loading in the atmosphere, working closely with the data the polar stations have been reporting. It seems that the dust loading has led to a reduction in solar energy passing through the atmosphere. I told him it was all theory, bullshit really. He made me come over and see the data for myself." He paused. "Cliff, glaciation is a fact."

Cliff sat in a stunned silence. Could Roscoe really mean what Cliff thought he meant?

"It's in progress in the polar regions," Roscoe went on. "You know John Van Muren, right?"

Cliff nodded.

"I've read the messages Van Muren has sent. Things are so bad up there his crew may not get out. The ski strip has been fractured by crevasses. The ice is expanding faster than anyone could have imagined."

Cliff looked at Roscoe with eyes widened in shock. Anxiety surged through him. Van Muren was more than just a colleague, he was a good friend. "I'm totally surprised by this news," he muttered, feeling as though he had been hit by a wrecking ball. "You actually read the messages from Van Muren?"

"Yes, I did," Roscoe replied. "They confirm Kronin's prediction of a massive cooling and growth of the ice pack not seen since the last ice age."

Cliff couldn't begin to respond. He hadn't seen the data, but he respected Kronin's work and believed fully in Van Muren. "If Van Muren says a deep freeze is in progress, I believe him," Cliff said.

"Good," Roscoe said. "As you would expect, Kronin asked for my cooperation, and I've promised him all the support he wants." With this last statement Roscoe's tone had dropped. Cliff saw a squall blowing up.

"What kind of support?" Cliff asked.

"Your modifier," Roscoe said, with no trace of emotion, no hint that he expected anything but complete agreement and cooperation from Cliff.

Jesus, no. It all came flooding back—the awful smell of putrefying bodies and the specter of Death that had haunted him since that day in Idaho.

Roscoe had lit a cigar. He peered at Cliff through a cloud of blue smoke, waiting for Cliff's response.

Cliff's mind raced. This wasn't just a matter of seeding a few passing clouds. Kronin wanted a major modification, one that might kill millions. "You're talking about a modification on a scale that will destroy more lives than it could ever save. By definition, CLIMODs destroy the environment, rather than salvaging or protecting it. They are *unnatural.* Didn't Idaho teach you *anything*?"

Roscoe waved his cigar. "It was an act of God," he said.

"Hell no!" Cliff shouted. "It was an act of man—of you and me."

Roscoe stared hard at Cliff. Cliff continued.

"Besides, CLIMODs were banned by the United Nations. Twenty-nine nations, including the U.S. and Russia, signed it. You can't do it."

"Don't play professor with me," stormed Roscoe. "I'm well aware of the U.N. resolution. The U.N. has also banned terrorism, torture, and starvation. So what? What has it ever changed? We are faced with a national emergency and we will take all steps necessary to protect these United States. With or without your help."

Cliff ground his teeth in frustration, knowing that Roscoe was treading the path to catastrophe.

"Brant, listen to me—"

"No, Cliff, you listen to me. Consider all your files both

here and at home impounded. If you won't play ball, I'll find someone who will. I've promised Kronin a modifier, and he'll get one." Roscoe was sweating, aglow with power.

Cliff stood up. "Those files are mine."

"Not so." Roscoe cited the regulation, the paragraph, and the section giving him the authority to impound Cliff's files and notes. Then, with staged calm, he brushed cigar ashes off his cuff. "I'm now ordering you to organize all the files so that I'll be able to turn them over to other researchers." He paused for effect. "I'm sure that Dr. Marshall will be interested in what you've been doing."

An alarm bell went off in Cliff's head. "Marshall?" he asked, his stomach knotted tight. "I know Marshall. I worked for him. He stole the idea for his modifier from an engineer named Ryker, the designer of the Panama Canal."

Roscoe dismissed Cliff's charge with a deliberate shrug. "If Kronin trusts Marshall, who am I to disagree with him?"

"Marshall's modifier is fatally flawed," Cliff said, choosing his words carefully, his voice low and somber. "Marshall," he went on, "never understood the theory behind Ryker's plan. You think glaciation is destructive? Wait until Marshall's modifier goes into action."

Roscoe blew a stream of smoke toward the ceiling, then dropped his eyes to Cliff and said, "Then give me your modifier, so that Kronin can choose for himself."

Cliff stood motionless. "I can't do it."

"Cliff, things are going to get chilly around here."

Cliff remained silent.

"All right," Roscoe said, ending the conversation. "I'll be sending someone for those files. You're dismissed."

The rain streaked down the windows of Pamela Wycoff's office as Cliff walked in with wrinkled brow, his mouth a tight, tense line. He appeared shaky, defeated.

Pamela glanced up, reading the signs in Cliff's face.

"I guess it didn't go too well." It was a statement, not a question.

"You could say that," he responded.

"Well, what happened?"

Cliff detailed Roscoe's request for his modifier, and his eventual order to turn over all of his notes and files.

"Just like that? With no discussion, no recognition of your concerns?"

Cliff nodded. "Just like that," he said.

"Unbelievable. What a bastard."

Cliff flashed a brief smile, then rose. "Better get started, I guess."

Pamela looked at him with concern and empathy. "Cliff, I'm so sorry. If there's anything I can do to help . . ."

"You already have," he said, heading out the door.

Cliff sat in his office with a sense of incredulity that his career—and consequently his life—was on the line because of a modifier he wouldn't consider.

Six years ago he had been asked to head the Cabot expedition. The mission: find and map hideouts for the "loitering" Trident submarines in the North Atlantic. It was during this Navy mission that he had made an exciting discovery.

In its long, embowed journey from the Gulf of Mexico to Northern Europe, the Gulf Stream bends sharply eastward south of Newfoundland. It is here that the stream breaks off into small curving tongues known as meanders. Resembling, on a map, the shavings coming off a carpenter's plane, meanders originating from the left bank of the stream take a northwesterly direction; southeasterly from the opposite bank. Even Cliff did not know the real reason for the meanders, though he theorized that their maverick behavior was due to the spinning of the Earth, the Coriolis Force. One of the meanders—the biggest as the processed data showed—was the J Current. It had an estimated volume transport equal to one-fourth the total volume transport of the stream.

Unlike the other meanders, however, the reason for its breaking off just south of Cape Race, Newfoundland, was something Cliff had learned on the return trip. Using the latest device Navy engineers had designed and developed for ocean-floor mapping, the side-looking sonar, he was able to obtain an accurate profile of the topography of the area.

To his surprise, he found that an underwater island existed in the spot where the J Current broke off from the stream. It was buried under a thick forest of long-stemmed weeds of the devil's apron variety, the laminaria weeds. Since the area had little military or strategic importance, no country had ever been interested in serious oceanographic research intended to establish the real source of the J Current and the moist air riding above it. It was just another meander.

Cliff named the island the "Hull." When he saw its three-dimensional shape projected on the screen of an imaging computer, it reminded him of a giant hull of a ship resting upside down on the ocean floor.

The Hull was clearly the maker of the J Current, Cliff reasoned—correctly, as later research proved. It stood like a giant fork in the road. It sliced off the stream's left bank, forcing it into the Mid-Ocean Canyon, which runs parallel to the Hull for twenty-one miles, then veers sharply left and heads toward Hudson and Baffin bays through the Davis Strait.

One didn't have to be a weatherman to realize that it was the J Current that fed moisture to the Arctic air masses— the reason behind the unusual amount of snowfall and ice north of the Quebec-Seattle line.

Back in Washington, Cliff accepted a personal commendation from Admiral Rickover, and the Hull, classified top secret, was soon forgotten like the waves on the sea above it.

But then one day something happened that changed Cliff's life.

One weekend, taking advantage of the long Columbus Day holiday, Cliff and his family went to a flea market along Route 1A. There Cliff's attention was suddenly drawn to an oval-shaped lithograph of the Gulf Stream stacked with a pile of old paintings and photographs. The glass was broken; the frame badly chipped, but the lithograph, which Benjamin Franklin had drawn and printed to give to his sea captains when he was postmaster of the colonies, looked undamaged beneath its cover of soot. Cliff bought it.

A week later, he began the work of restoring the lithograph. He noticed, to his amazement, that the tip of Greenland, that of Baffin Island, and the north shores of Labrador, which in modern maps are shaded in white to indicate snow, were painted a light green. Of course! Benjamin Franklin did not know about the J Current, so he could not have known that it supplied the cold Arctic masses with the moisture for the abundant snowfalls.

An idea flashed in his mind like a meteor.

Blow up the Hull, and there would be no J Current! Moreover, the forward momentum of the stream itself would carry the debris and block the entrance to the Mid-Ocean Canyon. For hours he tried to punch holes into the theory, but he couldn't. It was as flawless as an ice crystal, a perfect discovery, like that of Dr. Fleming and his penicillin. And no one had thought of it because it was so simple.

The following day, Cliff went to see Van Muren, who was organizing a research expedition in the North Pole prompted by the greenhouse effect. Van Muren seemed highly receptive to the idea of a modification. He felt that there was a need for science to address the problem of a likely increase or decrease of the polar ice sheet, possibly as the result of the damage being done to the ozone layer.

Van Muren encouraged Cliff to work on his modifier. And as the weeks went by, "Ocean Bypass" grew from a brief, seven-page description of the concept behind the modification to a voluminous collection of graphs, charts, soundings, sonar profiles, and computer printouts occupying a five-foot-high file cabinet.

When Cliff received a letter from Van Muren urging him to spend more time on his modifier, Cliff went to see

Roscoe and asked to be assigned to the climate modification section.

Then, in the car late one night in San Diego, the music stopped. *"We interrupt for a special bulletin,"* said the announcer. *"A tragedy of colossal proportion struck western Idaho this morning when a wall of water from a broken dam . . . "*

Cliff shook his head. Modifiers couldn't be trusted. The Idaho disaster clearly warned everybody that to attempt to regulate something as unpredictable and unknown as weather was suicidal folly indeed. Surely Kronin knew that. Anyhow, the odds that the Hull could be blown up before the polar ice sheet spread over the area were against modifiers.

It was dark when Cliff reached Rock Creek Parkway. Streetlights made sparkling pathways on the roads. To his right a long line of cars inched toward the Kennedy Center for the Performing Arts.

Something made Cliff pull up by the curb near the showroom of Liberty Oldsmobile at the corner of Reservoir Road. He stood in front of one of the large display windows, his body an exclamation point. He studied a red station wagon. In case of an evacuation, he knew, his survival could depend on it. The showroom was still open. A salesman approached him.

"How big a gas tank does it have?" Cliff asked.

The salesman arched his brows, surprised. "The gas tank, sir?" The salesman hesitated. "Fifteen," he said. "Twenty. I don't know, but I can look it up."

Cliff ignored him and pointed at another station wagon, smaller but with a rack on the roof. "Do you have a wagon in stock as big as this red one, but with a rack?".

"Sure," the salesman said. Cliff thanked him and walked back to his car, noticing a deep scratch on the right door of his Porsche. Probably it happened at Mekonhoe, he thought. Not that it mattered where it happened. Not that anything mattered that much now.

Cliff drove home slowly. He needed time to be alone and to think about the future. Marshall had to be stopped, that he knew.

The evening felt colder and damper, preparing him for a gloomier night. But it suited his mood.

He drove up Key Bridge, down George Washington Memorial, up Mason Bridge . . . The Potomac flowed turbulently, cresting with spring rains.

Ten o'clock. Cliff walked to his front door looking as if he had lived two lives.

Inside the house, as he read from Butch's recent letter, he began pulling out the summer clothes his son had requested. Then he checked to see what was left—a ski jacket, an old overcoat that was too small, a sport jacket, jeans, more jeans, and more sport jackets. Not a single parka or anorak. Butch would need a heavy parka, woolen socks, a heavy sweater. . . .

After putting the summer clothes into a carton, Cliff went to his study. It was a room normally cheered by sunlight because it faced south. Professional manuals with faded spines, books by Buckminster Fuller, Denis Hayes, and other writers of the National Staff of Environmental Action were neatly arranged on shelves covering two entire walls. On the floor by a comfortable chair was a copy of the *New York Times,* which he invariably skimmed through with a self-imposed time limit. There were no diplomas or degrees because he hated the way doctors and dentists decorated their office with them. Prominent was the Franklin lithograph in its original oval-shaped frame. It stood above the music stand, on which rested the flute Cliff had learned to play when he was a child. A folder with a few handwritten pages of the book Cliff was writing on the real function of the Gulf Stream rested on top of the desk. It was marked CHAPTER THREE/FIRST DRAFT.

Cliff collapsed in his easy chair, drooping over it like a puppet with slackened strings. He was mentally spent, physically beaten. He turned the stereo on. It produced a baroque concerto to which he listened long enough to decide that even his favorite baroque music was too much for him tonight. He had to rest, sleep, but how? There in front of him, locked in a fireproof cabinet, were half of the files Roscoe had impounded. Sticking out of the letter holder was the bank's reminder of his next mortgage payment on the condo. He was only forty-four, in good health, but plagued with the feeling that the future looked dark, and worried that glaciation might make it impossible for Butch to get the vital medications he needed.

The deck was stacked high and against him.

He remained seated, frightened of the future, fighting the seduction of despair.

With some effort he opened the windows wide, but the air felt heavy, gravid with consequences. The rain still poured down. Now, though, it was like the beginning of the biblical flood.

Yet it would be worse.

8

Going west from the old Red Square on Prospekt Kalinina Avenue, after crossing the nineteenth-century bridge over the Moscow River, one enters this new district of the city with its early-Manhattan skyscrapers. Here, red bricks and wood survive next to concrete and aluminum as they would in Boston or Philadelphia.

Across from the sprawling Kijerskaja Railroad Station is a massive rectangular building that catches one's attention because of its lemon yellow plaster and white painted columns. Despite the colors, it is austere, not obedient to classical proportions, and conceived with Greek and Roman architectural motifs. It's typically Russian—but for Kiev or Odessa, and not Moscow. A guard wearing a splendid doorman's uniform and no boots hints to the fact that 1228 Prospekt Kalinina Avenue is not one of the buildings run by the military.

Yet this is where the actual brains behind the Soviet army do their thinking, for 1228 Prospekt Kalinina is the residence of the Institute for Advance Planning, the first think tank of independent scientists and foreign policy experts entrusted with the task of advising the Kremlin on matters vital to the survival of the nation. Not surprisingly, it also houses the terminal of the hot line President Kennedy and Chairman Khrushchev agreed to install. Fearing that whoever was representing the new non-Communist government might use it to come to secret agreements with the president of the United States, it was moved from the Kremlin by unanimous vote of the Parliament.

For two weeks the institute's members had been discussing the threat of glaciation. As a body they saw mass evacuation, food distribution, looting, and violence as the major problems facing their society.

They offered suggestions and made recommendations, but as one of them put it, "What I can give you is purely theoretical. We have no history of a deep freeze close enough to use as reference. The unknown is our number one threat."

On May 23, Dr. Andrei Konlikov took the podium.

Sakharov Hall was a vast room that gave one a sense of the sky in the ceiling, which rose to a height twice that of a comparable building anywhere in the world. Heavy drapes over curtains of old-fashioned lace, Oriental carpets, red silk tufted sofas, and the barely visible portraits of Soviet men of science gave the room a feeling that time had stopped here sometime in the late nineteenth century. Shimmering chandeliers cast a golden glow, and a lemon-scented air freshener did its best to counter the smell of dark Russian tobacco.

"The biggest threat," Konlikov said without the traditional introductory statement, "is the United States. In a world of delicately balanced natural forces so predisposed to the domino effect, any attempt by American scientists to manipulate these forces can only have tragic consequences for us. As my colleague from St. Petersburg University pointed out yesterday"—he turned and nodded to the man on his left—"our weather is unfriendly as it is—if not outright hostile." He paused to assess his audience of twenty-five seated around a long oak table. Not one of them was in uniform, not even Konlikov.

To his right was Anatoli Marlinski, who, like Sakharov,

had been exiled for his views on academic freedom. Across the table was Natasha Karamzin, the professor from Moscow University who had camped for days inside the Parliament building during the recent unrest. And chairing the meeting was Apollon Federovna, a reformer and a member of the committee of overseers running the CIA-styled FID (Foreign Intelligence Division).

"Com—" Konlikov laughed, and his colleagues laughed with him. "After so many years, 'comrades' comes naturally. I'm sorry," he said, toying with his pipe and waiting for silence. "Ladies and gentlemen, unless we are willing to accept the reality of a United States modification, we will not prepare ourselves to counter it. As you know, tests on our thermoradiators indicate that we may be able to lessen the effects of glaciation. But the thermoradiators were designed with the present weather patterns in mind, not with a modification that could affect us adversely."

As one who had been involved in weather modification (he reminded his audience that his pet project was the proposed reversing of rivers in order to bring water to the parched Russian steppes), Konlikov went on to say that he was sure the United States was contemplating a modification. "One," he said, "that will affect us simply because some modifiers have the potential of becoming the catalysts of climatic reactions that favor one area at the expense of another."

A hand went up.

Konlikov nodded at the man, who asked, "We have surmised that much, sir. Tell us what you suggest?"

The answer came quickly. "That we begin gathering intelligence on the U.S. modifier immediately. Their plans, the personnel involved, ships and equipment to be used, et cetera. We are faced with a question of survival as great, or perhaps greater, than that posed during the Great War. We have faced much political strife and hardship these past years. Now we must set aside those differences that separate us and once again present a united front against a common enemy. We must again be a union."

He got plenty of nods; several clapped, and one even cheered.

Professor Karamzin asked, "You must have an idea about what the United States may be contemplating. Don't you?"

"Yes, I do," he answered, and explained that since ocean currents were the makers of weather, and the Gulf Stream ran along the eastern coast of the United States, a modification would have to involve the warm ocean current. "The stream is one huge thermostat at their control."

"Once we know how the Americans want to tinker with it, then what?" a woman asked from the far end of the table.

"Short of military intervention, that's something this institute must recommend."

Konlikov stressed again the need for an all-out intelligence gathering effort. "All we need are the funds." He looked at the FID chief, Apollon Federovna. "As the Americans say, dollars can move mountains."

He sat down.

Apollon Federovna began to smile.

A young man in an ill-fitting suit stood waiting outside Sakharov Hall. He got up when he saw Konlikov come out. "I have something for you, Colonel," he said, and smiled broadly. He opened a file folder and gave it to Konlikov. It was the printout of a computer search and file-matching program.

Konlikov began to read it:

```
SEARCH NO 00015
   DATA SECTION, STATE INTELLIGENCE
   SERVICE
   FILES COMPARED:39
   SOURCE:
           AMERIK DIRECTORATE,
           WASHINGTON
           LIBRARY OF CONGRESS
           UNION CATALOG, HARVARD
           UNIVERSITY
```

END SORT SELECTION:
　　　　LORENZ, CLIFF ADLEY
　　　　AGE 44
　　　　TERMINAL DEGREE, PH.D.
　　　　UC, DAVIS, CALIFORNIA
　　　　MILITARY SERVICE: NONE
　　　　POLITICAL ACTIVITY:
　　　　ANTIWAR ACTIVIST
　　　　***RECOMMENDED FOR RE-
　　　　CRUITMENT. NO ACTION
　　　　TAKEN***
　　　　WIDOWED.
　　　　ONE CHILD, AGE 12
　　　　NO PHOTOGRAPH ON FILE

PROFESSIONAL ACTIVITIES:
　　　　SPEAKER
　　　　SYMPOSIUM, OCEAN
　　　　CURRENTS, GENEVA, 1975
　　　　SYMPOSIUM, MANAGEMENT
　　　　OF OCEAN RESOURCES,
　　　　BARCELONA, 1981
　　　　SYMPOSIUM, REGULATORY
　　　　INFLUENCE OF THE
　　　　GULF STREAM,
　　　　SAN DIEGO, 1983

PUBLICATIONS:
　　　　ON THE GEOPHYSICS OF THE
　　　　STREAM, NATURE, MAY 1970
　　　　SOME DATA ON THERMAL AS-
　　　　PECTS OF THE GULF STREAM,
　　　　OCEANUS, FEB. 1971
　　　　TOPOGRAPHY OF GULF STREAM
　　　　MEANDERS, NATURE, MARCH,
　　　　1972
　　　　EKMAN TRANSPORT AND THE

GULF STREAM, OCEANUS, OCT.
1973
THE GULF STREAM AND GEO-
STROPHIC CURRENTS,
OCEANUS, JAN. 1974
EVAPORATION AND SALINITY
VALUES OF THE GULF
STREAM . . . 1978
THE INFLUENCE OF THE GULF
STREAM IN NORTH ATLANTIC
DURING WINTER, BRITISH
OCEANOGRAPHIC STUDIES,
OCT. 1980
SUBMARINE GEOLOGY OF THE
GULF STREAM, SCIENTIFIC
AMERICAN, JULY AND AUGUST,
1982
SATELLITE THERMOGRAPHS OF
THE GULF STREAM, OCEANUS,
1986

EMPLOYMENT RECORD:
SCRIPPS OCEANOGRAPHIC
INSTITUTE, 1971-72
WOODS HOLE OCEANOGRAPHIC
INSTITUTE, 1974-76
DEPARTMENT OF THE
INTERIOR, 1985-

MAJOR ASSIGNMENT TO DATE: HEAD,
CABOT EXPEDITION,
NORTH ATLANTIC,
SPONSOR: US ANTISUBMARINE
WARFARE DEPARTMENT.

Konlikov looked at the young man. "Good work, Antonov. Make a copy and bring it to me. Hurry."

Five minutes later, Konlikov went to see Apollon Federovna and gave him a copy of the computer search.

When the Berlin Wall came crashing down, and Germany once again became a unified nation, the Western intelligence services, like children set free in a candy store, rushed to seize and examine the files of East Germany's infamous intelligence agency, the Stasi. Among the secrets discovered was the existence of more than *two thousand* East German agents operating as members of the West German government. And the West Germans weren't alone in their embarrassment. Two East Germans, a husband-and-wife team, were discovered to be working not only for the Central Intelligence Agency and the Stasi, but also the People's Republic of China.

Also among the records found was evidence of more than *ten thousand* East German families that had emigrated to the Soviet Union, while other family members emigrated west. U.S., British, and West German intelligence agencies immediately began intensive efforts to uncover the identities of those who had gone west. For these missing individuals, thousands of them, were the sleepers, the agents sent into hiding in foreign countries, under false identities, tasked with blending in and becoming model citizens of their new countries. All the while, these sleepers were waiting for the message from home that would activate them, thereby opening a Pandora's box that Western intelligence agencies would do anything to keep closed.

Sleepers, by definition, lived in fear. Their families were nothing more than hostages, held in case the sleeper failed to perform his or her mission. With the fall of communism in the Soviet Union and the rise of the independent states, most had quietly burned their onetime pads, changed their phone numbers, moved to new towns. In effect, most sought to sterilize themselves, to separate themselves from their former keepers. After all, the penalties of being found out were still high: prison, or worse now, return to the former Soviet Union. Most sleepers had come to enjoy their lives in the West, an eventuality foreseen by their Soviet bosses when the sleepers' families were "invited" to live in the Soviet Union. But now the KGB was dead—at least as far as most of the sleepers were concerned—and the sleepers' families, like most citizens of the newly independent states, would have to fend for themselves.

For sleeper Jim Barclay—formerly Aleksandr Petrovski—the sudden appearance of a "policy renewal" from the Sunlife Insurance Company of North America triggered the end of his life. The sixty-two-year-old NASA administrator had entered the United States illegally, together with his wife, from Canada during the height of the space race, tasked with gaining a key position in the American space program. For thirty years, Barclay worked his way through a variety of positions at McDonnell-Douglas, JPL, and Lockheed. He had, for the most part, forgotten his primary goal. He had become a career NASA administrator, sweating funding cutbacks, and shedding tears when the space shuttle *Challenger* exploded.

When Jim Barclay opened his mailbox and found the policy renewal, the shock caused a massive coronary arrest. The paramedics declared him dead on the scene. Fifty-six NASA employees attended his funeral. During the eulogy, Barclay's superior described him as a great patriot, a member of a generation that had fought the cold war in outer space and won. Barclay's widow, herself a native of Leningrad, became so hysterical that she had to be sedated.

The ringing phone caught Fritz Hoffmeister just as he was leaving to meet his date for the evening. A beautiful blond researcher doing an internship at Woods Hole, she had captured his heart on first sight. It had taken several weeks to convince her that he wasn't as bad as the other women at Woods Hole made him out to be and that she should go out with him. He had the evening planned down to the last detail: a moonlit walk down the beach that would end at his beachfront home. He had just gotten back from Norfolk that morning and was looking forward to the evening with great expectation.

He picked up the phone.

"Mr. Hoffmeister? Moran of Sunlife here. How are you today?"

For a moment, time stopped. Every year Fritz received a mailing advising him of the benefits of having an insurance policy with Sunlife. He always checked the box asking for more information that also reassured him that "no salesman will call." Now a salesman was calling, and Fritz Hoffmeister felt an anxiety that loosened his bowels and left him gagging on the bile rising in his throat.

"Mr. Hoffmeister? Are you all right?"

Fritz swallowed hard and dropped into a kitchen chair. "Yes, I'm fine. Good afternoon. How are you?"

"Good. I finally got that policy approved," Moran said. Fritz struggled with the reality that he had just been activated, "awakened" from his sleeping state, a blissfully innocent state he had enjoyed for more years than he could remember. Moran's voice caught his attention.

"I thought I might drop the policy off at your home."

"Well . . . ah . . . I was on my way out," he said, trying to react calmly. "I have a—"

"Better if you cancel your plans," Moran said, his gruff voice firm in its direction. "The policy has to be signed today or you will lose the grace period."

Fritz sat on the verge of tears, realizing that he had just been informed that if he didn't respond to his activation orders, his life would be forfeit. *So much for the death of the Soviet Union*, he thought.

"Of course," he said. "When shall we meet?"

"Two hours, at the news agency. All right?"

"Agreed," Fritz said. The line went dead in his ear almost before he finished speaking.

Falmouth, Massachusetts, is eight miles north of Woods Hole at the southern tip of Cape Cod and linked to it by Woods Hole Road. At exactly 6:15 P.M., Fritz entered the Cape Cod News Agency to pick up a message from a man—Moran—he had never seen, nor would he ever. One cannot betray what one doesn't know, he remembered from his days at the former Leipzig Intelligence Center.

And in a bright flash of recall he saw in his mind's eye the building in Leipzig where he had been trained and heard the voice of his intelligence tutor.

"Most sleepers," the tutor had said, "never get activated." And Fritz, the fool, had believed that. Now he wondered what his assignment would be. He knew that the nearby Otis Air Force Base had just installed a new and highly sophisticated radar system. And in the days when Bear bombers had tested the United States' patience by flying down the coastline, information on that antenna might have been of interest. But today? Fritz didn't think so.

Fritz also knew that his ship, the *Knorr,* was sometimes used by the Navy for ASW (anti-submarine warfare) testing, but again, the world was now a different place, and he couldn't imagine what could have prompted his masters to wake him from his long rest.

Fritz entered the news agency and maneuvered his way through the crowd, buying the evening editions of the Boston papers and the *New York Times.* He stopped at the magazine rack and bent over to pick up the second-to-the-bottom copy of *Popular Science* from a large stack. The magazine did well in this area. For a few moments, he browsed through the magazine, as though trying to decide whether or not to buy it. Finally, he walked to the counter and handed a five-dollar bill to the clerk. Pocketing his change, he walked out of the agency and back to his car.

In his car, Fritz fought the instinct to throw away the magazine and escape. He knew he wouldn't be allowed to live unmolested. His instructions were to read the magazine and nod. Quickly, he opened the magazine and thumbed through it. On page sixteen, written along the edge of a subscription form, he found the words he had nearly forgotten: *You have been chosen for a vacation by Sunlife. Wait for travel instructions via agency.* Fritz forced a smile for his invisible control and nodded.

• • •

Across the country, in Los Angeles, a stocky man with the nose of a prizefighter went up to the news kiosk outside Twentieth Century Studios on Olympic Boulevard and bought the third-to-the-last copy of the *Hollywood Reporter*. The man, named Charles Donovan, bought the magazine regularly. As a Hollywood stunt driver who specialized in "fly swatting"—pinning a target automobile between his car and another, or a wall—he had won acclaim for his work in *The French Connection.* After reading his instructions, he nodded and walked out.

Across the United States, in Washington at the National Weather Service, in Houston at the Johnson Space Center, in Florida at the Kennedy Space Center, at centers for oceanography at three universities in California, at Boeing in Seattle, and at sixteen different naval installations, sleepers were awakened. Some tried to ignore their instructions. Two committed suicide almost immediately. One took the time to kill his family also. Most, with surprise and shock, fell back on their training from so many years past, just like Fritz Hoffmeister.

9

The days continued to get colder at NP/5. But John Van Muren and his crew thought they knew what they were in for. It wasn't anything like what followed.

On the twenty-forth, Transarctic Express flew one more flight, though the pilot remained on the far end of the ski strip only long enough to let Jeff Robertson off and unload some equipment.

"Welcome to the leper colony," Ed Larson called to Robertson over the raging winds, as he led the way back to the Snow-Cat.

During Robertson's absence, tension over the final evacuation date had continued to grow. Decommissioning was scheduled to start in the evening, and Robertson had come back with the assurance from the Juneau Air Force Base commander that by the twenty-sixth there would be helicopters at NP/5.

S-hour (shutdown), as it was called, was set for eight P.M. Everybody had been warned to stay out of the exclusion area and told not to interfere with the operation. That went for Van Muren as well. Dosimeters were passed out, as mandated by the Nuclear Regulatory Agency; Geiger counters were located at strategic areas throughout the station; radiation alarm sirens were tested and on-line.

These were only precautionary steps, though, and heightened the crew's anxiety little. All NP/5ers were briefed at length on nuclear power plants before departing for the polar station. They knew about allowable monthly dosages of radiation, the potential for cataracts, abnormal fetuses, and cancer. They knew that no nuclear explosion was possible with the low-enriched fuel used in fission reactors, as contrasted with the highly enriched uranium or pure plutonium used in nuclear bombs.

But no nuclear plant had ever faced expanding ice before, and even low-enriched fuel rods could release high levels of radiation if the ice affected plant operations.

In Little Bertha's control room, senior reactor operator Rip Nelson and his crew worked hard to check the condenser cooling pump and replace the defective gauge. But it didn't take long for them to realize that neither the pump nor the gauge had anything to do with the rise in temperature.

They began to suspect an obstruction in the condenser cooling system network. Yet they weren't concerned enough to sound the alarm. There was no place to run to, as Nelson put it. And, like all nuclear plants, Little Bertha had been designed with backup systems, engineering safety systems, and defense-in-depth strategy procedures that would assist the operators in case of trouble.

Tired and stretched thin, Nelson stared at the meters of the control panel. They were the windows of the reactor, just as the eyes are those of the soul. Fission continued. The water temperature was rising, and so was the steam pressure, but slowly. That is, if anything could be slow inside a nuclear reactor.

Nelson had been made SRO because he was resourceful, calm, and an adroit control operator. His plan was to reduce power output so that preliminary decommissioning could begin while, most important, allowing his colleagues to keep warm until the copters arrived.

At eight P.M., as scheduled, he stood behind Robertson,

who was seated in the RO's swivel chair, and began evaluating the plant's parameters.

"Drain flow in condenser cooling system is minus two point three percent, up point two from previous recorded reading," said Robertson. It meant that the amount of hot boiling water draining from the reactor to the condenser, where it would cool, wasn't flowing through the network of pipes at peak rate. Nothing serious, as the reduction in flow rate remained within given limits.

Nelson nodded. "Understood," he said loud and clear, eyes on the Symptoms-Based Chart. Like a chart used by nurses in intensive care units to evaluate a medical crisis, this one listed possibly mortal combinations of nuclear emergencies.

Experience and hundreds of drills had taught Nelson what steps to take in a real emergency. But following the chart was the only way to avoid a human error like the one responsible for the tragedy at Chernobyl.

Still studying the chart and knowing what the answer would be, Nelson asked, "Is there a rise in temperature?"

Robertson confirmed Nelson's belief. The temperature had risen from 905 to 950 degrees. As expected, the pressure inside the reactor increased as the hotter water produced more steam.

"Steam pressure is now one thousand eight psi, up thirty from last recorded reading," Robertson reported.

Nothing appeared critical yet, but all indicators were gradually swinging toward the red portion of their respective scales.

As the chart made clear, it was time to choose one of two possible steps: (a) insert the control rods one hundred percent to stop the nuclear reaction and shut the plant down; or, (b) activate the reactor core isolating cooling system, which was designed to increase the drain flow.

Without deliberation, Nelson elected to keep NP/5 warm. He ordered, "Activate RCIC."

"RCIC on," Robertson sounded off, and less than a minute later he announced that the drain flow was improving.

More water was now flowing into the condenser. As colder water flowed into the reactor, the temperature slowly dropped. And with that, the pressure dropped as well, as the steam within the system began to condense.

"All readings normal. All indicators in safety zone," Robertson reported.

Having satisfied himself that he had the parameters where they should be, Nelson was finally ready to cut the power down in anticipation of the decommissioning operation.

In a reactor, power is reduced to desired output by reducing the nuclear reaction, and this is achieved by partially covering the fuel rods with neutralizing control rods.

At Nelson's signal, hydraulic motors kicked on, activating the mechanism that lowered control rods one-third of the way between the fuel rods. Filled with neutron-absorbing boron, the control rods quickly slowed down fission.

Robertson checked the control panel and then spoke. "High-range neutron monitor indicates four zero reduction."

"Understood," Nelson said, and exhaled a long sigh as the reports continued: temperature down; pressure down; drain flow normal.

Nelson nodded. "Good work," he said, and kept an eye on the control panel for another half hour. Then, after one last reading of the panel meters, he flopped into a chair by the back wall, tipped his head back, and closed his eyes. "Watch it, Jeff."

Though everyone knew what was taking place in the control room, calm prevailed at NP/5, so the task of maintaining the station's vital activities continued.

At least for the next five hours.

As night fell with minimal solar radiation during the three hours of daylight, ice conditions worsened. Pressure ice running from the banks of the nearby lake continued to build. Surges, some five and six feet high and hundreds of feet in length, grew everywhere like long loaves of bread in a hot oven. They cast eerie shadows in the outdoor fog lights.

"These are ideal conditions for crevassing," one technician muttered. He had climbed on top of the chest of drawers to look out of the bubble-shaped Plexiglas window. "God help us," he repeated.

At dinner, Van Muren again expressed his confidence that things were going well in the control room and looked forward to rest and recuperation at Eureka. Helicopters would soon fly everybody there.

Then, just past six the following morning, a tremor ran through the living quarters, faint and sustained. "The ridge by the fuel bladder broke!" yelled one technician returning from the Snow-Cat pool. She had been driving around NP/5 checking seismic activity on her instruments. "Jesus," she exclaimed out of breath, "you should see it. It looks like a huge cracked watermelon. It must be two hundred feet deep . . . more!"

Van Muren thanked her. "That was your last trip out, Lois. You leave the day after tomorrow."

"Good!" she said, smiling. "I've had enough of this damn ice."

Suddenly, from the public address came a warning: "Crevassing at the east end of the tunnel!" It was the area of the nuclear reactor.

A deep booming resounded throughout the camp. Then another and still another after that. A long silence followed. Then came a creaking sound, barely audible, mixed with the tingling of water glasses touching. Minutes later, a quiver. It felt like a huge bowling ball rolling down a lane.

That did it.

Hysterical, Ned Gray came running down the service tunnel shouting, "We're dead!"

Ed Larson saw him pass by, chased him, and brought him down. "Shut up or I'll crack your skull open," he said, covering Gray's mouth with one hand while brandishing a wrench with the other. "The rest may believe you and panic. Do you—"

Just then there was another stronger, sustained quiver.

By the mess hall exit door, Van Muren tried to ignore the vibrations of the floor as he met his two assistants prior to going out. Shrieking katabatic winds had picked up again. In the paralyzing, knifing air, they could see Hut 4 enveloped in steam. "Oh, my God!" shouted one of them. The trio froze at the sight of a crevasse cutting across the tunnel that connected the women's hut to the heating shed. Sections of broken pipe pointed up, blowing clouds of steam that immediately froze in the frigid polar air.

Van Muren, his face bleeding from the sting of the wind-driven ice crystals, ran to the radio shack located in the hut adjacent to the mess hall. There the radio operator was trying to contact the IGCS. But the interference was too strong on shortwave frequencies. Washington was only intermittently readable. The other frequencies were not usable because the satellite was not within line of sight.

"I've never heard anything like this interference before," the operator said, looking up to Van Muren. "No filter cuts it out. Nothing."

Van Muren listened. Lines of strain creased his clam-gray face.

" . . . *will do our best,"* a voice came through the speaker. It was that of the expedition desk officer at the IGCS.

Abruptly, Van Muren tore the microphone from the operator's hand and shouted, "Just what do you mean, 'do our best'? Where the hell are the helicopters we've been promised?"

"They are at Eureka," blared the voice from the speaker. "Helicopters can't buck those winds. No way. However, two heavy C-4s, I repeat, figure two-Charlie-hyphen-figure-four, planes with extra-long skis are en route to Great Bear Lake from Thule. A Canadian Arctic Air Rescue Squadron is also en route."

Van Muren put the microphone down and wiped his forehead. He turned to the operator. "Keep talking and don't sign off, understand?" His voice was strained. "Tell jokes, recount your life history, read an article from *Playboy*. Keep him talking, understand?"

The operator stared at Van Muren wide-eyed, his face paler by the minute. "Does this mean I won't get on the plane?" he asked.

Van Muren frowned. "I thought you had guts," he said.

"I'm scared, sir. I know what's going on."

Van Muren jammed a finger into the operator's chest. "Listen carefully," he said, squinting his eyes. "You volunteered for this job; you asked to come here. You attended all the orientation meetings. You heard what they said about life in the Arctic. Now, put those shaky hands of yours on that radio and don't drift off frequency, understand?"

The operator blinked, then nodded.

Van Muren smiled. "Call me when the C-4s get within range," he added, and left the radio room only to return a few minutes later. "Call assembly. I want everybody here. I mean everybody," he shouted.

Forty-five people gathered in the mess hall. Some peered through the window facing the ski strip, some milled around talking softly to each other. One man paced back and forth in front of the door to the radio room. Blankets blocked the wind entering through an opening under the main door; a blue anorak stopped it from entering through a crack in the north wall.

Van Muren came in and asked everybody to be back in less than an hour, ready to evacuate the station. "C-4s are transport planes, not the Concorde. Bring everything you've got to keep warm."

As they raced to their huts, Van Muren and head geologist Dan Morgan climbed the meteorological observation tower to check the condition of the lake used by large supply aircraft. They gasped at the sight of the shimmering image of active ice. In the fading sunlight, the lake looked like a huge empty dinner plate with four unevenly spaced dark stripes running diagonally across it, the shadows caused by the pressure ridges. Now they measured three feet high and over fifteen feet wide at the base. For a few minutes neither one said anything. Then Van Muren patted Morgan on the shoulder. Morgan shook his head, ice crystals glittering yellowish in his beard.

"Don't worry, Dan," said Van Muren, "those guys flying C-4s are daredevils. They get their kicks landing on ice and snow, the same way fighter pilots love to land on a carrier at night. They like it better than sex. Come on, let's get something hot."

The mess hall was well lighted, steamy, and smelled of roasted chicken. It would be the last time the cook would use his propane oven.

A dozen or so scientists and technicians were already seated around a long rectangular table next to the kitchen counter. More came in with their duffel bags, backpacks, and suitcases. They talked loudly now, and there was even some laughter. Large Sterno cans kept coffee and hot chocolate warm. The jukebox played oldies: Frank Sinatra sang "My Way."

Van Muren and Morgan poured themselves some chocolate and joined those at the table. He sat next to his secretary, the oldest of the women at the station, and talked quickly to her. The group looked as if the four A.M. shift had stopped for something to eat before going to bed. But they were noisy and ate and drank with gusto.

Suddenly, a dull roar silenced them as another pressure ridge split open half a mile from the mess hall. Lights flickered. The needle of the jukebox skipped the track. A door creaked.

A nuclear technician entered the mess hall and waved at Van Muren. "Rip thinks it would be better to cut power a bit more. The creep meter just outside the concrete containment building shows signs of stress. Not much. But he's declaring the first emergency level."

Van Muren nodded. It was the "unusual event" level, and it didn't require special action. "Tell him to go ahead. They"—he tipped his head in the direction of the kitchen counter where the cook was putting trays of hot food—"will be eating soon. They eat fast. Tell Nelson to wait only a few minutes." He patted the technician on the shoulder and dashed toward the double door leading to the radio room.

A sharp snap, like a clap of thunder, froze Van Muren at the door. Another pressure ridge had split open. A tremor ran through the station. The mess hall shook. Plastic trays slid down the counter. Coffee spilled from cups; a door jarred open; the ceiling lights bounced, then swung in a circular motion. Van Muren held on to a steam pipe to keep his balance.

And that was only the start.

Another sound, long and sharp. A huge chunk of ice over six hundred feet long and more than two hundred feet wide broke off the crevasse's wall and dropped, carrying with it a Snow-Cat and two bulldozers that had been parked outside the repair hut.

The mess hall shook again. Then came the grinding crash of masonry coming apart; the creaking of splintering wood. Rivets sheered, prefabricated paneling cracked, pipes bent, pictures dropped to the floor, glass shattered.

There were loud gasps. People ducked under the tables and covered their heads with their hands. Then the shaking stopped.

The speaker blared, "Van Muren to the radio shack."

Van Muren struggled with the door, its bottom edge scraping the floor. He finally lurched in.

"Contact!" shouted the radio operator. "I've made contact with the C-4s! Line-of-sight communication. No interference."

"Thank God!" He ruffled the operator's hair, and quickly put on a pair of headphones, listening as the pilot of the lead plane gave his coordinates, altitude, and visibility. "I can see all the way to Peoria," the pilot said. Van Muren and the operator smiled.

Minutes later, the sound of turbofan engines overhead rumbled like an alpine waterfall. People cheered.

In the radio room, Van Muren pressed his hands on the headphones and fixed his eyes on a wall map to the right of the radio console. It was a map of the Fifth Polar Region.

"We're beginning an observation loop over the camp," the pilot of the lead plane said in a metallic voice.

There was a pause in transmission.

The pilot's voice came over the air again. "We have the camp in sight . . . we should be able to land this monster near it. No sweat. Over and out."

Three times the huge C-4s flew over the station at low altitude and from different headings. Then, as the planes gained altitude each time, a frown creased Van Muren's smooth, high forehead.

"What happened? Do you have a problem? Over," he shouted into the microphone, his eyes looking distantly in the direction of the roar of the engines.

"That's a roger," the pilot said clearly. His voice came through the console's speaker as well. "As far as I can see, there are ridges right across the area marked on my map as the only safe landing area, and there are crevasses. These don't worry us. We could slide over them, no sweat. But those ridges . . . they could catapult us into the air like a ski jump. I'll fly over the camp once more. Out."

Silence fell in the radio shack and the mess hall.

"It's hard to believe, sir," the pilot said on completing the fourth loop, "but I don't see a strip near the camp long enough—"

"The lake," Van Muren shouted. "How about the lake? The ice is fifty feet thick there."

The speaker cracked, "Negative," and went dead for a few seconds.

"I see ridges there, too," the pilot said, a note of helplessness in his voice.

Van Muren waited, then put the microphone down.

"Ridges everywhere," the pilot continued. "Judging from the shadows they cast, the smallest must be six feet high, maybe more. Over to you, sir."

Van Muren did not answer.

"NP/Five . . . NP/Five, this is Captain Elwood. Did you copy my last transmission? Over."

Van Muren put a hand over the shoulder of the operator again. The operator turned around. "The Canadians should get here soon. They have experience. They'll be able to land. Won't they?"

Van Muren forced a smile. "A plane is a plane," he said. His smile faltered. He left the radio shack. The voice of the pilot asked if there was anything he could do.

"Negative," the operator said. "Negative," he added. He took his headphones off, then checked the beacon transmitter. It was sending a steady string of dots and dashes: NP/5 . . . NP/5 . . .

As the percussive rumble of the engines faded, the chatter stopped in the crowded mess hall. Bundled up in goosedown Arctic gear, the men and women of NP/5 looked like oversized stuffed animals. Some stood up holding their luggage, some were packing, many sat on the floor with their gloved hands dangling over their knees. They were quiet, absorbed in the silence, as if expecting to hear the sounds of airplane engines again. At the corners of the mess hall, four emergency lights flickered with the livid glow of vigil candles. A woman blessed herself, a young man dropped his gym bag.

One hour passed and then another.

By morning there was still no news, no sound of airplanes. But the lights were on and the temperature held steady at thirty-four degrees.

At about nine A.M., Van Muren walked in ashen faced and with blood caked on his cheeks. Heads turned. He climbed on top of a wooden instrumentation box and, standing delicately erect, he told his audience that the planes could not land because they needed a smoother, longer runway. "But the Air Force hasn't given up," he said. "Success doesn't come with every try . . . and who knows that better than we do? Right?"

There was no response.

He went on. "Well, more planes are on the way. Smaller ones, of course."

A murmur of disbelief ran through the mess hall, muted, mixed with the occasional sound of the wooden floor creaking. Canal, the journalist from *National Geographic*, put the lens cover on his camera. "That's it then," he said.

Wordless, Morgan took out his wallet and flipped through pictures. Next to him, Van Muren's secretary wiped tears from her eyes. Van Muren saw her and whispered something to her. She looked up and forced a smile. "I came here because I wanted company. Well . . . I have it." Van Muren kissed her on her forehead, then, smiling nervously, he shouted, "Listen, everybody. These planes are Canadian, and Canadian pilots can land on snow more easily than anybody else can land on dry tarmac. Isn't that right?"

Again no responses.

Van Muren looked at them. They seemed confused, speechless with fright, helpless as he was.

Slowly Ed Larson unzipped his anorak, put an arm around the youngest of the female scientists, and looked away. The buzz of voices ceased. Many removed their gloves, anoraks, woolen caps. They knew they weren't going anywhere. Walking slowly and with his head down, the cook went back to the kitchen. Somebody kicked the jukebox, and it stopped playing. Silently, under a light in one corner of the mess hall, Ned Gray read from the Bible. Then, quietly, he began to read aloud. Soon he was surrounded.

The sun reappeared again a few hours later, and a DeHavilland ski plane of the Royal Canadian Air Force attempted to land on the lake. It crashed five hundred yards from the station. Van Muren himself led a caravan of skimobiles to rescue the crew, but found only one survivor.

For one more day the radio operator continued to maintain contact with the IGCS. Outside, at minus seventy degrees, mechanics tried to jury-rig a homemade bulldozer blade onto one of the Snow-Cats to smooth out the landing strip.

In the control room, the first sign of more trouble came when the temperature in the core began to rise, causing a safety valve to open and trigger the HICI (High-Pressure Cooling Injector), a high-powered pump that added water to the reactor.

The real problem arose when Nelson, exhausted and drained, failed to size up the situation correctly. Panicking, pushing Robertson away, bypassing the step-by-step instructions in the Symptom-Based Chart, he tried to focus on the readings of the dozens of meters and display panels. Convinced that the valve had opened because of a malfunction, when in fact it had not, he shut the HICI off manually.

In vain Robertson tried to persuade him to reopen the valve by pointing out that the needles of the panel meters were reaching the red zone.

"Oh, Jesus, what am I doing?" Nelson cried out, eyes wide with fright.

It was too late. The meltdown had begun.

As the level of cooling water dropped, the top portion of the fuel rods became exposed and the heat-resistant zirconium casing began to overheat. Temperatures inside the core shot up to 5,000 degrees. Water boiled off; steam pressure rose as the core grew hotter with a runaway surge of power—the positive void coefficient.

Seeing Nelson panic, Robertson took charge and together they tried to stop the meltdown by inserting the control rods one hundred percent and opening the core spray inlets to flood the reactor with all available water, but the hell inside the reactor was beyond control. With the coolant gone, the superheated core began triggering the feared chain reaction.

As the water level continued to drop, a greater portion of the fuel rods became exposed, growing red hot. And as the heat increased, a steam bubble formed in the steam-dryer assembly in the dome of the reactor and began pushing down on the steam-outlet fitting with 7,000 psi of pressure. The gasket began to crack. Fissionable material hissed out of the core through the damaged fitting. And finally the fuel rods became incandescent and cut through the bottom of the steel vessel with the melting power of fifty-four giant arc welding torches.

A loud, fearsome siren went off in all the huts as a burst of burnt orange illuminated the sky like the primal death of a star. The polar ice sheet quivered.

At 1:17 P.M., NP/5's beacon transmitter went dead.

A silent radio beacon is like a darkened lighthouse. It attracts attention with its absence.

The pilot of the H-3 Pelican helicopter en route to NP/5 was the first one to notice the absence of the signal, and reported it to the director of the Eureka station. "SATNAV will get us there no problem but . . . should we continue on?"

The director knew what the pilot meant. Before the helicopters had taken off for NP/5, the topic of conversation at Eureka had been the decommissioning of the reactor, especially during Robertson's brief visit. The reason for the silent beacon could be an accident at the nuclear plant. But what if the cause was nothing more than electronic troubles caused by plummeting temperatures? He told the pilot to continue on, but to approach the station from the north-northeast to stay clear of a possible radiation cloud.

Major Brian Convey, the lead pilot, immediately set a new course, one that would take him to a point sixty miles north of NP/5. His altitude was about one hundred feet. To fly low seemed safer. Radiation clouds were known to rise miles into the atmosphere. Five minutes later he radioed the director. "Hello, Eureka. This is Air Rescue Three. Do you still read me?"

"I read you five by five," a clear voice answered.

Major Convey reported his new course. "All sensors on," he added.

With Barbeau Peak to his left and Archer Hill up front as reference points, Major Convey turned right to a course of 122 degrees and reported his position. "Ping-Pong conditions now," he added, referring to the sensation of flying inside a Ping-Pong ball caused by the whiteness of the terrain, the surrounding snow-covered hills and peaks, and the thin cirrus clouds overhead. Long hours of Ping-Ponging caused "whiteouts" and fainting spells.

Less than fifteen miles from NP/5, the copilot saw something—dots blipping across his computer screen. "Look," he said to Major Convey, "what the hell is that?"

"Who knows?" He shook his head. "But if you wanted me to guess, I'd say that they're electrically charged solar particles being deflected by the earth's magnetic field. But I've never been this close to the North Pole before."

Five minutes later, more dots came blitzing across the screen. Then, from the Geiger counter, came a weak poppping sound, and then another much louder.

"Let's get the fuck out of here," Major Convey shouted, and while climbing with full throttle, he wheeled around into a wide arc. The H-3 trembled under the sudden surge of horsepower.

Within minutes, the huge H-3 was half a mile high, the other helicopter close behind.

Suddenly, the copilot tapped Major Convey on the shoulder. "Look over there," he said, and pointed.

Two miles ahead stood a building with its roof blown off, smoking like an iron works. Major Convey and his copilot looked at it stunned, unbelieving. "It must be the containment building," Major Convey said, craning his head for a better look. Left of the plume, he could see a dense, luminous cloud edged with tiny purple bubbles similar to soap suds. "Oh, my . . . ," he uttered with a drawn gasp that choked off his voice. His mind spun with grotesque images as he watched the cloud in astonished silence.

He called Eureka and reported what he had seen. "I can only describe it as a primordial cloud," he said. "If what I'm looking at isn't hell, I don't know what else it could be."

And now more dots blipped frenetically around the screen. The popping sounds became louder. "The needle on the Geiger counter is nearing the red zone,"

Major Convey radioed. "This area is practically glowing."

"Air Rescue three. This is Eureka. Do you see anybody?"

Major Convey strained to see. "Negative. Negative." The hand holding the mike dropped to his lap.

Then, as the helos completed a wide arc and were about to head back to Eureka, the spotter came on the intercom. "People at three o'clock."

"What?" Major Convey shouted, coming halfway out of his seat in a spasm of shock. He felt momentary panic as his mind raced ahead.

"Can't you see them? Right over that ridge where that orange Snow-Cat is. I count four, no . . . five people waving. Jesus, now what?"

Major Convey leaned left and saw an orange passenger Snow-Cat wedged between ice ridges with people around it waving. He wanted to wave back, but something told him to wait. He wheeled his helo into another wide arc, then looked down again, his eyes blurred with indecision.

Air rescue crews were trained to pluck pilots downed in enemy territory, trained to get shot at, trained to fly into storms, trained like a big city's fire department rescue squad. They were programmed to fly into danger. But this was beyond the training, beyond even heroic expectations.

Major Convey's fingers moved toward the mike, stopped inches from it. Beads of perspiration appeared along the edge of his flight helmet. He took a deep breath and felt his heart hammering erratically in his chest. How he wished he were somewhere else—anywhere else! To his right, the copilot, seemingly intent at his controls, was candle white, his eyes fixed in horror at some point on the horizon.

Major Convey composed himself, grabbed the mike, bent forward, and spoke into it. "Hello, Eureka. This is Major Convey. I have five survivors in sight. Do we pick them up? What if they are hot?" he asked. "Covered with radioactive dust, I mean."

Silence.

"Do you want us to pick them up just the same? Over."
Major Convey held his breath.

There was a scratchy, static-heavy sound of shortwave reception.

"Hello, Eureka. Did you copy me?"

He waited. "Eureka, do we pick them up? Over."

"Negative. Return to base."

10

Cliff jumped in surprise, so intense was his concentration on the file in front of him, when the phone rang. He had spent the morning going over notes and separating the information Roscoe had demanded from what he would keep. He closed the file and balanced it precariously on a pile that was already in danger of sliding off the desk. He grabbed the still-ringing telephone.

"Lorenz," he said.

"Hi, Dad," a cheerful young voice said.

"Hey, Butch! How are you?" Cliff's surprise showed in his voice. He hadn't expect this call. Suspicion snaked its way into his thoughts and he asked, in that expectant tone all fathers use, "What is it this time?"

"Soccer shoes."

"You made the team, eh? That's great. I'm proud of you, Butch."

"Are you coming to see me play? Next week is our first home game."

"You bet. How's school?"

"Good! I'm working on a new project in computer class and . . ." Butch then went into the details, which seemed typical of every young student. Cliff listened attentively, forgetting for a moment the catastrophe looming in the near distance.

As Butch finished relating the story of a practical joke the boys had played on their dorm monitor, Cliff's laughter stopped suddenly as he remembered an important question. "Butch, when did you see Dr. Beck last?" he asked.

"Yesterday," Butch answered.

"Well . . . what did he say?"

Butch told him that his doctor had instructed him to continue with Humulin-N, his new insulin medication. It seemed to be working well. "I feel better, I think," Butch said, and then changed the subject. No one, he said, including his science teacher, could explain why the caterpillars in the class's insect experiments had such uneven color bands this year. "What do you think, Dad?"

A chill ran through Cliff. He *did* know the answer to this question, and it terrified him—glaciation. But he couldn't tell Butch the real answer. "Simple," he said. "It means we're going to have a colder winter."

"No, that's not a good answer," Butch said. "That's the same answer we found in the Farmer's Almanac. I want a scientific answer."

Cliff thought for a moment. "Okay, are you ready?"

"Shoot."

"The unevenness in the width of the black and brown bands is due to a deficiency in solar energy. That deficiency is called Maunder Minima." He spelled it for him, then explained the cyclical nature of the Minima, and the effects of reduced solar energy on all forms of life. "Did you get all that?

"Yeah. I knew you'd know. You always have all the right answers."

Phil Jackson and Cliff Lorenz usually met for breakfast at least once a week to discuss matters relating to the Ergo II, an indoor rowing club they had founded.

Jackson, wearing a walkie-talkie and, much to Cliff's surprise, a holster with a .38 police special clipped to his belt, sat down at Cliff's table. He put the briefcase he was carrying on the floor. Cliff pointed at the weapon and asked, "What's with the heat? Somebody stealing office supplies again?"

Jackson didn't smile, but did button his blue blazer over the holster. He looked Cliff straight in the eye and spoke. "No jokes, buddy. I was over at the Feebies' headquarters until two this morning. I am not a happy camper."

"The FBI? What are you doing hanging out with them?"

"Getting briefed on how to protect all you scientist-types from the big, bad Reds."

"The Russians?" Cliff laughed. "Why would we need to be protected from them? The cold war's over, remember? They lost."

"Well, it's warming up again, buddy. It seems that over the past few years we've found out a few things and kept some tabs on a few folks. They're called sleepers. For the most part, they stayed quiet after the Soviet Union fell apart. Oh, a few went over to the Chinese, and a lot just disappeared, but a bunch stayed around, just being good Americans. The pressure was off.

"But, according to the Feebies, four or five that they've been keeping track of just started acting real hinky, you know, weird. They're following random patterns, acting like they're looking for tails and stuff."

"Hold on. You mean the FBI has been tracking former Soviet spies all these years, while we've been pumping billions of dollars into the Russian economy?"

"Yep. Gotta justify those departmental budgets. Right?" Jackson shifted gears then, going on, "And it's been worth it. Like I said, the Feebies say a bunch of these sleepers seem to have been activated, given missions."

"What kind of missions?" Cliff asked.

"Well, that's what I was getting to. Cliff, it seems that the guys the Feebies were tailing were all in high-tech and scientific positions. And, it seems a lot of them were working on atmospheric and oceanographic projects. The Feebies think the Russians are looking for weather modification data. And maybe for the people to interpret it. Cliff, they could have orders that go beyond stealing information; they could be looking to kidnap a key scientist."

Cliff put his coffee cup down angrily. "Phil, I'm not working with modifiers. I haven't for years."

"I know that. But they don't, do they?"

A chatty group of office workers sat down at the table next to Cliff's. "But they should," Cliff countered in a low voice. "I declared myself against the use of modifiers on the national news after the Idaho disaster, remember?"

Jackson nodded. "Sure. But will the Russians believe it? What if you changed your mind?"

"This is bullshit." Cliff clenched his mouth tight, a bubble of fear and frustration rising in his throat. "Is it just me, or does this mean that Butch could be a target?"

Jackson hesitated before speaking. "I don't know. Maybe. But, given the situation, I doubt they feel they have the time to bait you by taking Butch."

"Great. Will the FBI give me protection?"

Jackson sighed. "From what I heard last night, the Feebies' last worry is for one guy and his kid. No way are they going to spare the manpower to protect you and Butch, especially since they *know* you aren't working on a modifier. I got a list from Roscoe before I went to the briefing. They *will* put security on the people on that list. But you *ain't* on it, buddy."

"Goddammit!" Cliff said, slamming his palm on the table. The women at the next table looked over at the disturbance, but Cliff ignored them. "I'm damned if I do and damned if I don't," he told Jackson.

Jackson placed a calming hand on Cliff's shoulder. "Look, Cliff, just take it easy. From now on, all you have to do is be careful, be on the lookout. Try to vary your patterns: go to a different deli for lunch, pick up your dry cleaning on a different day, take a different route home, maybe check your rearview mirror a few more times than usual." Jackson picked his briefcase off the floor, opened it, and took out a book, which he handed to Cliff. It had a brightly colored tiger on the cover, but no title. Cliff looked at the book and up at Jackson.

"It's a book Exxon did," Jackson explained. "It's for all of their executives who had to go work in countries hostile to Americans. Read it. Everything that goes for Libya goes for D.C., too. Avoid big crowds, keep the car doors locked, don't get boxed in, keep an eye out for motorcyclists, et cetera. It's all in there. And don't hesitate to call me anytime, day or night. Understand?"

Cliff nodded as Jackson closed his briefcase and got up to leave. "Day or night, I said." Cliff nodded.

Cliff walked into his office and found an envelope marked *Personal and Confidential* on his chair. He tore it open and read the handwritten note from Roscoe: *Cancel everything. Be in CR-130 at 4:30 sharp this afternoon. B.R.*

Cliff was tiring of Roscoe's command performances, but there seemed to be little he could do about them. He settled down at his desk to continue his inventory of data for Roscoe. The day went quickly.

At 4:25, Cliff left his office and headed for conference room 130. He found Roscoe waiting in ambush for him outside of the conference room door. Roscoe walked up to Cliff and pointed a finger at Cliff's chest. "Listen," he growled, "you are still director of marine affairs. I expect you to carry out the policies of this department, and my orders in particular, with professionalism and good faith. You smile when you go in there. The people in there can smell bad blood, and they'll go after it like sharks. I don't want them to know there's even a drop of it in this department. Understand?"

Cliff nodded silently. Clearly, Roscoe wasn't through with him yet.

Cliff felt friendless as he entered CR-130. The room was crowded with DOI, IGCS, Army, Navy, and Air Force personnel. A menacing cloud of cigarette smoke hung in the air.

As his gaze swept the room, Cliff saw a man in a conservative jacket talking to an Air Force officer. Even from the back, there was no doubt as to the man's identity: Marshall, Professor Orville P. Marshall.

Trim and tweedy as ever, Marshall still had the arrogant look of tenured faculty, and he still borrowed so much hair from one side to cover his bald head that it looked as though it were growing out his left ear.

With Marshall's back to him, Cliff remembered the day the three-member personnel committee of the Oceanography Department met in Marshall's office to decide on who would get the assistant professorship—tenure track. Four floors below, Cliff, a recent Ph.D. graduate with a story about the real purpose of the Gulf Stream in *Time* magazine, waited in the Science Hall cafeteria. How the students had cheered that story in *Time*. Cliff was popular among students, which pleased Cliff but not the older members of the faculty. They considered his popularity a threat.

Cliff didn't have to wait long. An hour later, one of the two professors and Cliff's friend gave him the bad news. "Old man Marshall broke the deadlock," his friend had said. Cliff wondered how much power Marshall had now.

When his old professor sat down, Cliff's gaze fastened on him.

Marshall—thirty-five years of Ivy League politics behind him—managed a wintry smile, but Cliff put on an outward sign of civility and gave him a proper-for-the-moment silent "Hello."

Roscoe, now seated at the head table, watched the exchange of glances between Cliff and Marshall with satisfaction. He loved to encourage rivalry.

Minutes later Kronin walked in, eyes clouded with worry. He stepped to the head of the table with an apology for being late. "We must act," he began, "to prevent the destruction of civilization. You have had the time to study reports about our polar station NP/Five."

He immediately referred to the report sent by a group of scientists to the president, which he had read that morning. It described "modern life in an ice age." Copies of it would soon be delivered to all those present. "We have classified the report top secret," he said, "to prevent the media from causing chaos . . ."

A knock sounded at the door.

Kronin stopped talking, annoyed, as a handsome naval officer in gold braid brought him a note and waited for a reply.

Kronin raised his eyeglasses to read the message. "Notify the NSA liaison that I'll be leaving shortly," he said to the officer. When he spoke again, his voice had a tone of urgency. "The only alternative left to the administration is the use of modifiers," he said, and paused. "The cabinet and I have recommended them to the president. I am, therefore, ordering each of you to review the status of the modifier you've been developing. Report the status to my office. We will then schedule presentations to determine the most viable in this crisis. We'll pick one primary and one secondary, a backup, if you will."

This isn't a nightmare, Cliff thought, *it's a nightmare come true.* Involuntarily he shook his head.

Soon all eyes were turned in his direction.

"Yes?" Kronin raised an eyebrow.

"Considering the unpredictable, unstable, and untested nature of modifiers," he said, ignoring the surprised murmur from those around him; Roscoe stared at him flushed with anger, "couldn't we be adding to the impact of glaciation?"

"What alternative is there?" With deliberate slowness Kronin took off his glasses and waited for an answer, then panned around the table, as if counting votes of confidence.

Cliff did the same but didn't see a flicker of agreement on any of the faces. And Marshall was looking at him with a self-satisfied grin.

"You know what it would mean," a general said, glancing up at Cliff, "if we just did nothing?"

"CLIMODs may be untested," another general said, "but the technology that developed them is not."

Kronin nodded at him, this time with a smile.

Cliff felt gooseflesh run down his arms. He was in a pool of sharks, all right.

Kronin got ready to leave. His eyes in the direction of the Air Force colonel, he said, "Needless to say, it's a race against time. I'm eager to hear what you propose to modify the climate. So"—he took out a pocket calendar— "let's make the twenty-fifth presentation day." He nodded at the naval officer in gold braid and rushed out.

Kronin's black limousine left the parking lot just before five, when traffic was still heavy. He ordered the driver to hit the siren and braced himself for a tortuous ride to the National Security Agency monitoring station in Arlington, Virginia.

"Lester Pym . . . It's still going strong," said the NSA specialist to Kronin, as he got out of the limousine.

Kronin followed Pym to the laboratory, a small, windowless room. The only light came from the blue-green glow of various oscilloscopes and illuminated instrument dials. There was a strong odor of burning wire.

A large Sigma Analyzer, a table TV-sized apparatus with a nine-inch video screen and surrounded with switches and knobs displayed a pattern of interference—a horizontally stretched-out spring. The NSA's high-tech radio antennas, located around the globe, had been receiving it for days.

Kronin put a hand on a knob and made some adjustments. For five minutes he studied the pattern, made more adjustments, and took notes. Then he glanced at a panel meter that registered the audio strength of the interference.

"S-Nine," he said finally. "Incredible!"

"It is, sir," Pym agreed.

"Tell me," Kronin said, "you've been monitoring signals for years. What do you think it is?"

Pym, a spindly, aging man, looked as if he had been waiting for the question. He hesitated, gathering his thoughts, and then told Kronin that only once before had he heard a similar sound, when he was with the U.S. Army Signal Corps in Albuquerque. "One night," he said, "I experienced something I've never forgotten. I was monitoring signals from the Russian embassy in Managua. Suddenly, out of the blue, I couldn't receive that signal—or any signal at all—for a good four hours because of a strong interference just like this one. A solar flare-up, I said to myself. Then, a week later, I read in the papers that there had been an underground nuclear explosion the very day and hour I recorded the incident in my logbook."

"And that's why you said it was no jamming device, right?" Kronin asked.

"Right. It's something nuclear."

"Nuclear? Like a neutron particle beam?"

"I don't know what that is, but if it radiates thermal energy—"

Kronin gave an abrupt nod. "Thank you, Mr. Pym," he said, and walked out.

Kronin's limousine had just turned right on Lee Highway, taking Kronin home, when suddenly he knocked on the glass divider. "My office first," he ordered.

From there he sent an urgent telex requesting seismic reports from Palomar, RCA, Cal Tech—three observatories that monitored unusual terrestrial activities.

Within minutes Palomar informed him that there had been a series of low to moderate seismic "events" with epicenters in Siberia.

His glasses propped over his forehead, Kronin quickly studied the notes from his meeting with Pym. "Damn," he said, and dropped his glasses on his nose with a flip of a finger. "Pym was right. The interference is something nuclear. What the hell are those Russians doing?" He rushed out to see the president.

• • •

Another story broke three miles away. At eight-fifteen P.M., Major General (retired) Robert Carson, newly appointed head of Civil Defense, returned to Headquarters at the request of the Crisis Relocation Group (CRG).

Earlier, he had assured the president that Civil Defense would be able to handle the massive southward movement of millions of Americans.

He was wrong.

Now, as the president prepared to meet with the chiefs of staff, Carson had to tell him that the Crisis Relocation Plan developed by Civil Defense in case of a nuclear attack would not work. Reason: Of the many highways—exit roads—fanning out of major cities, only those running north/south could be used to evacuate inhabitants, provided icing did not restrict operations. Another problem was Canada. In order to guarantee the smooth flow of Canadian traffic through U.S. cities, the evacuation of Americans had to begin first—in six weeks at the latest.

"I have bad news," he said to the White House chief of staff. He briefed him on the findings of the CRG and its recommendation for an earlier evacuation of cities in the border states.

"Six weeks—no way," the Chief of Staff said, pointing out that news of an evacuation without gradually allowing people to get used to the idea of an impending deep freeze was dangerous. It was certain to create chaos, unimaginable drops in the value of real estate, a crash in the stock market, the closing of banks, and other unpredictable reactions. "Host" counties in the south were not physically and psychologically ready yet to accommodate hordes of angry, homeless, and financially bankrupt refugees. Furthermore, he doubted people would abandon their homes in response to an immediate order for evacuation. "We have another three to four weeks of seasonal weather ahead," he said. "Who's going to believe an ice age will hit us by Labor Day?"

• • •

Glaciation would not hit by Labor Day, but there were signs of its inexorable advance just south of the Arctic Circle.

On the morning of May 21, the ice-strengthened, double-hulled Norwegian cruise ship *Nordland Princess* was scheduled to sail up the Davis Strait and by three in the afternoon stop in front of the God Havn White Wall, the massive 400-foot-high ice cliff on the west coast of Greenland, one of the world's biggest glaciers.

But at 2:10 A.M. the International Ice Patrol warned the captain of the *Nordland Princess* that the leading edge of the God Havn White Wall glacier was draining on the water and breaking up. Hundreds of icebergs were moving south with the current.

The captain immediately turned around and headed for the other remote and unusual attraction on the cruise, the Ungaya Bay in north Labrador.

At breakfast, he announced the change to the high-paying passengers, who accepted his decision but wanted to know more about the icebergs. They didn't have to be reminded that in 1912 the *Titanic* had sunk after striking an iceberg that had broken off a draining glacier.

The captain could only repeat what the International Ice Patrol had told him. "I can only tell you," he said, speaking into a microphone, "that this is the first time in thirty-five years that I can't sail up the strait because of icebergs. In late May."

Traveling on the *Nordland Princess* was a retired geophysicist. Not knowing then that he would popularize the term seasonal reversal, he got up and explained that periodically during spring months, diminishing solar output attributable to astronomic causes could plunge temperatures below normal for several weeks. He reminded his fellow passengers just how cold it had been, especially at night. Then he said, "Glaciers grow during seasonal reversals, move faster because of the added weight, and drain into the water. They're just like rivers. Many of you will remember that in 1974, the year of the last seasonal reversal according to the books, the Klenjdal Glacier spilled over one hundred icebergs into Loen Lake up in the Nordsfiord country."

For over three hours Canadian marine telephone operators were busy handling the many calls from the *Nordland Princess.*

One caller was Sandra Tallbridge. A sales representative for station KDRS-FM in Decatur, Illinois, on her honeymoon, she reported all that she had heard that morning to the station's news director. Within minutes, seasonal reversal hit the airwaves. By seven P.M., all major television networks had picked up the story and broadcast it, adding interviews with International Ice Patrol officials and motion-picture footage of the *Titanic* sinking.

So the term *seasonal reversal* spread.

To many Americans the term was more ominous than it sounded. They phoned the Weather Bureau, NOAA, NASA, and even the White House to get the real facts.

Of course, the White House had been preparing for just such an event, so early the following day, the president met with his Crisis Management Team to discuss ways of defusing the iceberg story and to consider the best program for projecting calm in order to gain control of the situation.

It was decided that the president would call a press conference and talk about the seasonal reversal, which he did. The conference, carried live by CNN, lasted only ten minutes and achieved its purpose.

"We have had several seasonal reversals," the president said. "My science adviser tells me that they are quite common." He mentioned several of them, especially those that took place in 1831, 1883, 1903, and 1974, years corresponding to the eruption of volcanoes such as the Skapur Jokul and Pellee. "And, if you remember, we did have a quake in California just this past January." He promised Americans to keep them informed and returned to the Oval office. Not once during the conference did the president mention the word *glaciation.*

In the corridor he told Kronin that in 1961 President Kennedy and his planners had agreed that in case of a nuclear attack, the people should go about their jobs and pleasures unaware. "A twenty-minute warning would only cause panic. I agree," the president said to Kronin. He then stopped and added, "We have more time than that. Let's handle the news release of glaciation very gradually—if we can."

11

Not everybody accepted the unusual but inevitable news of the seasonal reversal as the real story. Many believed that since politicians seldom spoke the truth, what the president had revealed, as one editorial in *U.S. News and World Report* put it, was just the "tip of the iceberg."

Numbed by fear and bombarded by sensational stories with fanciful illustrations, for many personal survival was the only truth left.

Understandably, this was in the minds of the international crew of the *Rotterdam Star,* a supertanker with Liberian registration sailing on the Mayen shipping lane. She was headed for Halifax, Nova Scotia, where she was to arrive the following day and deliver an emergency supply of heating oil.

Dinner was always the high point of the day for sailors on the high seas, and on the *Rotterdam Star* the dining hall was like a Casablanca restaurant in the days prior to World War II, where languages and cooking and cigarette aromas competed with one another.

On this night, those who were eating did so quietly, for the *Rotterdam Star* was at 41, 27 north; 50, 8 west, the location all sailors making the North Atlantic run never forget—the spot where the *Titanic* had sunk.

In the wheelhouse, Captain Kanellopulous was leafing through the stack of messages the radio operator had brought him, electing to read only those from the International Ice Patrol.

Suddenly he turned to Second Officer Polein and asked him, "Which would you rather do: risk hitting an iceberg which could cause an oil spill as big as the one they had in Alaska and spend the rest of your life in court, or change course and risk getting fired?"

"Captain," the second officer answered shortly, "I'd risk getting fired any day."

Without blinking an eye, as if he had been expecting that answer, the captain turned to the helmsman, who was trying to suppress a smile, and ordered, "Steer course one one six."

"Yes, sir," the helmsman sounded off joyfully. "One one six."

An FBI memo had urged: . . . *conduct all business and social activities in a manner suggesting normality and in such a way as to arouse no suspicion.*

So, on Saturday, June 5, the departmental outing was held as scheduled.

Cliff headed for Old Fort Park, taking a different route from the one he would normally have taken. And as he pondered the merits of being unpredictable to make things difficult for a tail, he realized how difficult it was to behave in a manner suggesting normality. Since the conversation with Phil Jackson, every male and female driver looked like a potential threat. He drove with eyes flitting from the rear to side mirror like a nervous teenager, while his mind raced from NP/5 to Roscoe, to his modifier as an ecological breakthrough, to his modifier as the cause of an uncontrollable cataclysm.

He saw no motorcycles or familiar cars following him, yet sweat dripped from his armpits. It was a matter of time, he felt, before one would.

Suddenly, just before he was to turn left on MacArthur Boulevard, Cliff pulled to the side of the road, got out of the car, and peeled off the No Nukes sticker from the rear bumper. It would certainly aid in identifying his car, he told himself. It would also help if he removed the black wind spoiler. Tomorrow, for sure.

Maintained by the Department of the Interior, Old Fort Park had once been the headquarters of the Union Navy. A half-hour ride from D.C. proper, it was adjacent to the Federal Communications Commission Center.

As usual the picnic looked like a rerun of the year before, except for what was taking place away from the crowd. Occupying the study once used by Admiral Farragut as the Union Navy Headquarters, Roscoe, in his golf outfit, was busy holding meetings, dictating memos, making calls.

Next door, his administrative assistant and two cartographers were finishing—between hamburgers and beer—the updated report titled "Status of Federal Land in the Sun Belt," which was due at the White House that evening.

Cliff always parked his car where it wouldn't get scratched. Today he parked in a narrow space between other cars and in view from the playground. That done, he instinctively looked for Phil Jackson and his other colleagues, but without success. Puzzled, he stopped ostensibly to look at the picture of Old Ironsides shelling Charleston Forts, which was on display at the entrance of the carriage house. But he wondered instead where all the division directors were. Perhaps caught in traffic . . . though unlikely, he thought.

Groups of adults were seated on blankets around their coolers; children crawled all over the old siege guns that decorated the five-acre lawn. The sky, a cerulean blue only two hours earlier, was now heavy with livid blisters of clouds, and a thin mist danced along the bank of the nearby Piscataway Creek.

Wearing an expression of holiday mood, he began making his rounds. He chatted with his supply man, threw a Frisbee with an assistant, and had some strawberries with his secretary and her date.

A drumroll of thunder sounded and then rain poured down.

Everybody took cover under the roof of Admiral Farragut's porch, where Cliff, relieved, saw Pam waving at him.

"Am I glad to see you, Cliff," she said, "and then I'm not."

Cliff sensed tension in her voice. "I'm glad to see you, too—and then I'm not," he said.

The silence that followed was telling.

"Where are they?" Cliff asked, bracing himself for the answer.

She pointed a thumb up.

"A coincidence?"

She shook her head. "A meeting," she said, and told him that if he went upstairs, he would see all the directors. "And, Cliff . . . ," she hesitated, "Mel Josephs is also up there." She was referring to Cliff's division deputy director.

"The old man moves fast and on schedule," Cliff heard himself stammer. "He took my files and locked them in the vault. Have you any idea what those files mean to me?" An armed courier had come to the house the night before, sealed the file cabinet with a steel band, and left.

Her pained expression was the answer.

Now anxiety dulled Cliff's eyes. On relieving him of the responsibility of the modification, Roscoe had also taken away some of Cliff's privileges and duties. Thus Cliff would have to resign himself to a new assignment and to a slow bureaucratic death. He wondered what would befall him next. Devoting his life to science was not a goal he had ever equated with ostracism, humiliation, or getting kidnapped by a foreign agent. "God knows how long he's been waiting to stick it to me. Old soldiers never forget, and he never forgot that I didn't serve in the war."

"And that you—and I—opposed him on the offshore oil exploration proposal."

Cliff leaned against the post, blankly watching the clouds close in like a manhole cover. For a moment he looked as anxious as a child struggling with something beyond his understanding.

"Cheer up. I'm also down here," she said, and moved closer to him in a gentle, spontaneous act of affection, one that suggested a familiarity she probably hadn't intended.

Theirs was the kind of relationship that was all emotion, one that seemed to call for a closer association. He could feel an affection coming from her that was as sincere as his. Their closeness filled him with daring, and his instinctive response was to gaze at Pam with eyes softening at the sight of hers.

Wycoff was flattered by his attention and interest, but she had different ideas. "Cliff, don't fall in love with me," she began, and her voice, though quiet, had an ominous tone. "My work is what fulfills me now and it's no less an ennobling way of looking at things than getting ready to become a superwife or a supermom. Anyhow, you shouldn't be tied to someone who sees things the way I do now. You already know how the idea of oceanographers going out to sea for months has never appealed to me." She grabbed his hand. "Really, Cliff, both you and I ought to be free."

It happened so unexpectedly that it was like a movie splice. Cliff listened, surprised and hurt. He loved her, even though at that very moment love had dissolved into a kind of antidote for his anxieties and the need to be close to someone. "We could try. Things might work out better than you think now," he said lamely, barely keeping his voice under control.

"No, Cliff," she said with conviction. "I've thought about us a long time, but longer about my work. My mind is made up. I'm sorry."

Cliff said nothing. Pam's words had a tone of finality that was devastating.

And so they pretended to enjoy their drinks without talking, each pondering what had just transpired.

Cliff remembered the days when they had worked together on environmental issues. Opposing offshore drilling or the sale of government property to developers was a ritual that renewed the exhilaration of antiwar demonstrations. Working together had thus become a ritual, one that strengthened their friendship and was an indispensable part of their lives. He had to keep his relationship with Pam.

Glancing up at the darkened sky, Cliff broke the silence. "Anyhow, for now we can still play tennis. Can't we?"

She smiled broadly. "Of course," she said cheerily. "After all, we do make a terrific team."

"In that case," Cliff said in a jesting but forced way, "why don't we obey the directive from the FBI and play some mixed doubles with the Jacksons in order to keep suggesting normality? I'll call you to confirm date and time."

She was amused by his good humor and laughed richly. "I'd love that, Cliff," she said, and wrinkled her pretty little nose at him.

It was time to circulate, and for a few minutes they made polite conversation and drank gin-and-tonics with other people.

Her glass empty, Pam excused herself for leaving, and Cliff accompanied her to the car.

He opened her door and waited for the engine to start. But then he saw Pam roll down the window and look up at him. "I'm sorry to spoil the picnic, but I wanted you to know how I feel."

Cliff resisted touching her shoulder through the open window. "I appreciate that," he said, and smiled. "Sincerity is one of the virtues one comes to appreciate in D.C."

Their eyes met in a moment of understanding before they said good-bye.

"Don't forget to call about the match." She waved.

The rain fell, cold and unwelcome.

• • •

Roscoe was waiting with a folder in his hand as Cliff passed by the main entrance to the admiral's house.

My new assignment, Cliff thought. It hung over his head like the blade of a guillotine.

"Come," Roscoe said, and led the way to the study, a red-paneled room with nautical brass relics and faded Navy uniforms from the Civil War.

A cloud of cigar smoke accompanied Roscoe in. When Cliff had closed the door, Roscoe looked at him pointedly. "I have something I want you to read now," he said by way of addressing his subject, and told Cliff that it wouldn't take him more than ten minutes. "I'm going to have something to eat," he said, and put a hand on the doorknob. "Call me when you finish. I have something else for you."

Cliff, accustomed as he was to Roscoe's Chinese torture technique, simply nodded, opened the folder, and pulled out a thin ream of papers in a black plastic binder.

It was the report to the president, entitled, *Glaciation— Danger to Our Human and Social Communities.*

For a moment Cliff felt a sense of relief that it wasn't his new assignment.

Cliff sat at the desk trying to absorb the material, beginning to feel as though he were being informed of a crime about to take place and planning—beforehand—to do nothing about it.

He leafed quickly through the report the way he would sift through an article of minor interest just for some facts, all the while feelings of guilt rising from deep within him.

But then—quite involuntarily—his eyes stopped at the words *Systems Breakdown* and scanned the section with the header "Food and Medical Supplies Shortages and Related Violence." With growing anxiety, he planted his elbows on the desk and returned to the beginning:

An estimated 100 million Americans will be forced to move south. The consequences of such an enormous exodus present a condition of critical instability with regard to our dependence on complex systems such as food distribution, medical assistance, traffic control, communications, and law enforcement.

And so it went for thirty-three pages. Simple statements written thoughtfully and free of the usual federal prose. The frightening thing was that in their simplicity and clarity they had the smoke and thunder of the prophets.

Cliff pinched the bridge of his nose. While waiting for the tension headache to abate, he scanned the next few paragraphs, the reality of the deep freeze no longer a doubt; the details describing glaciation were well documented but not terribly relevant. He read on.

While migratory birds (knots and plovers in particular) will provide the first visual signs of a premature winter to the trained observer, anomalies in the behavior of animals in the wild will cause speculation and fear—even panic—in the general public. Arctic wolves and rodents will be driven southward. . . .

No fewer than three pages were devoted to the infestation of rodents and the likely spread of diseases; another two pages dealt with wolves and their dangerous practice of roaming in packs.

Shifting position, Cliff pushed the chair back and propped his feet on the edge of the desk. Instantly he felt relief, as blood drained from them. But the tension headache was still there—as was the lengthy section recommending triage in order to give "the healthy more opportunity for survival," and the demand placed on antibiotics, vitamins, insulin, milk, high-protein powder, and other life-sustaining products by the predicted breakdown in food distribution and hoarding.

Sweat started matting his hairline. Lord! The need for special medicine so vital to Butch's health had not crossed his mind up to now. Nor had the thought that his mother might be left behind when Manchester was evacuated.

Our large agricultural and medical surplus, even though capable of meeting a foreseeable crisis, is too vulnerable to panic and violence. . . . In order to provide an adequate distribution, the presidential committee recommends that the Army's quartermaster general draw a plan. . . . It is now imperative to set straight myths and misconceptions about camp life, climate-related ailments, clothing, identification of poisonous herbs and snakes.

Someone—possibly Roscoe—had circled in red the section with the header "Behavior." The bluntness of the opening statement shocked Cliff. It read:

When survival becomes the first responsibility of each individual and his family, people will act for their own self-interests. . . . Consequently, for most Americans the terrors of glaciation will be equal to an accumulation of social and political injustices culminating in a political act of violence. . . . A more serious threat to our social communities will be the growth of the socially and ecologically disaffected, who will find in chaos the opportunity to release natural instincts . . . Law enforcement units will disintegrate as the individual officer—considering himself a poorly paid town or city employee and not a soldier—will not report to work in order to stay with his family.

He was even more shocked to read that the simple defection of a console operator at a major electric power distribution center (e.g., St. Lawrence International

Consortium) could stop the flow of electric power to traffic lights, radio stations, hospitals.

> The domino effect of the Great Blackout of 1966 is but a microcosm of the breakdowns likely to plague the nation under glaciation siege.

Thunder boomed in the distance, a dramatic sound track appropriate to his reading.

Eyes narrowing within worry lines, he flipped the page over and saw in bold letters:

> Lastly, Mr. President, the following is a preliminary model of our community during glaciation. It was originally constructed in case of a nuclear war for the Hartford Symposium by the Institute of the Future (August 1979). Here are some excerpts:
> "The patriarchal community will form the basic nucleus of our society. . . . The majority of people will live in tents, campers, Quonset huts, and portable hangars, using these shelters in shifts to sleep, cook, etc. . . . People will adjust slowly to the new regional and social environments, but only those mentally and physically strong will be able to endure the initial hardships. . . . All daily activities will be centered around the satisfaction of basic needs, the protection of property, and improving shelter, hunting tools, and weapons. . . . The major task will be survival. . . . Violence will be common in the struggle to maintain personal privileges and to increase possession and power. . . . Money will be worthless, as tools, guns, canned food, vitamins, drugs, jewels, and other non-perishable items will constitute more stable units of exchange. . . . Typologically, communities will form along religious, ethnic, ideological lines. . . . Religious and ethnic wars will erupt between groups, testing how effectively our democratic experience has been able to destroy old resentments, racial hatred, and prejudice. . . . Mafia-style organizations, each with its own private rules, secrecy, and methods of terrorism, will

typify the internal structures of communities. . . .
Patriarchy will prevail as a social system. . . .
Vigilantes will organize to guarantee social order
and to guard against the encroachment of left-wing
groups. . . . Homage, tribute, and service, in grateful exchange for protection, may reintroduce old
feudalistic relationships, especially between patri-
arch and member. . . . Physical strength will be
a valued, highly rewarded asset. . . . The all-too-
human combination of collective interests and
power will determine the success of each community. . . . <u>Liberty will not be a constitutional right,
but only the luxury of self-discipline</u>.

Cliff sat frozen in his chair. "My God," he said, his
emotions in turmoil, erupting.

There remained two more pages to read—the committee's recommendation for the use of modifiers, he thought.
He was right. Quickly he scanned them, stopping at the last
words underlined in red:

Alvin Toffler once said it well: "<u>Unless we are willing
to change the future, we shall endure it.</u>"

Respectfully yours . . .

Twelve signatures followed.

Staring at the blank space that followed the signatures,
Cliff shook his head. Nothing about the report seemed possible. It belonged to another reality, to the futuristic view of
the world scientists called nuclear winter. In fact, nuclear
bombs and glaciation led to the same ultimate disaster—the
assassination of civilization. Kronin was right.

Triage, food shortages, violence burned in his stomach.
And there was the report itself now taking on a personality
of a living thing inexorably shaking a threatening finger
at him.

Yet he had to prevent an inadvertent modification from
making things even more catastrophic. He had to, regardless
of the consequences.

12

The Russians were planning a full-scale test of their modification, and Konlikov, recently named deputy coordinator of the National Bureau of Weather Resources, flew to St. Petersburg for the occasion.

Long in development and secretly guarded, the Macronda Thermodiffuser had a lot in common with the modifier NASA would soon present to Kronin. Both were designed to raise air temperatures to tolerable levels.

For years Russian scientists had been working on a system capable of producing macrondas, a form of low-frequency radio wave of the type used by submarines for communications. Only recently were they able to develop the all-important thermionic converter. This sophisticated, high-tech component transformed electrical energy into macronda energy.

It was during an experiment that they discovered that if high-speed switches turned the emission of macronda waves off and on, an extremely useful pulse developed. Useful, because it caused air particles to vibrate and create friction, which in turn gave off heat. The analogy the scientists gave to non-technical people was that it was like two hands being rubbed together and the heat this produced.

Konlikov spent the morning touring the first of the thermaloops, the series of concentric circles of half-inch hollow copper tubing or filotrons connecting the thermionic converters. Fastened on miniature high-tension towers by long ceramic standoff insulators, the thermaloops encircled St. Petersburg. Then he watched scientists prepare radio-sondes for release. Of the type used by weather stations to measure weather conditions up to 40,000 feet and carried aloft by balloons, the radiosondes permitted telemetering of precise changes in both temperature and humidity.

The test got under way at around one P.M., with the activation of the outermost filotron of the thermal loop. One hour later, the other two filotrons started emitting macrondas.

Konlikov's smile never faltered from the moment printers started plotting the information radioed back by the radio-sondes. He could plainly see the initial rise of one-tenth of a degree centigrade temperature at the 500-foot level at the end of the first six-hour-long emission test.

"Of course," a scientist told Konlikov, "one of the by-products of this system is that as we reach peak height—about two thousand meters or so—we'll have an inversion, which will act as a lid. The temperature will increase with increased altitude, holding down the warm air below." He paused before he gave the bad news. "Another by-product is radio interference in the medium- and shortwave bands, one that will force us to rely on satellite communications almost exclusively."

"Not a bad trade-off," Konlikov said, loading his pipe. "We can certainly live with that until the seasonal reversal ends."

The scientist agreed. Not a bad one under the circumstances. There was yet another negative characteristic of the macrondas. Like all radio waves in the AM band sensitive to electrical storms and other atmospheric disturbances, macrondas were additionally sensitive to humidity. "As you can see here," he said, pointing to a recorder plotting the relationship between heat and humidity, "the more moisture there is in the air, the less friction is generated by the pulse."

"Which means," Konlikov offered, "that any extra amount of humidity would greatly reduce the effectiveness of the thermodiffusers."

The scientist nodded. "We must find out, therefore, if the American modifier has the potential to increase moisture levels," he said, but he didn't have to offer any suggestion, for Konlikov told him that he would personally provide him with the information. "What the Americans are planning is something I want to see for myself, and if it looks suspicious, I will suggest what to do," he said, and tapped tobacco out of his pipe. "But I can guarantee you that of the modifiers the Americans are considering, one will surely involve the Gulf Stream. I'd bet my life on it."

Cliff still sat at the small desk in rigid discomfort, as in his mind the whiteness of the last page of the report dissolved into endless glaciated snow fields.

Outside, children ran to the parking lot using trash bags as umbrellas.

What if his modifier didn't backfire? Those children would be there next year for another picnic.

As he pondered old arguments, Roscoe walked in accompanied by an aide, who quickly put a reel-to-reel player on the desk, plugged it into an outlet, and left.

Time to face the music, Cliff thought. He could tell that by the way Roscoe's eyes flashed at him with a combination of anger and impatience.

"I want you to hear something," Roscoe said, pointing at the tape player.

Cliff nodded.

"This is the reel of tape that was on the voice recorder of an H-3 Pelican helicopter that tried to rescue the poor bastards trapped at NP/Five," he said. His voice, though unusually restrained, had a foreboding quality. Then his face went grim and he pressed a button.

From the speaker came, *"Hello, Eureka. This is Major Convey. I have five survivors in sight. Do we pick them up? What if they are hot? Covered with radioactive dust, I mean. Do you want us to pick them up just the same? Over.*

"Hello, Eureka? Did you copy me?"

"Eureka, do we pick them up? Over."

"Negative, Return to base."

Oh, my God, it's like a dialogue from hell, Cliff thought, shuddering inwardly as he imagined the painful scenes that had taken place in the helicopter, at Eureka, at NP/5. Immobile, he stared at the player with a glazed look of anguish.

He heard Roscoe say, "God knows what else glaciation has in store for countless millions. And what you've heard is only half the story." He took out three photographs from a folder and gave them to Cliff. "That's how NP/Five looked when the SR-71 plane took the picture you're looking at. You can see the ridges and the crevasses, can't you? The nuclear plant is still smoking. Now look at the next picture. See those colored dots? They are people wearing parkas and anoraks. What's the date along the border of the picture?"

"Four May, thirteen-fifteen hours."

"Go to the next picture."

Cliff did.

"What's the date?"

"Seven May, fourteen hundred hours."

"The dots haven't moved in relation to nearby objects, like that trailerlike building over here." He pointed. "Have they?"

No answer.

"Have they, Cliff?"

Still no answer, but Cliff's head bent.

"First burned by radiation, then left to freeze to death knowing that nobody wanted to come near them, let alone help them inside a rescue helicopter. Not a pleasant way to go, is it?" Roscoe snatched the photographs away from Cliff's hands and put them back in the folder, ready to leave.

"I cannot believe," Cliff finally said, "that a technology has not been developed to save people exposed to radiation."

"Would you believe that there is a technology to save millions from freezing to death, and that there are people not willing to use it?"

Roscoe started walking away. At the door, he announced, "I'm going to put another oceanographer in charge of your modification. After all, Cliff, you worked on it while a high-salaried federal employee. Can't waste Uncle Sam's money, you know." He opened the door. "One more thing, Cliff. You may have brains, but you certainly have no balls."

Cliff experienced the waking nightmare of the Gulf Stream modification gone wrong. Just as he had envisioned the phases of one that worked, Cliff had also thought of the sequence of reactions that would follow a modification going out of control.

In that scenario the Hull is blown off all at once, its debris falls into the Mid-Ocean Canyon and blocks the J Current. There is a significant drop in the amount of moisture in North America, as planned.

But because of a miscalculation in the size of the dynamite charges, the powerful blasts dig an enormous channel. The waters of the stream flow through it and begin to form an eastward channel with its tremendous forward momentum. The channel gets bigger and wider. Soon the stream has a new course and heads for Portugal and Spain. It's the ultimate catastrophe. Northeasterly warm winds from the Sahara spread the moisture brought by the stream over the Iberian peninsula and into southern Europe. In a matter of days Portugal, Spain, France, Italy, and Yugoslavia are a steaming jungle. The mercury rises to 140 degrees F in Madrid; 135 degrees in Paris, where the humidity is an unbearable 96 percent—too high for human existence under the intense heat. Rome, Naples, Nice, and Zagreb are as inhospitable as the valley forests of the lower Amazon. Children and the elderly are first to die. Millions afflicted with respiratory diseases choke to death; thousands die slowly, weakened by the relentless wave of hot, humid weather. Roaches, maggots, and rodents proliferate by the billions, causing outbursts of plague that soon spread to the rest of Europe, the Balkans, the Middle East. Elephant grass grows everywhere. It buries roads, houses, bridges. . . .

But what if a perfectly constructed computer model could guarantee that the modification would be successful? Wasn't it a computer model that guaranteed the success of the moon shot?

The sun had barely set when Cliff sat in his kitchen for a light supper and moments of self-doubt and sorrow. By the time he made himself another cup of coffee, the moon was about forty-five degrees above the towers of Georgetown University.

Alone at his table, he stirred his coffee—and his past. Twenty years of study, long ocean trips, endless research, and a future that stretched before him like the Indianapolis racetrack—a road going to nowhere.

Inches away, a white phone stared at him, and Cliff stared back at it with eyes immobilized by lack of resolution. Should he call Roscoe or see him first thing in the morning?

It was a moment of intense emotion. But Cliff had no time to nourish his feeling of pride, or recall the scene in the armory. He had to confront the situation, believe that a well-planned modifier would work, get some kind of protection for Butch. . . .

Inbound traffic was a "snail trail," the helicopter spotter said, and Cliff considered other means of getting to Roscoe's office . . . even running a couple of miles. Roscoe moved fast. He would move faster to put another oceanographer in charge of Cliff's modification.

But when he finally parked his car just a few yards from

Roscoe's big black Buick, he didn't hurry to shut the engine off. The thought of seeing Roscoe chilled him, and he just sat there. The clock ticked.

Suddenly he got out of the car, climbed the stairs by twos, and asked the receptionist to let him see Roscoe.

As Cliff had feared, Roscoe was "out of the building."

"I accept the fact that Mr. Roscoe has meetings," he said to the receptionist, out of breath. He planted his long, slender fingers on her desk like a tent and, looking at her as if he had X-ray eyes, he added, "You just tell him that Cliff Lorenz is waiting outside. I wouldn't be here at this hour if I didn't believe he'd want to see me." His voice was authoritative, firm.

Roscoe, still angry, suppressed the urge to refuse Cliff's request. Well he knew that too many of his counterparts had failed because they let emotions prevail over political expediency.

He swiveled his chair 180 degrees and glanced across the lawn into the empty suite of the secretary of the interior. Recalling the day when the White House had called to inform him that the president was about to choose somebody else for the Cabinet post, and that he, Roscoe, was a candidate, a sense of opportunity welled inside him. Of course, nothing would please him more than to see Cliff suffer. But in D.C., the character of a government official could be prominently revealed in a crisis . . . and Cliff was a genius.

He lighted a cigar and waited for Cliff to come in.

"When can you start?" Roscoe said, still facing the window, his back to Cliff.

"Tomorrow." The cigar smoke smelled disturbingly acrid.

"Sooner," Roscoe said, turning his chair to face Cliff. "If I remember correctly, hundreds of shot holes have to be drilled into the—"

"Hull."

"The Hull, that's it. And then they must be loaded with dynamite." Roscoe rose, extending a hand toward Cliff.

"I'm sorry . . ." Cliff's voice trailed away. He had said enough.

For a moment Roscoe seemed out of words. "Sorry for what?" he said, shaking Cliff's hand. His tone was conciliatory, almost fatherly. "We can't waste precious hours," he said. "Marshall, on Kronin's order, is already setting up his modification."

"But it's flawed." Cliff's eyes were big round Os of astonishment. Hearing himself speak that word, Cliff shuddered. He was gripped by suspicion that politics—not science—was going to prevail.

"Flawed or not, Marshall has a head start—and with Kronin's personal backing."

So it was politics. Cliff burned. He was seldom troubled by nepotism and political favoritism. He was more often troubled by the thought that an oceanographer with connections might get grants and congressional support to carry out experiments with the stream. No one had done more research on the current or knew its behavior as well as Cliff did.

Roscoe nodded and went on to say that during the last cabinet meeting, Kronin had broken down modifiers into two groups: those taking advantage of existing natural forces and those using high-tech resources. "As far as I know, Marshall's and yours are the only two that fit the first category."

The dead end of hopelessness.

"It will never work." Cliff mopped his forehead "If anything, Marshall's plan would make things worse," he said, holding back the scream clawing in his throat.

"Yes, yes, I understand." Roscoe put a calming hand over Cliff's shoulder. "But Marshall will never get to use it if Kronin believes your plan for a modification holds more promise. Besides, the president wants each modifier to be a backup for the one chosen."

"Good idea. So what news have you about the other CLIMODs?"

Roscoe shrugged. "Also being readied. But . . ." He

paused, then leaned over and in a lower voice added, "At that cabinet meeting, Kronin also said that—theoretically—natural modifiers were the best. Besides"—Roscoe leaned even closer—"would you rely on NASA if you had to go somewhere on a certain day, or on a Weather Bureau forecast when planning a picnic?"

Cliff didn't react, but he could feel his blood pressure rise. "I'll get going right away."

"Good man, Cliff," Roscoe said with a quick slap of a hand on Cliff's knee. "Now, you damn well think of what you need and let me get it for you—even if you ask for the whole U.S. Navy. Yes?"

And that was it. As they walked to the door, Cliff stopped and said, "I really will need the Navy later, at least part of it. But for now I want you to make sure my son Butch doesn't get hurt."

Cliff didn't have to explain, for Roscoe nodded his compliance without asking for clarification. "I'll get on the phone first thing in the morning."

Cliff looked at him straight in the eye. As a team player, he was committed and uncompromising, and the way he held his gaze showed it. "No, now," he said.

Fritz had been activated because of his solid cover at Woods Hole, which Konlikov had identified as a likely—if not obvious—place where a climate modifier would be developed because of the enormous influence of the oceans on climate.

Seemingly ideal fishing-trip company (friendly, funny, and full of good stories, according to Cliff), Fritz was almost unimaginable in the role. He taught scuba diving for the YMCA; was popular with the girls; sang with the choir of the Chatham Lutheran Church. He was also chief engineer on the *Knorr,* as well as deputy operations officer and research coordinator.

Not surprisingly, on June 8, after two weeks of driving to Hyannis to see if the control had an assignment for him, Fritz got one. As he took Route 28 just outside Woods Hole and passed Bass River Road, he noticed a can resting smack under the *P* of "Airport" of the large blue-and-white road sign. It was the signal that his control had made the drop. Instructions were waiting for him at the local mall cinema. *Jesus!* he thought. He had to retrieve his assignment before sundown—before seven-thirty P.M.

Fritz felt a shortness of breath. He slowed down and stopped, his heart pounding at his chest.

For a long while he just stared at the can—hypnotized by the sight. He thought it funny that his big moment had finally come, yet he wished it hadn't. After years of an incredibly good life, spying on friends and neighbors seemed unthinkable. America had Americanized him; the process had taken place gradually. He remembered the story he had read in the *Boston Globe* the day an American petty officer was arrested for passing secret information to the KGB. "A man of Walker's character will not hesitate to violate his own sister for the sake of money. . . . He's the sleaziest drop of sewage ever to drip into a cesspool." Fritz closed his eyes in horror and saw the sun falling behind the jagged outline of a mountain.

He thought of Oleg Penkovsky, the KGB agent who became a CIA informant, and who was hurled alive into a crematorium the day after he had been shown the acid-distorted face of his wife and the mutilated bodies of his two daughters. All doubts vanished from his mind.

He looked around at the people. . . . One of them was his control, he was sure of that. Controls spied on spies.

Quickly, Fritz brought his Stingray to highway speed and headed for Hyannis, his mind on the drop. Without a doubt, his intelligence activities would involve him with research secrets kept at WHOI. The institution had been his assignment for years. But at least Cliff was no longer a research scientist there. He wouldn't have to worry about betraying his best friend.

Downtown Hyannis was crowded with sunburned vacationers in colorful summer clothes, and the air was filled with the smell of french fries and charcoaled hamburgers.

Fritz parked his car at the Stop and Shop and, following the instructions given him earlier, bought a ticket at the mall cinema.

He sat through a Tom Cruise movie, seemingly absorbing his control through the pores of his skin and wondering who the man with the seersucker suit seated five rows behind him was.

There was a burst of applause and the movie was over. People left, but he remained seated.

Finally, he took a deep breath, got up, and headed for the rest rooms.

The man with the seersucker suit walked behind him, then continued on out. Fritz laughed at his imagination.

The stalls were occupied, so he stood in front of a urinal, legs apart, eyes on the invisible stream.

Fritz washed his hands, combed his hair. Finally he entered the toilet stall.

He started to remove the chrome cylinder that held the roll of toilet paper by pushing in one end of it. The cylinder didn't collapse, but a pair of shoes came into view under the door . . . and then another. He tried again. Nothing. Had he fallen into an FBI trap?

The sweet smell of deodorizer was making him sick.

The shoes went out of his sight, and Fritz decided to try again, pushing from the other end. It worked. But the cylinder slipped from his fingers, shot out of the roll, and fell on the floor. Before he could reach for it, it had rolled to the next booth. He managed to laugh. Someone laughed back and kicked the cylinder in Fritz's direction. Unsmiling, he waited until the man in the next stall left, then pulled the cylinder apart. Visible through the metal spring was a piece of paper. It was a quarter of the society page of the *Cape Cod News*. It had some obscene words written on it, a woman's name in red, two pornographic doodles, and a telephone number. To anyone finding it, the page would appear a pimp's way of advertising. To Fritz it contained a hidden message. At once he held it to the light and read only the words with a pinhole through the dot of the letter

I. It said, "Station five. Lincoln Emporium. Precisely eight. Pick"—there was a pinhole over a numeral 2—"ring." Fritz threw the paper in the bowl, flushed, and made sure it didn't float up.

Again as instructed, he drove to the Lincoln Mall, parked his car, and headed for the bank of phone booths to the left of the entrance of the K-Mart department store. He began to shiver, a sure sign of anxiety. At the appointed time, as Fritz approached them, one of the phones rang once, then twice. Fritz knew his control was watching. He quickly took the phone off the hook. "The sun is rising," a gruff voice said over the line. A knot of fear tightened in his stomach as he said, "I'm ready."

As if dictating, the same gravelly voice of earlier contacts announced, "Identify scientists working on proposal to modify the flow of ocean currents. Learn about sailing schedules of all research vessels. Leave antenna of your car fully collapsed the day of the drop—Falmouth bus terminal, booth two. Urgent. Nod to acknowledge."

Heavyhearted but managing to look calm, Fritz nodded and hung up.

He wanted to wipe perspiration off his upper lips, but he thought it unwise. Instead, he put a finger in the coin-return slot—no dimes, but it must've looked as if he had all his wits.

There was still plenty of orange-tinted sunlight when Fritz walked to the car, forcing a spirited gait.

13

It was week six in the glaciation calendar.

At the monitoring station thirty-five miles south of San Jose, California, UCLA volcanologists were sampling the quality of airborne particles along the San Andreas Fault. Using special equipment capable of segregating particles deposited in "collectors," and counting them with a technique similar to one used by laboratories for blood analysis, the volcanologists determined that gases were continuing to escape at a constant rate, and that the layer of reflective crystalline particles now girding the Earth was thickening.

Their findings explained the drop in temperature—a significant 0.3 degrees Fahrenheit—from the previous air sampling conducted six days before.

In the capital the first signs of glaciation began to appear, though hardly visible to the untrained eye. For three days a brilliant, ultramarine sky curtained its classic skyline. Tungsten-colored sun rays glinted off the tip of the Washington Monument like those from a mythical sun god. Trees, houses, buildings looked hue enhanced, as if seen through a glass of light tea. The moon, ocher in color, had yellow rings around it.

Nobody seemed alarmed by the beautiful colors, which many observers of the Washington scene attributed to smog trapped over the city by a temperature inversion that kept the smog from rising into the atmosphere.

But in Madison, Wisconsin, glaciation appeared with less subtlety. Chester Braden, a golf professional, was on the course giving a putting lesson to one of the members of the Green Bay Golf and Tennis Club.

Suddenly, he stopped talking and kneeled down to look closely at the grass. "It can't be," he said. He motioned his student to kneel down, and together they examined the grass. "Yeah, it does look like crabgrass, Chester, but it isn't. Crabgrass comes up in August."

"No, Mr. Wilford, I know what I'm saying," Chester Braden told him deferentially. "I've spent my life walking on grass, half of it on this very course." He yanked off a clump of grass and put it in front of Mr. Wilford's eyes. "That's crabgrass."

"Almost three months ahead of time."

Chester Braden nodded.

Mr. Wilford took a ball out of his bag, dropped it on the ground, and putted. Then turned and saw the pro still holding the clump in his hand. He said, "If that is crabgrass, I'll eat a bowl of it in the dining room in front of the other guys."

He had to.

At the White House, the Crisis Management Team (CMT) studied ways of evacuating the terminally sick and those with communicable diseases without alarming the population. The primary problem was the relocation of the afflicted—4 million, according to some estimates—without the consent of the host people in the Sun Belt. "Not to mention the need for medical personnel willing to travel with them," the co-chairman of the CMT said. He recommended triage.

One floor below, speech writers worked on the language of the announcements about glaciation, and at the Pentagon, while analysts worked over reports of Russian troop movements along the Black and Caspian seas, officials scheduled the calling out of the National Guard, now designated as the "prime riot, traffic, and fire-control force."

Meanwhile, as Professor Orville Marshall flew out of Andrews AFB for Cape Race, where his modifier would be put into effect, stunt driver Charles Donovan was landing at Dulles Airport. After he had picked up his suitcase, he went to stand by the bank of phones next to the Hertz rental agency, his eyes scanning the arrivals concourse, as if he were waiting for someone.

It wasn't long before one of the phones rang, and he was welcomed by Moran, his control, who quickly told him that he would call him again at the hotel where Donovan was staying. "The dough is in the drop," Moran said. "If you heard what I said, nod twice."

Donovan nodded, and Moran hung up.

June 20, Monday.

The pain in the back of his neck, the red itching eyes, and not being able to sit for more than half an hour told Cliff he was suffering from techno stress. He was ready for a workout in the Ergo Club.

But a phone call forced him to cancel his plans.

Cliff had ordered the drill ship *Glomar Challenger,* sister ship to the *Glomar Explorer,* known for its super-secret salvage of a sunken Soviet submarine at the height of the cold war, to return to Norfolk from San Diego. However, the caller, Captain Jay Wilson, informed Cliff that the ship's sensitive steering mechanism had broken down. "Just metal fatigue," Wilson said. "I'm not too concerned about it, other than for the time factor."

What a way to start, Cliff thought. He hadn't worked on the modifier for a day, but the gremlins were already screwing things up for him. He hoped it wasn't an omen.

Without the *Challenger,* they could never remove the Hull in time.

"When can you leave San Diego?" Cliff asked Wilson.

"I don't know. Navy maintenance says that we aren't the only ship that needs repairs."

"I'll get you out of there fast," Cliff said, and told Wilson that he was leaving for San Diego that afternoon. "I'm bringing out a specialist. Someone who knows ships better than any of the Navy guys."

Cliff hung up and immediately dialed the number for the Woods Hole switchboard. No one knew ships like Fritz Hoffmeister.

Fritz looked up and read 6:45 PM FLIGHT 811 SAN DIEGO . . . GATE 30, a line on the departures monitor. Fritz's throat tightened at the idea that in a few hours his betrayal of Cliff would begin. His worst nightmare had come true. But the specter of his control floated somewhere nearby, reminding Fritz of his priorities. He boarded the plane and settled down to catch up on his sleep. But past the Mississippi, he was still awake. He wondered how he would look his best friend in the eye and lie.

The next day, after a troubled night's sleep and a light breakfast with Cliff, during which Fritz acted jet lagged to avoid small talk, a Navy staff car picked both men up outside the Marriott and drove them to Pier 7 of the U.S. Navy Yard.

Guarded by SPs with salivating German shepherds, the *Glomar Challenger* floated like a leviathan risen from the deep.

Originally used by the Navy in the laying of undersea sonar arrays for tracking Soviet ballistic submarines, the *Challenger* wore proudly the number 17,500 painted on a crossbar of its huge derrick to indicate its record-breaking drilling depth.

Upon boarding the ship, Cliff and Fritz were logged in and given security passes by an SP wearing a side arm. Security seemed to be tight.

After inspecting the damaged steering mechanism, Cliff

and Fritz met with the ship's captain, Wilson, and his chief maintenance officer.

"I figure four to six weeks to install the new steering mechanism and get us back to sea," the maintenance chief said.

"Four weeks seems reasonable," Fritz said to Cliff. "But I could do it in three." The captain looked to the maintenance chief, whose temper seemed ready to flare.

"There's no way—"

"Easy, Chief," Wilson interrupted. "This is a priority job, and if Mr. Hoffmeister thinks he can get it done faster, then we'll welcome his help. Understood?"

"Aye, Captain. But I'll believe it when I see it."

Cliff smiled and thanked the captain, then turned to Fritz. "Just let me know what you need. I'll be on the phone to the chief of naval operations for whatever it is—mechanics, spare parts, the works. Okay?"

"No problem," Fritz reassured Cliff. Fritz was pleased. Working on the *Challenger* would give him new access, beyond what he had working on the *Knorr*, to potential information of interest to his control. "But what is the big hurry? Are you planning a project you have not told me about?" he asked.

Cliff hesitated before answering. Fritz had not yet been briefed on glaciation, since he wasn't part of the modification program. And Cliff didn't think Fritz had a "need to know" just yet. "No," he said. "The Navy's got some hush-hush project the DOI is monitoring. That's why I'm involved."

"Ach, I see," Fritz answered, knowing that his friend wasn't being completely truthful.

Cliff looked at his watch. "If I hurry, I can catch the two-fifteen flight to D.C. I'll leave this in your capable hands."

"What is the rush, Cliff? You have just come here," Fritz said.

"No rest for the weary. I've got plenty of work to do back in D.C. And you don't need me here. The harbor master and maintenance know this is a priority job. I'll call to check on your status in a couple of days, okay?"

"Sure, please do," Fritz replied, and with an affectionate slap on Cliff's upper arm he said, "I will take care of everything."

As Cliff headed down the gangplank to the waiting staff car, Fritz knew that there was more going on than he was being told. But that was all right with him. He could wait.

One hour into the flight, Cliff sat in his seat, pen in hand, head shaking.

Reshaping the course of the Gulf Stream—long the dream of many—was about to become reality. And he was in charge! Playing God again!

He felt ice flowing through his veins, and he would quickly have become a victim of second thoughts had he not forced himself to think of other matters. On top of his yellow pad he wrote: *Phase One: Operation Data.*

For a while he just looked at those words written in black ink. Slowly ideas started to organize. First, he reasoned, one group of ships must profile the Hull to determine its rock formation and cleavage. While the profiling was going on, a second group would be taking echo sounder images of the area around the Hull. . . . The task of recording density and current velocity should be given to a third group.

All without the Russians knowing what was going on.

By the time flight attendants served lunch, Cliff had almost filled his legal pad with notes. For a long time he looked at the food, wondering if he really knew what he was doing. Six years ago, when he first drew the modified course of the stream on a napkin, he had almost convinced himself that he did.

Now he was beginning to wonder.

14

June cooled into July.

And in France everybody was talking about what was happening to the snails.

Instead of retreating into crevices and holes to hibernate, as they did in fall, they were dying near the vegetable plants they fed on. Millions of them. Temperatures at the Franciscan Monastery of Clermont Ferrand, high in the Massif Central, ran an average of twenty-two Fahrenheit degrees lower at night.

Their death was not a total mystery. Since the middle of the twelfth century, when Clermont Ferrand Abbey was built, monks had meticulously chronicled life at the monastery. Many passages in the chronicles dealt with snails, and some had been translated to modern French as background information for the lucrative snail industry.

In the translation of manuscript page XXIII (guerrite n.19, tome II), which begins with an illuminated *D*, with garlands and foliage of the late Gothic and ascribed to Abbot Kacquamart de Purcel, the coming of what was later known as the Little Ice Age was chronicled. The last paragraph read:

. . . but the little snails, which are so delicate
and graceful and which are usually plentiful around
the abbey thanks to our Lord, have not caused the
usual mischief this year nor have they invaded
the vegetable garden of brother Antoine . . . nor
were the villagers in the valley below compelled
to lay cabbage leaves to attract them away from
the vegetables, which seldom grow big enough to
be used in soups. The snails were dead before the
harvest of the vineyards, which in this year of our
Lord 1375 were totally ruined eight weeks before
the picking time because of frost at night and then
snow. . . . The snails could have lived in hibernation
had they eaten plentifully before the snows came
the day after the feast of the Assumption of the
Blessed Lady August 15. These snails are certainly
our silent sentinels of change. . . .

Bloodthirsty martens proved to be sentinels of change of
a different kind.

It happened in Chinook, Montana. When Doug Melchior,
fifty-eight, arose on the morning of June 24, he knew at
once something was wrong. His chickens and roosters were
quiet. He looked at the clock—5:45 A.M., past the time
his animals would waken him. He turned to one side and
noticed that his wife was awake. "Louise," he whispered,
"the chickens . . ."

"I know," she said. "They've never done this before.
Something's wrong."

Putting on his overalls, Melchior ran outside. It was cold,
and the sky was still dark except for a band of bluish pink
light in the east. With vapor jetting out of his nostrils, he
opened the barn door. "Jesus," he cried, covering his mouth
with one hand, "who would do this to me?" He walked
around the barn, mouth open, eyes wide. He shook his
head. He looked as if he were going to vomit. Everywhere
there were half-eaten chickens; roosters with bloody broken
beaks. Bloodstained feathers stuck on walls and rafters. The
air was damp, dense, foul with the smell of entrails and

excrement. As he ran out of the barn to call the police, he spotted the body of an animal resembling a weasel.

When the local veterinarian came to Melchior's farm at the request of the police, a quick examination revealed that the animal Melchior had found was a breed of the pennant marten. "This far south?" asked the veterinarian, shaking his head. "A bloodthirsty marten around here? I don't believe it."

Later that day, when the veterinarian was interviewed on station WTJW, he explained that martens were known to attack chickens and human beings, "if driven by something."

"Driven by what?" the morning disk jockey asked him.

"Who knows?" The veterinarian thought for a while. "In this case, I'd say unusual weather," he answered. "They're sensitive to changes, you know. And adapting to a new environment can make them desperate."

"That's a lot of bullshit," croaked Owen Silby, fifty-two, when he read about the martens that evening. "Phony-baloney Doug is at it again!" he said to his daughter. "Oh, well, there ain't been a good story in this fuckin' newspaper for months. Shit!" He rolled a cigar from one corner of his mouth to the other. Dropping the newspaper on his lap, he glanced around the room. "Jill," he called to his daughter, "go see where Billy is." He went back to reading his paper.

Suddenly, from the garage, came a scream. "Daddy, quick!"

Silby dashed out. There, in one corner of the garage, was his daughter. Hysterically repeating the name of her brother over and over, she rocked back and forth with the bloody little body cradled tight in her arms.

Silby was horrified. Aghast, he leaned against the garage frame, eyes on the dozens of skin punctures on the child's body—spaced and deep like those from a carving fork. The child was still alive.

Billy was flown to Gerry Falls by National Guard helicopter, but his life could not be saved. He died of blood poisoning. There was no antidote for the marten bite.

News of the "martens on the loose" spread.

By two A.M., the CMT voted to have the press secretary admit that the White House was studying reports from the scientific community dealing with unseasonable weather changes evidenced by the behavior of some animals and plants.

"How long has the White House known about these weather changes?" asked Lee Jackson of the *Los Angeles Times* at the press conference that followed. "What is the administration doing about it? Is anybody in danger?"

"The president has been informed of these changes and he will meet with his cabinet and science adviser . . . ," the secretary replied. "And the answer to the last part of your question is no. No one is in danger."

It wasn't true.

Packs of foraging Arctic wolves were moving south by migratory instinct. As night fell, one pack stopped half a mile from A-9, the Air Force radar site in the Kilbuck Mountains, Alaska.

Technical Sergeant Theodore Hicks was having supper when he got a telephone call from the crew monitoring surveillance radar. There was a "burn" on the screen of the long-range PPI (Present Position Indicator) radar.

"I'll see what's causing it," he said, and left the mess hall.

A look at his ammeter told Hicks that the antenna's motor current drain had dropped, hence the burn. Something was causing the antenna to rotate at lower rotations per minute.

Hicks, a solid-looking man in his thirties, decided to go to the generator shack and investigate. He put on his fur-lined parka, grabbed his toolbox and walkie-talkie, and went out. It was four degrees below zero and clear, with a steady wind from the northwest. Minutes later, he returned to

pick up his M-16 rifle. He checked the ammunition clip—
three rounds. He again headed for the generator shack five
hundred yards away.

Less than thirty yards from his destination, he stopped,
put down the toolbox, and took out the walkie-talkie from
his pocket. "Hicks to Control," he said. He sounded calm.

Somebody with a bored voice answered, "Control
here . . . Go ahead."

"Call the dog unit and find out if any of their beasts are
still around."

"What's the matter, Hicks? You scared, eh?"

Hicks cupped a hand over the microphone slot of the
walkie-talkie. His voice low, he said, "Cut the shit and do
what I tell you."

A few minutes passed.

"Control . . . goddammit . . . Where the Christ are you?"

A chilled voice replied, "You can get a court-martial for
using foul language on radio. Over."

Hicks crouched on the snow and lowered his voice. "Do
what I told you. Over."

"Yeah, hold on," the same voice said.

More minutes passed. Hicks panned around, eyes wide
open. Without making any noise, he disengaged the safety
lock of the M-16. "Control to Hicks."

Hicks turned the volume down. "Go ahead, quick," he
whispered.

"Dogs are in. Repeat . . . dogs all in."

"They can't be." He raised his head and squinted to see,
focusing on something. He pressed the talk lever. "Hicks
to Control."

"What now, ghosts?"

"Listen, you bastard"—Hicks spoke as if dictating—
"there are big dogs around the generator shack and the dome.
Have someone meet me halfway. Bring ammo. Repeat.
Bring ammo. Over."

"What ammo? It's all locked up. Anyhow, them dogs
won't eat you. You're too tough. Ha!"

Hicks looked left and right. "Hurry up, you bastard,

they're coming at me. I can see—" A shot rang out, and then another. They reflected like fireflies in the luminescent bluish eyes of big animals around him.

Hicks fired again, his last shot echoing in the valley below. "Hurry!" he cried. He stood up, fumbling with the walkie-talkie and the rifle. He dropped the rifle on the snow. "Get out . . . get out," he yelled, cocking the arm holding the walkie-talkie, eyes straining in the darkness.

The animals were all around him. They were salivating, vapor belching out of their mouths. He counted them: two, five, ten . . .

"Hello, Hicks, do you read me?" asked the man in the control room.

Hicks bent his knees. Fumbling, he touched the lock of the toolbox where his hunting knife was. "Go away. Beat it!" he cried.

The walkie-talkie crackled. "Hicks?"

At that moment, an animal jumped on Hicks's back, knocking him down onto the snow. He covered his face with his hands, kicking. "Help!" he shouted in a voice distorted by the jerks of his body.

Shots rang out from the door of the control room. Then a beam from a powerful searchlight cut through the darkness and flooded the area stained with Hicks's blood. The animals—white Arctic wolves—ran in all directions. In less than a minute they had torn away Hicks's ears, hands, buttocks, and throat.

That evening, after placing the remains of Hicks's body in a makeshift coffin, the colonel commanding the monitoring station, in violation of Pentagon policies, raised the number of ammunition rounds from three to a full clip.

Ornithologists were puzzled. A number of red knots that had been banded and color-coded in the Hudson Bay region by an international team researching the birds' migratory habits had been spotted as far south as Manomet Observatory. "I literally froze," said Michael Hubbard to his colleague. He had banded the birds in May and he had not expected to see them feeding in the area for another eight weeks, since the red knots leave the northern reaches of Hudson Bay for the Bay of Valdes, Argentina, early in August. "At first I thought I was seeing things," Hubbard added. "But then I recognized the yellow paint on the underbelly of three of the birds and I knew something was wrong somewhere. You can set your watch by the flight of these migratory birds. I can't figure it out."

Man also sensed the coming of natural disaster.

It was now early July, and the nation continued to enjoy near-seasonal temperatures during the day, slightly lower during the night. A quirk in the weather, many believed. Erratic behavior of the jet stream, others said. And there were those quick to point out the reliability of the *Farmer's Almanac*, now better than 80 percent accurate.

Yet outdoor activities did not reflect it. Weber claimed a record sale of half a million barbecue gas ovens in a month.

Adults watched "oldies" with Bette Davis and Roland Colman on TV or rented them from video stores. Youngsters went back to the sound of the big bands.

"I suppose there is some kind of logic to new preferences," wrote Tom Neil in the *New York Times*. "Man always seems to find expression in nostalgia when things go bad and worse times to come are anticipated."

Nostalgia and anxiety are what characterized the International Summer Show, which opened at the Art Institute of Chicago. "In general," art critic Chris Bene wrote in the program note, "it is in the exploitation of the color blue, as in Picasso's *La Vie*, that one will sense despair. . . . The skies seem alien and hostile. . . . The people, deprived of their flesh colors, move in their world overcome by the failure of nerve."

But it was at Brandeis University's Spingold Theater that man's intuitive powers found expression in the new play, *Noah,* which opened the summer season. In the first scene, the ark builder tells his family, "I have heard sounds of frightened birds and animals . . . of angrier, colder winds."

15

Presentation day. The Pentagon.

Cliff was there even though he had had only three days to prepare a presentation, which he had limited to only the theory behind his modification. He had no model, no visual aids, not even an assistant. But he knew that if he could sell the theory, Kronin would give him an opportunity to make a full-dress presentation.

Despite the uncertainties, he felt excited and looked forward to a momentous event in the history of science and human ingenuity. A new scientific era was beginning that day.

As Cliff glanced about the hearing room he noticed a disturbing smile on Marshall's face. It hinted that his modification was on schedule or that he knew something nobody else did.

Yet the cold and impersonal mask on Kronin's face, like that of a judge at a hearing, reassured him. Any judge, Cliff mused, believes only one-half of what he hears. A good judge, however, knows which half to believe. Cliff looked at him wondering what Kronin would believe.

The setting was familiar to anyone who had watched a

Senate hearing on TV, though it took place at the Pentagon. HR-4, with a privileged view of the Tidal Basin and the Jefferson Memorial along its northeast wall, resembled the lecture hall of an old college. It had been chosen because it was equipped with the latest in audiovisual equipment and security electronics. A semicircular table with clusters of chairs around it and the traditional complement of green blotters, microphones, Thermoses, and glasses filled the center of the room. Large photographs of military hardware and men in action in Iwo Jima, Anzio, Midway, and Kuwait hung on the wall. Long battles over this or that weapon system had been fought here. Its very air smelled of bureaucratic conflict.

To Cliff, the layout, the uniforms, and the unsmiling, strange faces contributed to the feeling of cold war summit conference. Perhaps HR-4 was a good choice, after all.

It was obvious from the props being brought in that the modifiers to be proposed differed not only in the method used to reach the goal but also in the identification and definition of the goal itself. It would make the task of choosing the right one difficult for Kronin.

The piece of equipment the U.S. Weather Bureau wheeled in, for example, was an instant attention-getter. People stood up, walked to it and around it, examined it, wondered about its function. It piqued everyone's curiosity even in a room full of jaded scientists.

Cliff himself didn't realize how long he had been staring at it, marveling at its simplicity and wondering about its purpose. The words *USWB Weather Chamber K-5* did little to satisfy his curiosity. The giant stainless steel machine resembling a pressure cooker was so unreadable that Cliff figured the CIA must have had a hand in building it. If it was a machine.

Whatever it was, Cliff could identify a NiCad battery power supply, switches, one panel meter reading DC output, and another measuring some kind of electron flow. He was utterly baffled by the thousands of tiny copper wires sticking out from the top section of the weather chamber to form an inverted bowl about five feet in diameter.

Less mysterious was the apparatus bearing NASA's logo. It resembled a tall louvered window with highly polished slats. Next to it stood what appeared to be a miniature space satellite with solar panels, telescopic antennas, and sensors of various shapes and sizes.

Both pieces looked harmless, Cliff thought, not like the stream.

Marshall was first to make his presentation and began by stressing that he had relied on a "logic-based approach to ecological simulation modeling."

Having done so, he turned on a wide-screen TV monitor. It showed various LANDSAT pictures of Cape Race, Newfoundland, and the Gulf Stream taken from 440 miles up during several passes then stitched together by computer. Covering an area of 20,000 square miles, the seamless overview of the North Atlantic and East Coast was spectacular. And telling. Everyone could see how close a meander of the stream (colored sulfide green against a deep blue ocean) was to Cape Race.

"If the cape protruded just an extra five miles out into the Atlantic," Marshall said while working a mouse-operated pointer, "it would block the meander and deflect its warm water westward. Because Cape Race peninsula does not, I would build in shallow water, an artificial continuation of the cape in the form of a jetty eight miles long made of interlocking concrete cassoni." As he spoke, all three monitors showed various views of the cassoni, the prefabricated structures resembling container boxes.

Now CAD (Computer-Aided Design) images appeared sequentially on the monitor with three-dimensional wire-framed views of the cassoni, how they interlocked and stood on the ocean floor to form "a man-made arm stretching out into the Atlantic to catch the much-needed warm water of the stream."

Then the graphics showed how the climate would change

because of the jetty. Together the images made up an information flow model with excellent scientific visualization. It was like watching a serious Walt Disney cartoon.

Cliff was impressed, though convinced that the modification was flawed. He took copious notes, wondering if he could top Marshall's high-tech, mind-bending presentation, wondering if salesmanship more than the right modification for the country was going to be the deciding factor.

"Glaciation," Marshall said as he concluded his presentation, "is the absence of warm moisture in the air."

It wasn't until he stressed his point for the second time that an icy realization surged through Cliff, and he was sure that Marshall was a victim of self-delusion. With grim certainty he knew that Marshall's proposal was extremely dangerous. It would be more dangerous if nobody tried to prove his error. Marshall had to be stopped now. Cliff leaned into his microphone and said, "If you bring moisture, you make precipitation possible."

The hammer had struck the flint stone.

A hum of whispering broke out among the conferees. At first Marshall made no comment, but his body language did. He just stared at Cliff with a combination of incredulity and anger. Then, regaining his composure, Marshall said, "True. But warm moisture also means higher temperatures. For us it would mean getting rain instead of snow."

Cliff had studied the Ryker plan, which had inspired Marshall, going carefully over that portion of the congressional record with the testimony of scientists opposed to Ryker's attempt at making the northeast "another Florida." He had done his homework. He had also read the works of prominent climatologists, one of whom was in the room. "Dr. Maxwell of NOAA, whom many of you know for his contribution to climatology, may want to say something," Cliff said, turning to a pouchy man with an Abraham Lincoln beard.

All eyes were now focused on Dr. Maxwell.

Technicians switched his mike on, but he seemed hesitant. Climatology was his background, politics his daily life.

He waited. Marshall, with his failing-heart look, just stared as one would at a firing squad.

"It's both a temperature and moisture problem," Maxwell said in a wooden tone, as if programmed with that line.

"That may be true," Cliff told him. "Temperature is one problem, but moisture would feed blizzards." He shook his head. "Dr. Maxwell," he said, facing the audience as though they were jurors, "how can you say that when you write—"

"Gentlemen," Kronin interrupted, and called for a brief recess.

No computers or videos were needed for the next presentation.

"This is our Krypton-five inhibitor," Dr. James Stoddard of the Weather Bureau said. Tall and ungainly, he made a rather gangling figure. "It's actually a denucleating engine," he added, and went into a scientific explanation of its purpose.

Simply put, he explained that precipitation, rain or snow, took place only after "nucleation," the all-important accumulation of microscopic moisture particles around a nucleus of dust. This nucleation caused the formation of drops, which fell when they reached a certain weight.

"If we inhibit nucleation by shielding the nucleus of dust with negatively charged ions, the formation of rain droplets will not take place. I'll prove it," he said, and got ready for a demonstration.

At a signal from him, steam from a giant vaporizer billowed out and began collecting under the ceiling of HR-4. It dissipated quickly after the vaporizer was turned off.

Stoddard said, "Now let's see if steam will collect with the inhibitor on." As he spoke, an assistant flipped a couple of switches and immediately millions of minute sparks danced purplish along the copper wires. The room filled with a smell of ozone, but when the vaporizer was turned back on no steam collected under the ceiling.

"Well, as you can see, negatively charged ions have

accumulated around particles of dust and have prevented nucleation. That's obvious," he said, his voice mixing with a low-decibel crackling sound creeping into the P.A. system through the long microphone cord acting as an antenna.

He announced how fifty factories could build enough Krypton-5 engines so that a string of them could be placed along the Arctic Circle spaced a quarter of a mile apart; he revealed that tests on animals had shown no harmful effects from massive doses of negative ions, and that the Krypton-5 system had been tested successfully in valleys prone to morning fog.

"But has it been tested to see whether the billions of negative ions might play havoc with VHF and UHF communications?" a bearded man sitting to the left of the deputy director of NASA asked. "I could hear the hash over the P.A. system when your Krypton-five machine was turned on."

The answer came fast. "No, it has not. A test of that magnitude would require hundreds and hundreds of inhibitors, and our budget is limited."

"What you're saying is that if your modification is executed, we might find that it interferes with telemetering? Without telemetering NASA might as well close shop."

"Sir, it's either no precipitation or no telemetering. We cannot have both. I'm—"

"Wait a minute—"

"Gentlemen!"

Cliff noted with interest how different each modifier was, obviously because Stoddard and Marshall had seen glaciation from different points of view. For Stoddard glaciation was precipitation; for Marshall, it was lack of warm moisture. And for the gentleman now speaking, it was low temperature. He listened.

"Cold Arctic air will be our enemy during glaciation," Emery Baker, senior engineer of NASA's Atmospheric Research Group, began. "So, NASA proposes to raise mean temperatures by capturing the rays of the sun passing by

Earth on the way to space and by deflecting them toward North America."

The purpose of the tall louvered window was now obvious, and judging by the number of heads nodding at what Baker said, it made a lot of sense.

His modifier was indeed simple and, given NASA's experience and equipment, very viable. It didn't take long for Cliff to realize that. Indeed, the more he looked at the louvered window, the more he was convinced of its potential effectiveness with little danger of backfiring. According to Baker, NASA proposed to place thousands of fifteen-by-forty-five-foot tinfoil reflectors in geosynchronous or stationary orbit. They would be arranged in "venetian blind" fashion, two miles apart and stacked for one hundred miles along a concave line.

Standing by the tall louvered window, he said that the scale model gave a good idea of the size relationship, angle of refraction, and material used. The shuttles *Columbia* and *Atlantis* would be able to place 20,000 sheets each during a four-day mission using a "dispenser" made in Canada. "The modification," he went on, "can be regulated or adjusted. Telemetering units would allow us to monitor all aspects of their function. And . . . yes, the reflectors have been tested over Antarctica during one of our classified missions. Using only fifteen hundred reflectors, the temperature on a one-hundred-square-mile area rose fifteen degrees—just as our mathematical model had predicted."

There were no questions, and Kronin smiled.

For his part, Cliff sighed with relief, feeling almost weightless knowing that the burden of the responsibility to modify the weather lay not just on his shoulders. Judging from the way some of the discussions went, there were at least two colleagues ready to execute modifiers. This did not change his agenda for the day, however. Despite everything, he knew his own modification was superior to those presented because it would change nature by rearranging nature. He had entered the Pentagon to sell an idea and he would leave with a purchase order. That was his task, one made more difficult by the lack of a supporting model or even a series of graphic images like the ones Marshall had used.

Cliff's turn came and he took his time.

Looking trim and businesslike in a double-breasted suit, he looked a bit more like a banker than a scientist. But the look worked for this audience. Unhurried, Cliff first glanced at his watch, filled his glass with water, then tapped on the mike.

It was all deliberate. He knew that in a tense atmosphere every motion—insignificant as it might seem—increased the listener's level of attention.

Memories were long in D.C. People would remember him by what he said and did today.

His talk, focused mainly on the theory of his modification and delivered in front of a tired audience, was good. Of course his experience as a lecturer, speaker at various international symposia, and the numerous appearances before Senate subcommittees on behalf of the DOI, had polished his style.

His presentation was also short and so devoid of techno-babble and scientific terminology that even the two military MPs standing at the door were able to follow Cliff without losing concentration once. He spoke slowly yet loud enough that an amplifier hardly seemed necessary. He looked often at his notes, paying careful attention to his marginal reminders about voice inflection, pauses, and gestures.

Using a simple map, he pinpointed the location of the Hull, described how its shape contributed to halving the Gulf Stream, talked about the effect of the J Current as a supplier of moisture in North America, then asserted how that supply could be eliminated by blowing up the Hull.

Ten minutes after he began, he concluded, "One of the first things I learned as a boy," he said, "is that moisture is the principal component of rain, snow, and ice. Moisture is glaciation, and we can prevent the assassination of civilization, as Professor Kronin called it, by cutting off whatever moisture we can—not by bringing it in, as has been suggested."

The atmosphere in HR-4 grew suddenly tense and unpredictable. Cliff's last remark was yet another denunciation of Marshall's scholarship and understanding of the complexities of climate. Many of the conferees shifted uncomfortably in their seats.

A hand went up.

"Could you tell me how many drill holes you would need to properly dynamite your Hull?" a woman asked.

That was the question Cliff had asked himself a thousand times. He answered, "If after subsurface exploration, we find that we can take advantage of the cleavage of the rock, I'd say about two hundred drill holes. The model I plan to build will give me the exact number. I need three weeks to build one." He turned to Kronin. "I request that I be granted a hearing to complete my presentation."

Kronin, obviously interested in the proposal, and impressed with Cliff's grasp of his research, granted the request.

There was a follow-up question. "You mean to say, Dr. Lorenz, that you plan to drill two hundred holes in weather conditions getting progressively worse because of an advancing glaciation?" the same woman asked, and shook her head incredulously.

"Yes. But I know what our drill ships can do."

Cliff looked around. He saw Roscoe with a big smile on his face but the reaction he had expected from Marshall did not come. He was puzzled. But he was sure it was only a matter of time. Indeed, minutes later, he noticed Marshall, visibly smoldering with fury, raising a hand. "Yes, Professor?"

Marshall pinched his forehead. "If my memory serves me right, isn't the area around . . . whatever you call it, infested with laminarias, the same fifteen- to twenty-foot-tall weeds that prevented Jacques Cousteau from reaching the Spanish galleon *Virgen del Rosario*?"

Cliff was taken off guard and he knew that Marshall was

going to fight him on a different turf. Cliff cursed silently
and gave him a quick questioning look. "Yes, the same type
of weed."

"Well, Dr. Lorenz," Marshall continued, his voice cold
and harsh, "since the holes cannot be loaded by the same
pipes that drill them, who will you send down there to do
the job?"

For a moment their eyes met. Underwater horrors flashed
through Cliff's mind. "Volunteers," he replied.

"Volunteers, I see." Marshall paused for effect. "Would
you go?"

Instinctively Cliff replied, "If it's necessary, yes."

Marshall passed a hand over his carefully combed hair
and smiled. "That I would like to see, Doctor. That I would
like to see."

Cliff needed not descend onto a jungle of laminaria
weeds to get trapped. A trap was being set up on land at
the Capitol Motor Lodge on Georgia Avenue, where stunt
driver Charles Donovan was staying.

As promised, Moran of Sunlife called him and told
Donovan to go ahead with the plan to put Cliff Lorenz
out of action. The FBI's warnings had not been completely
on target. The Russians were not planning to kidnap any of
the scientists working on modifiers. They didn't have time
for any such niceties.

The following morning Donovan waited along Reservoir
Road, thus covering all possible routes a car leaving Cliff's
home would take. He was driving a long van with a dozen
or so cinder blocks piled loosely just behind him.

After only a few days on the job, he knew the location
of every large tree on any street in northwest D.C., the
time cycle of traffic lights, traffic patterns at various times
of the day, the schedule of police cruisers. He could even
tell you at what time a given truck made its delivery. He
also had learned to identify Cliff's car in the dark because
it had a muffler with chrome-plated double exhaust pipes
that made a noise like that of a speedboat on idle. It was

also the only Porsche inside the Beltway with a nose bra.
Piece of cake.

It was seven-thirty A.M. and drizzling, and the morning
fog blowing from Glover Park gave the tree-lined street the
landscape look of a Chinese watercolor.

At 7:40 A.M., Donovan spotted Cliff lifting the hood of
his car. Immediately Donovan drove some five hundred
yards down the street, made a U-turn, and parked on the
right side of the road. From where he was he could see the
top of the hill and the intersection where Cliff had to take
a right.

Which he did. Then Donovan saw Cliff stop at a gas
station a block from the intersection.

Traffic was light; there were no cops or police cruisers.

Donovan decided to move. He pulled out of the parking
space when he saw Cliff leave the station. He pushed hard
on the gas pedal. Smoke shot out of the tail pipe; the old rattling van picked up speed, barrelling along like a runaway
locomotive as its tires churned up high plumes of spray.

And then came the most dreaded sound.

Eyes burning with the thrill of the chase, Donovan saw
the red Porsche moving toward him and got ready for the
slugger's swing. He picked up speed, hit the horn, jammed
on the brake, turned hard left, while his screeching tires
laid smokey marks on the road.

Its front wheels locked, the rear of the van turned left
but the momentum of the shifting blocks was too much. It
skidded furiously over the thin sheen of engine oil and water
covering the highway, roared past the Porsche, ripping its
front bumper with a sickening sound, slamming against a
pile of old tires, and coming to a stop in a cloud of steam
that shot up from the radiator.

A dreadful sound. The familiar shuddering, rattling sound
of metal hitting metal.

Cliff's neck whiplashed, but the head rest and seat belt
saved him. "Where did you learn to drive?" he shouted to
Donovan.

Sirens wailed.

Soon traffic came to a halt and above the wailing sirens one could hear the voice of a paramedic reporting to the station via radio: "No P.I. Driver of Porsche looks shaken. Auto drivable. Taking him to Memorial Emergency for mandatory X rays against his will. Over and out."

The X rays were negative.

As Cliff was on his way to his office, Donovan was being questioned by the police.

Donovan's neck was damp and cold. He had imagined that his career would end in traction, never in a police station or in jail.

"Faced with either life imprisonment or cash and a new identity," spymaster Allen Dulles wrote, "agents opt for the latter."

He was right. That night Donovan promised the police full cooperation and described Moran the best he could.

The police didn't have much, but a lead was a lead.

Simferopol, Crimea.

In the office of the director of Ukraine's Armed Forces Personnel Files building, a robust captain kept shaking his head as he read the list Dr. Andrei Konlikov had given him. He hit the paper with the back of his fingers. "Damn," he said, "we used to have dozens of specialists right here at the base. But now," he said, shrugging, "only a handful, not the number you need."

"Where are they?" Konlikov asked. "Home, I suppose."

The captain nodded and told Konlikov that with the major cuts in the Ukrainian military budget, things had changed drastically. "But the law requires that they serve in reserve units."

Konlikov wondered if there was a way of going back to the time when the Red Army could count on thousands of specialists ready to move out on a minute's notice. It was not the time or the place to get into an argument. He said, "I knew that. But would they volunteer for a dangerous job now?"

"Of course," the captain answered. Nothing had really changed because of the soldiers' military status. They were still people who got their kicks doing dangerous and unusual work. Take the Navy Underwater Commandos. Practically all of them were itching to dive but couldn't because they didn't even own a snorkel mask, let alone a wet suit. Besides, many were unemployed and waiting for something to come along that promised a salary. "If they got the call, they'd come."

The real problem, however, was getting in touch with them. Some might be home; others, God only knew where they might be. "The task facing me is to round up as many as you need," the captain said. "That will not be easy. But I will do my best. I come from Gorky, and it gets very cold up there, even without glaciation."

Konlikov leaned back on the chair heavily, his jet-lagged eyes red and half-open. He knew he had no choice but to resign himself to the idea of having to make do with fewer specialists. He toyed with a book of matches and said nothing for a while.

There was only the sound of rock music coming through the window facing the parade ground.

"More than your best, Captain," Konlikov said. He made it sound like a favor, not an order—even though he held the rank of colonel.

That seemed to please the captain, for he smiled benevolently, and Konlikov pressed on. "I desperately need underwater cameramen," he said, and circled a line on the sheet of paper. "At least four."

Then he asked for demolition experts, hydrophone mechanics, experts in sonar images, laser theodolite and underwater acoustic technicians, and deep submergence divers. And the list went on with six more specializations.

When the time came to discuss logistics, Konlikov already had everything figured out. He suggested that as soon as the specialists reported to the base, they were to fly to Cuba and from there they were to be ferried to the *Dokholov*. "I'll be boarding it late tomorrow night in Panama in order to take charge." He shook the captain's hand and thanked him.

16

So much to do, and with so little time left!

But Cliff dared to dream of total success. He put the pen he'd been taking notes with down and called Fritz in San Diego to tell him to get back to Woods Hole and have the *Knorr* ready for a data-collecting trip. "Three, four days max."

"*Gut!*" Fritz said. "We have just received the goods." He was referring to the new steering mechanism for the *Challenger*. "Can you delay departure . . . forty-eight hours?"

Cliff said he couldn't. "A Navy intelligence officer will explain what's happening. Now tell me, how's work progressing?"

Fritz's eyes opened wide. Explain what? "Fine, fine," he answered. "If I press she should be ready in a week."

"Then press. And, Fritz . . ." Cliff had an idea.

"Yes."

"Have the Navy tow her to Woods Hole while they work on it. You get on a plane. We sail Saturday."

So that's where she's going, Fritz thought. "Can Captain Edwards put together a good crew in such short time?"

"If he doesn't, we'll have to make do."

Fritz hung up the phone, a shade paler yet grinning slightly. With all he was about to find out, he'd be able to risk a drop to his control—his first good drop.

No one could be expected to visualize, plan, and execute a major geological restructuring of the ocean floor in a few days. But Cliff had been thinking about his modifier for months, years even. He knew what he needed.

Above all, he felt that the key would be to develop an accurate computer model that would allow him to test his hypothesis under controlled conditions. There was no other way of foreseeing possible disaster.

But first Cliff needed fresh data. A model would only be as good as the data it used.

Take salinity. It determined the weight of the water, which when factored with the speed of the Gulf Stream quantified "forward momentum," or the ability of the current to sweep debris from the Hull into the Mid-Ocean Canyon and block it. It had to be ocean engineering at its best.

Needless to say, Cliff didn't have the time to collect the remaining data he needed himself, such as geostrophic flow, gyre, temperature, and solar constants. He would have to rely on the reputation of the oceanographer who had collected the most recent readings.

Cliff's operation data had three major goals: (a) profile and complete a subsurface study of the Hull in order to determine the proper location of the drill holes; (b) generate a topography of the surrounding area to determine potential bed or beds through which the stream or parts of it might flow after the modification; (c) collect fresh data on density and current speed.

Six research ships would be needed to do the job, and that was hardly a problem for an experienced oceanographer who had the cooperation and the assistance of the chief of naval operations.

By noon Monday, the office of the CNO sent special orders to all research ships operating in the Atlantic or docked in East Coast ports to sail for the Hull area. Along with the order, the CNO issued specific assignments, coordinates, and rendezvous points. The ships were the *Knorr,* the *Atlantis II,* and the *Glomar Challenger* of the academic fleet; and the *Dolphin, Oceanographer,* and *Mizar* of the United States Coast and Geodetic Survey.

Early Tuesday morning Cliff visited with the director of the U.S. Bureau of Mines and the president of the American Science Foundation to get referrals for the two scientists he needed. One was Nevil Adams, a geologist and dynamite wizard who had pioneered and developed ESE (electronic subsurface exploration) while working for Exxon Corporation; the other, Adrian Scott, twenty-nine, a computer programmer, was also a geologist. He had recently received a Ph.D. in earth sciences and was a "demigod" at M.I.T.'s famed Artificial Intelligence Laboratory.

Cliff liked what he knew of Scott's experience in building models, including his computer animation of particles flowing through the wing and the fuselage of the first human-powered aircraft to fly for over seventy miles, the *Daedalus,* and a model of the atmosphere showing how the Earth's winds and ocean currents interact.

What also impressed Cliff was the fact that Scott had helped develop a new number cruncher described as a "teraflop parallel computer." Making a quantum leap, this computer, instead of using a single central processing unit to solve problems one step at a time, divided the problem into parts and used hundreds of central processing units to do the job simultaneously at incredible speed—a trillion calculations a second.

Cliff would need that kind of speed to process the enormous amount of data his team would be collecting. He felt good, pleased with the recommendations. He had already chosen Pamela Wycoff as the fourth member of the team.

Special Secret Service couriers rushed to deliver copies of Cliff's proposal to the selected individuals.

Two days later Cliff flew to Boston by private jet.

"It's a gating project, Dr. Lorenz," Adrian Scott said, using a buzzword that Cliff translated as interesting. He was correct.

"Putting it in other words," Scott went on, looking at Cliff with dark, distant eyes that appeared anatomically too small behind his thick lenses, "it's a programmatically attractive superconcept, one that interests me."

Shorter than Cliff, Scott was pale, bearded, and a bit untidy. He wore a blue Oxford button-down shirt—the pocket bulging with colored pens—jeans, and jogging shoes.

His office, on the tenth floor of the Earth and Planetary Science Building, consisted of a king-size cubicle that recalled the passenger sphere on the *Alvin*, except that it had a cot and a small refrigerator. Two minicomputers, a laser printer, and a graphic plotter filled the space. They faced a rack full of circuit boards, cards, ribbon cables, little white boxes, empty cans of Coke, and numerous gray widgets—frobnitzes, as Scott called them. A floor-to-ceiling bookshelf with nothing but user's manuals covered one wall. The cubicle smelled of lo mein.

"You see, Dr. Lorenz—"

"Cliff, please. Doctor ages me."

"You see, Cliff, modeling your modification is not like nailing jelly on a tree. On the contrary, you have presented me with a concept that I'd love to interface with because it's made for neuro-networking.

"Though we still don't understand how it works," Scott said, "neuro-networking mimics the brain. So, if you combine the ability of the brain with the computational speed of a teraflop computer, you're getting close to God's mind."

Cliff felt an electric tingle, knowing he'd found the right man. "Computers have certainly leaped forward," he said, feeling behind the times.

"And in addition to all this," Scott continued, "there is the fact that all aspects of your modification can be translated into a mathematical problem. What I mean is that since all the information we need can now be digitized—and that includes charts, traces, contours, and the like"—

Scott smiled, straightening a paper clip—"it offers a real challenge to AI and VR."

Artificial intelligence was one, but the other? "I didn't catch the last one."

"Virtual reality, the computer-generated synthetic reality that will allow you to look at your modification not only from the outside in, but also from the inside of a monitor out," Scott said, sounding a bit impatient.

He had come to the right man, all right, Cliff thought. He'd better not sound computer illiterate and look like a nerd. He shrugged. "Yes, of course. VR as a method of interfacing with the modification."

"Exactly." Scott threw the paper clip on the floor and reached for another. "Programmatically attractive," he said, with a nod toward the folder Cliff had sent him.

With that, Scott went into specifics. He thought Cliff needed two models. The first, a simulation model, would allow Cliff to visualize what he could not see. "Sort of telepresence," Scott said, "except that instead of a TV camera mounted on a remote-controlled robot, I will make artful use of computer generated graphics and images to produce three-D representations. This will be especially useful in studying fluid dynamics, the flow of stream and meanders. Of course, I need to work out certain equations first."

"Navier-Stokes, I suppose."

"Exactly."

The second model would be a mathematical one, needed to find a numerical solution to the biggest problem of all: the release of energy. This meant calculating the proper amount of dynamite and other high explosives. "After all," Scott said, "you wouldn't be just modifying the weather, Cliff, you would be modifying the Atlantic. And you have chosen to do it very close to a delicate ridge and fault system."

"I'm aware of that," Cliff said. "That's why I need your models."

It was now one-thirty P.M., and Scott suggested lunch.

The student center was a bright and modern cafeteria with lots of open space and tall windows facing the Boston skyline on the other bank of the Charles River, but offering food that was the very antithesis of culinary art and technology.

Dipping a couple of greasy french fries in ketchup, Scott said, "So you see, Cliff, my job will be to give you a visual and numerical overview of the modification." His voice now had a rasp of excitement. "And I can do that because the laws of physics can be expressed in mathematical equations as well as in physical models."

The rest of the meeting focused on details.

On the plane home, Cliff's mind thought about Scott. The man lived in another world, a . . . cyber-cosmos—that was a good word for it—where men and computers lived together for mutual programming purposes.

The following day, Pamela Wycoff was talking spiritedly. "I'm dizzy. I feel as though I've been inside a washing machine during the spin cycle," she said to Cliff with a trace of laughter, her eyes darting humorously back and forth. "In less than twenty-four hours, I was relieved of my old duties by Roscoe himself, given new ones by him, during lunch no less, briefed on glaciation by one of Kronin's aides, and on security by Phil Jackson, visited by Secret Service agents who carried your proposal in a briefcase that looked like the black box . . ." Pam stopped to catch her breath. "Told to read it overnight, reminded of my clearance, and ordered to get in touch with you by no later than noon today. Phew." She passed a small, delicate, well-manicured hand over her forehead. "Well, here I am, all washed, rinsed, and ready for the drier," she said, and dropped her shoulders in mock collapse.

Cliff laughed. Pam never looked as charming or as beautiful as she did at that moment. He wanted to kiss her but settled for an openly admiring look.

They were in the Grill Room of the Hyatt Regency, ground zero for maker and shaker watching.

A waiter came, and Cliff ordered his own creation—stock mergers (half-dry, half-sweet Stock vermouth).

Turning back to her, Cliff found Pam's big blue eyes on him and had the feeling that they hadn't happened to be looking at him just at that instant.

Her eyes skittered across him quickly, leaving Cliff tingling, alert to a new phase in their relationship. "They don't have Punt e Mess," he said, a bit confused, "and I know how much you like Italian aperitivi. What I've ordered comes very close to it."

But as he spoke, he tried not to hold his gaze too long for fear that Pam might think he had asked her to join his team for other than professional reasons. He needed Pam not only as a true environmentalist with years of experience and scientific background, but also as someone he could talk to.

"When I read your theory of the modification," she said in a low, composed voice, "I couldn't help thinking of Einstein and what he had said about general relativity— theoretically too beautiful not to be true."

"Thanks." Cliff smiled with warm spontaneity and squeezed her hand with an intimacy he had not intended.

The drinks mixed and served, he talked about the specifics of his plans and the problem with time. "The way things stand," he said, "we may not be able to drill the necessary shot holes. You heard about the icebergs."

She nodded. "Cliff . . ." Pam hesitated, looking at him straight in the eye, "I have serious misgivings."

"Yes?" Cliff braced himself.

According to Pam, if the United States had to depend on fish for its food supply with ice covering the wheat belt, it would be suicidal to destroy entire areas full of a variety of sea life with the tons of high explosives needed to blow up the Hull. "Without this precious source, how are you going to feed America?"

Cliff listened carefully. He said, "What if one were to ward off the fish before the charges go off?" His own tone told Pam he doubted the validity of the idea.

"How?" she asked.

Another problem to think about—and he hadn't spoken to Nevil Adams yet. "I don't know, but you have less than a month to figure that out."

When Cliff was finally able to reach him, Adams had not finished reading the proposal.

Two hours later, Cliff called him again. Adams needed more time "to think it over."

Cliff waited another hour, soothing his impatience with a cognac, and double-checking the details of Operation Data for the tenth time.

"I must have your answer now," he said firmly but politely to Adams when he called him back.

"I'm afraid I . . . can't join your team," Adams answered with a feeble voice.

"Why?" Cliff asked.

"You'd better ask someone else."

"Is it your health? Moral or ethical reasons, perhaps?"

"Please ask someone else."

"I may have to do that," Cliff said, "but you haven't answered my question."

The line was silent for a while.

"Dr. Lorenz," Adams began wearily, "for forty-odd years I have dealt in cubic yards of rocks and boxes of TNT. Simply put, I'm not ready to deal in cubic miles of rock and trainloads of TNT."

"Magnitude . . . size, is that it?" Cliff asked, anticipating the answer, an honest answer.

"Yes."

"For Christ's sake, Dr. Adams," Cliff exploded, anger erupting, "how can a man of science, like yourself, give such an answer? I'm shocked. Had you given moral or ethical reasons, I would've understood you. But magnitude, size? Come on!" He paused not only for breath but for dramatic effect, his face brick red. "Sir Hillary, Dr. Adams," Cliff continued, his voice cracking like a whip, "made it to the top of Mount Everest because modern technology made it possible. Man has landed on the moon because . . ." He went on and on. "Neither height nor distance was a factor."

"I realize that. Still, please ask . . ."

Cliff thought for a moment. As a scientist he was as straight as a slide rule, but as a leader he could make a canny Boston politician act like a saint. He sighed gustily. "Okay, I will ask someone else. For now I need a profile of the rock. You can at least do that for your country."

No answer, which Cliff took as a silent yes.

"See you at Andrews, then." Cliff gave the details of the data-collection mission, starting with a flight over the modification site.

At a signal from the pilot, Cliff tapped Adams on the shoulder and motioned him to look down. "That line separates the Atlantic from the king and pope of the Atlantic," Cliff shouted to Adams as the two-engine plane banked gently left at the start of a wide arc over the Hull.

"I suppose the other line is out of sight," Adams said over the noise of the engines. He was a man of medium height in his late sixties, with a quiet, oval face, a mane of gray hair, and sly, melancholy eyes.

Cliff nodded. "Eighty miles away."

Five minutes later, Cliff tapped Adams on the shoulder again. "We are passing over the southern tip of the Hull. As you can see, right there"—Cliff pointed—"where you see the apex of the V formed by the two light-shaded branches of the stream. The one going west is the J Current."

"How long did you say the Hull is?"

"About sixty miles. A lot of rock."

"A lot of drilling."

"How deep?"

"Three hundred fathoms."

They studied the scene below in silence as the sleek Lear Jet flew along the axis of the Hull at an altitude of fifteen thousand feet. It was a clear, cloudless day with a glassy blue sky, and a glassier sea.

"And how tall is this Hull?"

"I figure one and a half miles."

"An island, eh?" Adams sounded both interested and skeptical at the same time.

"However," Cliff said, raising a finger, "one miscalculation and the British will live in a hot steaming jungle the rest—"

"Fuck the British," Adams shouted. He turned to face Cliff. "If those bastards could find a way of sending their bloody fog over to us, they'd do it."

Slowly Cliff's mouth lifted in a rare, intimate smile. "Yeah," he said, nodding, "fuck 'em."

They looked at each other and laughed.

Having traveled the length of the Hull, the plane banked left, leaning gently into a wide turn. Soon it headed for Cape Cod, leaving the stream to port.

Pensive and wordless, Cliff just stared at the stream beneath them. Boundless and mighty, it stretched away, alive with quicksilvery shimmers that danced like bright flames. To its left, a small meander uncoiled itself from the current and headed for Cape May.

Adams, who had remained seated on the starboard side, moved closer to Cliff. "So that's what you've researched for years?"

Cliff nodded. "Yes. That lighter blue water over there. Lighter because it's warmer. That meander is but one small part of an eighty-mile-wide river," he said. "Without which the Atlantic would be as polluted as the Med."

Adams's face darkened, as if finally aware of the awesome power of the stream. "Eighty miles wide?" he exclaimed, his thin, reedy voice sounding as frightened as his eyes looked. "Aren't you afraid to manipulate that much water?" He looked at Cliff, waiting for some reassuring words.

"Terrified," Cliff answered without hesitation. "But I also know more about the stream than anybody else, just as you know more about explosives than anybody else." He gave

Adams the reassuring pat on the shoulder he needed. "It follows that if it must be modified, I must be the one to do it, and do it well."

They went back, studying the stream, receding into silence, each wary of the task facing him.

The rest of the flight was uneventful, as was the ride from Hyannis Airport to Woods Hole. Only after they had turned left on Route 28 did Cliff talk to Adams about the home he had built years ago in Sippewisset, a small town of houses with weather-stained shingles. "Up that road," Cliff said, all excited, as they crossed Widows' Hill Lane. "And straight ahead is downtown Woods Hole. Real nice. Marla didn't think much of it. 'It's not the end of the world, Cliff,' she said to me when we first drove down this road, 'but one can certainly see it from here.' "

Consisting of a few brick structures with white window trim and small stores with weathered shingles, Woods Hole, at six-thirty P.M., looked like a college town during exams week.

Once past the Fishmonger Cafe, the *Knorr* came into view.

With its length of 247 feet, the research ship had the blue and white colors of an ocean liner, the beamy displacement of a tugboat, the antenna farm of a spy ship. Built by the Navy, it was every oceanographer's dream of a research ship because of its library, the well-equipped laboratories, the compact video submersible it towed like a sled, and the food, which deserved four forks in the Michelin Guide.

"Permission to come aboard, Captain."

"Permission granted, Doctor," said the skipper, Nick Edwards, who greeted Cliff like an old friend. A big-featured man with a crew cut and steel blue eyes, he wore the uniform of the merchant marine.

Cliff stepped on the deck and looked around. For a moment he seemed happier than any fisherman casting for bluefish that afternoon. "Nothing has changed."

"Not on the outside," the skipper said. "But wait until you see the inside."

In the library, which also served as wardroom, the skipper made his report: Fritz had gone to pick up a circuit board they needed and was due back by daybreak; the rest of the equipment had checked out; the weather forecast was good for the next two days, stormy after that. But Edwards hadn't been able to reach several of the crew members on shore leave. He needed another day. "I'll get you another good diver at least."

There was no time. "Besides, Nick, did you forget that I learned to snorkel even before I could walk?" Cliff said in mock admonition.

The briefing over, Cliff drank a mug of hot chocolate and went to his stateroom, a small, wedge-shaped space with electrical cables and steam pipes crisscrossing the ceiling. Located on deck C just one floor above the radio room and covered with hard vinyl walls, it had just enough space for a berth sitting on top of a chest of drawers, a metal desk, and swivel chair. Despite the jet of fresh air sucked in by the fan of a venting snorkel, Cliff's "second home" smelled of old gym sneakers.

Cliff untied his duffel bag and a number of thoughts as well. As chief scientist, he was going to be the *Knorr*'s master. So, he had better make the best of it, for his behavior would determine that of the crew.

A lavatory stood between his stateroom and Adams's, and Cliff stepped through to see him. "By the way," Cliff said in a cheerful tone, "you'll know where you are on this ship by the smell of things: diesel—engine deck; disinfectant—toilets; week-old fish—lower lab; cheese—mess hall, and you'll never have to guess where the sleeping quarters are."

Minutes later he was on the aft deck, amid booms, winches, and two vans Cliff hadn't remembered seeing before. They were about eighteen by eight by ten, and obviously portable workstations. He entered the first and immediately realized he was inside the video van he had once seen pictured in *Time* magazine. All the monitors were turned off but he could imagine the excitement when suddenly on one of them appeared the forward crane of the *Titanic* captured by the video camera aboard the *Argo*, the unmanned vehicle with optical-imaging systems the *Knorr* could tow. How could he have missed such momentous events in the history of oceanography and technology?

The other van was clearly an oceanographic recorder van. It bristled with the latest high-tech gear used for the study of the ocean's surface and subsurface. The skipper was right. It was almost all-new equipment.

A technician with a boyish face was running static tests. "What's that recorder you're testing? The one above the radio current meter. I haven't seen one of those before," Cliff said.

"Oh, that one. I love it. It's a new precision depth recorder. As you can see from this trace resembling an outline of a mountain ridge drawn with a charcoal pencil, the PDR has produced a continuous profile of the ocean floor by timing the returning echo of electromagnetic sound pulses."

Cliff leaned to look at the trace. "A fancy fish finder or echo sounder, I'd say."

"Yes, in a way it is because it works on the same principle of transmitted sound waves reflected back by fish or the ocean floor," he said, pulling a long sheet of paper out of a drawer. "Except that the PDR produces a sharper profile because it uses a very narrow beam. Look here. No echo sounder would have drawn a profile so sharp that you can see these details." He ran the tip of his finger along the contour line.

Cliff listened, feeling that he was listening to a younger self talk. "And that one?" He pointed to another instrument twice the size of a stereo amplifier. It had a wide paper tape scrolling down its front half. "It's also new, isn't it?"

"Yes, it is. It's the CSP by Beckman."

"Well, well. Beckman has come out with a new continuous seismic profiling receiver. That's good news."

Although Cliff had never used it, he knew that the CSP recorded and traced echoes on paper from a 100-pound dynamite shot fired by a ship a few feet under the surface of the water to achieve deeper penetration than acoustic sound waves transmitted by echo sounders. It worked on the principle that part of the sound energy is reflected back by the ocean floor, while the remainder continues into the ocean floor and is reflected back by different layers of rock or sediment. Since the speed of sound in seawater is about 1.5 km/second, and that of consolidated sediment and rock is 1.7 to 2.8 km/second, the arrivals of the returning echoes differ in time. Geologists had learned to interpret the difference in time and to identify the type of sediment or rock that produced them. Oil companies had spent millions developing and perfecting seismic profiling because it allowed geologists to spot the telltale tilting of rock over salt domes that help entrap petroleum.

Tomorrow the first dynamite shot would be fired over the Hull and Adams would know how hard its rock was. In a way what the Beckman CSP would trace alternately thrilled and frightened him.

Cliff stepped out of the van and took a deep breath of air, still not quite believing where he was. The air was salty and full of snap, and breathing it in made him feel a sailor.

Noisy couples were leaving the Black Duck Restaurant. Gleaming white, the tugboat *Santa Maria* plowed by the channel marker, and soon beer cans bobbed alongside the *Knorr*'s hull.

Seeing a young family on the pier, Cliff's internal alarm went off. He remembered that there was a public phone inside the machine shop and called Butch. "Let's say you and I have a day together."

"When?"

"In a couple of days. I'll call the moment I disembark."

"You mean . . . on a school day, Dad?"

"Why not, if your grades are still up there."

A moment of silence and then, "Is that a promise?"

"Yes, and you know that I keep my word."

"Awesome! Thanks, Dad."

Cliff laughed, relieved for a moment of the burden weighing upon him.

Home was where the oceanographer's labs were. Cliff took a walk, heading first for the main lab on the same deck. Occupying more spaces than any other enclosure on board, the main lab was the largest of the three on the *Knorr* and was long, narrow, and wet. Cliff stood by the door. God knows how many hours he had spent there! As a graduate student, his first assignment had been to wash and maintain all the instruments that went into the water: temperature sensors, radio current meters, drift bottle, and the biggest of all, the STD (salinity-temperature-depth). Cliff walked to it. Resembling a miniature space station, the "rosette" had a cluster of pod bottles that opened on command from the ship. Cliff inspected it carefully. It was so well maintained that it appeared almost new. Next to it was the CTD, a conductivity-temperature-depth sensor that looked like a smaller STD. It, too, was in good shape.

Pleased with that inspection, Cliff headed for his cabin and a shower. Tomorrow would be a busy day.

It was a splendid day—as only Cape Cod days can be in early summer. A morning wind swept down from hills, scooping up a thin band of mist, and smoke rose from the chimney of the Fishmonger Cafe. Eager yachtsmen slipped out of the harbor after spending the night at anchor. But Cliff was fuming.

Fritz had not arrived yet, and sailing without him was out of the question. "It would be like taking off on a jumbo jet without a flight engineer," Cliff said to Adams, who had climbed up to the bridge to keep him company. Winding his watch backward, he searched for a blue-and-white truck passing over the Route 28 bridge. Tall and commanding in his multi-badged Woods Hole jumpsuit and baseball cap with scrambled eggs, Cliff had been waiting on the port overhang since dawn. A fresh breeze made a flapping streamer of his yellow scarf. "Damn. Fritz knows damn well how changeable the weather is in the North Atlantic."

Just past nine o'clock Fritz finally called and told the skipper that he would be at Woods Hole before three in the afternoon.

The skipper believed him, not knowing what had happened to Fritz when he drove to Provincetown, the location of the electronics supplier. Fritz never went anywhere now without first making sure that there were no drops waiting for him. So instead of driving north to pick up the MidCape Highway to Provincetown, he went to Hyannis first. Passing slowly by the airport sign, he saw the signal.

After removing the message from the chrome cylinder and picking up the pay phone outside the Martha's Vineyard ferryboat dock, he heard the same gruff voice giving him instructions.

As he had anticipated, Fritz was to gather information on the purpose of the trip, the type of equipment used, radio frequencies, etc. But then the voice concluded with, "Above all, keep a close watch on Cliff Lorenz. Good luck."

"Thanks . . . thanks a lot. I mean it," Fritz said in his best English, hardened by a strong German accent.

He nodded twice, even though he hadn't been asked, then hung up, ashen faced.

Shock hit him first, then the shakes. Watch Cliff? Why? Cliff hadn't told Fritz about his involvement in a special mission.

Fritz remained lost in shock, shivering, soaked in cold sweat.

• • •

At five-thirty P.M. the *Knorr* moved out, the sea frothing furiously under the cycloids (vertically mounted propulsors resembling eggbeaters). Past the last channel, it slid forward, gained speed, then knifed through Woods Hole's harbor, leaving behind a widening trail of churning white foam. Overhead, a flock of whistling geese flew by, their wings fluttering in a V formation.

"The cycloids give the *Knorr* the maneuverability of a helicopter. Excellent for oceanographic work," Cliff said to Adams as they watched from one corner of the wheelhouse. "The *Knorr* is the only ship in the world that has no helm—only joysticks."

Soon the navigator took his last land fix, the plume of smoke from the Edison Electric plant disappeared, and Cliff could taste the salty tang of the Atlantic on his lips. "All ahead full," the captain rang down to the engine room.

Half an hour later, using the public-address system, Cliff greeted everybody on board and told them what their mission was. "For now, keep your mind full," he concluded in a humorous tone, "your bowels empty."

Sunday, a clear day.

In one corner of the mess room Fritz and Cliff sat to have brunch.

"So far, so good. All systems are go," Fritz said, his accent strong. The only problem was the number of hours crews had to work to make up for the shortage of hands.

"It's only for three days," Cliff said. Three days . . . Fritz forced his food down, his stomach twisted shut by guilt. One way to save Cliff was perhaps to put him out of action before someone killed him. Fritz feared his control's order to watch Cliff meant that he had been targeted for termination. Putting Cliff out of action would give him some sort of a chance. But how?

His plate empty, Cliff got up. "I gotta run. See you at supper." He frowned at Fritz. "And don't look so glum."

Fritz did not look up from his plate, his mind on his mission.

Cliff walked into the main lab at the sound of the eighth bell, and for two hours he talked, demonstrated, rehearsed, told jokes, and gave out warnings. The planning progressed quickly.

Arrival day—Monday—had dawned slowly. Eerie, vaporous curtains of steam rose sluggishly, as if from a brewer's vat. The Atlantic looked like an enormous hot pool in some mythical place.

With a mug of coffee in hand, and wearing a watch cap and yellow Windbreaker, Cliff had been on the deck C bridge overhang since the *Knorr* crossed the stream at 58.32 degrees west, 45.27 degrees north—when the water digital thermometer went from 59 to 71 degrees in thirty seconds.

Suddenly thirty-five miles from the tip of the Hull, the radar antenna on top of the bridge began rotating at twice the speed. The *Knorr* bucked and slowed down to five knots. Running, a sailor took his lookout post at the bow. With fog all around him, he looked like a black paper cutout stuck on ground glass.

The P.A. system blared, "Dr. Lorenz to sonar room."

Cliff's head snapped like an alarmed bird's. He dropped the mug and dashed upstairs.

An operator listened to sonar echoes as he moved a pointer toward the sixty-six-degree marker on the display. "There's something straight ahead," he said. "It's submerged and stationary . . . about a hundred forty feet, maybe more."

"That's almost C.D.," he said, referring to critical depth, the point where divers were only half as intelligent due to narcosis.

"Just about."

Cliff stirred. "Any ideas?"

"Not yet, but these photographs may give us a clue," the operator answered, and began comparing the echoes on the monitor with those in a notebook.

Cliff stood behind him, rubbing a hand over his chin. "A minisub or submersible is out of the question, I suppose."

The operator nodded. "There's no motor, pumps, or screws noise. It's something else."

"Keep looking," Cliff said, fighting the temptation to wind his watch. He always did that when he was nervous, but had tried to break the habit because it revealed that he was not in control of himself. And he wasn't going to let old sailors' superstition have the best of things.

"I've got it," the man cried out finally, and told Cliff that the echoes were probably those from a "snooper," a listening device that could have been dropped by a low-flying aircraft or released by a submarine. "Look, sir," he added, tracing a blip on the monitor with a finger, "the vertical beam follows the cable to it."

It was a snooper, as further investigations confirmed. Powered by colossal nickel cadmium batteries and sensitive receivers, it eavesdropped on radio communications between ships and relayed them to intelligence satellites. It could even monitor walkie-talkie communication on the *Knorr* during the mission.

But whose snooper was it?

A coded cable was radioed to the chief of naval operations asking for clarification and/or instructions. The answer came back at once: "Cut it loose and let it flow with the current. Exercise extreme caution, as device may be booby-trapped."

The urge to dive was instantaneous. "I'll go down," Cliff said to the skipper who had just come in with Adams. "I've had experience in these waters." He held up a hand before the skipper could interrupt. "We can't wait until we get a specialist. It may take a day, even two."

"What's another day?" Adams said, running behind him.

Cliff kept walking. "It's something I don't have many of, and you know it."

Adams grabbed him by the arm. "Cliff, listen to me. Don't dive."

"I have experience." He pulled himself away.

"Experience in what? Narcosis, booby traps, sharks?"

There was no response.

Cliff was in the divers' shed, selecting his scuba gear, when Roy Felton, the newest diver to have come aboard ship, stormed in, out of breath. "I'll go down with you, sir." His large, almost timid eyes expressed nothing but sincerity.

Diving was dangerous enough even if God came along, and Cliff had become suspicious of strangers. "That's kind of you, Roy," Cliff said, "but I'll ask Mr. Hoffmeister. We have our own sign language and have worked more hours underwater than above it. You know how it is, don't you?" he added, and before Felton could say anything, he reached for the wall phone. "Fritz?" he shouted. "Get up here on the double. We're diving."

17

Cliff was first to emerge from the divers' shed completely sheathed in a green Parkway wet suit. He flashed a smile at Adams and said, "Do I look like Kermit?"

Adams shrugged, then moved closer, his aquiline nose white and pinched with rage. "Don't be a fool, Cliff," he said, and gave him a disapproving look. "Do what you have to do, but don't take chances. You heard what Navy Intelligence said, the snooper may be booby-trapped."

"Yes, yes . . ." Cliff nodded with excessive nonchalance, then looked over his shoulder to see if Fritz was coming.

Fritz had already suited up and was about to come out on deck when he suddenly took his flippers off and ran to his cabin. There he took out a plastic box from the drawer and spilled its contents on the desk: alcohol wipes, a test strip, a Becton and Dickenson bottle of insulin, and a 1/2 cc syringe. He held the syringe in his hand and looked at it as if it were the pistol he was about to kill himself with. And as he did, he began feeling his sanity ripping loose. He feared that he might have second thoughts about putting Cliff out of action. He knew only too well that if he chickened out today, it would become increasingly easier to do the same tomorrow. And the day after. Until he had no more time left. He plunged the needle into the insulin vial and loaded the syringe.

"Mr. Hoffmeister, please call the divers' shed," Felton's voice came over the P.A. system.

He reached for the phone and dialed P.A. "Coming," he said, a threat of hysteria in his voice.

Quickly Fritz unscrewed a cap from the top of the handle of his Ranger knife and placed the syringe inside a narrow chamber, dropped the rest of the insulin kit in the drawer with one whipping motion, locked the desk, and dashed out.

Pale, Fritz walked onto the aft deck and finished suiting up. Strapped just below the right knee, his long Ranger's knife stuck out like a six-shooter. "I had forgotten to spray my nose." He sniffled. "Breathing easier now. Sorry."

Carrying their masks, Cliff and Fritz toddled to the end of the aft deck, where crews were hooking the diving platform to the number one crane. From the back they appeared as twins.

Summer days in the North Atlantic could be like tepid, bubbleless champagne, and today was no exception. But at around five P.M., the sharp and cutting wind from the northwest had the wolf of winter in it. A kerchief of sulfur-colored mist hung over the deck, shrouding sailors in oily light. From the ventilator above the galley came a warm, fragrant air. It seemed to scent the whole North Atlantic with wine sauce. At once Cliff and Fritz went through the regulation checklist, giving each other a once-over before inspecting the individual scuba parts.

"Who would've thought we'd be diving again," Cliff said.

The joy in Cliff's voice deepened Fritz's sadness, and he felt his whole body liquefy into some vile substance. "How about that?" he managed to say cheerfully, and they got ready for the dive. It would be their last.

A few feet away diver Roy Felton, acting as dive chief, supervised the procedure, moving his lips as if going through his own checklist.

Behind him, a gray-orange band of light now separated sea from sky, and clouds forming over the stream pressed down with the threat of rain. "Let's hurry," he ordered.

To watch Cliff at work was like watching a fastidious cop frisking a suspect. He searched Fritz's suit for tears in the wet suit, looked for telltale chalky deposits around the chrome-plated brass fittings, pressed a finger on the buoyancy regulator to see if it had enough air. He noticed that a quick-disconnect shoulder buckle was not right and snapped it in place.

"Weight feels a bit too tight," he said, tugging at it.

"Does it?" Fritz tried to loosen it, but his fingers seemed too stiff, so Cliff had to do it.

Fritz did his thing slowly, trembling—shivering, he claimed—choked by the flow of memories of past dives. Girding himself with resolve, he went through a mental checklist.

With reduced air flow, Cliff would lose consciousness for the few seconds Fritz needed to inject sodium amytal in his body using the syringe he had placed inside the handle of his Ranger knife. The insulin label was a ruse. The sodium amytal would produce a highly susceptible state of mind that would cause Cliff to talk about wholly imaginary and incoherent episodes. Hopefully, his condition would prompt the skipper to think that Cliff was suffering from some form of narcosis and airlift him to a navy hospital, where he would remain under observation for a few weeks. By then, Fritz reasoned, he would've made his drop and satisfied his control with good information. And saved Cliff from any real harm.

That much was easy; the rest was not. If the loss of oxygen lasted too long, Cliff would suffer irreversible brain damage. Involuntarily he looked down, his knife seemingly leaping at him from the scabbard.

He felt along Cliff's air hose running from the mouthpiece to the tank. It seemed okay, but the air valve knob was of another design. Pretending to check its condition, Fritz saw

what made it different, then turned it slightly counterclock-
wise, enough for what he had in mind.

And then, as he tried the weight belt, he spotted the
Dacor Dive Pouch he had given Cliff nine years ago as a
Christmas gift. He realized now that it was an inexpensive
accessory, probably made in Taiwan, and an extra piece of
equipment serious divers did not use to hold their keys or
watch. But Cliff must have cherished it anyway, to have
carried it aboard. "You're all set," Fritz said with a slap
on the tank, his throat a swollen lump.

"Okay, chief, let's have them," Cliff ordered.

As if defusing a bomb, Felton unlocked a wooden box
and took out two aluminum tubes—shark darts. Five feet
in length, they were fitted on one end with a cylindrical
steel bottle from which protruded a foot-long, thick needle.
It was the best weapon divers had. The pressurized CO_2
could blow a hole the size of a grapefruit in a shark. "I
hope you won't have to use them," he said.

A horn blast signaled that the *Knorr* had reached its
station directly above the snooper. Holding it would be a
tricky maneuver, for higher RPMs meant greater and more
dangerous centripetal pull for the divers; lower RPMs, more
drift off target.

Felton spat a long, whistling spurt of brown fluid. "Ease
on the throttle," he shouted into a microphone. "More . . .
more."

With one eye on the diminishing turbulence caused by
the cycloids, Cliff wet the inside of the mask with saliva to
prevent fogging, then calmly stepped onto a small platform.
As soon as Fritz joined him, Cliff pointed a thumb down,
and the crane operator swung the platform over the side.

Steam billowed from a porthole aft, and off-duty personnel looked on from the C deck overhang.

With the platform floating on the water, Felton lowered a hundred-pound lead weight by a yellow nylon rope
equipped with tennis ball–sized wooden markers that had
bright orange numbers painted on them. It was the regulation descent line; the numbers marking the depths at which

Cliff and Fritz would wait to decompress and prevent the bends.

"Twenty minutes. And not below a hundred and fifty feet. That's all." Sulking, Felton sounded like a reform school teacher. "Surface slowly. Stop at the ten marker. Look at the chart. Okay?"

Cliff and Fritz made a circle with thumb and forefinger. "Go!"

It was exactly 6:05 P.M., and the Atlantic looked like a dark, bottomless inkwell.

Cliff jumped feetfirst into the water, found the descent line, and started sucking air. The flow was steady, and the air rushed out with a regular cadence. Breathing, however, seemed more difficult than he remembered, but then, months had passed since his last dive.

He descended with the sure grace of a dolphin, as the familiar, frightening sensation of going straight down like a stone swept over him. The worst moment. Always. And he could feel the throbs of the cycloids pound like beats on a jungle drum. If there was no other danger in the mission, the cycloids were enough. Their centripetal pull was unforgiving. He had to hang on to the descent line.

He looked up and saw Fritz silhouetted against a patch of light green water and surrounded by a widening stream of emerald-colored bubbles.

Cliff descended more, penetrating deeper into the heart of darkness and, as always, unprepared for the magnificence of the bottom dwellers—noctilucas gleaming like stars; lace-like sargassum fish; something resembling big-eyed scad but translucent and with fins delicate as frills of chiffon. The stream felt cold on his face, but his body temperature was already heating up the insulating layer of water in his suit, giving him the familiar sensation of being wrapped in a warm, moist towel.

The ninety-foot marker went past. Now the North Atlantic became Laminaria, the dark world of the eel-like weeds by that name, and Fritz, peering with fishlike curiosity through his mask, wondered why Cliff showed no signs of breathing less oxygen. Probably the knob had a different shut-off–turn ratio. He aimed his flashlight at the knob. A school of silvery minnows flitted by, moving in drill fashion, as if sharing the same brain. Tiny herring battered against the flashlight like moths against a light bulb.

At the 110-foot mark, the throbs of the cycloids faded, and the stream grew darker, denser. Cliff began to feel the old sinus squeeze in his head and pressure in his ear canal. Nothing new. But a sudden spaced-out feeling came over him. Similar to the light-headedness that comes with taking antihistamines, it worried him. He reached the 140-foot marker.

His ears hurting now, Cliff anchored himself to the descent line, mindful of the harmful nitrogen absorption taking place at that depth. It acted like a mind-altering drug. Was it acting on him? He checked the elapsed time and noticed that four minutes had passed already. Quickly he gave Fritz two short flicks of the flashlight, their way of saying "join me." Swallowing to release pressure in his ears, he let his feet be lifted by the current, then regulated the buoyancy compensator until his body was 120 degrees to the descent line. He rested for a moment, overcome by the sense of weightlessness that the silent and supportive body of the stream gave him.

The search for the snooper began at once, and Cliff and Fritz began their communication in the unfailing short-hand that had developed after diving together hundreds of times.

Holding on to the descent line with one hand and working the flashlight with the other, they looked, turned in all directions, looked some more. Nothing. Time passed. Five minutes, six, seven . . .

They descended another five feet.

Finally Fritz tugged at the descent line, even as he wondered why the reduced oxygen was not affecting Cliff. He had spotted something. Cliff looked in the direction Fritz indicated and there, not ten feet away, was a cylindrical metal object shaped like a cat-o'-nine-tails bent by the wind.

Cliff got near it, careful not to touch it. With Fritz watching for sharks, Cliff took a good look at the thing—about eight feet long . . . with a retractable whip antenna . . . large heat exchangers . . . radio frequency connectors . . .

It was a snooper, just as the sonar operator had described it. He checked the time underwater—nine minutes. He moved the beam of the flashlight around the snooper and made sure that there were no trip wires anywhere, then moved closer and saw small barnacles on its underside . . . on the stabilizing fins facing north. *This snooper,* Cliff thought, *is dead.* He could . . .

Suddenly, without reason, the sound of the air flow changed pitch, and he felt a weight over his shoulders. Cliff jerked in spasmodic shock, frightened. Jesus, what was happening? Quickly, he let go of the flashlight and let it dangle by its strap, grabbed the snooper's cable with one hand for balance, then reached for the knob on top of the tank. *Not Fritz . . . No!* He felt Fritz's hand around it. Had Fritz gone crazy? He couldn't be joking. Air was life underwater. *Why Fritz? Why?* He writhed and jerked his body. Nothing. Fritz's seemed to possess the strength of a man gone mad. Air! He took a deep breath but he couldn't hold it. The exertion was forcing him to exhale. Another breath. Same thing.

And now the airstream had almost stopped. His nose started running. Fluid dripped to his throat. A glob of phlegm clogged his windpipe. It sickened him and he wanted to vomit. *Butch . . . Pam . . .* He swallowed. Another glob of phlegm. He had to suck air through his nose, but there wasn't enough of it. His chest muscles went into spasms as he gasped for air. Sweat dripped into his eyes, stinging them, blurring his vision. Cliff was losing control of himself, but if he panicked, his lungs would fill with water. Breathing slowly now to conserve air, he blinked rapidly to clear his vision. He could see better.

Narcosis? Had Fritz absorbed too much nitrogen? Whatever, the man holding the regulator was a killer. At once he reached for the knife and swung in terrifying slowness

in the direction of the knob and hit something. It felt
like thrusting into a potato. Suddenly, the pressure on his
shoulders eased. Straining his throat muscles to suck air,
he let the knife dangle by its tether and at once reached
for the knob and tried in vain to turn it. Too tight. *Damn!*
His teeth biting on the mouthpiece, he turned the knob in
the opposite direction. Ah! There was a loud, exhilarating
inrush of air. Lots of it. Breathing wildly in long gulps, he
savored it like swallows of elixir.

Where was Fritz?

If Fritz wanted to kill him, he could do it with his shark
dart. Cliff had to disarm him.

His arms weighed a ton, his chest hurt, and the dangerous situation demanded an all-out physical effort. He
reached for the flashlight and pointed it up, the beam cutting
through the water like a rapier. Pink-colored water swirled
around Fritz.

Sharks! Fritz's blood would surely attract them. How
they loved a bleeding human. Why hadn't he brought the
suit of chain mail . . . or the jawbreaker? Fritz! Where the
hell was the bastard?

Fritz was panicking. Having failed in his mission, he
knew he'd better stop Cliff before Cliff killed him. He
could claim that there was an accident. He had no choice.
Quickly he decided to arm the shark dart.

Cliff saw him reaching for the safety pin, and he knew
that all Fritz had to do was to stab him with the needle and
his body would explode.

His eyes straining in the dark, Cliff judged Fritz to be
about five feet away. Suddenly, he was flooded with a
bright beam. It felt like a depth charge blowing up in
his face.

Cliff's eyes froze on it—Fritz was moving toward him,
steadily, deliberately. Cliff recoiled, descending a few feet.
But Fritz kicked hard on the flippers, and soon Cliff saw the
tip of the dart—a long, thin, ugly needle. It was going for
his right leg like a torpedo. Cliff looked at it and he knew
that he didn't have a chance.

Quickly, turning off his flashlight, he gave one sideways kick with his left leg, skinning his knuckles on the weight belt as he swerved to the left and closed his eyes.

Air bubbles purled by him—Fritz had missed him! Instinctively, Cliff turned his flashlight on, the beam bouncing off the aluminum tube of the shark dart now inches away. Fritz was almost upon him. He managed to grab hold of the shark dart just past the cartridge and push it away from his body. Now they both had a grasp on it. Fritz lurched to one side, trying to yank the shark dart away from Cliff. Cliff held on to it, his survival instinct flowed through him with strength and anger. Again Fritz tugged and pulled, but the effort seemed weaker. Cliff waited, biting on his mouthpiece, holding on to the shark dart with all his strength. Suddenly, it felt as if Fritz was releasing his grip. He was! Cliff swung his arms to the right as far as he could. Fritz's shark dart was his! He dropped it; saw it disappear.

Breathing with effort, Cliff wagged the flashlight. At once the beam caught Fritz grimacing in pain, his face distorted by the mouthpiece, eyes wide. It was the look of panic. Blood oozed out of Fritz's wrist and trailed in long stringy blobs.

Cliff looked around. No sharks yet.

His senses were alert now. Every nerve of his body, every cell of his brain was keyed up. Adrenaline surged through his body like a magic tonic; he was ready for an attack with the Ranger knife. But it didn't come. Was Fritz surfacing?

Exhausted, he clung with both hands to the descent line, resting.

Fritz! He was out of sight. Using the descent line as a guide, he pointed the flashlight upward. He saw Fritz flinch, fumble with his gear, tug with one hand holding the descent line. Cliff followed him. The 80-, 75-, 50-, 45-foot markers went by.

Fritz was surfacing too fast. Fear of losing too much blood was obviously urging him toward help. But they had been at the 135 marker for roughly thirteen minutes. If he didn't stop at the ten-foot marker and decompress for at least five minutes, Fritz would hemorrhage internally because of the rapidly expanding gases. Somehow letting Fritz get the bends shook Cliff more than the desire to escape further danger.

Cliff grew desperate. He wanted only to stop Fritz from surfacing—only that. He tugged hard on the descent line and moved up a few feet, trying to catch up to Fritz. But Fritz surfaced faster, kicking his legs in a scissor motion so that Cliff would not be able to grab them. *Christ, doesn't he ever give up?*

He moved after Fritz and then saw the twenty-foot marker pass by. He had to stop and decompress. He tried not to think of Fritz's blood gone with the current. Sharks would home in on it like heat-sensing missiles.

The fifteen-foot marker. Fritz's flippers were inches away, barely visible amid the cycloids' bubbly turbulence. In a burst of energy, Cliff tugged on the descent line and managed to grab one flipper. Fritz kicked, then pulled his leg up, freeing his foot from the flipper. Then Cliff tried to stop him by grasping the strap holding the knife. His fingers held on, stiff as bird claws. Fritz kicked.

The blow on the head came suddenly, knocking Cliff's breath out of him. It was numbing, disorienting. . . . A muffled cry of shock gushed out of his nostrils, followed by a rush of opaque fluid. Was it blood? Cliff grimaced. He closed his eyes and saw pinwheels and shooting stars. His mind whirled in darkness, and he began reeling in nauseous dizziness in the eerie, noiseless stream. But he didn't black out. He felt a tooth-gnashing pain at the base of his neck. Blood vessels welled in his head. His pulse raced, roaring in his ears. Perspiration dripped into his eyes, and they stung. Yet he had to keep them open. Suddenly his stomach was a solid knot. Cramps . . . If he got cramps, he was sure to die. His heart trembled, head pounded, hands shook. Phlegm started clogging his nasal passages. Oh, Lord! He felt a tremor, loosening muscles, a letting go. Was this the end?

But he thought of Fritz, and the need to know why Fritz had tried to kill him seemed to energize him. He heard the hiss of the air rushing in, then the gurgling sound of bubbles wriggle out. He fixed his eyes on the marker. He could still read the number on it: ten. He could make it. He held on to the descent line—his life. Was this what life just before death felt like? Cold, helpless, and all alone? Lord, please!

He had another six minutes of air, but experience told him that he should remain at the marker at least three more minutes for good decompression. Now if only he didn't get cramps in his hands. He had to hold on to the descent line.

Breathing slowly, his lungs aching, the vibration from the cycloids beating on his chest, he looked up and saw only the platform.

"Jesus, what happened?" Felton cried out, ashen faced, when he saw Fritz surface in a pool of blood. He groped, swore, strained himself to keep Fritz from slipping under. Finally he pulled him onto the platform by the tank straps. "Mr. Hoffmeister?" Felton took Fritz's mask off. "Do you hear me? Is the doc all right?"

The answer was a weak, tortured groan.

Fritz's eyes were closed, but Felton could tell that he was still alive by the rapid and spasmodic breathing. "You'll make it, sir."

"Oh, my God." Captain Edwards stared at the blood-stained platform beneath him. He dashed back to the ship's intercom.

Just then the alarm sounded—a shrill, piercing, frightening bell. Running footsteps pounded on C deck. Off-duty personnel streamed out with CPR equipment, first-aid boxes, stretchers. . . .

Little talk. Only commands. "Resuscitator here . . . You, come with me. Bear a hand, you guys. On the double. Move!"

Leaning over the guardrail, Adams kept shouting at

Felton, "Where is Cliff? Is he all right?" Turning his head hysterically around, he ran to Edwards. "Captain, do something," he implored.

"Clear out of here," the skipper ordered. Gesturing broadly with his arms at the bridge, he ordered the cycloids stopped. "*Stop 'em, damn it.*"

On the platform Felton was instructing a confused assistant who had gone down to help him. "Take him to the infirmary. I'm diving." Then he screwed his face up and yelled, "Get me a tank, *move!*" He quickly put Fritz's mask on.

"Where the fuck is the tank?" Felton yelled.

Twelve feet beneath the platform Cliff was counting his second minute of decompression: a thousand five . . . a thousand six . . . He looked up, down, left, right. No sharks—yet. A thousand seven . . . a thousand eight . . .

But he was too weak and dizzy. He tugged on the line and began to surface. He reached for the platform but was unable to hold on to it. He slipped under.

Felton dived in, grabbed him by the tank straps, and managed to jam a crane's hook around Cliff's weight belt, then pushed and shoved him onto the diving platform.

"Christ." Felton yanked Cliff's mask off. Cliff's skin was livid and seemed to have shrunk on his face and it was covered with phlegm. The lips were purple; the eyes cold and unblinking, like those of a dead fish.

"Did you decompress? Answer me," Felton cried out.

Cliff nodded and wiped his mouth. "Hoffmeister . . . t-tried to kill me," he stammered.

"What?" Felton paled.

Cliff nodded again and passed out.

When he opened his eyes, Felton was giving him pure oxygen.

"Where's Hoffmeister?" Cliff asked.

"Do you recognize me?"

"Just answer me, Roy."

Felton wiped his forehead in gesture of thankfulness. "In the infirmary," he said.

Cliff pushed the oxygen mask away. "The infirmary?"

"Take it easy. They opted to stitch him up before taking him to decompression." His voice dropped. "Losing too much blood."

An awful foreboding rose to Cliff's throat and all he could do was nod. Then, as Felton shut off the oxygen tank's valve, Cliff put a hand on Felton's powerful arm. "If you weren't on that platform," he said, "I would be keeping the weeds company." He gave the arm a squeeze.

Five minutes later, Cliff headed for the infirmary, leaving a trail of sea water behind him.

Just past the gyro room, his face tightened at the sight of Edwards and the first mate, wearing a pistol belt, moving in his direction. Numb, as if a dark premonition had paralyzed him, Cliff stopped walking. And with every step of Edwards, a fist of fear grew bigger in his stomach.

"It wasn't narcosis, was it?" Cliff said to him in a flash of terrible logic.

Edwards shook his head. "He said . . . 'I've tried to spare his life.' " He hesitated. "I heard Fritz say that before they took him to decompression."

"What else did the bastard say," Cliff asked bitingly, his eyes now red with rage.

"Nothing else."

Cliff nodded, then passed a hand over the spot on his head—still aching—where Fritz had kicked him. *Sucker,* he told himself, aware of the maddening urge to finish Fritz off himself.

The decompression chamber was open and Felton and the pharmacist's mate were standing silently by the double door, looking in. It was an eight-by-fifteen steel room with a wooden floor, equipped with oxygen masks, large pressure gauges, and medical instruments. Damp, cold, and with a foul air, it had the feeling of an abandoned walk-in refrigerator.

Cliff braced himself.

"We did what Dr. Barret and I thought best," the pharmacist's mate said on seeing Cliff. Dr. Barret was the ship's biologist. "I've given him morphine," the pharmacist's mate went on, lowering his voice to a whisper. "He's got a bubble in the spinal cord. . . . Death will come as a mercy." He looked at Cliff and shook his head. "I wouldn't go in, sir."

"I have to," Cliff said, and pushed the mate aside.

He froze as he crossed into the chamber. As much as he had anticipated gratification in having Fritz suffer, he was overcome by what he saw. Fritz lay on his back on a wooden bench under the low ceiling. His only recognizable feature was his hair. Blood oozed out of his left ear and his eyelashes were barely visible in the swollen slits of his closed eyes. His body, still clothed in the diving suit that had been cut away from his spine, curved upward, as if from some invisible horrifying pressure. His skin was taut, almost translucent. What was he feeling now? That's what Cliff wanted to know. He shook his head. It all seemed another world; Fritz, another man.

Cliff's hair hung damply over his forehead as he drew near the bench. Fritz's breath came in wheezy gasps and his ribs shook convulsively.

In Cliff's mind, the decompression chamber became the *Alvin*, and his memories of their many dives together exploded like fireworks. He again heard Fritz's voice full of nervous excitement as he fixed the leak around the penetrator with the hose clamp. Fritz had always been at ease with everything around—the gauges, wires, conduits, the smell of body odor, and salt water. But now his breathing roared in Cliff's ears like the bellows of an infernal forge.

Unzipping the forearms of his wet suit to release the pressure, Cliff shook his head, annoyed at himself. He would have liked to feel anger, but the only sensation he was really aware of was bitterness at the world. Water began dripping from his wrists.

Slowly Fritz passed his tongue over his lips a couple of times. They were edged with a pencil-thin line of caked blood. His eyes were still closed, and a thin, gluey line of mucus dripped from his nose. Cliff felt nothing but pity.

From the C deck above came the squeaks of a hatch door being tightened shut. Cliff turned and called the pharmacist's mate. "Have you arranged for an airlift?" he asked.

He had, but it would not take place before daybreak. "Too dark now." The pharmacist's mate paused. "But I'm afraid—"

Fritz mumbled something.

Cliff silenced the pharmacist's mate with a hand and moved closer to the bench.

In the dim light of the decompression chamber he could see that a waxy pallor was slowly covering Fritz's face like a gray veil.

"I . . . tried, Cliff." His voice was a feeble, ghostlike sound coming from a distance. "Tried to spare you from a horrible accident or certain death. He'll have to . . . kill you now," Fritz's eyes blinked but wouldn't open.

"Who?" Cliff knelt beside him. "Tell me."

Fritz gasped, arched his back like a leaf as his fingers dug into the palms of his balled hands.

"*Tell me.*" Cliff clutched his arm.

"My"—Fritz coughed—"my control."

Cliff moved closer. "What's his name?"

Fritz moved his head from side to side. "I . . . can only tell you that he speaks as though he has a sore throat. But . . . it could be a disguise."

"Is he American?"

A nod. "From the South."

Cliff just stared at him and could see Fritz's lips getting grayer, bloodless. The lies they had told!

"Be careful. He will kill you, Cliff."

"With a shark dart, too?" Cliff rose to his feet.

"I didn't want to use it. Then I saw you . . ."

Cliff stared at him. His whole being ached with anger. He longed to leave him in the chamber without air.

"Come closer . . . please."

Then the cycloids started frothing the sea again.

"Cliff . . ."

The P.A. speaker blared, "Getting under way. Lookouts, man your stations. Yeoman Benda, report . . ."

Fritz uttered something, which was lost in the announcement. Then he arched his back one more time. Cliff drew near. The breathing got more irregular.

Cliff remained standing. He was a mournful figure— face pale, eyes tragic, head bent forward and shaking from side to side. In less than an hour, he had escaped death, learned who Fritz really was, lost faith in friendship. What came next?

Then his eyes got red and liquid, and he wept.

When Cliff walked into his stateroom, Adams was there with a bottle of cognac. He looked shell shocked and shaken. "I don't believe you're alive," he said, to Cliff.

"I don't, either." Cliff sat wearily on the bunk without removing his wet suit and gestured to Adams to give him the bottle. "You must've heard that Fritz tried to kill me," he said with a terse, cold voice. The very name made him choke on his words. He took a long swig, then exhaled audibly. His expression was wild, angry; his face so flushed it looked as though he had been strangled.

Adams shook his head. "Why?"

Cliff blew his nose with a decisive honk. Diving left him with a running nose for hours. As he had expected, he could think of no answer other than the one that sounded the most plausible. "I guess he remained an East German, a Vopo, a Communist." He blew his nose again. "I suppose he always kept his values in the right order—duty, country, friendship," he said, almost as if he despised all those who did. "There are people like him. Skinheads and neo-Nazis act that way . . . and neo-Communists will act that way soon."

Adams nodded. "You've got to say that much for him."

Cliff recoiled. An obsessively devoted individual himself, he didn't expect Adams's remark. He said nothing, suddenly assailed by a shameful consciousness of his own sense of duty. He saw himself telling Roscoe he wanted nothing to do with modifiers, and slowly turned to one side, afraid that Adams might notice the blush of shame he felt coloring his face. "Values or not, he'll get what a traitor deserves," he said, his voice lacking conviction. "There's nothing like the bends." He snapped his fingers at Adams's face. "Nothing."

And Adams, quietly, "Well you did what you had to do," he said with a gentle, reassuring tone, as though offering the ultimate consolation.

As Adams turned to leave, Cliff tumbled into his bunk, his blood surging, head aching, chest hurting.

An hour later, he was owl eyed and sleepless. In just a few minutes he had had to learn to kill, while his sense of humanity was squeezed out of him as if by water pressure. But now he knew the true meaning of survival. It transcended love, friendship . . . even reason. Incredible.

Eight bells.

A pair of binoculars hanging on a hook near the mirror swayed like a pendulum, and Cliff's head moved synchronously from side to side. He was finally asleep, exhausted.

On the yardarm above the bridge, the anemometer whined. Signal flags flapped and frayed, and the acquisition radar antenna bore through the air as though it were a giant corkscrew.

The storm hit with the violence of an anathema. And almost without warning. Suddenly the *Knorr* pitched, its bow hitting the water hard, as if it were a rock. Everything shook. Cups, staplers, pliers jingled. Raindrops pelted the porthole.

Then a gigantic wave hit the *Knorr* broadside, forcing her to list to port. Oil drums rolled; wooden boxes grated on the decks. The cycloids spun in the air. In the engine room the telegraph repeater read: "All Ahead Full," but one could have guessed that order blindfolded. There was a strong odor of burning engine oil as the ship's engines fought to keep up speed.

Nine bells. A strong wind howled, setting cables, wire

antennas, and halyards in motion. A metallic hum provided sinister accompaniment. It resounded like a bass note in a cathedral. And the *Knorr* pitched, bobbed, and shuddered, shaking everything and everybody.

After nearly four hours, the wind speed finally dropped to twenty-five mph, and the P.A. system crackled with a terse voice, "Damage control to bridge. Move!"

Cliff sprang to his feet, his face gray as modeling clay. Damage could mean inoperative equipment, no data. He headed for the bridge, struggling to keep his balance in the slippery passageway cluttered with life jackets, uncoiled fire hoses, broken pieces of glass, and sand that had spilled from the ashtrays. The air was acrid with a mix of urine and bilge water.

He stood quietly and out of breath as the first mate made his report.

Cliff played it cool. "And . . . the cranes?" he asked almost without emotion.

"Number one is okay; number two has water in the motor housing."

"Not bad," Cliff said, optimism in his voice. "And the crews?"

"No broken bones, no serious injuries, no—"

"Good. We're lucky, all right."

"Sir . . ." The first mate hesitated. "Mr. Hoffmeister . . ." He let his voice trail off.

Cliff stiffened. "What about him?" he asked with a face like granite, but unable to give his voice the rich timbre it had.

"He didn't make it."

Cliff stood with battleship solidity as the skipper ordered the mate to ready Fritz's body for burial at sea.

At dawn, Cliff watched from the bridge overhang as two crewmen got ready to lower the weighted body bag into the water. The aft deck was otherwise deserted except for the skipper, who seemed unfamiliar with the book in his hands.

And it wasn't until the crewmen swung the body bag over the side, as though it were just another oceanographic instrument, that Cliff experienced something not totally unexpected, a stab of warm feeling cutting through the fog of his anger and disappointment like a laser beam. Fritz had done what he had to do for his beliefs . . . and, perhaps, even for his friend.

Bareheaded, the skipper intoned from the Book of Psalms: "Blessed is he whose iniquities are forgiven; whose sin is forgiven. Blessed the man . . ."

Cliff began to pray. It came easy.

"So, now that we know dust trapped in the atmosphere can cut down solar energy and reduce temperature drastically, and we know that moisture can become snow and ice, let me explain to you how scientists, including myself, are trying to save the world from a deep freeze," Cliff said to the technicians and sailors assembled in the main lab. "My modification . . ." He went on and described it in detail.

"Any questions?" he asked.

The technicians and sailors were too startled to raise a hand.

"Okay then," Cliff said. "Let's get to work."

With a sense of rising excitement, one that seemed contagious, Operation Data finally got under way.

As the *Knorr* headed for the southern tip of the Hull, the other five ships were also maneuvering in position in accordance with the original instructions Cliff had sent them and revised at Scott's request.

Profiling of the ocean floor was the responsibility of the *Dolphin* and the *Oceanographer*. Sailing U-shaped 100-mile-long, 5-mile-wide courses running perpendicular to the axis of the Hull, they would use Precision Depth Recorders and navy AN/UQN sonar sounding sets to chart the geology of a 1,500-square-mile area of ocean floor.

Also using PDRs, the *Glomar Challenger* was to profile the entrance to the Mid-Ocean Canyon, then record the speed of the stream along the seabed at predetermined locations using a new radio current meter.

The task of towing the big egg-shaped underwater side-looking sonar to obtain continuous profile images of the Hull was given to the *Atlantis II*.

It was chilly and damp, with frequent breaks in the clouds, but the sea was calm, as if someone had poured oil over it. The air thudded with the sputter of motors. The deck was alive with equipment going through self-test sequences, with booms and crane arms moving like those of a friendly giant.

Yet Cliff grew uneasy. He was used to logic, mathematics, scientific proofs, and he did not believe in omens. But after the bout with death at the hands of a friend, he wondered if the devil was running things.

At two-fifteen P.M., the *Knorr* came within a quarter mile from the southern tip of the Hull. The *Mizar*, following five hundred yards behind, exploded a hundred-pound dynamite shot to produce seismic waves.

One and a half seconds later, a device that looked like a long and fat garden hose, a hydrophone streamer, towed behind the *Knorr*, picked up the acoustic waves refracted back from the surface (2,200 meters) and subsurface layer of the Hull, and transmitted them to a recorder for digital processing. At once, horizontal lines representing geological contours appeared on fan-fold paper.

Cliff and Adams were in the portable van when the ink pens began tracing one mile=one inch refractions on paper. Narrowly spaced, the tracings looked a bit like tombstone rubbings.

For almost a half hour, Adams, seated in front of the recorder, studied the contours as if they were MRIs of his own brain and marked the paper with symbols and abbreviations.

This and the silence were too much for Cliff. "Well," he said, "what's the verdict?"

Adams shrugged. "I don't know yet," he answered, but the tone had an ominous quality that made Cliff say, "I think you do. Come on, let's have it."

Adams circled a large area of tracings and explained that,

from what they showed, the Hull was made of igneous rock from an underground volcano. Nothing new. The cleavages, however, did not run vertically, or nearly so, but twenty degrees from the horizontal plane. And that was not all. There were three cleavages, each marking volcanic eruptions millions of years apart. This was no good. He said, "If you had, say, two hundred vertical cleavage lines from where we are"—he pointed to the southern tip of the Hull—"to the other end, all we'd have to do is drill halfway down the first cleavage, load it with dynamite, and blast it. Then go to the second cleavage and so on." Adams smiled. "Like slicing big chunks of salami."

His attempt at cheering Cliff failed, for Cliff appeared not to have heard the remark and kept moving his head from side to side while pressing his lips hard in disgust. "But I don't have two hundred cleavages, do I?" he asked, and pounded the van's wall.

"As you can guess," Adams began slowly, searching for the proper words, "the structure of the Hull requires that we drill down to each cleavage and pack it with dynamite every—"

"That just means," Cliff interrupted, "more drill holes, doesn't it?"

Standing up, Adams nodded and sighed.

"Damn. Damn. But we don't have the time for more drill holes."

"Yes and no. That all depends on when we start, how many drill ships we can get up here, and . . . if the Russians don't make trouble." Adams spoke as if what he had said was not a tall order. But it was.

"Easier said than done."

A thudding sound coming out of the recorder's speaker followed by more paper scrolling out of the recorder indicated that the *Mizar* had fired another shot.

While Adams leaned over to look at the tracings, Cliff paced back and forth, head down, right hand on his chin. "Damn," he whispered, and the muscles of his jaw bunched.

Quietly Adams scribbled something along the right edge

of the paper, then offered, "If worse comes to worst, we blow only one-third or half of the Hull."

Cliff had thought of that. "If the model says it will do any good. But I doubt it."

They were silent against the scratchy noise of the pens inking the paper. "Well," Adams said, as he sat down in front of the recorder, "what if the pattern of the cleavage changes as we sail north? Cleavage lines reflect nature's capricious ways, you know. . . . There goes shot number three."

And so Operation Data continued.

Crews worked, ate, rested, worked again.

Like a giant dragonfly over a pond, the *Knorr* hovered here and there around the Hull, and sheet after sheet of new data piled up without interruption—data on temperature, echo soundings, profiles, current speed. . . .

A rhythm developed, and soon Operation Data took on a soul of its own. His flight suit greasy and torn, Cliff went from lab to deck talking to crews like a minister reassuring believers that they were doing God's work.

Data day four.

It was plain that the weather was cooperating. The sun was high and warm and it bleached the cloudless sky. But as everybody knew, it wouldn't be for long. Frost crystals resembling ground pumice had glittered at dawn like tarnished Christmas tree tinsel.

Cliff stopped for a moment to look at the frost crystals covering the density meter. The sight chilled him. Now there was the danger of slipping on the ice, of men falling overboard.

It was time he ran on all eight cylinders, he told himself, and walked to the fantail, where crews were having a hard time getting the density meter ready to be lowered into the water.

"Okay, George," he ordered, "let's move the boom right over here. That's it . . . good. Billy, give me a hand with this baby. Watch your fingers. . . . Easy, now. We don't want to do this again tomorrow night, do we? Watch your fingers, Billy. . . . It's in the water. . . . Okay, good . . ."

And so it went.

"You know how to make coffee?" Cliff shouted to a sailor who was waiting to go on watch.

"Sure I do."

"Navy style?"

"Hell, no."

"Good," Cliff said. "Go down and make some for all of us."

Watching a crew of three getting ready to sink an acoustic positioning transponder from the divers' platform, he shouted, "Are you sure you guys aren't Mario Andretti's pit crew?"

A voice sailed back. "No, Doc, pit crews are too slow."

Cliff grinned, then he searched the horizon with his binoculars. A couple of hundred yards off the starboard beam the *Glomar Challenger* continued its surveying.

Finally, with the retrieval of the density meter after its twentieth probe, Cliff's mission ended.

And as far as research missions go, it was successful. There were no injuries, the equipment worked "gremlinlessly," as Cliff would say, and on schedule. A five-foot-tall stack of fan-fold paper in the portable van was the proof that lifted Cliff's spirit.

At once, wearing the sort of smiles that forced one to smile back, Cliff walked through every passageway to thank mechanics, radio operators, crane operators, yeomen. In the galley, he ordered a special dinner. "One they'll never forget," he told the chef.

That night they gathered in the mess hall with a crossing-of-the-equator mood.

"Ready launch!" the skipper barked from the port bridge overhang soon after breakfast. Minutes later, Cliff and Adams were waiting on the aft deck to transfer to the Coast Guard H-4S seaplane, a stout all-weather aircraft capable of landing on a runway because of its retractable wheels.

● ● ● ●

Felton came to Cliff carrying an envelope. "I found it in Mr. Hoffmeister's stateroom, between the pages of a Dylan Thomas paperback. You should have it, sir."

Cliff looked at it with cynical weariness. "Thank you," he said. "It's something the FBI should have."

Felton stuffed the envelope in Cliff's pocket. "No, sir. It's of no use to those guys."

As the white Coast Guard H-4S gained altitude, Adams's eyes were glued on the *Knorr* down below. "It looks like a toy," he said. "And during the storm, I would have sworn it was."

Cliff, seated next to him, didn't even hear him. Gazing into private space, he held a sheet of paper full of scribbles and erasures in one hand. It was in Fritz's cursive handwriting and it read:

> I, too, will leave love
> and die in such a way
> that my friends will not forget me.

Roscoe had come by limousine to Sparrows Point, Maryland, to pick Cliff up and take him to Washington. He stood silhouetted against the white Coast Guard station building, his chin up, ignoring the cold rain falling.

It was nearing dusk when the plane touched down. It was cloudy, socked in, and the lights along the pier cast a dull glow that seemed to accent the leaden silence of the scene.

Roscoe was friendly, effusive. "Welcome back," he said, beaming. "You're a real hero. Captain Edwards has kept us informed."

"A hero?" Cliff shook his head. "Just an ordinary nerd."

The greetings were brief. Cliff, a borrowed scarf covering his mouth to keep him from inhaling the cool air, said good-bye to Adams, who was going home for a few hours. With that, he walked toward the limousine with a hunched back, his hands in his pockets, and his mind on Roscoe's unusual warmth and thoughtfulness.

Phil Jackson got out of the limo to shake hands with Cliff, and the two exchanged brief greetings. Once inside the comfortable and warm automobile, Cliff sunk in the seat and let out a sigh of relief. He was behind schedule, he thought, but he was alive and he had the data he needed. Soon he would meet with his team. Meanwhile he had to contend with the lack of sleep. "If you don't mind, we'll talk about Fritz later," he said churlishly and closed his eyes.

Ten minutes passed.

Roscoe shifted position, then cleared his throat. Cliff sensed something was really up. "What is it?"

Roscoe hesitated. "Cliff, you are not going home," he began, and went on to explain that the FBI was convinced that Russian operatives had Cliff framed inside a rifle's cross hair and that they would keep him in there until he was dead. "You have survived two attempts, your luck may not hold for the next one."

"Two attempts?" Cliff opened his bleary eyes wide, nerves tensing.

Phil Jackson told him when and where the other attempt took place. "So, you see. These are determined people, and they'll do anything now to get you. God knows how many operatives have been assigned to bump you off. One has been arrested already."

At this point, Cliff felt momentarily beyond danger. "A southerner with a gruff voice, I bet," he said.

Phil Jackson and Roscoe looked questioningly at each other as if to say, Is he all right?

"No, no southerner. Anyhow, where did you get those details?" Roscoe asked.

Cliff told them. "Are you sure he wasn't from the South and that he had a gruff voice?"

"We are." It was Phil Jackson who answered. "I read the report the FBI sent us—and you know how fussy they are with details."

Cliff sat up straight. "Are you really sure?"

A state police cruiser passed by, and then an ambulance. Sirens screeched. The traffic slowed down.

Against the background of revolving lights, Roscoe answered, "We are, and that is why you and your team will be living in an FBI safe house."

"But I've promised Butch to spend a day with him."

"We'll arrange something," Phil Jackson put in. "Give us time. For now, know that Butch is himself in a safe house with special tutors, a nurse, the works."

Inwardly, Cliff boiled like a volcano. "And he understands why?"

Another police cruiser sped by.

Turning to face Cliff, Phil Jackson said, "A smart kid like him? Of course he does."

The limousine sped along the Washington-Baltimore Parkway, its yellow fog lights lending an aura of vagueness to the road ahead. Wet leaves, dripping road signs, darkened trees . . . all swept gloomily past Cliff's questioning eyes.

He leaned back in his seat, exiled in his worries, forced to consider the new crisis in the light of some thoughts of his own.

To be sure, he had never imagined that someday he would live with a high-powered rifle pointed at him or that Butch had one pointed at him also. So he never had had any thoughts about it. Now they came in a rush. Were safe houses really safe? What made them safe? Did they have bulletproof windows?

One more turn of the screw.

18

"The weapon of the post–cold war era is the EMP," the head of the NSC, James Sellwood, told the president in the National Security Council Situation Room in the basement of the West Wing. "The Russians would be crazy not to try an EMP if they were convinced that whatever we did to modify the weather would adversely affect them."

Sellwood was referring to the new danger facing the high-tech world—an electromagnetic pulse from a high-altitude nuclear explosion. The bomb, he believed, would be dropped either from a high-flying bomber or via FOBS (Fractional Orbit Bombardment System). As Nuclear Regulatory Agency tests in the Pacific had revealed, EMPs "zapped" chips, the tiny pieces of semiconductor material on which thousands and thousands of transistors and other electronic components are microscopically etched.

Chips burned out easily when hit with an EMP, Sellwood explained, because the radiation and wave propagation from a nuclear explosion include cosmic rays, photons, and gamma rays, which require thick layers of dense material, such as concrete, lead, or water, to stop them. With the exception of a few specially hardened rooms, like the one they were in, no other buildings in the United States housing computers offered protection against an EMP. "None whatever, Mr. President."

"An EMP, rather than military action?" the president asked. A handsome, sixty-four-year-old compact man of medium height, he was so young looking that one cartoonist saw him as a young college student walking to the White House still wearing his graduation robe. But recent events had aged him considerably.

"Yes, Mr. President," Sellwood answered. "EMPs destroy chips, not cities. But the destruction of the chips could lead to that of cities." Taking out a telescopic pointer from his breast pocket, Sellwood walked to a map of the United States. "An explosion here," he said, and placed the tip of the pointer to a spot in the Atlantic some two hundred miles east of Boston, "could render useless all computers at M.I.T., Harvard, and those inside every building along Route One Twenty-eight, famous for its electronics industry. Along this high-tech road are located Raytheon, G.E., IBM, Mitre, and Digital, to name a few defense and computer companies."

"And I suppose," the president said, "two hundred miles east of Boston means that such an explosion is over international waters." He paused. "Yet an explosion two hundred miles east of here would . . ."

"Create a problem impossible to visualize, let alone solve."

The president stared glumly across the long rectangular table for a long time, seemingly unaware of the expectant look in the eyes of the fourteen advisers seated left and right of him.

Finally he spoke. "So now what do we do?" he asked, and looked around. The answer came from the secretary of defense, who was seated to his immediate right. "Mr. President," he began, "the greater our suspicion of Russian intentions is, the greater our incentive must be to go on the offensive."

"Are you talking of a first strike?"

The secretary of defense nodded. "Yes, a selective strike, of course. I've always championed the shoot-look-shoot policy and I recommend that we adopt it now."

"Attack, see what happens, attack again," the president muttered quietly, but one could practically hear the alarm bell going off in his head. "What if they counterattack, look, and attack again?" he asked uneasily.

"What alternative is there?" Kronin asked. As chief of the CLIMOD program, Kronin had achieved temporary cabinet rank and attended all meetings during which the threat of glaciation would be discussed. In short, he attended all White House meetings now.

"Let's meet this afternoon to discuss this further," the president said, addressing the chief of staff seated four places to his left. "Now, let's hear what the Russians may be planning."

"Are planning, Mr. President," Sellwood corrected. He went on to say that the Russians were maneuvering a number of suspicious-looking freighters at both ends of the Panama Canal in order, presumably, to scuttle them as they passed through the locks.

"What in the world would be the purpose of blocking it?" the president asked, flushing with anger.

Kronin answered him. "Simple, Mr. President. If they block the canal, the *Glomar Explorer* would be forced to go the Cape Horne route, a trip that could last six weeks or longer. As you already know from our discussion, Dr. Lorenz needs the *Explorer* for his modification. She's indispensable."

"The one-upmanship game continues, doesn't it?" The President thanked Kronin, then, turning to Sellwood, he said, "And you still believe that the Russians will try to stop us from modifying our weather because they fear our modifier could worsen their weather?"

"Mr. President," Sellwood answered, his tone deferential, "I haven't taken a poll. But I can guarantee you that half the people in this room believe that modifiers have the potential of making our own weather, let alone that of the Russians, as inhospitable as the weather on Venus."

The meeting adjourned.

• • •

The manager of the safe house, an FBI agent himself who walked around with the customized pistol grip of a big M-39 sticking out from under his left armpit, was a rugged man with ears that looked as if he had been a boxer. He took Cliff on a tour of the facilities in anticipation of the changes to be made.

Located on a hilly twenty-acre lot in a quiet residential area just off Route 120 and within walking distance of the Arlington National Cemetery, the onetime residence of Justice Daniel Winthrop was anyone's idea of a late-nineteenth-century mansion. Though the dark furniture, the yellowed doilies, and the chipped English china gave it a hint of decadence, the kitchen was well equipped. A North Korean diplomat who had defected had been its last guest.

"A great old house," Cliff said. No dog lover, he reluctantly patted the Doberman that had followed them during the tour of the house.

The manager nodded. "Well built. Same roof . . . dry cellar . . . no termites, either." He paused. "But the electrical system isn't holding up well," he said. He angled his head in the direction of an antiquated fuse box visible through the pantry door. "Kept blowing fuses last week. Somebody had put lower-amperage ones—maybe as a desperate measure—and then forgot about them. No more problems now. I've replaced all the fuses. But someday . . . Anyhow, GSA has promised to look at it." He shook his head. "Well, you know GSA . . ."

Cliff nodded his "yes, I know GSA and their promises" and made a mental note to phone Roscoe and have him send an electrician to replace the old fuse box with one having automatic circuit breakers.

Then, clipboard in hand, Cliff began requisitioning some comforts. Think tank or not, the place was going to be home and health club rolled into one. It would sweeten the self-imposed isolation he foresaw for total success.

Though the FBI had provided Cliff with the latest in

communications gear, the team would not use it to call
home and vice versa. The occasional contacts with spouse
or children were to be mostly one way.

Cliff converted the library into a conference room
equipped with imaging equipment, and had two more
bedrooms on the second floor turned into offices. He
indulged himself by seeing that fresh flowers from the
garden be displayed daily in Pam's room, which he had
selected for her for its view of East Potomac Park and the
Jefferson Memorial to the left.

In keeping with Cliff's concept of a health club, he
checked the condition of the tennis court and ordered a rowing machine and a small Nautilus. He also had a wireless
intercom system installed so the team would be able to communicate with one another from their different workstations
without having to hold a receiver in their hand. Finally,
aware of the tendency on the part of scholars to research
things ad infinitum, he plotted the advance of the icebergs
on a map using white push pins and mounted it at the
entrance of the dining room.

By noon he was standing by the main door wondering if
there was anything he had omitted.

And by five that afternoon the safe house had the look of
a posh ivory tower. Team members worked undisturbed at
their desk; agents moved quietly about installing equipment,
bringing refreshments, and running errands.

Cliff walked into the safe house living room, where his
team had gathered, carrying a folder. He looked younger,
stronger in jeans and open collar, and his face had the
flush of impatience, as if the hard task ahead was what
he needed.

Adams, Scott, and Wycoff were there. *Four scholars in
all*, Cliff thought, *each with a penchant for seeing things
through the narrow viewfinder of his own discipline*. To
keep such individuals working as a team would be tanta-
mount to having four soloists, each with his own idea of
tempo and loudness, make good music.

He spoke with authority, laying down the ground rules.

"Daily meetings will start promptly at eight A.M. Supper is at eight. Requests for supplies and assistants are to be made to the house manager. Smoke, if you must, outside."

Cliff kept the meeting short, and as they left, he wished everyone good luck.

With that, Operation Model got under way.

Though four days behind schedule, it did so in an atmosphere of guarded optimism. One reason was that the H-Team (Hull-Team), as Cliff had named it after an old TV show his son loved, had subscribed to the principle that in science the best ideas were the simple ones. And Cliff's idea was so convincingly simple, as Adams put it, "that it could've been drawn on the back of an envelope."

Well, simple to a point. Just to code program instructions so that the computer performed flawlessly the sequence of steps leading to the solution of a single problem was almost as difficult as decoding the DNA.

Atmos-1, the ecological model Scott had built two years before, showed, by visualization, the interaction between winds and ocean currents without attempting to forecast the weather.

CLIMOD-1, however, would have to simulate conditions during and after the modifications, and predict the flow patterns of the stream and its meanders.

And that was just for starters. CLIMOD-1 required a prediction of tidal wave motion, the influence of the advancing polar ice sheet on ocean circulation, and the parameters for TNT detonations without prompting an apocalyptic magma flow.

A lot of modeling.

Without miscalculations.

Scott had put together his "ergonomic" room with furniture and computers designed for optimum comfort and efficiency. Having studied what the problem was, he worked out a set of instructions coded in programming language, and planned the order by which problems would be solved according to structure charts. He was now ready to start building CLIMOD-1.

Cliff was present when the "ground-breaking ceremony" took place. "Let's start by downloading data from the United States Coast and Geodetic Survey," Scott said, as he sipped Coke from a can. First he typed the number 1044/1244RA on the computer keyboard. It was his secret account number. Then he typed the password DORSEN provided by the FBI.

TYPE DATA BANK NAME AND ACCOUNT NUMBER, read the prompt.

Scott typed it. Seconds later the word ACCEPTED flashed. Scott was in the network. He had entered the fast electronic highway system on which he could now travel by telephone to any government data bank.

Scott typed USCGS/0137522, and within seconds his monitor displayed a long list of files in alphabetical order, each followed by a date.

"I'll start scrolling," he told Cliff. "You tell me which files you want."

Cliff studied them carefully, noticing the date, and indicated the ones he needed.

"This one," Cliff said, pointing with a finger. "And this one, and . . ."

And so began the process of transferring data from twenty-four data banks—from the Weather Bureau, the Hydrographic Office of the Navy, the U.S. Coast and Geodetic Survey, the Naval Oceanographic Office, the Submarine Signal Division, the Environmental Science Services Administration, the Bureau of Mines, the Naval Chart and Information Center, the Geodesy Information Center. . . .

Like a newly appointed coach, Cliff was demanding of his team, as they were of him.

"Where in hell are the *Challenger*'s drill specs you promised me?" Adams said to Cliff one evening. "Do you expect me to figure things out without them, eh?"

"I'm sorry . . . I . . ."

"Sorry, hell. Just have them E-mailed to me at once."

Scott asked later, "Cliff, at what intervals were the seismic records taken?"

"Six usually. Let me check."

"Don't bother. That's close enough for now. . . ."

"Cliff," Pamela called through the intercom, "I must talk to someone at Aquatech Industries," she said, her voice musical even through a cheap two-inch speaker. "Do you know anybody there? If you don't . . ."

Phones rang, cursors blinked, printers hummed on standby.

Day one passed, two followed, then came day three, day four. . . .

And from his hip pocket out came a leather daily appointment book, which he used to scrupulously put down what he had done that day. For as long as he could remember, he had always carried one. It gave him tangible proof of accomplishments—or the lack of them.

As excitement competed with exhaustion, computers solved problems, sought flaws, offered alternatives, created new problems. Especially new problems.

But Cliff was an experimental scientist. To him glitches and gremlins—or the "G squared factor," as he called them—and everything else that made life on earth difficult were only temporary obstacles.

Adams completed his visual model in record time because Scott needed it to study it using virtual reality techniques.

Adams had wanted to see the Hull in a manageable form, rather than what the five-foot stack of fan-fold paper offered him, and CAD (Computer-Aided Design) gave him the graphic images he sought.

What made this possible was the fact that CAD images are based on mathematical coordinates. As the computer saw them, mathematical coordinates were nothing more than points drawn on a graph and connected with a line like those used to show the ups and downs of the stock market.

He had the coordinates. They were the traces printed on paper by the side-looking sonar and the Precision Depth Recorders and stored as digital electronic data on hard disks—which Adams fed easily to his computer using CAD language.

It was just after three in the afternoon of day five when Adams called Cliff to his office.

"So that's it?" Cliff said, looking at the orange-colored wire frame of the Hull projected on a high-resolution bright blue monitor. Though Cliff had seen CAD images before, he stared at the monitor like someone watching TV for the first time. The Hull looked exactly as he had imagined, with its contours smoothed out over millions of years, yet standing like a mythical ship defying decay.

He said, "I know that you haven't completed your analysis, but from what you see, what can you tell me? Good or bad?"

"Which one do you want first?" Adams asked.

"The good."

Adams reached for a ream of fan-fold paper. "This is the subsurface profiling," he began, and showed Cliff that, contrary to Adams's earlier predictions, the Hull was actually made up of a layer of lava, a thicker layer of limestone, and a newer, thinner coating of lava on top of that. Having done so, he pressed some keys on the keyboard to display an enlarged view of one section of the Hull. "This is the southern half," he said, and pointed at the two lines that separated the layers. "Now," he continued, "if we can drill all the way down to the cleavage between the first layer of lava and the limestone, and if we can load the holes with enough high explosives, the limestone should break up easily, causing the outer layer of lava to drop and shatter like plate glass." He paused. "That is, if we can load the holes with enough high explosives. Remember, there is magma flowing under the first layer of lava."

"The layer of limestone looks very thick in relation to the others."

"It is, Cliff. But it also has lots of faults running through it. Do you see these?" Adams pointed to lines running vertically through the limestone.

Cliff nodded, eyes on the monitor.

"Now the bad news."

"I'm ready," Cliff said, and tensed.

Holding a piece of paper in his hands, Adams explained that to blow up the two layers of rock they would have to drill four rows of holes for a total of 240 holes, many more than the original estimates. "Maybe less, I don't know yet," he said.

Furrowing his forehead, Cliff did some quick mental calculations. "Too many. Too many. Even if we had six drill ships—which we don't—we wouldn't make it. As I see it, icebergs should begin descending over the Hull area three weeks after we start drilling." He tried to discipline his voice to retain the optimism of the last few days, but a tone of disappointment, if not defeat, had crept into it.

"We could blow up as much of the Hull as possible and reduce moisture proportionately, could we not?"

"I honestly don't know. The virtual reality model Scott wants to build could tell me if it's worth the try."

But Scott had to construct first the mathematical model that was the foundation of the VR display. That took time.

Nevertheless, he was also moving at record speed.

Virtually locked in his room and feeling good about the logic-based system Scott had selected to build the model with, he was now ready to process the data downloaded from the USDN and the data Cliff had brought back from the Hull.

His first task was to set up algorithms, the logical sequence of precise descriptions for solving problems using mathematical operations and actions expressed in a language the computer understood.

The first problem Scott wanted to solve was a key one because it would tell Cliff whether the Gulf Stream would continue on its present course without the Hull, or stray dangerously in other directions.

In order for Scott to get the information he wanted from the surface to the bottom of the ocean, he needed millions of algorithms. Algorithms that would reveal the influence of pressure, of the weight of the water, of the Coriolis force, and the all-important angle of the slope of the Continental Shelf.

But Scott had experience with artificial intelligence, the technique computer scientists use to make their machines reason almost like human beings. AI would generate the millions of algorithms Scott had no time to prepare.

Enter the parallel computer. It first divided the algorithms according to problems, channeled them to numerous central processing units (CPU), then began printing the information at the ten-foot level.

"Cliff," Scott shouted in the direction of the intercom, "I have values for the fifty-foot level and it looks good."

The work progressed so well that Cliff began the twice-postponed task of reading the dossiers of the navy divers who had volunteered for the job of loading the drill holes.

After the fight with Fritz, diving triggered images of death, and the idea of sending young men into an underwater forest of long weeds transformed those images into horrible Dante-esque visions not wholly fantastic. Jacques Cousteau, the first oceanographer ever to see the weeds through a remote-controlled TV camera, had called them "an undulating, macabre sargasso of long, lamenting arms . . . reaching out like those of infernal souls."

Cliff also found the time to assemble a flotilla of special ships for Operation Drill and Load, a relatively easy task for someone with the organizational skill of a field marshal who had masterminded the Cabot expedition.

Pamela Wycoff walked in as he was reading, and Cliff offered to make her the "perfect" drink for the afternoon, a cappuccino.

"I'll be sorry when it's over," she said, settling into a large rattan chair. She was wearing a white blouse, a plaid woolen skirt, and a blue sweater over her shoulders. "This is the ideal academic life—no dishes, no shopping, no cooking."

Loading the finely ground coffee into the filter basket, Cliff listened with the strange sensation of hearing himself on playback, a string responding to the vibration of another playing the same note.

Perhaps it was the sharing of setbacks and the promise of success. Perhaps it was the sharing of such a big secret. Whatever, today she was a kindred spirit, one which he in a way resembled.

Cliff turned the lever to caffè, and soon the solarium filled with the pungent and spicy aroma of French-roast coffee.

He brought her a cup, put his on a small table, and sat facing her.

She said, "You do make good coffee, Cliff."

"Well, it's actually the machine," Cliff said. He leaned back in his chair and, cup in hand, allowed himself to study her. Pam was striking, with an oval face, widely spaced blue eyes with hints of green, and rich and abundant auburn hair. And how richly her body filled her clothes. He looked at her so admiringly and with so much desire that Pam dropped her eyes.

"Well, I must go back to my office," Pam said, licking the last bit of froth off the rim of the cup.

"Stay."

"You want me to make my deadline, right?"

Cliff put his cup down. "I do, but I also want to spend some time with you. I love you, Pam."

She looked at him with an expression of mellow tolerance. Perhaps it was inappropriate, but it was what she did. "Men are all alike. They fall in love as easily as they fall asleep," she said, but her tone lacked the accusing sting of the words.

Cliff sighed, feeling helpless under the spell of her eyes. "Don't you know there are times when it is only a woman that is indispensable in a man's life?"

She just looked at him, aware of the intensity of his feelings.

"It's true," he said, convinced that Pam fascinated him even more because she always found a way of frustrating his will. "But you keep resisting me," he added.

"I'm not," she protested with such an uneasy look that he pushed on.

"Woods Hole. Is that it?" He reached for her hand and held it firmly, a delicate, slender-fingered hand . . . smooth and creamy.

"In part . . ." Pam caught her breath and saw his head bend over and kiss her hand. "But soon," she continued, lips quivering almost imperceptibly, "we'll be facing an awful and dangerous future. Getting emotionally involved now would be a mistake, an added complication to the difficulties ahead."

"But that's precisely when people need each other," Cliff interrupted. "Let's face it together, Pam. Love eases the pain. I know I couldn't bear having you somewhere far away from me. I couldn't."

She hesitated. "Cliff, I like you but there is no room for love in my life right now. Things are too complicated already."

There was slow reluctance as she pulled her hand away. "Stay."

"I . . . it's late, Cliff. Time for work, don't you think?"

"See you at dinner?"

She didn't answer.

Cliff would never forget day seven.

He had finally begun to think he might be able to leave for the Hull ahead of schedule because of the progress made on the model and its preliminary positive results when the unimaginable happened.

It all started soon after midnight.

As usual, Scott was at his workstation but having a short break. He was nibbling on some left-over butter-fried shrimps and laughing as he read the poem the colleague who was running Scott's projects back in Cambridge had sent him via E-mail, the electronic mail automatically passed through computer networks by modems. Suddenly the *A*s in the lines began to streak down to the bottom of the monitor as if they were drops of condensation on a pane of glass.

OUR PROGRAM WHO ART IN MEMORY
HELLO BE THY NAME.
THY OPERATING SYSTEM COME,
THY COMMAND BE DONE . . .

Scott was petrified. "Oh, my God, no," he gasped. "Oh, no," he repeated. His eyes, aghast, were riveted on the *B*s as they began to drip away slowly.

His first reaction was that a hacker at M.I.T. had broken the encryption program Scott had written to protect his files. "Whoever the fuck you are I'll find you, you bastard," he muttered.

The truth, however, was that the "cracker" was at Georgetown University. A year earlier he had cracked the password for the USDN and was using the network to tap data from the United States Weather Bureau in order to have weather maps displayed on his screen even before they appeared on television. It was an illegal tap, but harmless.

During the last four days, the cracker had noticed that a new account was using the network—Scott downloading the USDN network. Believing it to be another cracker that might spoil things for him, he decided to foul the information Scott was receiving.

Dim-eyed from the long hours of work, Scott kept watching the monitor, anticipating what might happen next. But nothing did. After a while the monitor filled with the rest of the poem.

This worried Scott, for he knew that crackers always left something behind—usually a logic bomb, a program that disorganizes algorithms or causes some other destructive function.

Being the computer wizard he was, it wasn't difficult for him to run through some tests first, and discover that the data already processed had symptoms of An Infected Disk Syndrome (AIDS).

Specifically, he noticed that the bathymetric data, for example, seemed to be infected with a decaflop virus, a program that automatically rounded off numbers after the decimal point to ten.

Not much, to be sure. But because the data had gone through millions and millions of operations, the error had become dangerously magnified.

The ultimate humiliation.

It was time to call Cliff.

"You silicone nerd . . ." Cliff walked out of his bedroom, putting on his bathrobe and feeling that the whole operation was jinxed.

Leaning against a Digital minicomputer, he listened as Scott told him what had happened and debated with himself whether he should fire him first and decide what to do about his replacement later.

He decided against it. After all, Scott was the best computer modeler. All right, he had been broken into, but nothing was safe these days. Probably not even the house they were in. And he had learned long ago that one had to keep his cool if one hoped to see things in their proper perspective.

He heard Scott say: "I should've worked on the encryption program longer. But I said to myself: two days is plenty."

"You did your best," Cliff said, and found enough generosity of spirit to put a reassuring hand on Scott's shoulder. "Forget it. It's done with," he said, "but tell me what's next and please say it in plain English."

One corner of Scott's mouth moved up into a slight smile of relief. "Obviously I must rewrite another encryption program, then run more tests. As far as the rest," Scott said, "actually, it's a rather interesting problem. You see, Cliff," he added, seemingly fully recovered from the setback, "a constant error means a bug with only one infecting feature. Easy to find, easy to fix. I'll detail my plans off line."

"Plain English, I said."

"Later, I mean."

"That's fine. Now answer this: how much time do you need to get back to the stage you were at before you got raped?"

Scott hesitated. "Couple of days," he answered not too audibly.

"Two days? Do you know how many holes the *Challenger* can drill in two days?" Cliff hit his forehead with the palm of a hand. "Jesus!"

Scott seemed not to hear him. "I also need some kosher data, especially density data, that would tell me whether I'm still inside the ballpark or outside." He pointed to a monitor filled with rows of numbers and added, "Something to compare these with."

Cliff tightened the belt of his bathrobe. "You go to work, I'll get you the data."

"Super. Where can you get it?"

"From the vault of the Department of the Interior."

As Cliff waited for the director of documents to break the seal of the impounded file cabinet at the Department of the Interior, his eyes focused on a black notebook hanging under the red-and-blue Civil Defense emblem. He reached for it and opened it to the first page: *What You Should Know About Nuclear Power and Nuclear War.* He flipped through it casually. One sketch and a photograph called his attention. It was that of the Interior Department building in relation to ground zero (Andrews Air Force Base), the radioactive fallout, the predicted condition of the building. What intrigued him more was the photograph just below the sketch. It showed the crater created by an underground ten-kiloton explosion. It was enormous, as if dug up by a huge meteor. Using the dimensions of a trailer truck parked near the rim of the crater as a reference, Cliff guessed at those of the crater itself—about 6,000 feet in diameter, 800 to 1,200 feet deep. He was awestruck. *Lord, and that was only a ten-kiloton bomb, a small bomb*, he thought.

A swift train of thoughts flashed through his mind. Faded. Flashed again, brighter. *Blow the Hull with nukes*, went the voice in his head.

Eyes fixed in a stare, his expression froze in a mid-frown. All he could think of was the report to the president he had read at the picnic. A series of images blurred his vision: food shortages, violence, life in the nomadic community. . . .

Nukes? Yes! YES!

But what about radiation?

It was madness. Nuclear bombs were concrete, apocalyptic devices that could destroy the world.

What if the model showed that they were practical? They stopped a war. They could stop glaciation!

Rolling whales wasn't a very good idea at first.

Cliff stalked about the porch like a restless ghost. He had been there in the morning chill for two hours, considering the pros and cons of nukes. His only desire was to come up with a decision that for two days had eluded him.

Nothing distracted him—not food, not work, not even Pam's company. The strategy of using nukes clung to him like a burr. If he opted for nuclear blasting, it would solve the problems of time, number of shot holes, the logistics of transporting tons of TNT, and wiring and priming them under the threat of sharks and weeds.

That much, at least, worked in his favor.

He stood by the screen door, seeming as tall and still as an obelisk. Only his eyes moved, calculating. To explode dozens of nukes could induce more powerful seaquakes, higher tidal waves, start bigger magma flows. It was a madman's scheme.

One hour later, he was still there running his fingers through his hair. He had made his decision, yet he did not dare to act.

Then, suddenly, he knew there was nothing else for him

to do but go to the Princeton University Nuclear Research
Center and get all the facts.

Unlike his previous trip to Boston, the helicopter flight
to Princeton was eventful because he could see how quickly
things were changing.

The skies above him were the skies of autumn, filled
with migrating birds and dark clouds edged with translucent
outlines.

Below him he noticed that the leaves of trees lining Route
95 just south of Philadelphia had lost their sheen and looked
tired, the way they do at the end of the summer. Lawns had
a yellowish patina, public swimming pools had few bathers,
traffic was heavy in the southbound direction—the opposite
direction it moved during the summer.

Cliff met with Professor Ifraim Gallego, a tall, clean-
looking man with a neat hairline moustache who wouldn't
have been out of place in a bullfighter's suit of lights. He
had become an overnight household name when he had
proposed to open a canal in the Israeli occupied zone of the
Sinai Peninsula using nuclear bombs. This second "door,"
Gallego had believed, would have given the West access to
the Red Sea in case Egypt again blocked the Suez Canal.
The proposal, which received a most favorable response,
had been shelved when Egypt and Israel signed a peace
treaty in 1979.

The shelving had so depressed Gallego that he spent
months in a hospital to recover from severe depression
and a nervous breakdown. His plan for the canal would
have been a proof of the safe and practical use of nuclear
energy.

Calmly, Gallego put a cigarette in a gold-tipped holder
and leaned back in his chair. "My dear fellow"—pure con-
descension, Cliff thought—"the use of nuclear devices isn't
just practical. It's cheaper, less bulky, easier to handle, and
in many cases safer than TNT," he said, lisping slightly.
"Just consider this: one one-hundred-kiloton device the

size of a butane bottle of gas equals two hundred truckloads of dynamite sticks." He stopped to light his cigarette with a slim Dunhill. "That's quite a ratio."

Cliff ignored the tone of superiority. "What about radiation?"

"Radiation?" Gallego repeated, and swiveled in his chair to face the Einstein Physics Lab, visible through the window to his right. "My dear fellow, in that building," he said, pointing, "there is enough radiation to incinerate everybody from here to Chicago. But it's contained in man-made vessels—as it is in all nuclear subs."

"Yes, I know," Cliff said, "but in my case . . ."

Gallego grinned with grating tolerance. "In your case, my dear fellow . . ."

"Cliff." He smiled.

"Cliff," he began again. "In your case we aren't just talking about an underground explosion," he said, and sunshine broke across his face. "We are talking about an underground explosion . . . *underwater*. In other words, an explosion contained within a vessel—the Hull—which is itself contained within a bigger, God-created vessel. The ocean, I mean." He paused and concluded: "So, the little radiation that fails to get locked into the melted rock will be dissipated by the best dissipator of all, the billions of cubic feet of water passing over the detonation site." He smiled broadly, revealing his evenly capped teeth.

It was his lucky day. "I see, I see," Cliff replied hesitantly, not believing his luck. Gallego's words, he thought, were like a benediction.

Even before Cliff could breathe with relief, Gallego said: "Dissipated, that is, if the mushroom cloud doesn't rise above the surface of the water. Only the precise knowledge of displacement power and weight of the water will keep the mushroom down."

Christ! Can't a day go by without ifs? Cliff nodded. And if the charges were too powerful, there was also the danger of starting a massive magma flow.

"You realize," Gallego went on with killing frankness,

"that if the cloud is permitted to rise, winds might carry the radiation eastward—toward the United States."

"It all boils down to math. Isn't that it?"

"Yes."

"In that case, I have the best mathematician in the world—Adrian Scott."

Gallego nodded. "The genius at M.I.T.'s Artificial Intelligence Lab. In that case, it all boils down to him."

They talked, theorized, planned.

Later, in the faculty lounge, where they went for some refreshments, Cliff asked Gallego to join the team.

Gallego thanked Cliff, then said: "As a student of Keller, it's my duty to continue his crusade on behalf of the peaceful use of nuclear power and . . ." His words faded away to an academic drone. "I come from an old line of conquistadores," he concluded with pride, "the Gallegos from Valencia, and you are giving me the opportunity to conquer the fear of nuclear power. I accept."

"And the nukes?" Cliff asked

"Test devices. I mean assemblies of nuclear and other explosive materials and fuses normally used in tests. Small charges. One to three kilotons, I would guess, fired in groups of three or four at predetermined intervals."

Cliff nodded. "Comparatively speaking, what—"

"*Little Boy*, the uranium bomb dropped on Hiroshima had an explosive power of 13 kilotons."

Cliff exhaled a long sigh of relief. "Small devices, indeed."

"Yes, that's why they are perfect for our purpose." Gallego put his index finger up. "*If* they fit inside the drill holes."

19

Nobody in the administration was really surprised when it happened, certainly not the president.

It was late afternoon, and at Dulles Airport crews rushed to taxi an Aeroflot jetliner to ramp 16.

Inside the international terminal, TV technicians were setting up lights and microphones with the feverish anticipation of a media first.

Six miles away, a motorcade of three cars bearing the diplomatic plates of the Russian embassy and two police motorcycle escorts snaked along Dulles Airport access. In the first car rode Sergei Sovenko, the Russian ambassador who was suddenly returning to Moscow for "consultation" with his government, according to the communiqué released to the press by the embassy shortly before noon.

Speculation ran high—it ran even higher after the first secretary of the embassy phoned the director of the National Press Club and told him that the ambassador would hold a press conference at the airport.

"Mr. Sovenko's Departure Linked to Military Buildup in Caspian Sea," began the lead story in the special edition of the *Washington Post*. In the Oval Office, the president sat

238

feeling utterly defeated. Neither FCC nor State Department experts could find ways of keeping the ambassador from holding his televised press conference, scheduled to begin at eight P.M. that evening. Prime time.

Gate 16 served as the conference room. Lesser-known reporters and journalists jockeyed for better positions. In the forefront were the popular veteran newsmen from the major TV networks.

Lights burned, cameras rolled, and 95 million TV screens filled with the image of the energetic diplomat taking his place in front of a wall of microphones.

Without preambles the ambassador nodded to a reporter from ABC News, and he fired the first question:

"Mr. Ambassador, is the considerable buildup of troops along the shore of the Caspian Sea an indication that the military is running your country? You must admit that the political situation there is far from stable. And, sir, isn't this a violation of the SALT One agreement, especially with regard to the limitations of troop movements allowed under the provisions of that agreement?"

The ambassador spoke through his interpreter. "My country has never violated any agreement. The troops in question are not combat but logistic units—communications vans, for the most part. I'm sure your spy satellites are revealing that. Anyhow, the units have been transferred not for military reasons but for what has been known for some time: namely, the predicted rapid fall in temperatures and its catastrophic consequences." The interpreter put his mouth closer to the microphone and said: "In short, glaciation."

Another reporter said to the interpreter, "You wanted to say a rise in temperatures because of the greenhouse effect, right?"

The interpreter, irritated, repeated himself. "I said 'fall.' "

The reporters frowned, giving each other questioning glances.

From the back a man spoke up. "I'm sorry, did you say glassation?"

The interpreter leaned very close to the microphones. "I said gla-ci-ation, a short—"

"Do you mean a short *ice age?*" a front-row reporter interrupted.

The ambassador, nodding like a pigeon, answered, "Yes, yes."

"Hold goddamn commercial. Close in on interpreter," the news director at ABC control room ordered.

At Gate 16, reporters rushed for the few public phones.

The show had the vibration of an earthquake about it.

Washington shuddered.

Public reaction proceeded at first with chaos, then with the coherence of an unstoppable tragedy. High-ranking officials—mostly congressmen and senators—appeared on television to calm the people. But no one paid attention to them. Most Americans were convinced that since they had not been told the truth about the icebergs, they should act according to their own sense of survival. "It smells bad. I'm going to Florida. What the hell, I only rent a small apartment," a tubby New York nurse told her friend.

Like a knife blade, the show severed trust from reality.

At the White House, limousines, like bees at the end of the day, were returning with media specialists and advisers picked up by presidential request. There, after a brief meeting, the official position of the government was decided upon: To play down the importance of the Russian ambassador's TV appearance, the president would go on the air with a simple prepared statement intended to buy time in view of the forthcoming choice of climate modifier. And, notwithstanding NSC head James Sellwood's opposition, the president ordered the mobilization of key military units.

On the following day, the National Guard was called out as a crowd-control force. But the action backfired. The sight of soldiers in battle gear confirmed the speculation of an imminent war in the minds of those who believed that glaciation would lead to world war in the Middle East.

As expected, the stock market reacted with a drop of 305 points, with southern utilities and real estate companies in the south posting impressive gains. On the commodity exchange, wheat jumped five dollars a bushel from the previous close. Gold rose sixty dollars an ounce; at Wilson in New York, diamonds sold at one-third the price per carat higher. Firearms of all kinds sold with any price tags, as did camping equipment, dry food, batteries, canned fruit, and cans of high-protein supplements such as Sustacal and Ensure. Gasoline went up fifty cents a gallon, motor oil thirty cents a quart. By three in the afternoon, life-sustaining drugs such as NPH-U100, Tenormin, and Digoxin disappeared from shelves.

In Europe, prices dropped sharply on London's Royal Exchange and on the Borsa di Milano during a day of "neurotic trading," as E. F. Hutton's chief account executive in Paris put it. But at the Banco Nacional de Mexico in Tijuana and the Banco Comercial de Costa Rica, tellers offered an incredible 12 percent interest to American depositors.

On Monday evening the president held his televised press conference, and for the first time since he came to the White House, a makeup artist was called to work on his tired face. Reading the statement speech writers had drafted and redrafted for two days, the president alluded to a "mild" seasonal reversal taking place in the Arctic region. With unusual calm, he answered a total of nine questions from reporters, all restatements of what he had read earlier.

His calm was only for the cameras. Now, an hour later, the president paced in his private study on the third floor of the White House. The chief of staff, Kronin, and Sellwood were with him for the post-mortem. Dimmed floor lamps cast a weak, pale light on the scene, and especially on the president, who looked as faded as twilight itself. Earlier, he had complained to the chief of staff that the crisis demanded that he think clearly, but that urgent dispatches had interrupted him constantly.

Still, he seemed pleased to hear that according to inform-
ers within the press corps, he had achieved what he had
hoped.

"Yes, you have bought the time you needed," Sellwood
said. "But I also believe that the mobilization was a mistake.
Americans now have both a war and a deep freeze to worry
about."

"But the Russian embassy has a new cipher code, and
four nuclear subs have quietly left Russian ports. Isn't that
indication enough that the Russians are up to something?"

"Perhaps, but I'm sure they'll try something non-military
first."

Squinting, the president said to Sellwood in a ruminating
voice, "You know . . . the only time those bastard Russians
ever let the cat out of the bag was the day before their two
orbiting spacecraft successfully linked. Some cockiness!"
Then, turning to Kronin, seated on a couch opposite him,
he asked, "Could it mean the Russians have a surefire
modifier?" He sipped his scotch and water.

"Well . . . ," Kronin answered, and thumbed his eyeglasses up, "if the radio interference continues, it will mean that.
Years ago they started working on thermodiffusers, heat
exchangers allegedly fueled by nuclear power—possibly
fusion. The Russians are very secretive. They share little
with the world even now."

"And we don't have a surefire modifier?" It was the
feisty, craggy-faced chief of staff. He had been casting
worried glances at the president.

Nobody said anything.

"Well?" the president prodded, still facing Kronin.

"The Russians have spent more money on climate control
than we have," Kronin answered. "However, our computer technology is far ahead of theirs." He shrugged. "So,
what you lose on the Ferris wheel you make up on the
merry-go-round."

"Dr. Kronin," Sellwood asked, "what if there are
delays?"

A phone rang. The chief of staff answered it.

"Then," Kronin continued on, "the evacuation of some cities and towns will be inevitable. What alternative is there?"

Ice cubes tinkled in the president's glass. "That means that D.C. will have to evacuate before Philadelphia, Philadelphia before New York, and New York before Boston—all using the same north-south highway. I can imagine the traffic jams and the fights already," he said, his voice faltering.

Kronin nodded. "The direction of the exodus and the sheer number of vehicles make it a very good possibility. And there are other unsettling predictions," he said, and paused.

The president closed his eyes, as if expecting a blow. "Go on."

"Breakdowns should close at least one lane on major highways; ice and snow some of the other lanes." He shook his head. "And why not? The problem with evacuation plans is that they create illusions, not solutions. However, I'm sure the Russians will have their hands full, too. All boats rise and fall with the tide. But . . . ," he began hesitantly, "what worries me most is the unstable situation in what was once the Soviet Union. So, if we wake up tomorrow and find the Kremlin in the hands of a general who had the wisdom to get out of bed first and who also happens to be a hawk, we may have him to worry about, too."

Suddenly the president rose from his rocking chair and walked to the tall window. It was a self-protective habit that his staff and friends recognized as one calling for silence.

Those behind him stood motionless, drink in hand, silent as their own shadow on the floor. Rain hummed against the skylight overhead.

"You'll be confident with the choice of modifier, Mr. President," Kronin said, barely managing to remove the thrill of alarm his tone had before.

The president turned. "I'd better be."

Professor Orville Marshall rode through Cape Race in a Jeep with his assistant and driver.

"My God," he cried out, smiling broadly. "I have waited all my life for the opportunity to put the stream to better use and now I have it." He waved the dispatch he had received from the U.S. Army Transportation Corps.

A long column of trailer tractors moving toward the shore, carrying cassoni, came into view.

He pointed to it. "With the other two thousand trailers the army has put at my disposal, I'll have no problems setting up my modification before the arrival of the polar ice sheet." He nudged his driver with an elbow. "Step on the gas, Lou."

Near Toque, Quebec, five hundred miles to the northwest, black rats were moving, spurred by a migration instinct seemingly as powerful as a battle cry.

"The furrows of the potato field," Miriam Oswald told the police by phone, "seem to move like the waves of a black lake. They are huge, I tell you. Huge and ugly. What do I do?"

A surge of panic rose within her as she spoke. In a few seconds the sight of the black beasts had reduced her from the woman who "did the work of three men," to a quivering mass of hysteria. "Quick, tell me, what do I do? Tell me, tell me."

"Just close front and back doors," the police sergeant said calmly, "and make sure all windows are closed, then take some steel wool and put it around the drainpipe under the kitchen sink and into any other openings they could get through. Make sure there's no way they can get in. You have steel wool, don't you?"

"Oh, yes. Jack used to keep lots of it down in the garage."

"Is the garage door closed?"

"Yes."

"Good. Now, do what I've told you and don't hang up. I'll be right here. Okay?"

"Yes. Thank you."

Shaking, walking tentatively as if the floor were about to cave in, Miriam passed by the fireplace to pick up an iron stoker, then opened the door in the hall leading down to the garage.

She put the light on and looked around. No rats anywhere. She walked to the workbench and quickly grabbed the package of steel wool resting on top of an old radio. She raced upstairs, closed the door.

"I have the steel wool, Sergeant."

"Good, Miriam. Now, start by packing the hole around the kitchen drainpipe."

It was as if the rats had been listening in on the conversation, for Miriam, kneeling, pressed her ear to the kitchen cabinet door and heard nothing.

"I'm opening the cabinet door," she yelled, in the direction of the phone resting on a chair near her.

At that instant, about a dozen black rats jumped on her. Miriam fell backward, letting out a long scream, then covered her face with both hands and froze.

"Miriam?"

No answer came.

20

How to convince the team to use nukes? That was the question in Cliff's mind since he left Princeton University.

As he saw it, the team was a microcosm of the larger body of presidential advisers who would make the ultimate decision. If the team went along with the idea of nuclear blasting, the advisers might follow suit.

Two days later Gallego arrived at the safe house, and Cliff immediately asked the others to come and meet the Princeton University professor who was going to help with the model.

Once the introductions were made and everybody settled down around the library's conference table, Cliff asked the team to brief Gallego on what they were building and to "state in realistic terms what the chances of succeeding in executing the modification" were.

Adams, who talked about the geological components of the model, reiterated what he had been telling Cliff. Namely, that it would be impossible to blow up the Hull in its entirety because there wasn't sufficient time to drill the number of holes his model called for. "And that's too bad, because now that the cat is out of the bag people will panic even if the forecast is only for rain. I've been listening to some of the talk shows. I know how scared they are. And," he groused, "that's too bad, because Cliff's plan for a CLIMOD isn't just good, it's great."

Pam echoed Adams's words. Then she added that from her point of view, the modification would not change the volume of water. Therefore, all carbon dioxide–using organisms would continue to bind this gas into their own bodies and keep it in check. "Bottom line," she said, "no appreciable environmental impact. The Atlantic will continue to control the weather. Ecologically speaking, however, I'm very much concerned about detonating tons of TNT inside a delicate biosphere. I'm worried about triggering tragic events in the food chain. There may be a way to prevent them by seeding the area with acoustic devices. I don't know yet."

A mathematical model and a visualization of it was what he was working on, Scott told Gallego. "I'm days behind because I goofed, but if all goes well, Cliff will be able to see the mathematical problem as a three-dimensional display that will be a close approximation of reality. I'm excited about it."

"I forgot to tell you, Ifraim," Cliff added, "that to analyze the modification with a water tank model would've been difficult because there is no way of preventing dyes that simulate flow fields from mixing with the water. So, the virtual reality model is all we've got." He didn't sound excited about it.

Gallego thanked each one, then turned to face Cliff and waited.

Without preambles Cliff said, "Suppose we only needed a fifth of the drill holes because uranium is vastly more effective than TNT?"

"You mean nuclear power?" Scott said, aghast.

"Yes, Adrian. Nuclear blasting. Why not?"

Taken by surprise, Scott didn't answer, and Cliff repeated the question. Then added, "If you're thinking about radiation, let me tell you that there will be only small amounts—whatever little escapes from an underground nuclear test."

Still no reaction.

It was not enough for Cliff.

"What do you say?" he asked, turning to Adams.

Adams raised his arms. "What do I say? An hour ago I was frustrated because there were too many holes to drill. Now you tell me that we need to drill only a fifth of them. I say yes—if we can bang on the wall without knocking it down." He shook his head incredulously. "Nuclear blasting! Is that what we are considering on top of everything else? I don't believe it."

"Well, if you come right down to it, we are facing a mindless enemy," Scott said, his voice low and serious. "We can either lose the battle with the ice or win the war with thermonuclear heat. Let's nuke."

Everybody turned to Pam. "I'm not surprised by what is being proposed here because when scientists think of CLIMODs, they think the unimaginable," she said, and paused. "For now, I say yes."

That was it. The team had accepted the idea of nuclear blasting! Cliff nodded, rendered speechless by a strong sense of unreality. "All's fair in war," he said, looking at Scott, and felt his knees go weak.

The divers—the other hurdle.

It was time to pick those who would load the drill holes. In turbulent water—worse, in a jungle of long weeds. Worse yet, while handling explosives.

Cliff excused himself and left the library. But in the corridor he found it hard to walk into the living room and meet the divers.

Two days ago, the color picture of Jeremy P. Nelson had wrenched Cliff's heart as he read through his dossier. "Skip" had a baby face and an innocent smile that seemed to leap out at him. And his eyes, a pair of inquisitive, jade green eyes, had stared at him even from the passport-sized photograph.

His record had also leaped out at him: mine removal in the Persian Gulf; training with dolphins; rescue of the crew of a sunken minisubmarine. . . . "Excellent diver," Skip's last commanding officer had written in the personnel evaluation section of the dossier, "hard worker, resourceful, and very curious. I recommend that he be promoted to . . ." The word *curious*, Cliff noticed, was underlined.

"You must be Skip," Cliff said, shaking his hand. He was the youngest-looking but highest-ranking member of the UDT (Underwater Demolitions Team) standing in front of the living room fireplace.

"Indeed I am, man—I mean, sir." He smiled—a smart-ass little grin.

"What do you like besides diving?"

Skip smiled suggestively.

"But women are expensive."

Skip shrugged. "But diving pay is good now, and when I get out of this outfit, it will be too good to be true. A cool two hundred bucks a day welding the underwater tunnel between Boston and its airport." He snapped his fingers. "Good, easy bucks."

"When will you start?"

"In a year, two months, and . . . thirteen days, sir."

"If we stop glaciation . . ."

"You don't know me or the other guys of the UDT."

Cliff studied him. "One more question."

"Shoot." Skip looked confident.

"Why did you volunteer, knowing how dangerous the mission would be?" Cliff asked.

"Because, sir, diving is all I know and I do it well. Right, guys?" Skip looked at the others, who nodded.

"And you're Anthony," Cliff said to the boy on Skip's left with the look of a mean-street survivor and eyes so penetrating they could've been ice picks. His dossiers had read something like Skip's: foster parents; high school diploma through a correspondence course; mine removal in the

Persian Gulf; twelve dives over a "classified" site (a sunken nuclear submarine). "Fast worker with the tendency to rush," his last crew chief had noted.

"Yes, sir. Anthony Baldi."

"What got you into this business?"

"Well," he answered, "the attention you get from everybody during a dive, I guess—like what a boxer gets between rounds and . . ."

"And the money. Say it," Skip nudged him with an elbow.

"What will you do when you get out of the navy? Commercial diving, too?" Cliff asked.

"No, sir. I'd like to open a certified air station. Sell diving equipment, give lessons. Well, you know the sort of business."

"I do. Treasure hunters multiply by the week. A good business, to be sure. Good luck."

Cliff moved along. "And you are . . ."

After he had met and talked to each one individually he said to them all: "How long have you been together?"

Skip answered for the others. "For so long that we can sense if one of us is in trouble just by the way bubbles behave."

How many times Cliff had watched Fritz's bubble rate of escape to see if it was regular or irregular, this last one a sure sign of trouble!

"You're real divers," he said, and they nudged each other, cocky and sure.

Cliff said good-bye to the divers and from his office he phoned Jackson and learned that the *Glomar Explorer* had gotten through the Panama Canal. "Apparently, the Russians decided not to risk a serious incident by scuttling a freighter while it was in one of the locks," Phil Jackson said, his voice a bit distorted by the scrambler phone. "But," he continued, "the *Dokholov* is still very much in the picture."

"How so?"

"The CIA says that a known Russian scientist by the name of . . . Konlikov, I spell it . . ."

"You don't have to, Phil. I know of him."

"Good. Well, according to the CIA, Konlikov has boarded the *Dokholov*."

"Phil?"

"Yes."

"Ask the Coast Guard to track her and to report to me here. Thanks."

Cliff hung up.

A minute later, he called the deputy chief of naval operations and told him to send a fleet to the Florida Strait. "Sub tenders, old machine shops, crane barges, anything. Konlikov must be made to think that we are interested in the area where the stream begins to form."

Still holding the receiver, he called Kronin and set up a date for the second half of his presentation. "A week from today," Cliff said, "and I promise you no postponements."

The weather began to change. Drastically.

Along Chesapeake Bay a strange, thin fog would roll in now from the sea just before noon. And for hours, houses, trees, and people looked as if seen through a thin curtain. Then, about three hours later, as the fog lifted, the sky would break into thin and wispy clouds that to children looked like endless layers of gray spun sugar. At dusk, as the temperature dropped to near freezing, the fog would roll in again. This time denser than before and with ice crystals forming luminous bluish halos around streetlights.

Clinton, Ontario, is a long way from Washington.

There, two inches of snow had fallen during the night, and more of it was in the forecast.

"How much more?" Debbie Howlett asked, turning the radio off. A nurse at St. Claire Hospital, Debbie was home because she had decided to move her six-year-old daughter stricken with bronchial asthma to Atlanta, Georgia, where her former husband was working.

A plump, happy-faced young woman in her late twenties, Debbie thought of going to the bank to withdraw the four thousand plus dollars she had in her account. She had cashed her paycheck two days before, but she knew it wouldn't take her far.

Not wanting to leave Janie alone, she bundled her up and drove off with her.

Clinton was a typical provincial city, a hodgepodge of commercial and residential areas with an occasional high-rise building, narrow streets, and railroad tracks going in all directions.

As Debbie approached downtown, she turned right on Victoria Avenue and slowed down. Behind her, a TransCanada locomotive came blowing its whistle ahead of a long train of boxcars.

"Is there an accident up ahead?" she asked, waving at a motorist going in the opposite direction but waiting for the train to pass.

"Nope. That's the line for the drive-in teller. It's the only one open at this hour."

"I know that. But are you sure this is the line to it."

The motorist, a spiky redhead, nodded.

"Ten blocks long?" Her words reflected shock.

"That's why I've turned around," he said. "I've already wasted a quarter of a tank of gas—and there isn't much left of it in Clinton. Esso up ahead is closed, so is BP."

Debbie glanced at her gas meter—almost half. "Say, who's got gas, do you know?"

"Richy."

"By the skating rink?"

"That's him. I'd hurry, though."

She thanked the man and remained in line. Two blocks in thirty minutes. The needle of the gas meter had hardly moved—almost half. But she knew it wasn't accurate. It moved faster once past the halfway point. "How're you doing, little one?" she asked her daughter as she began to ponder the question of whether she should go to Richy's and get gas or stay in line. "We'll be home soon, all right?"

From the backseat came a wheezy "Yes, Mom."

"Go to sleep, now. I'll wake you up at McDonald's. All right?" Debbie turned and put a blanket over her child and checked to see if she had a fever. She didn't. Thank God for that.

She moved another ten feet. Perhaps gas is more important than money, she thought. Besides, there is a branch of La Banque de Quebec in Sudbury . . . but why lose my place in this line? She shut off the engine to save gas, then turned it on again when the people behind her honked when she didn't move.

At Richy's there was a line but also gas. A green flag on top of a pump was still flapping in the wind.

Debbie reached for her Visa card.

"No Visa," the attendant said, unscrewing the cap of the gas tank. For a moment Debbie was too annoyed to speak, mouth twisted in exasperation. "And why not? You've taken it before."

"Cash or move along."

"Okay . . . okay, cash. But why no Visa?"

As if thinking aloud, the attendant answered, "Are you kidding or what? It will be at least three weeks before I get the money from the Visa bank. By then there'll be ten feet of snow here. Do you know what's going on, eh? How much gas?"

Debbie hesitated, then gave him the money.

The attendant counted it. "Fifty. Ten gallons coming up."

They filled the tank.

Debbie drove off cursing herself for having gone to work after the Russian ambassador made the announcement. *Who do you think you are, Florence Nightingale*? she asked herself.

"We had better go home, Janie. I'll make something good and hot for mommy's little . . ."

Debbie thought of something.

She grabbed her cellular phone and dialed Mountain Properties Real Estate. Busy.

She pushed the redial button. Busy.

Finally someone answered.

"Marge? Debbie Howlett. I'm short of cash and I need some money fast. I'm putting the condo up for a quick sale. Anything you—"

"You and a hundred like you. Besides, we're closing." The phone went dead. It was like a slap in the face and it left her bewildered and a little frightened.

Traffic was slow on Northern Avenue. She turned the radio on to her favorite talk show. " . . . *oh, yes, ma'am, it's true. Clinton has six big snowplows, but only one operator today. All the others have reported in sick. Five of them! How do you like that? . . . Yes, sir, you are on radio. What's that again? Turn your radio off, then ask the same question. Vasotec? For blood pressure? I don't know. Have you tried Shoppers Drug Mart? Then try the Clinton Council for the Aged, all right? . . . Good evening, ma'am. You're . . .*

Seven-thirty P.M. Home.

After a quick supper, Debbie began packing—everything that felt like wool, old parkas and ski pants, socks, earmuffs. Then she filled two large cardboard boxes with all the canned goods in the kitchen cabinets, and every prescription bottle she could find.

Having loaded the car, she went around collecting documents, jewelry, flashlights, her daughtier's medical file. But there were no Sterno cans. Damn it all!

It was four in the morning when she stretched out in her bed, still fully dressed.

Two hours later she left the condo without even checking to see if she had locked it.

As it had been forecast, snow was falling again. But thirty miles an hour, she thought, wasn't bad for a single-lane country road leading to the highway.

Yes, maybe she could be on the other side of the Saint Lawrence River before midnight, after all. She had a full tank, the car was new, and her child's asthma seemed to have eased.

But right away she ran into problems.

As she approached the up ramp, she saw a hand-painted sign tacked on the side of a Royal Canadian Air Force van that read in English and French: Attention: Fast Lanes One and Two Are Closed to *ALL* Civilian Motor Vehicles Due to Priority Military Wide-Load Traffic. Violators Will Be Court-Martialed on the Spot.

"My God," Debbie gasped on seeing the snail trail of trucks, buses, tractors, vans, mobile homes, recreational vehicles, and trailers of all descriptions stretching for miles along Route 1A South. The automobile in front of her was so heavily laden with passengers and bundles perilously tied on the roof that the muffler scraped on the pavement. Motorcycles were the only vehicles that moved faster than fifteen miles an hour.

There were even abandoned cars, some with steam billowing from under the open hood. A gang of youths was cannibalizing one of them for the tires and battery.

The air echoed with long engine grunts and growls, blasting horns, the loud sputter from cars that had lost their mufflers, the unending screeching, and the piercing sirens of military vehicles ahead of long platform trucks with plainly visible missiles.

Driving was difficult because the braking distance between vehicles was a few feet, often less because of drivers constantly shifting lanes. There were rear-end collisions by the hundreds. Emotions ran high.

Debbie passed by two motorists having a fight. One had a knife. She looked straight ahead, right foot on the brake pedal. But where were the police?

"Mom, I've got to go to the bathroom."

Oh, God, not now, Debbie fretted. They'd never get back into line if she pulled over. "Hang on, Janie."

"But I've got to go."

"Just a little while more."

Repent, read a sign on the other side of the Route 3 overpass.

Another, with an arrow pointing to a tent in the parking lot of St. Stephen Episcopal Church said, *Survivalist Service Every Hour.*

There were more signs ten miles north of Sudbury, and more closely spaced. They announced special sales of tents, camping equipment, lanterns, firearms, kerosene stoves, axes, hand saws, inflatable mattresses. Still further, vendors stopped to barter with motorists. They ran when traffic moved and shouted "bargain prices" for knives, fishing rods, seeds, hoes, candles, Sterno cans, army pup tents, insect repellants, dried food, powdered milk.

Prices were high: thirty-five dollars for a six-pack of baby food, fifty for a tube of dental adhesive, seventy-five for a box of sanitary napkins.

"And just where the hell do you think you're gonna find a highway supermarket where you're gonna buy toilet paper, eh?" a melon-breasted woman shouted to Debbie. "In the States," she went on, "they're askin' thirty bucks, shithead." She held the roll of paper in front of Debbie as if it were a bouquet of cut flowers. "Twenty bucks, or nothin'," she shouted.

One booth of many that lined the road sold only Howard Ruff's survival books. Another was full of large white boxes with the handwritten words: Survival Kits $3,500.

Shotgun prices began at $6,000.

A Handy House could be used for thirty dollars, but those who used them—mostly women—were often forced to wait in line as long as an hour.

There were sellers everywhere. Loudmouthed knickknack vendors between lanes, well-dressed condo salesmen by the side of the road, leather-jacketed youths weaving in and out of cars with auto parts, cigarettes, birth-control pills, condoms.

Debbie shook her head. *I don't believe it. This is bizarre— a carnival.*

And a mile from the Sudbury exit, a bald-headed man with a beak of a nose shouted the same verses from the Bible over and over with the aid of a bullhorn: "God looks from heaven upon the children of man to see whether there is anyone who knows and seeks God. There is none who does good. *There is not even one*. God looks from heaven . . ."

Forget going to the bank, Debbie, she told herself. *Keep moving. You have a half a tank. . . . There will be plenty of money where you're going.*

"Mom. I really got to go. I can't wait."

There was an old weigh station up on a hill and Debbie inched her way to it behind other cars. She took out a Kleenex from her glove compartment and gave it to her daughter. "That's all we've got."

It took Debbie one hour to get back in traffic. And on entering the Algonquin Provincial Park, snow began to fall heavily. Visibility was poor. Twice she got within inches of hitting the bus in front of her. Getting into an accident now would certainly be the end. Her fear got more uncontrollable by the mile. *Keep your head, Debbie! Stay awake!* She opened her Thermos bottle and managed to have some coffee without spilling any of it.

Florida Real Estate Five Miles, had been painted on the side of a railroad bridge.

Debbie drove on, wondering if those living in Florida were on their knees thanking God for their good fortune. Probably not. People get used to good luck. Anyhow, luck is coquettish, she mused. She comes to you if you don't run after her.

It was getting dark. Now the strain of constantly watching the taillights of the bus in front of her and its hypnotic effect was playing havoc with Debbie's concentration. And she could feel her lids getting heavier. Her right leg had pins and needles, and it felt as if it no longer belonged to her. She realized she'd have to stop and get some sleep. An hour would do.

There were a half dozen vehicles inside the next rest area, and Debbie pulled in behind the last one. It was dark there. Headlights were off because, to save gas, none of the engines were running.

Debbie gave Janie some cookies and milk, set a portable alarm clock, which she placed on top of the dashboard, and curled against the high pile of clothes on the passenger seat. Almost at once she fell asleep.

It couldn't have been more than five minutes later that the occupant of the van in front of Debbie's car opened his side door facing the woods and, with a cylindrical tank resembling an oversized garden sprayer in his hands, walked on his knees to the lid of her gas tank. He waited and listened. Then, pushing down on the latch with a putty knife, he opened the lid, unscrewed the cap, and after inserting a rubber hose in the tank, began siphoning gas out with a slow pumping action. It took him five minutes to drain most of it out; two minutes to leave the rest area.

Debbie woke up and started her car with no problems. And because of a break in the traffic, she was soon back on the highway.

"Darling, go back to sleep. I'll wake you up when it's time for a break—"

The car bucked.

What now?

It bucked again.

Water in the gas? She paled. *Oh, no, I have no gas! I have no gas!* The realization that she wasn't going anywhere now hit her with such force that momentarily she remained frozen on the steering wheel.

There was a claxon blast. Another. And then the driver of the car behind her touched her rear bumper with his.

Trembling, she got out of the car and walked to the one behind her. "I'm out of gas."

"So?"

For a moment Debbie didn't know what to say. "Could you push me?"

The driver nodded, breaking into a sleazy grin. "Yeah, I'll push you—off the road."

Someone in his car giggled.

"But I have a sick daughter. She'll freeze."

"Freeze?" he said, gesturing Debbie to go. "We'll all freeze if you don't move."

She found herself on the side of the road in the snowstorm. She held her daughter in her arms and watched motorists go by, praying that someone would stop and help them.

"Good luck," someone shouted.

Border Closed, read a large sign barricading the Mexican Customs booths at Tijuana.

Just beyond it, a gang of Mexican youths in a seemingly party mood were draping one of their own signs over the windows of an old bus. It read: We Don't Need Rich Wetbacks.

"Fuck you lazy bastards," shouted a driver from the window of his mobile home. He had been waiting for five hours to get through. "Is that what I get for wanting to spend my money in your filthy country, eh?" He stepped down and threw a frothy can of beer at the bus. He missed—much to the delight of the youths—then walked red-faced to the Winnebago behind him and shouted to its owner, "Would you believe this shit, Mac? Would you, huh?"

So began the nightmare of the highway.

Thousands of campers and vans from Oregon, Nevada, and Washington lined both lanes of Route 101a South and the side roads leading to it. Some had broken down, others had run out of gas.

By nightfall, unable to move in either direction, many abandoned their vehicles and sought refuge and shelter in nearby homes. But soon the shortage of food forced residents of San Diego and its surrounding towns to refuse to take people in. New homes, empty homes, homes under construction were confiscated in the name of humanity, compassion, God himself.

Despite a city ordinance prohibiting residents to bear arms, thousands armed themselves. In Otey and Chula Vista a curfew was declared on request of the selectmen, and the National Guard was asked to patrol the streets with orders to shoot. "But who is the more criminal," asked a young guardsman, "the refugee or the resident?"

News of the closing of the border, first relayed by truckers stuck along Route 101a, hit the local media and rippled out.

Again the president went on national television to promise assistance to those stranded on the California highway. Then he talked about the weather. His speech—reworded and reedited by speech writers and rehearsed under the guidance of media experts—was not prompted by the events in San Diego. He spoke of an ice storm in Minnesota, a late killing frost in Nebraska and Iowa, the snow that had capped the mountains in Maine, New York, and Vermont.

The president acknowledged the veracity of the obvious signs of a major change in weather patterns and admitted that the problem was of worldwide concern. "Since these changes are likely to affect parts of the world differently, each nation has elected to deal with its problem according to its needs and conditions."

Using a pointer and a map of North America, he explained how the United States had been blessed with a system of high-speed winds aloft—the jet stream—which had acted as a big fence holding back the cold air from the Arctic. "But now," he said, "the fence is weakening, bending southward and no longer able to hold back the cold air. That's the reason for the early snow and frost."

He reassured Americans that his administration had foreseen the possibility of a deep freeze and had funded research in modifiers. Secular in design, fantastic in concept, and mythical in power—those were his words—modifiers were, however, "infant" creations of science. "They are like experimental drugs," he said. "They can cause injuries in the attempt to save lives."

The camera moved in for a tight shot, and the president talked about evacuation. It was necessary because of the uncertainty of the success of modifiers and the severity of the deep freeze. However, since the U.S. government could not be made responsible for any losses in the event that climate conditions fell short of predictions, the decision to evacuate had to be a matter of individual choice. The White House press secretary would keep the nation informed with twice-daily bulletins. Law and order, he said with a serious demeanor, had to be maintained to safeguard the principles of American democracy. He announced his decision to give the military authority over other institutions. He talked about martial law. It was not a press conference; there were no questions.

Even before the president finished listing the counties in Montana, the first state to evacuate, Military Police jeeps had occupied key checkpoints. Gasoline stations were ordered closed, and armed guards were posted to protect the pumps. Riot police and canine units took positions around super-markets, drugstores, and food warehouses. Along city streets and avenues, mobilized Montana National Guardsmen in full battle gear kept a close watch on all activities.

Just as the military takeover appeared to be going well, several dispatches received at the White House Communication Center piled on the president's desk:

—Operators of the Seabrook power plant could not cool
  down the reactor by August 15, the deadline.
—Doctors at the Centers for Disease Control warned that
  if victims of AIDS and other communicable diseases
  were not moved immediately to a "medical enclave,"
  the spread of deadly viruses would be disastrous.
—The U.S. ice cutter *North Star*, with 200 scientists, technicians, and sailors on board reported herself trapped
  in McMurdo Sound.
—Ice in the Bering Strait had become thick enough to
  support a T-60 Russian tank . . .

"Tell me something," the president asked the chief of staff as he leafed quickly through the dispatches, "if I don't have the time to read these, how will I find the time to act on them?"

21

"Good as math models are," Scott said to Cliff, "when you finally finish building one, all you get is numbers. But virtual reality makes math come alive. Wait until you see your modification simulated realistically," he added with a voice choked with excitement.

Cliff just smiled, a bland, tight-lipped smile.

"Cliff," Scott went on, frowning at Cliff's cool reaction, "VR will give you a way of visually testing your hypothesis and will confirm what the mathematical model has revealed."

"Well, I can hardly wait," Cliff finally said. But his voice was not that of the first man on Earth to see how a CLIMOD was going to perform in a three-dimensional color simulation.

The reason for Cliff's skepticism was that to him only mathematics could interpret ideas accurately because it was pure science. Only mathematical equations, such as the Navier-Stokes, could express the reality of fluid dynamics. Mathematics was the key to good ocean engineering.

But if VR could give him an extra eye with which to see his modification, he wasn't about to refuse the offer. The more eyes, the better, of course.

Scott continued his briefing. "By the way, all visualizations are data base–based simulations. They will be generated from the data you gave me and what I've just received from NASA."

"NASA is into virtual reality?"

Scott nodded several times. "And in a big way," he said, and explained that at the Numerical Aerodynamic Simulation Division at Moffett Field, California, NASA engineers were able to create a computer-generated wind tunnel that allowed them to see how air moved along the surface of the wings of the space shuttle. The virtual wind tunnel had all the features of a real one but with the advantage of placing the scientist inside the tunnel without disturbing the airflow.

And that was only one aspect that the wind tunnel showed. By inserting thin streamers sensitive to airflow, engineers were able to pinpoint areas of turbulence and vortices that affected wing stability, and go inside them to examine their structure. Obviously, it was a test impossible to conduct inside a real wind tunnel. "Cliff, this is a godsend."

"I don't follow you."

Scott's eyes grew bigger than Ping-Pong balls behind the thick lenses. "Why? The Hull is shaped like a wing. And, Cliff, don't air and fluids obey the same dynamics laws?"

Cliff thought, then nodded. "Of course." He pinched his forehead in embarrassment. "That means that—"

"You'll be able to see if with the Hull removed, the stream will develop chaotic patterns and assume an erratic course."

Cliff's face brightened. "I'll be darned," he said, and smiled. "How long will it take you to build the VR model?"

Scott shrugged. "I don't know, but I promise you won't have to cancel the appointment with Kronin."

Scott's VR model was a hacker's dream.
First, Scott designed a virtual water tank and used NASA

data to simulate the flow around the computer-generated Hull Adams had worked on.

That done, he contoured the ocean floor with rises and ridges charted with echo-sounding equipment. He did this carefully because they would later reveal how the water behaved as it passed over them.

Then Scott created a sequence of images to show the circulation of the stream before, during, and after the modification.

Lastly, he created a simulation to analyze if the course of the stream and its forward momentum were strong enough to push the debris from the Hull into the Mid-Ocean Canyon and block it.

Throughout it all Scott ran on caffeine.

In just three days he had debugged the program, and built and tested the model. It was late Wednesday evening, and Scott waited impatiently for Cliff and the rest of the team. Scott needed a shower badly, and a good shot of mouthwash.

On entering the room, Cliff thanked Scott for his efforts. "Before we begin this hacking run," he said, using techno-babble terminology, "I want to express my gratitude to you for wanting to juggle eggs in a real gang bang of a data bank."

Scott threw his head back and laughed. "That's nice of you, Cliff. But tell me one thing. Where did you get all those words, from a hacker?"

"Hell no," Cliff answered. "I had the manager buy me a copy of *The Hacker's Dictionary*. The day I met you I realized that before I could understand what you were doing with these computers—big irons, as you say—I had to understand what you were saying."

They laughed, especially Pam, who had been looking at him with longing and admiration.

The hardware was certainly the most interesting component of the VR environment. It was also what surprised, if not disappointed, Cliff, because at first sight there seemed to be no plausible correlation between the unsophisticated-looking hardware and what it allowed one to see or, as he put it, get between "the basic high-tech nuts and bolts and the lofty scientific purpose."

VR's business end was the tele-head. It had two four-inch television display screens mounted like binoculars in order to create a wide, three-dimensional field of view in color. A cable connected the tele-head to the graphic workstation and a minicomputer.

"When I first saw it, I thought it was a welder's mask," Cliff said when he picked up the tele-head. "And just as light," he added, adjusting it until it sat comfortably on his head.

"Ready, Cliff?" Scott asked from his workstation.

"Oh, wow!" Cliff's first impression was that of dazed surprise. "Granted," he said, "it's a computer-generated Hull but . . . it's like watching it from the *Alvin*'s view port. Now I'm cruising on top of the Hull . . . moving in front of its southern tip . . . and along the eastern slope. Incredible."

"Really?" Pam and Gallego asked in unison.

Cliff nodded. "Absolutely. For one thing, it's not like watching the Hull on the monitor screen Scott is using, but it's . . . How shall I put it? . . . It's like watching a color Walt Disney cartoon in three D. The Hull looks so . . . so real, I feel I could touch it. And I feel completely surrounded by the ocean environment—the ridges, the rises, the canyons, part of the Continental Shelf. Everything is there but the fish."

Scott typed another command on his keyboard and wavy thin lines, the streamers, began flowing around the Hull and along the ridges and rises of the ocean floor, simulating the stream's flow field. "Streamers are to VR what smoke is to a wind tunnel," Scott said.

Shaking his head in disbelief, Cliff said: "Now, because of the streamers acting as dyes in a water tank, I can see how water moves along and around objects . . . how certain currents converge for no apparent reason."

For the next hour the team forgot that the world was freezing over, as each team member tried the tele-head in turn.

After the "demo," Scott elected to show what the model revealed to Cliff alone.

"One fundamental feature of virtual reality is to set up test conditions that are difficult, if not impossible, to achieve conventionally," Scott said to Cliff while handing him a glove onto which were fastened wires that looked like the electrodes of a cardiogram machine. The "dataglove," as it was called, sensed the position and gestures of the hand, which the computer recognized in order to place one or more three-dimensional cursors in the flow field.

"So my next job," Scott continued, "is to help you grasp an overview of the modification before, during, and after the removal of the Hull to give you the best opportunity for analysis."

Cliff listened attentively, leaning back, gloved hand rigidly on the armrest, eyes on Scott. So now it was all up to Cliff. He swallowed dryly a couple of times and so conspicuously that Scott realized that Cliff was struggling with himself. He said to him, "If glaciation had started two years ago, all you would've gotten was a pile of fan-fold paper with rows and rows of numbers. But today I'm able to give you the opportunity to see the modification from start to finish, as if on playback. It should be quite an advantage."

Cliff took a deep breath. "I'm ready," he said, and Scott sat down at his workstation.

After giving Cliff instructions on the use of the dataglove, Scott pressed a number of keys on his computer and simultaneously a bird's-eye view of the Hull appeared on his screen and on Cliff's tele-head.

"This is what we have out there today," Scott began. "If you lift your gloved hand and move your index finger down, a cursor will appear with a string of tiny dots appearing as dotted lines emanating from it. That's the first streamer."

"I see it."

"The streamer is now showing you how water is flowing. Can you see that?"

He could.

"Is it showing how water is moving around objects?"

Cliff nodded, one hand pressing on the tele-head.

"Keep that in mind for now," Scott told him. "What I will do next is to show you the vertical view of the first group of shot holes and the approximate area of the Hull the nukes would blast away."

Cliff studied the display, paying particular attention to the flow of the stream. "Freeze here and print me a copy of what I'm seeing," he said, and a few seconds later a graphic printer whirred to life.

There followed the second, third, and fourth rows of shot holes, and how much of the Hull the charges would remove.

Then came the fifth row and a disappointing moment.

Technically the modification was working. The flow of the right portion of the stream appeared smooth, undisturbed, and steady on its course. That was the desired outcome.

But the amount of debris falling into the Mid-Ocean Canyon didn't seem to be reducing proportionately the all-important flow of the J Current.

And there seemed to be no apparent reason why that should be so.

At Cliff's request, Scott repeated the simulation. "Could it be that we got some inaccurate data?"

"No." Cliff paused to think, then he moved his index finger and placed a number of cursors in the flow field. He was perplexed to see that the streamers emanating from them got funneled in a chaotic vortex in front of the remaining Hull. Inserting a cursor inside the vortex, Cliff moved inside of it and was able to study its structure. He quickly realized what was happening. Multiple vortices were forming in front of the remaining portion of the Hull. This turbulence was so powerful it was scattering the debris in all directions, thus preventing it from being deposited inside the Mid-Ocean Canyon. "It's exactly what happens at the bottom of a powerful waterfall," he said.

"What's getting into the act?"

Cliff didn't answer right away.

"You must know, I'm sure."

"I'm not sure, but I think it has to do with the way the Hull is left after the blasts, for the stream hits it as if it were a wall. That's not what happens at the southern tip of the Hull, which is shaped like the bow of a ship. Streamers show that we have serious chaotic regions in front of the remains of the Hull."

"In that case, why not drill holes in patterns capable of producing a wedge-shaped rock formation?"

Cliff shook his head. "That won't do, either. The charges have to be placed near the rock cleavage."

For the next two hours Cliff sat inside his virtual water tank and studied the remaining aspects of the modification. "Well," he said at last, eyes clouded with an odd mingling of weariness and excitement, "the math model tells us that the modification will work. VR confirms it. I'm satisfied. And the vortices prove that a partial blasting of the Hull would result in an inadvertent modification."

He thanked Scott for developing the groupware that allowed each member of the team to work with the others. "It was the ultimate in teamwork." He paused. "And what can I say about the VR model? I feel as though I borrowed God's eyes." He gave Scott's arm a squeeze. "Thank you, also, for making it possible for me to meet Kronin's deadline as scheduled."

Awkwardly, Scott cleared his throat, his eyes large, glittering black buttons of pride. "I've enjoyed every byte of it.

"How about some downtime, now."

"Plain English."

"A break. I'll make the coffee."

As they left the VR room, Cliff shook his head regretfully and said, "And that's too bad. Though I've never admitted

to Adams, he had me convinced that blowing up half of the
Hull was better than nothing."

Feeling a thousand eyes staring at him, Cliff looked at
his notes.

He saw that his next statement, in a room where even the
most hawkish generals developed cold feet from the fear of
nuclear power, would announce his intention of using nukes
to blow up the Hull.

It was difficult to tell whether it was his delivery or the
uniqueness of the modification that was holding the attention of Kronin and those who had listened to his previous
presentation almost four weeks before. But he had it. Cliff
knew it and said, "You may ask . . ." He sipped some water
not for effect but because his mouth was suddenly dry.
"How could a sixty-mile-long underwater island such as
the Hull be removed in less than six w——"

"Nuclear bombs," a wart-faced, bug-eyed air force general said aloud.

People gasped as one and the room went deadly quiet. It was as if that general had detonated a nuke right
in there.

Suddenly the hall erupted with a flurry of wordless
sounds, voices filled with ominous inflection, gestures,
the ear-busting whistle of microphone feedback. Hands
went up.

"Is that true?" Someone shouted.

"Yes," Cliff nodded. "Nuke blasting."

A technician turned the mike volume down too much.

A chorus of stunned voices said "What?" in unison.

"Nuke—"

"You don't—"

Hoots of denunciation.

A question came to him from the rear. "Do you really
mean blasting with nuclear bombs?"

More objections.

But Cliff had his debate face on. "Yes, nuclear devices.
Why not?"

"Again!"

"Why not nuke blasting, I said." He sounded stiffer than before. "Let me—"

Someone cut in on him. "Preposterous—"

"*Gentlemen!*" Kronin shouted.

But the disorder continued. And it was only then that Cliff really seemed to become aware of what he was proposing.

At a gesture from Kronin, Howard Long, the Senate majority leader, asked, "And what about radiation?"

An amphitheater of heads nodded.

It was now Gallego's turn, and he was all science, all authority, smooth.

Interlacing every other sentence with "Princeton Nuclear Research Center" and other references to his experience with the United States Underground Nuclear Testing Program, he discussed the nuclear physics of nuclear explosions, the absorption factor of rock and sand on radiation, the chemical properties of water as a dissipator of residual radiation, uranium as an alpha emitter, the size of the nuclear devices. He walked to a blackboard and wrote: 1 = 2 10; CL uranium/tritium 1 c 1, or C 14 per Kt. He said, pointing, "Hundreds of underground charges have gone off because of the reliability of this equation. Had the Hull been above ground, I wouldn't have considered nuke blasting as readily. But fortunately the Hull is underwater, under billions and billions of cubic meters of water constantly moving at six knots." He paused to let this sink in.

"But some low-level radiation is bound to escape," a doubting voice said.

"Yes, some." Gallego shrugged. "But it wouldn't be harmful."

"*What?*" a woman shouted, disbelieving.

"Yes, yes"—Gallego nodded a dozen times—"not harmful because—"

"Go tell it to the Physicians for Social Responsibility," a man in the front row said. "Yours is scientific heresy."

"Heresy?" Gallego managed to laugh. "I've been exposed

to low-level radiation all my academic life and I'm still alive. And let me say this for the record. Since we, the British, the French, the Chinese, and the Russians have detonated hundreds of nuclear devices for test purposes, we should certainly explode a few of them for our survival. I see no—"

"Soldiers who were forced to witness the detonation of a nuclear bomb in Nevada, my dear professor, are dying of cancer."

"Sir"—Gallego raised his booming voice—"there is no conclusive evidence to support that allegation."

"Dr. James of . . ."

A thump.

"*Gentlemen*, please." Kronin stood up. "Let him speak."

"As I was saying . . ." Gallego went on with his strong yet controlled voice and repeated that low-level radiation was not harmful. "It's like assuming," he said in the disquieting buzz of two people whispering, "that because hot water scalds, you should never take a warm bath because warm water might, I repeat *might*, have long-term effects—though no one ever died from it."

More questions for clarification followed.

"How about the biosphere? Has anybody thought of that?"

Pamela answered and explained that high-pitched noisemakers similar to acoustic pest-control devices would be dropped before the detonation to clear the area of fish. "These underwater transducer units, or UTUs, worked during our nuclear tests in the Pacific, and are used by high-minded oil companies engaged in offshore drilling. More will be dropped to keep fish away until all traces of radiation have disappeared. For your information . . ."

Cliff listened with an imperceptible, triumphant smile forming on his lips. It was all over.

It was now five-fifteen P.M., and an aide leaned over to remind Kronin of his appointment with the president.

Kronin nodded, then addressing Cliff, asked, "Do you have any final words to add, Dr. Lorenz?"

How glad Cliff was to hear that.

Itching to read what it had taken him so long to write as a concluding statement, he answered. "I do, sir. Do you know what it would mean, if we could use the very bombs designed to kill people . . . to save humanity?"

He sat down.

"Thank you," Kronin said, then looked around and waited. "Very well," he went on, and gave each team the go-ahead with preparations because he wanted as many backups as possible. Problems, he reminded his audience, were inherent to technology, and the president would have to rely on a modifier to ease the evacuation of millions. "He is very, very worried—and you can see why. Let's suppose we do manage to put these millions on the road. Will the people in the South wait for them with open arms . . . or with loaded firearms? One thing is sure. The events in San Diego tell us that xenophobia is a dreadful disease." A pause. "Last night a foot of snow fell on Calgary." Another pause. "I will consider all proposals very carefully. I believe we have the means to stop glaciation. Thank you," he said quietly. He thumbed up his glasses and walked slowly out of HR-4, bowed down with unutterable burdens.

Roscoe came down the aisle to congratulate Cliff. He was all smiles. Cliff thanked him, and with that he turned his mind to other matters.

The idea of the backups was a good one, and Cliff had anticipated as much three weeks before, when he began to assemble his flotilla.

So as the amphitheater emptied, he and his team stayed for a quick strategy session. Gallego was to leave at once for the Nuclear Regulatory Agency Headquarters in New Mexico to supervise the placing of the charges into special canisters; Adams for Wilmington, where the *Challenger* and other drill ships were being outfitted with larger drills. And while Scott would remain at a safe house developing the computer program that would fire the charges, Wycoff would organize the dropping of the UTUs, also from there. "I'm flying to Norfolk by helicopter. The flotilla must be ready to sail in a couple of days." He thanked his team. "Well," he added, "if nothing else, we did our best."

Yet he felt no joy, no triumph. Only the fear of something unimaginably dangerous and inhuman.

Then, seemingly as an afterthought but more to lift his spirits, he took out a piece of paper from his wallet. It was a quote from an article in the *New York Times* of November 8, 1912—the article covered Ryker's plan. Cliff had carried it with him since he had begun researching Marshall's modification. "I did not see my old professor in the hall, and that's because he's working on the modification Ryker had proposed back in 1912. Anyhow," he said to his team, "just substitute the name Marshall where it says Ryker." He paused then read: " 'Mr. Ryker does not say what would happen in Northwestern Europe after his big dike has been built off Cape Race. Perhaps he doesn't care. The Brits, after all, are human—or almost—and we have always been told that if the Gulf Stream did not run just where it does now, their present climate—which is none too good— would be no good at all.' "

There was a brief explosion of laughter.

The FBI limousine whispered along silent and smooth.

But now a stunned Cliff had his eyes on the scene he had avoided on the way to the Pentagon.

Along both sides of Second Street, there were army vehicles of all kinds: ambulances, field kitchens, personnel carriers, buses, communication vans. Parking lots were filled with wooden boxes, row after row of oil drums, helicopters, tents. Armed soldiers were posted at intersections; military policemen with white gloves and white cartridge belts directed traffic.

The once-majestic, heavy-foliaged maples that graced parkways and boulevards had wizened and now looked torpid. Cold chestnut trees drooped onto streets. Geraniums had withered and coiled amid flattened grass, as if poisoned by smog. Squirrels chirped about searching for the acorns that would never fall. Sparrows, hundreds of them, were wheeling, sweeping, chittering around an army olive green garbage pail. Chickadees, or dive bombers, as Fritz had called them, twittered for leftovers.

A veil of bad memories fell painfully at the back of Cliff's eyes, and he quickly shook his head, as if it helped remove images of his old friend, and looked up. Timid crows were flying high, waiting for a chance to land for food, making Cliff wonder if anyone was feeding Fred, his pet crow for five years. To the east, flecks of fleecy clouds floated with the wind like a rally of white hot-air balloons. They seemed to be the only carefree things in a world of dying plants and frightened animals.

A scarlet sun colored Arlington. It felt weak on Cliff's hands. The solar minima had started. Glaciation was really on its way.

How he wished he was going home—and to Butch.

"Lord," Adams murmured next to him, "and this is only August."

22

As Cliff flew to Norfolk, Andrei Konlikov was trying to make sense of the presence of numerous U.S. auxiliary ships taking position south of Key West, Florida.

"Have they moved at all?" Konlikov asked a young naval officer.

"No, sir. At least not enough to be considered a course change."

They were in the chart room of the *Dokholov*, a ship that looked like a giant version of the *Knorr*. In reality it was a highly sophisticated oceangoing intelligence center. Its telecommunication section alone occupied one deck with fifteen bays specializing in VHF, UHF, and low-frequency eavesdropping, submarine cable tapping, radio jamming, and underwater acoustic detection. It carried a complement of twelve divers, sonar specialists, numerous photo analysts, interpreters, and code clerks. It was the jewel of the former KGB.

The officer handed Konlikov a sheet of paper. "These are the specs of the *City of Denver*," he said, and remained rigidly at attention.

"It brings the number to—"

"Fifty-five, sir. The Intelligence Directorate says the specs are the latest, but—"

"Fine, fine." Konlikov waved a hand, and the officer left.

A bright Gulf of Mexico sun bathed the *Dokholov* and cast a blinding dazzle of light on the quiet sea. It was almost noon, and the temperature in the chart room had risen to an uncomfortable thirty-two degrees C. The air was heavy with moisture and had the burned-oil odor of machinery. Sea gulls waiting for the next barrel of garbage wheeled overhead like vultures and dropped their waste on sensitive antennas.

Mopping his forehead, Konlikov walked to the large chart table and meticulously printed the words *City of Denver* on a spot over the sheet of Plexiglas protecting the map of the Florida Keys. The spot corresponded to the coordinates the officer had given him.

Then he stepped back and, nervously tamping his pipe with a finger, studied the map. *Why*, he asked himself, *should a ship that was used as prepositioned food supplier come to join the others, unless extra personnel was expected? And what would they be doing there*?

The more he looked at the specs of the *City of Denver*, the more the odds seemed to suggest that a large contingent of troops or workers—maybe divers—was on its way to the gulf.

Everything seemed to be laid out for a construction operation—8 dock landing ships, 12 dredgers, 10 crane barges, 16 pile drivers, 7 steam shovels, a hospital ship, and now a food supplier.

Even though Russian intelligence had informed him that there was unusual traffic to and from Cape Race, Newfoundland, Konlikov still believed that if the United States scientists were planning to modify the weather by manipulating the Gulf Stream, they would do so where it originated. Hence his request that all the "pikemen" in Cuban ports be put on alert. These were the small two-men attack submarines often taken for pleasure boats because of their size.

Trust your instinct, he told himself.

Quite unprofessional. But natural.

He lit his pipe, picked up a wall phone, and rang up photo intelligence. "Konlikov speaking. I want our freighters to take sonar profiles of the following American ships as soon as possible," he ordered, and spelled out the names of ten of them. These ships are as deceptive as the mirages of the desert, he told himself. But you can't fool all of the people all of the time, can you?

"Come on, Dad," Butch shouted, his gray-green-flecked eyes on the monitor of Cliff's rowing machine. "Three hundred meters to go," he added as the display neared the 2,500-meter mark. "Come on, Dad. If I could do it, you can, too."

At twelve, Butch wasn't tall for his age but he held himself as if he were. Cleft chinned, with blond, curly hair and all the bloom of adolescence, he looked like an aspiring surfer.

"Phew!" Cliff grabbed the towel Butch tossed him. "I'm really, really . . . out of shape," he said, out of breath, and buried his sweaty face in the towel.

Thanks to Phil Jackson and the house manager who planned it, Cliff and Butch were able to spend an afternoon together in the Ergo Room in the Department of the Interior basement.

"Imagine me doing only twenty-five hundred meters. In fourteen minutes?" he said to Phil Jackson, barely able to straighten up.

"Well, what do you expect?" Phil Jackson told him. "You haven't rowed for . . ."

Cliff put three fingers up.

"Three months. That's a lot, Cliff."

"That's . . ."

"Two minutes more than me," Butch said, grinning.

"Yep, and all anaerobic because I was out of breath." He put a hand on Butch's head and messed up his hair. "I'm proud of you, son. One of these days we'll have to enter you in the indoor rowing regatta. You're sure to win in your age category." He paused to catch his breath. "Well, what do you say we hit the showers and then have something special for supper."

Butch opened his eyes wide. "We never have onion rings at school and I'd love some," he said, and suggested Mrs. B, a small student restaurant at the corner of Thirty-ninth and S Street and a few hundred yards from Georgetown University's medical and dental schools.

"If it's open," Phil Jackson said.

The place smelled of charcoal-broiled meat as they walked in, and it was brightly lit. Large blackboards listed the fifty hamburger specialties handwritten with colored chalk. There were wall-sized pictures of the Beatles, the Three Stooges, one of actor Ronald Reagan promoting Chesterfield cigarettes, numerous signs that once belonged to train stations, reprints of newspaper articles praising Mrs. B's "in the rough" cuisine. Normally a busy place because it catered to summer school students, the restaurant was almost empty. But all the same, WCXR, the students' favorite radio station, played classic rock.

"Do you like it, Dad?"

His mouth watering, Cliff looked around with a combination of amusement and curiosity. "You bet I do," he answered. "How did you find out about this place, anyhow?"

"Miss Wycoff brought me here once."

Cliff's face was quizzical. "Is that so?" he said, and noticed that Butch's face had brightened on mentioning her name.

"She knows a lot about basketball. And did you know that she has season tickets and that sometimes she has to give them away because of work?"

"No, I didn't," Cliff said, trying to decide what to have. "I wonder whom she gives them to."

Butch offered to order and he chose number twenty-three on the board facing them: hamburger Stroganoff and onion rings. "Miss Wycoff chose that for me and, man, did she hit it right."

It was August and D.C. wasn't the usual oven. Cliff ordered hot coffee; Butch, Coke.

"You seem to like Miss Wycoff," Cliff said, yet there was a tinge of anxiety in his voice.

"I do . . ."

A waitress in a red blouse and black jeans came with two baskets of food.

"Oh, wow, this looks great," Cliff said, then suddenly motioned Butch to be quiet at the announcement of a news bulletin.

They both turned to face the radio and listened: *"The United States nuclear submarine* Octopus, *a Los Angeles– class vessel, is reported to be missing in the North Atlantic and presumed lost. The* Octopus, *with one hundred and thirty men on board, was commissioned only a year ago and it's believed to carry sixteen nuclear-tipped missiles.*

"Secretary of the Navy Barrington has announced that a task force of rescue ships will sail from Norfolk and other East Coast ports and will attempt to rescue the trapped officers and sailors and recover the dangerous payload of nuclear weapons.

"All shipping interests have been warned to stay fifty miles off latitude forty-eight point two degrees west, and forty-four point four degrees north.

"In 1963, the atomic submarine Thresher *failed to sur- face after a depth test dive some five hundred miles south of the present location of the* Octopus. *More news as . . ."*

"Poor guys," Butch said. "Do you think they have a chance?"

Cliff tried hard to look shaken by the news. "Sure. The *Octopus* is in relatively shallow waters. I've been there. They'll rescue them. You should see what the navy has in the way of rescue ships." He motioned Butch not to think about the submarine and eat. He wished he could tell Butch that the announcement was disinformation and that the story of the *Octopus* was a cover-up for Operation Drill and Load.

They began eating with gusto.

"You never told me why you like Miss Wycoff," Cliff said, looking appreciatively at the thick hamburger topped with sour cream and sautéed with mushrooms.

Butch dropped another onion ring into his mouth before answering. "For one thing, Dad, she talks to me as if I was—"

"Were."

"As if I were her longtime friend. And then she's fun. You should've heard her talk about Meadowlark, one of the original Globetrotters. Did you ever see him play?"

"Yes, many times. Well," Cliff said, "I'm glad you like her. She's my best friend, one I care a lot about."

They ate some more, then Cliff's expression changed. He told Butch that things didn't look good weather-wise and that possibly Washington would have to evacuate before Boston did. He gave the reason. "Miss Wycoff may have told you about what I'm doing and why."

"She did. I'm really proud of you, Dad."

"And I of you. You seem to be taking all of this in stride. That's a big help. Someday I'll explain everything. Now I can't. And probably you know why."

"A secret?"

"That's right. Classified information."

"I understand. Mr. Jackson spent a lot of time explaining that."

"Good," Cliff said, and paused. When he spoke again, his voice had the tone reserved for feelings difficult to articulate. He said, "If Washington has to evacuate, I can't be with you when the order comes. Since you like Miss Wycoff, I thought the two of you could be together and watch after one another. Can you handle that?"

Butch nodded, but Cliff could see that he was a little scared. His eyes were clouded with anxiety.

"That's the spirit!" he said reassuringly.

A pause.

"You bet, Dad." Butch smiled.

Logs hissed and crackled in the fireplace.

Pamela Wycoff put her book down, and her mind drifted. Glaciation, health, home . . .

She was all alone. Adams and Gallego were on assignment; Cliff was on his way back to the safe house after meeting with Butch; Scott was in his room.

She wondered if she'd be spending the evening any differently had she been at home. Not much differently, really. The luxury of an evening at home was rare, but even so, long and lonely. Pity. One's reactions and ideas on a book or the new CD re-release of Glenn Gould playing Bach's *The Well-Tempered Clavier* were made to be shared with someone. God knows how many times she had heard or played selections from Book One, never feeling so different about them as she did tonight.

Thinking about that, she felt the need of a companion. Though in a limited way, Cliff had been a good one during her stay in the safe house. She would miss him. He shared everything from the proper way of making cappuccino to his dream of making his CLIMOD work. And his way of looking at women started fires within her. How many times had she included him in her fantasies? She heard the front door open and Cliff's greeting to the dog. She made a decision.

As he walked down the hall Cliff heard Pamela say, "Come join me."

Cliff turned.

Pamela, her honeyed, auburn hair draping her shoulders, was seated on the deep-cushioned sofa like a woman in an Ingres painting.

Was she waiting for someone?

"Thank you, Pam," Cliff threw his jacket on a chair, suddenly gripped by the feeling that something unusual was going to happen to him—a sense of an impending event, the realization of a lifelong dream.

"With nobody here but the manager and his dog, things have been quiet." She held up a Baccarat glass. "How about a drink—a real drink. It could be our last," she said with a combination of blue-eyed swagger and a bright, slightly frightened smile that made Cliff feel uncertain and protective at the same time.

"I'd love a drink," he said. "I'll mix it."

He walked to the buffet and measured exactly two ounces of orange juice, which he poured into a wide glass. He carefully examined the contents of two bottles of rum, chose the darker of the two, and added one precise jigger of it to the orange juice. He dropped three ice cubes in the glass and slowly stirred the mixture. "It looks like a specimen sample of the Potomac," he said, holding the glass up, "but it's a really good drink."

They sat cross-legged on opposite ends of the sofa and watched the fire in silence.

And as he sipped his drink, he noticed that his right foot and her left one pointed to each other, a kinesics pose he took as a meaningful sign.

"Please." She held her glass up to him. "I'll have another drink," she said with an indulgent glint in her eyes. "Not too much ice."

He mixed her drink as if one of the ingredients were nitroglycerin, and she watched him, fascinated.

"Here," he said, and as she reached for the glass, he covered her hand with his for a long time. It was a gentle, instinctive caress . . . and he dared to pulse his secret urging through it. The warm, smooth feel of her hand spread over him like a hot, rushing torrent.

"What are you feeling?" she asked.

"Memories," he said quickly. "For instance, as I admire you, I'm reliving a similar scene that took place years ago, with Marla popping into my mind. And as she does, it rekindles the feeling of falling inexorably in love for the first time." Tenderly, his eyes dissolved into hers. "Pam, it's what I'm again feeling now. It's something no other woman but you ever gave me."

Neither one knew what to say.

"Are you leaving early tomorrow afternoon?" she asked.

"Yes, and I feel good about going. I've finally accepted the fact that nature is no environmentalist, no conservationist, either. Not with its waves reshaping coastlines and its glaciers reworking the land like giant bulldozers, and its lightning setting fires to thousands—"

"I'll take care of Butch, if . . . He's a wonderful boy."

"He likes you a lot."

"He reminds me of you," she said almost shyly.

"I'll come and join you when I can," he said, and moved close to Pam.

She sat silent and immobile, but the same pair of big blue-green eyes looked at him with dreamy abandon.

The logs settled, leaving glowing red coals burning in the ashes.

"Soon, I hope," she said.

"Very soon." He brushed back her hair and kissed her forehead. "I love you, Pam," he said, and suddenly felt a warm, tender hand on the back of his neck. He kissed her again on her lips. It felt like his first kiss.

"I'll love you always," he said, getting up.

"Stay."

He did.

Beyond the luminous scrim of a saffron mist, the safe house loomed on a lawn with blemishes of thatch-colored grass. Yellowed leaves plumed up and swirled as a black limousine with Orville Marshall in the rear right seat raced up the driveway.

Cliff waited in the hall, tensely aware of his old professor's arrival—unusual though not totally unexpected. He had sent him a revised, detailed copy of the proposal, and had spoken to Marshall's assistant about nuke blasting when he called.

Now with his hands behind his back, he wound his watch and tried to control his emotions.

From the day Cliff met Marshall, he had never found anything good about him, especially his academic jealousy and his tendency to keep his scholarship secret. Only later, however, would Cliff discover that it was this very jealousy and secrecy that kept the ivory tower from falling down on him.

The front door opened, and Cliff and Marshall stared at each other. "Nice to see you," Cliff said, finding a small smile.

"You look swell, Cliff," Marshall said in a "good old boy" voice. His face defined arrogance. Wearing a double-breasted, wide-pinstripe charcoal suit that made one wonder if Al Capone's tailor was still working, he had hard, quick eyes, a presence about him born of years of teaching and lecturing.

Cliff returned the compliment. "Coffee?"

They sat on the library's massive tufted leather sofa, a long silence stretching between them.

"Cliff, I've read and reread the details of your proposal very carefully," Marshall said, waving an envelope. "It's suicidal."

"All modifiers can be suicidal. And that includes yours."

The remark was unexpected. Marshall flinched, with a look that combined disbelief and resentment. For a moment tension hung between them like an electrically charged storm cloud.

"Maybe so." Marshall reached for the attaché case and put it on his lap. "But my modification can be stopped, altered, or nullified anytime. Not yours. Yours would be permanent. Nobody—not even God—could reverse it once it has begun," he said in the spitfire tongue of his. He opened the case and took out a map of the North Atlantic, which he spread over the coffee table. "It is here"—he jabbed a finger on the map—"just east of the Milne Seamount where the tons of TNT would go off. True?"

The explosive power of nuclear charges is measured in terms of tons of TNT. Cliff nodded, and Marshall spread out a chart. Prepared at the National Marine Geodesy Insti-

tute, it showed an undersea ridge of newly risen mol-
ten rock in black, against a multicolored background. One
distinct characteristic of the ridge—besides its horseshoe
shape—was its fracture or fault lines of weakness running
toward it. Bridging an area between the southern coast of
Newfoundland to a spot 330 miles out to sea, the ridge
resembled a section of a bicycle rim; the fracture lines, its
spokes.

"Have you seen this?" Marshall asked him with an ominous inflection.

He had not.

"You're honest. Not published yet. A recent graduate of
mine sent it to me, God bless him. You see, Cliff," he said,
face brightening with an omnipotent glow as he ran the tip
of his index finger along the ridge, "an elastic wave in
an area of geological activity would be cataclysmic. The
sudden relaxation of strain accumulated along these geologic faults can only result in one thing—the collapse of
interfracture areas and the formation of a new eastbound
course along the ridge."

Cliff understood what Marshall was saying: with powerful explosives going off in an area younger in age and,
therefore, in constant state of formation, a seaquake was
likely to occur. It could easily change the contour of the
ocean floor along the horseshoe-shaped ridge and force the
Gulf Stream to flow in a westerly direction. He didn't have
to say that a new course implied the sudden flooding of
millions of acres of populated areas along the eastern coast
of the United States.

Cliff had listened with a mixture of scholarly curiosity
and terror. Yet didn't reward Marshall with the slightest
change of expression.

The model was a success, the flotilla was assembling
without problems, and Cliff was finally feeling good about
going. Things were better than he had expected.

And now the fracture lines—as if the magma flow
Adams had warned about was not enough of a nightmare. But they were not going to stop him. Not now.

"First of all," he said calmly but firmly, "I was forced—"

"Forced? Bullshit," Marshall interrupted, face reddening, nostrils flaring. "No, Cliff, you are simply playing the role again. The role of noble victim of circumstance, while all you care about is to maintain a possessive grip on research about the Gulf Stream."

Cliff shrugged his shoulders. Yes, there was a kernel of truth in what Marshall was saying, but Cliff had to get ready for Operation Drill and Load and wasn't wasting his time on academic issues.

"In the second place," he went on louder, his tone intimidating, "my model, which includes geological data, warns of no seaquakes. I trust it. That's all for now," he added, like a man sure of his own truth.

"You're pretty cocky, considering you've been out of the mainstream of research for . . . what is it? Ten years?" A quivering sneer.

"I know what I'm doing. Good day, Professor."

"Bullshit." Marshall flared, and walked to the door. He turned and pointed a finger at Cliff. "Just remember this: in a permanent weather modification, it isn't getting what you want, but wanting what you get."

23

Cliff would never forget the evil winds of August.

Icebergs were beginning to drift further south, but more worrisome were the floes, the small chunks of ice advancing ahead of icebergs. If they moved far enough south to meet the Labrador Current, they would be over the Hull before drilling and loading were completed. With a forty-knot wind, a floe became a battering ram with the hole-punching power of a torpedo.

And the weeds . . .

At last, the skipper of the *Glomar Challenger* set the engine telegraph to "one-third," and the flotilla left Norfolk and headed for the open sea. It was one-thirty P.M.

Just below the bridge on the open deck, Cliff, in a blue turtleneck and wool cap, watched as the *Glomar Challenger* swung up astern east of Fort Monroe at the southern tip of Chesapeake Bay and rounded Cape Charles to port.

The day had dawned exceptionally cloudless and clear. The sun was bright but it did not warm.

Trailing behind the *Glomar Challenger* was the *Glomar Explorer*, also rigged for deep-sea drilling. Lumbering astern and chugging along like a chubby, short-legged bulldog were the drill ship *Cass* and the *Catamaran II*, a twenty-thousand-ton, double-hulled high-tech ship. Right behind them, towed by navy tugboats, was the *Charibdes*, a superbarge with three cranes and giant winches used for salvage operations. The only "decoy" was the *Preserver*, a salvage ship with two helicopter pads. The *Knorr* went boiling up front. Down under were the escorts—two attack subs of the Los Angeles class.

Two hundred nautical miles north was the supercarrier *Nimitz*, the floating command post responsible for the protection of the flotilla and the security of its mission. On its decks, crews in red flight caps and blue parkas were arming the missiles under the wings of F-14 Tomcats. Pilots sat in the briefing room and listened to the squadron commander review the rules of engagement. "Despite all the electronic brains aboard this carrier," he said, "it will be your human brain that will decide whether to shoot or not."

High in the sky, specialists seated in front of large screens monitored air traffic in the North Atlantic on their AWACS early-warning radar. More AWACS were on their way to strengthen the radar surveillance lost with the evacuation of stations in northern Canada.

And, completing a very wide loop around the Hull were two Canadian destroyers. Their mission was to seed the ocean floor with sonar buoys and other antisubmarine acoustic devices. "This is not a free peep show," said Rear Admiral Mazel, skipper of the *Nimitz*.

The moment all ships cleared the last channel marker, the skipper of the *Glomar Challenger* ordered "Ahead full."

Cliff's amazement at the sheer power and capabilities of the *Challenger* never ceased. The ship's drilling derrick, with its lower legs straddling the middle of the ship and rising 142 feet into the sky, looked like a miniature replica of the Eiffel Tower.

The drilling rig itself consisted of a long string of rotating pipes coupled to a giant diesel engine. Its business end was the diamond-cutting bit, a cylinder of steel that bore fixed black diamonds around one edge that would project alternatively beyond the outside and inside edges of the cylinder. It was capable of piercing through soft limestone at the rate of fifty feet an hour.

An automatic pipe rack, which could store and dispense 24,000 feet of drill pipe, sat on the foredeck.

One deck below was the support equipment—threaded couplings, chains, drums of oil, outboard motors, pumps, generators. . . .

Deck C housed the longest lab Cliff had ever seen. There geologists examined fossils and core samples for their age and traces of oil. Drilled out with a hollow bit, a core could be collected as the bit worked its way down. One sample core was two hundred feet long. Cliff stopped to study one such geological calendar that showed him how sediment had become rock during a period of 5 billion years.

The only part of the *Challenger* that looked like any other ship was Deck D. That's where the mess hall and the sleeping quarters were. Like the other three decks above, it was wet, slippery, and so noisy that it sounded to Cliff as if demons were practicing drumrolls on the steel bulkhead.

On paper, Operation Drill and Load was cookbook simple: The Hull was divided into three blast areas—lower, middle, and upper. These areas would be drilled by the *Glomar Explorer, Cass,* and *Glomar Challenger* respectively. A fourth drill ship, the *Humble,* was the spare.

The ships were assigned specific latitudes along which they would drill two holes to computerized depth and spaced 3,600 feet apart, then move up three miles and repeat the operation until they drilled eighteen holes each.

Divers would then insert the canister containing the nuclear charge and the conventional charges into the hole, cap it with a metal plug, and wire the primer to the firing/retrieve box.

At four P.M. of August 22, when the flotilla reached the southern tip of the Hull, the ships deployed to their prearranged positions.

At a signal, the *Knorr* dropped sonar beacons around each drill ship. Minutes later, the beacons began transmitting acoustic signals or pings back to each drill ship's navigation rooms. Here, state-of-the-art computers sensed the drift of the ships in relation to the beacons and automatically sent corrections to the many outboard propellers mounted along the individual ship's hull. Since these faced in different directions, it was possible to make the ships move forward, backward, sideways, or rotate. The system held the ship virtually motionless in position and precisely over the drill hole all the time.

On the *Glomar Challenger* the time came to hand things over to the tooler or chief roughneck, and he started barking orders as if he were a prison guard supervising a chain gang on a road job.

Cliff, who had learned that crews on research ships tended to regard oceanographers with the same contempt that guards and tackles show for quarterbacks, stayed well away from roughnecks while they worked.

A knock sounded at the door of the op room. "Dr. Lorenz?"

Roy Felton stood in the doorway. "The divers are waiting in the ready room, sir. I had them go through a dress rehearsal."

"How're they doing, Roy?"

Felton shrugged, eyes averted. Even to a veteran of many dangerous night dives and rescue efforts, the idea of descending over a jungle of long weeds led to nightmares. "Fine, I guess," he answered in a thin voice.

Skip, the lead diver, and Tony, the third arm, were seated on a bench next to the communications console, their heads in traditional red caps sticking out of the locking neck rings of their yellow, thermally insulated Viking dry suits. They preferred this type of suit, as it allowed them to stay underwater longer and work more comfortably because one stayed dry. With their Kirby Morgan helmet on their lap, they looked like astronauts sitting for a preflight picture.

The other divers, in jeans and work shirts, were seated on folding chairs arranged in a semicircle. Air hissed out of the safety valve of a giant DCS, the dive-control system. Dry and wet suits hung from the walls like giant colored-paper cutouts. The place had the gummy smell of latex and baby powder.

"There isn't much I can add to the earlier briefings," Cliff began, and quickly recapped what the divers were to expect. A thermocline was first. According to the recent soundings, the thermocline was at the two-hundred-foot depth. The temperature drop, Cliff said, would be extremely rapid, almost thirty degrees.

"What about visibility?" Tony asked.

"Not like in the Bahamas," Cliff answered, and explained that the water was denser because it got heavier and sank as it approached the freezing point. They would see plenty of "snow," the underwater particles blown by the cold current. "All told, you should have thirty to forty feet of visibility with the halogen lamp. And speaking of currents, the one you will encounter will not be a strong one." He looked at his chart. "Forty centimeters per second, about a knot.

"And now the . . . weeds."

Involuntarily, the way he said it was unsettling, and Skip, who had appeared calm—even bored—as he listened, now looked at Cliff with an apprehensive sideways squint. His buddies shifted uneasily.

"We don't know a hell of a lot about them," Cliff continued, the tone of his voice giving away his apprehension. "They remain one of oceanography's mysteries."

Skip cocked one eyebrow.

Cliff turned to him and explained that nobody knew how they grew. "We just don't know."

"Think there's going to be trouble down there?" one of the divers asked.

Cliff knew that the divers must be pondering the same ugly images of entanglement that were rushing through his own mind.

The weeds had to be feared if one hoped to surface alive. He said, "If you don't rely on your instinct and experience, yes. I'd say lots of trouble."

He looked around. "Here's what you'll do," he went on. "You'll descend over the weeds slowly until you see their tops. Stop. Drop more—but not below the tops—and cut them off. Drop again, cut. Talk as you work. Felton and I have to know what you're doing so that we can advise you. Understand?"

They nodded.

"Sir, this ain't the first time we cut—"

Cliff cut Skip short. "Just do what I tell you. All right? This is like diving in Boston Harbor." Cliff looked at the others. "Any questions?"

Not one.

"Well, good luck," he said softly, and shook Tony's hand and then Skip's.

Adams, a rigger and an engineer of the ARC, took over, and the team rehearsed loading and wiring. Cliff, wanting all support personnel to do their job undisturbed, walked to op room to see if there were any messages from Roscoe or Kronin.

He wasn't back there a minute when the tooler signaled that everything was ready to drill shot hole number one. "Start engine," he ordered, his breath steaming in the wintry air.

The deck, flooded with large quartz lamps, seemed ready for a movie night scene. Hanging from a swivel in the center of the derrick was the square kelly, the first joint of pipe, the drill collar, and the bit. In that order. At a signal from the tooler, the bit passed slowly through the center of the turntable, followed by the first joint and a number of drill pipes. Minutes later, the tooler shouted, "Contact." Almost at once, the drill collar was locked in the turntable, the giant motor picked up speed, and the bit began to bite in.

Calmly, the tooler watched a panel on the control board. It told him how much pressure was on the bit. "Too much weight on the bit," he shouted. "It's getting embedded in the rock. It'll never get the chips out. . . . Okay, Jim, reduce weight by one-third. . . . Fine. Easy does it . . . All right, increase pump action."

At that command, drilling mud, forced down inside the drill pipe, began to well up around the bit, cooling it, and then flowed up the return pipe, through a wire screen, and into a tank.

Roughnecks moved around as the tooler barked orders. Smoke billowed out of the motor's exhaust as the kelly picked up another joint of pipe and brought it over the center of the hole. "All right, let's screw it nice and tight," the tooler said.

Then he started counting the number of feet of penetration and estimating the hardness of the rock by the way the drilling was going.

"Ten, eleven, thirteen . . ."

A cloud of bluish-brown smoke billowed out of the exhaust pipe of the giant diesel engine driving the heavy steel turntable through which the sections of drill pipes were fed. The air filled with an ominous thrumming.

"Rock hardness . . . three. Not bad!" he shouted enthusiastically.

Second day of drilling. Late afternoon.

It was raw with only a wash of orange light in the west, suggesting warmth. In the east the horizon had disappeared in a low overcast, and the Atlantic looked wrinkled and flecked. A cold wind fluted through the maze of antennas and guy wires.

Cliff stood on the open bridge alternately watching the sea and the roughnecks at work, wondering how they could do it. They were covered with mud, the deck was slippery, and a Labrador wind showered them with a frigid ocean spray. A ghostly vapor rose from their body in a mix of breath and perspiration. Two yards away the diesel engine that drove the shaft roared with power, while the rack-and-pinion mechanism of the overhead crane squeaked. With a wind-chill factor of minus fifteen, pain accompanied every task and hastened crew burnout. They talked little.

Suddenly came the announcement. "Shot hole one ready," the tooler shouted. "BD is seven, niner, zero." He was referring to burial depth, the maximum depth Adams had specified for that hole. With that announcement came a change in motor pitch, and the drill shaft idled.

It was now just past six P.M.

Not far from the shed housing the motor, the crews assigned to the divers were running through one more checklist. The intercom was working; the supply of oxygen and helium checked out; life and slack lines had been examined for breaks and punctures. The forty pounds of lead weights were laid out. And double-checking their work was Roy Felton.

A hatch opened and a tractor moved onto the deck pulling a coffin-like metal container with Special Ammunition Storage written in red and flanked by universal nuclear symbols.

Off-duty sailors came out to watch. At last the flotilla got into the brass tacks of Operation Drill and Load.

Using the drill shaft as a guide, Skip went down first. Tony followed twenty-five feet behind. He was carrying a bank of amber halogen lights.

"Skip, give me a short count," Felton said into a microphone, as he watched from the door of the ready room.

"*One, two, three . . .*"

Bubbles came up and broke; the lungs, the air compressor breathed easily; crews worked silently, their ears tuned to the speaker.

It looked and sounded like just another dive.

But things soon changed.

At fifty feet, the North Atlantic became an explosion of fish. A school of them resembling arrowheads turned as one around the drill shaft. Another seemed suspended to Skip's right, their fins fluttering for balance in hummingbird fashion. Transparent worms came straight at him, striking the Plexiglas faceplate. Swiftly, a formation of three swordfish buzzed him twice, obviously sensing prey. They gave him the feeling that he was being watched—curiously and with contempt. Swordfish could be mean.

"How're you guys doing up there?" he said jauntily. "We're taking it easy as we go through the thermocline. It's cold, all right."

Silently Roy Felton read the descent meter, mike in hand. "*You should be over the tops. Watch out,*" he said.

"No weeds in sight. But I can see contact point."

And that he did without straining because the drill bit had made contact over a ledge of rock so smooth and light colored it shimmered with shafts of reflected halogen amber.

But where were the weeds? "I'm parked just over bottom and I don't see nothing," he said. He signaled Tony to fan the lights and saw bottom, eyes alert at the slightest movement. His heart pounding in his chest, Skip looked around, drawn by a morbid curiosity.

"Let fifteen on the umbilical," he ordered, asking for fifteen feet of slack on the inch-and-a-half-wide nylon lifelines hooked on his shoulder harness and the round hose carrying the air mixture and phone wires taped on it.

Using the ledge as a reference point, he descended and touched bottom.

Slowly he turned around and there, not fifteen feet away, shining garishly under the halogen lights, were orange tube-shaped objects rising vertically like the columns of an ancient mosque.

And the tops? Skip walked a few feet, looked up, and saw long, foot-wide blades with bony, Velcro-like thorns growing along the spines, which fanned out like a crown on top of the tube-shaped objects, or stems, as he called them.

"I can see the weeds."

"What do they look like?"

"Weeds, man." He laughed. "Can you switch me to Dr. Lorenz in the op room?"

Felton flipped a switch and Cliff got on the line.

"Well, Doc, I can tell you what the weeds look like."

"*I'm listening*," Cliff said, and Skip described what he saw as best he could.

"Well, sir, I would say . . . they look like palm trees. Yeah, that's it."

"*How far apart are the stems?*"

Skip paused. "You could fit a two-car garage between stems. I'd say the trick is to drop through the space where there are no blades and walk to the drill hole. One could also . . . Hold on, sir."

He checked his air line and untangled it; listened to the five-second self-testing beep in the phone hookup. It was loud and clear. He was actually having fun, though his throat had clutched a bit. But his curiosity was greater than whatever was playing with his throat. And he thanked God for it. It made up for the lack of a high school education. How often does a high school dropout have the opportunity to contribute to oceanography? And solve a problem for his buddies above.

"Looking for a place where I can anchor the firing cables," he announced, and, having walked slowly toward the nearest stem, he reached for his knife and got closer to the stem.

That's when he made his mistake.

As he walked under the arch, he didn't foresee that the very tops of the weeds could touch his lifelines—which they did. Thorns by the thousand anchored on them.

Unaware of this, Skip started cutting the stem at the base. "I'm cutting a stem to see if it's easy in case you have one of them near the drill hole. But this fuckin' thing . . . A machete would be better. But wait." Skip cut through the stem as hard as he could. "There it goes. Whoa! Slack up," he ordered, smiling.

But when he felt no tugging on his belt, he suspected he might be in trouble.

"Slack up, I said. Wake up, you guys." The voice, like an S.O.S., had an edge of desperation.

Outside the ready room, Roy Felton tensed as he watched the winch operator shake his head and say, "Slack won't come up, Chief. Somethin's wrong."

A siren went off.

In the op room, Cliff cursed. Something had gone wrong. He was sure of it.

Beneath the sea, Tony had descended some twenty feet from Skip and was explaining to Felton that the blades were stuck onto the lifelines. "Like they were welded on."

"OK, Tony, don't get close to them. But you, Skip, see if you can cut some of those blades, all right?"

"Yeah, sure. No sweat," Skip said, but the sight of the weeds alone swaying toward him was terrifying. They spooked him, and he looked at them with glassy and unmoving eyes.

"I'm telling you guys, moving around these weeds requires real concentration. They're the ugliest fuckin' things I've ever seen. But I'll find a way to work around them, you know me," he said, but the words came out stuck together.

Having pulled down on the slack, Skip began cutting one blade off the lifelines.

It proved more difficult than it seemed because he wasn't able to get a firm hold on the weed. It had a slippery, squidlike texture. And then there was the risk of having his suit punctured by the thorns he could now see. At that depth, pressure would instantly balloon his suit with water.

He stood still for a moment, thinking about his next move. Since the current was moving the blades just over his head, he got on his knees for a better whack at them. It was cold, but he could breathe well. He took a couple of deep breaths.

"Skip, what's up?" Felton asked him.

"Just resting. You all right, Tony?"

"No sweat, Skip."

And then, suddenly, without warning, he felt an involuntary contraction of the flexor of his right leg. *Maybe not*, Skip told himself, worried. If there was anything divers feared more than sharks it was cramps.

Before he could straighten up, a sharp pain seized him. Now the muscle under his thigh knotted so hard he could feel it bulging out like a tennis ball. Jesus, he was getting a charley horse.

At once he dropped the knife and tried to stand straight. But he couldn't. If anything, he crouched even more. It felt as if his leg was a nutcracker squeezed by a giant hand.

"I've got a charley horse."

Felton swore, his thick, clotty voice bouncing off the metal wall. "*Try to relax and rub it.*"

"God . . . is it . . . painful."

"*Try again to rub it,*" Felton said and signaled to lower the rescue bell. "Did you try to stretch?"

"*This is Tony. Skip, try hard.*"

"I can't."

"*Skip, dammit, stretch it!*"

"Please, Tony, help me."

Felton broke in. "*Tony? You stay where you are. That's an order. Hang on those lights and don't move. Give me a roger.*"

Tony's voice came over the speaker. "*Roger . . . Skip, please, try.*"

When the muscle contraction reached its peak, Skip doubled over and fell into a fetal position—hardly a good one for the lungs to expand when breathing air six times the normal pressure. And as he fell, his air hose got squeezed between a lead weight on his belt and the rock, reducing his airflow.

Silt rose quickly about him, clouding the water.

Breathing was now even more difficult. A shudder of panic stole through his chest, and Skip began to shake with fear of mortal danger. "Is the lung working? . . . Somebody do . . . something, please. Little air," Skip said between gasps. He was now in terror, numb with dread.

In the ready room a diver put his head down and plugged his ears; another started swearing, still another pounded the bulkhead. "Damn, damn, damn."

"Don't worry, Skip. We're increasing air pressure." It was Felton with a calm voice as he nodded to the DCS operator who had motioned to him that no air was getting through to Skip.

"Please. Oh, please hurry. I think I'm going to die." Skip's vision was blurred; he couldn't see. He started choking convulsively. *"For God's sake . . . do something. I think I'm going to die."* He gagged; retched. His face was reddish blue and shining with sweat.

The DCS operator swore with a voice so anguished that no one ever forgot it. Dark premonition held the others speechless.

"I think I'm going to . . . die."

"Shut up and die like a diver," Felton said.

"Oh, my God . . . " Skip's voice trailed into silence, into a coma from which he would never awake. A day later the *Knorr* would take him twenty miles out for burial at sea.

So, Operation Drill and Load came to a stop.

Cliff felt a deep, personal grief. He hadn't studied the problem of the weeds long enough; he had sent Skip down with a minimum of instructions. Skip's death had put things in a different perspective: if the weeds had gotten the best and most experienced diver, what chance would the others have?

Tony had to pick up from where Skip had left off, despite Cliff's fears that Tony might not be the right man for the job. The comment in the dossier that Tony had the tendency to rush repeated in Cliff's head.

"Fact is, sir, you send Jimmy down," Felton had told him, "the confidence of the rest of the UDT will go down with him. The thing about navy divers is . . . well, they have their own goddamn sacred order of things."

It was 9:25 A.M., and the tug-of-war between wind and outboard engines that kept the *Challenger* on target had begun. It felt like a long earthquake.

A day and a half had passed since Skip's last dive, and the weather was changing. A somber, ashen sky threatened to bring the first snow.

"Just remember this," Felton said, passing a Kleenex over Tony's faceplate, his eyes watering slightly with emotion and not because of the wind, "all the nukes have to fire if the modification is to succeed. You heard Adams. We just can't afford misfires. Work fast but don't do things with haste." He gave Tony a pat over the helmet. "Go. God be with you, and know that I'll make sure you'll surface."

Tony nodded, his forehead glistening more with anxiety than with real perspiration.

His first dive was over an area that he could see was free of weeds. But his temperature rose and he began to breathe irregularly. It was then that he remembered Felton's last words to Skip.

There was a reading of 220 on the depth gauge. His lifeline was free. "Going down, and enjoying the view," he said, straining to sound cool and excited, but his voice still cracked with a thrill of alarm.

He automatically halted his descent slowly through the thermocline, making sure all systems worked. They did, but water was leaking through the left latex rubber cuff. Calmly Tony pulled it higher up on his arm. The leakage stopped.

The bank of six powerful, amber-colored halogen lights just above him made him feel good and warm, and let him see an opening free of weeds. He descended without difficulty, always aware that the blades were not far away.

The first drill hole, now visible through the murky water, was two feet beneath him.

Tony waited for the water to clear as jellyfish danced in front of him like translucent goblins. Not far away, Fred—the third arm—kept giving him the "no shark" hand signal.

Nuclear charges came in different shapes and explosive sizes, and were controlled by the Department of Energy. The ones Gallego had selected were built at the Nuclear Weapon Production Facility in New Mexico and of the type specially made for the military to reroute rivers, blow up dams, cause landslides. Called ADEMS, short for Atomic Demolition Munitions, they were four feet long and eleven inches in diameter. They resembled oxygen tanks.

Though he had worked on dummy ADEMS during training, Tony didn't feel like touching the first real one the special ammunition officer had sent him. For a while he just stared at it with stomach-twisting intensity.

He could see clearly the green, yellow and red sections of the nuke: top section, initiator; middle section, uranium-235 rod; bottom section, fissionable core. But his eyes kept returning to the green section and the two standoff posts sticking out like the jambs of a sea mine. That was where it all began.

"The principle behind the detonation of a nuclear device," Gallego had said during training in Norfolk, "is comparable to the sequence in an artillery round. Q.E.D. . . . TNT initiator blasts uranium rod projectile down to fissionable core; uranium and core react with explosion."

Motionless, like a man in wax, Tony couldn't keep his eyes away from the ADEM. One immobile moment followed another, his muscles frozen.

But he wasn't going to blow his cool. Not the day after he became lead diver.

He started humming some ad lib tune softly, eyes on the green section. *Imagine me, seeing a nuke, let alone handling one? On August such and such, navy diver Anthony Baldi loaded the first nuke that modified . . .*

That thought broke his paralysis. Now he was ready to load the damn thing. He reached for the tool basket hanging a foot above his shoulder, momentarily forgetting colors, firing sequences, kilotons of TNT. Carefully, as if the ADEM was pressure sensitive, he placed his hands around the red section and let it rest on the hollow of his right shoulder. His hands trembled as he held the ADEM in place. Now a warm sensation in his chest made him think that the energy radiating from the fissionable core was already frying his insides.

Pushing with his legs, he lined up the ADEM with the center of the hole. "OK, drop it gently—and I mean gently," he said in a whisper.

Tony could now feel the accelerating trip-hammer beat of his heart telegraphed to his left wrist, where the sealing cuffs were very tight.

Next to preventing the canister from banging against the rock and causing damage to the delicate internal mechanism, he had to make sure that the outer insulation of the cable didn't scrape off as it passed by the razor-sharp rim of the hole. Exposed inner conductors could short-circuit or bleed precious radio frequency power. That he knew from laying cable for antisubmarine hydrophones.

Like a piston in its down cycle, the ADEM slid smoothly into the hole, and Tony let his breath out in a long, slow sigh. And as the ADEM disappeared, leaving a spiraling trail of silt, he held the firing electrical cable and the chain used to lower the ADEM away from the rim of the hole.

In the cabin, a computer told the winch operator that the canister was nearing BD. Minutes later Tony looked up and saw the plug suspended a few feet above him.

As instructed, his job now was to fit a bassinet-shaped steel lid over the hole, unfasten the chain that brought it down, then see if the firing and retrieve box attached to the cap by cable had made it down undamaged, and that the self-testing/homing light was working.

Actually oval and about a foot high, the firing and retrieve box contained modules of the permissive action linkage, the all-important electronic "pass key" that authenticated the blue-green laser firing signal, then sent out authenticated signals of its own to the initiator on command. It was a miniaturized crypto room.

This last phase of the assignment was important. If the light wasn't glowing intermittently, the F/R box would not authenticate the firing command. Worse yet, in case the nuclear blasting was called off, it would not send out infrared signals to divers looking for it with homing receivers.

"Then anybody could get a hold on a nuke," the SAO had warned. "And there are a lot of loonies around."

In cooperation with the winch operator, Tony capped the hole. It took three minutes. This done, he got ready to disengage the chain.

He checked with the dive information center about time elapsed, pressure, etc., and started to work on the bolt that held the chain. All the while he kept an eye on Fred and gave Felton a blow-by-blow report.

But soon he ran into trouble.

The bolt wouldn't loosen up.

He worked it from a different angle. Still it wouldn't loosen.

"Way beyond torque. Who the fuck tightened it so hard?" he shouted.

"*We'll get the bastard later,*" Felton said. "*Just cut it loose.*"

Up in the op room, where a repeater speaker carried the crew/diver communications, Cliff's breath stopped in his throat at the word *cut.*

He knew that the bolt, being attached to the cap, was part of the common ground of the electrical circuit to which the firing mechanism was wired. If frictional static was allowed to build up during the cutting, a dangerous level of electricity would develop across the circuit. Water was a good conductor. Frictional electricity increased with speed—and Tony worked fast.

Cliff stormed out of the op room, followed by the chief engineer, who had obviously arrived at the same conclusion. Together they bolted through the passageways and down metal stairs. Human error was always the most costly.

"Tell him to shop cutting," the engineer shouted even before he entered the ready room.

Without an explanation, Cliff yanked the mike out of Felton's hands. "Tony, this is Cliff Lorenz," he said. "I want you to cut that bolt very, very, *very* slowly. Give me a roger."

"*All right, roger.*" Tony sounded annoyed. "*I know what you're thinking. If I cut myself, sharks will smell blood. I'll be careful.*"

"That and then some." Cliff didn't have to say more. He knew Tony was already scared enough to be careful. "Listen, Tony, and listen carefully." His voice kept rising. "You will cut the damn thing as I direct. One, forth; two, back. Get it?"

"*It's really getting cold,*" Tony's voice sailed back in cranky bursts and was distorted. Because the extra helium in the mixture he was breathing increased the velocity of sound, the pitch of his voice rose. He sounded like a discontented Donald Duck.

"It's cold up here, too. Now keep your mouth shut and do what I told you. *Ready*? One . . . two . . . ; one . . ."

Ten minutes later, Tony had succeeded in cutting the bolt and freeing the chain.

Wasting no time, he wedged the eyelet between the cleavage of the rock, pushed down with a hammer, passed the wires through it, then fastened them with an automobile hose clamp. That was easy. He looked around. No sharks . . . and no cramps.

Next came the firing and retrieve box.

"Look, you guys," Tony said, "unless you make the wires shorter, the current will push all the boxes into the fuckin' weeds."

"Will do," Felton said. It was a good suggestion and he thanked Tony for it. But the electricians would have to splice and fit connectors on the shorter cables. "It will take time."

"Five minutes?"

"More like . . . fifteen."

Shit! Tony thought for a moment. He wasn't getting a cramp, his muscles felt very loose, and he wasn't tired. Breathing was still easy. He could stay down a bit longer. If he didn't, someone else would finish the job. He really wanted to wire that first nuke.

He called Felton. "I gave the box a good look. It really isn't that close to the weeds," he lied. "I'll check it, but the next one must have a shorter cable."

"Sure?"

"No sweat."

The F/R box was floating twenty feet over his head and ten to his right. He started to come up to it and the closer he got to it the better he could see it. And the weeds.

Carefully Tony inched closer to the box until he could make out the spokes of the VHF turnstile antenna, the most delicate component. They looked intact. He turned it around and could see a red light glowing. "First nuke loaded and wired. Pull me up."

So the first report was coded and radioed out to Norfolk and to Kronin. "*Shot hole one ready. One fatality. C. Lorenz.*"

Still standing, Cliff took out his notebook and wrote down the same message he had sent to Kronin. Putting the notebook in his pants back pocket, he went to see Adams, who was in the jury-rigged situation room. There, fastened on the wall with electrical tape, was a chart of the Hull showing the first shot hole all inked with red.

Cliff put a finger on the hole and asked Adams, "The question now is, will it fire?"

Adams nodded. "From what Gallego tells me, yes. Strange as it sounds, there's never been a nuclear misfire. The system must work."

Still in the situation room, Cliff leafed through the latest dispatches the radio officer had handed him: one from the Navy Meteorological Office in Norfolk; one from the International Ice Patrol. Cliff read the one about the weather first:

NNNN
CLIFF LORENZ
USS GLOMAR CHALLENGER.
24 AUGUST 11:00 ZULU

A MASSIVE UPPER AIR LOW IS GETTING ORGANIZED OVER BRITISH COLUMBIA. WILL REPORT ON THIS DEVEL-OPMENT EVERY SIX HOURS.

BEST REGARDS
CHARLES E. DOWLING, CAPT. USN

Cliff swore to himself and read the other message. It reported sighting icebergs and clusters of floes about seven hundred miles north of the flotilla. They had moved slowly from the last reported sighting, but still headed toward the Labrador current.

Shot hole two was drilled and loaded. Then number three, four, five . . .

Alternately engines coughed into life, divers dived and surfaced, crews came and went, and the drill ships moved up another three miles. A rhythm developed, and everybody felt that a definite momentum had been established. Crews worked seemingly driven by anger as compressors hissed, buckles clanged, turntables squeaked, and chains clattered, mixing dissonantly with the sputter of the outboard motors thrashing the water. All of this while the ship yawed, jerked, bobbed, and lurched fore and aft, fighting to hold position in the increasingly turbulent Atlantic.

There were good days and days like no Arctic explorer had ever described. There was also the energy in the dream of outwitting nature. Nevertheless, it was a hard life.

But nobody had expected less.

24

In Duluth it had began at dusk, September 2.

In less than two hours, from a limpid, brilliant blue, clouds grayed the sky to a solid overcast like a dark curtain. The barometer dropped. So did the temperature—to fifteen degrees F. An east wind brought the first streaming snowflakes of the blizzard, granular for the most part. Within an hour, it rose to near hurricane force. Snow whirled, driving parallel to the ground like an North African ghibli. Then came the skidding, the accidents, the angry fights.

The blizzard struck Chicago next.

It seized the city with the brute force of a bear seeking revenge, as one newscaster put it.

By seven in the evening, O'Hare Airport had to shut down because of six-foot-high snowdrifts accumulating under the wheel carriages of planes waiting to take off on runway 32.

Downtown, power lines snapped under the weight of snow. Traffic lights went out first on Washington Boulevard, then at the busy intersection of Central Park Boulevard.

"Stay indoors," the mayor had warned that morning, but

thousands had ventured into the city for one last business day, to visit someone in a hospital, or go to the bank as suburban offices were out of cash.

Now, after being forced into center lanes because of high drifts on the windward side of major arteries, motorists going home had to fight desperate battles at every intersection where no policeman was directing traffic.

Fearing the much-publicized hypothermia, the falling of body temperature below normal, many had let their engines run and were overcome by fumes escaping through rusted panels and floorboards.

Overexertion, perspiration, and the bitter cold got thousands more. With winds lowering the chill factor to thirty degrees below zero F, exposed skin became brittle and cracked. Frostbite became epidemic and went untreated because doctors were treating more serious emergency cases.

Nor was Lake Michigan a faster route out for those who had anticipated an evacuation order.

Ignoring a Coast Guard report, the *Monitou Bell*, a two-decked ferryboat, left Green Bay shortly after nine P.M., with a load of high-paying evacuees. An hour later, a flat-topped ice floe, driven by the wind, rammed into its hull, gouging an eight-foot hole at the waterline. Icy water rushed through the hole, deluging the engine room. Hot steam billowed furiously up the aft stairwell. Hysterical passengers lurched, elbowed, pushed, shoved, clawed their way out to the upper decks and the lifeboats. But it was too late. The *Monitou Bell* went under bow first, and its passengers, like children on a pool slide, skidded to their death.

Trains were no surer means of escape.

As drift snow piled under bridges and on exposed stretches of track, trains started to slow down. The Floridian, which had been ordered to wait in the Illinois Central Gulf Station until priority military convoys had reached Gary, Indiana, never got out of Chicago.

By the afternoon of the second storm day, Chicago had

lost the city pulse. Her socio-systems—electricity, transportation, communications, food supplies—were virtually nonexistent. Walking was dangerous and children disappeared in the snow, as high as nine feet in front of the Mercantile Building. Roads were blocked; no traffic moved, not even military vehicles. Millions were left without utilities. Water mains froze and burst. Ice quickly formed and expanded. Walls gave in under the pressure of the ice and cracked. Windowpanes shattered, light poles tilted, cables snapped. Roofs collapsed under the weight of tons of snow. Fires raged out of control. Fire brigades were helpless. A smell like a burning garbage dump hung in the air. As night fell, from windows of residential homes, the faint light of candles and oil lamps shed a sickly yellow glow on the snow.

The Weather Bureau called the storm Alfi because it was the first blizzard of glaciation.

In the evacuation bus, mostly filled with blue-haired ladies in real fur coats and high boots, Pam stared back for another glimpse of D.C. with a consoling arm around Butch, who had had to leave a friend behind.

As the bus crossed over the Potomac and was waved on at the Wilson Boulevard checkpoint, a slim soldier stood up by the front door and gave his name, rank, division, and regiment information.

"You're traveling with a United States Army convoy," he said with a shrill jockey voice. "Therefore, you are subject to army jurisdiction. All I can tell you is that your destination is Bailey, Texas. Don't ask me near what city it is, or what our ETA is—that's estimated time of arrival." He wiped his running nose with the sleeve of his parka. "I simply don't know." And in the same breath he added, "I only know that (a) there will be no smoking; (b) the bus will stop only at designated areas; (c) you'll get some hot chow and coffee when we get to Greenville, South Carolina." He sat down, pulled his pile cap over his eyes, and went to sleep.

As the bus made a right turn on Spoutrun Parkway, the towers of Georgetown University were still visible on the left. It was in the Lauinger Memorial Library, Pam remembered, that Cliff would often spend a few hours looking through computer magazines and articles on the environment. It was his ivory tower. She thought of him wistfully and wondered what he was doing at that very moment. Then she took off her glove, leaned forward, and put a hand on Butch's face, which looked flushed. Not feverish. That was a relief. She took a deep breath, pushed the collar of her heavy car coat up, and closed her eyes.

She felt a nudge from the woman next to her. Pam turned, and saw her pointing to Pam's handbag.

"If you must sleep," the woman whispered, "do it with one eye open at all times—if all you own now is in there."

"Of course, thank you," Pam said, catching a trace of a British accent.

"And unless you remove your rings, you'd better not take those gloves off again. Rings will be better than cash soon."

"I never wear rings. But these were my mother's, and I didn't want to lose them," Pam said, and thanked her. She was a tiny, bright-eyed woman in her late seventies.

"And remember this."

Pam turned.

"Trust no one, and don't make friends."

"Don't make friends?" Pam looked puzzled. "Why not?"

The woman leaned toward her. "Making friends now will mean sharing with them what they don't have." She winked an eye. "Or claim not to have. I was in London during the war. I learned a lot." She nudged Pam and never spoke again.

With the convoy of buses carrying wives of congressmen and other high officials south of D.C., the evacuation of government documents and national treasures began trouble free.

Martial law, whose meaning and implications had been explained by the press and the television media, was responsible for the initial success. With roadblocks set up at major intersections and entrances to exit routes, hundreds of military vehicles moved around D.C. picking up sensitive documents and computer tapes from the CIA, Department of Defense, IRS, U.S. Mint. . . .

On the second day, items classified as "Primary Resources of the National Patrimony" were shipped out of museums and libraries. Of the 18 million volumes in the Library of Congress, only a fraction of the rarest and most valuable manuscripts and first editions were carted off.

"We have another three hundred miles of bookshelves in there," Dr. Malvin Fox, the chief librarian, said to the officer who had come to inform him that there was no more space in the trucks allotted to the library. "You know, Captain," he told the officer with a smokey whisper of a voice, "we don't want a repeat of what happened to the National Library in Madrid during the civil war—when booksellers, antique dealers, and dishonest academics ripped it off clean." As an afterthought, he added, "Of course, even if we locked our precious books in vaults, I don't think they could withstand the ravages of an ice age."

Of course, there was also a limit on what could be moved out of the many national museums and galleries. But the Declaration of Independence, together with the Bill of Rights, in their original glass enclosure and nine crates of manuscripts of the period from 1773 to 1779 left D.C. by guarded vans, as did Lincoln's statue by Daniel French, the *Spirit of St. Louis,* the *Kitty Hawk,* the *Apollo 11* Lunar Module, and a Lucite block with Lincoln's first and second drafts of the Gettysburg Address.

Because of the weight and volume of packing crates, only two paintings per artist in the National Art Gallery were permitted to be moved out of D.C. The remaining paintings were locked in World War II air raid shelters along the Mall, which were designed to protect artwork from falling bombs.

"Egg and tempera canvases, the oils of the great masters will simply flake off under sub-zero weather," curator Daryl Simpson explained when he walked to the White House to plead for more trucks. "Imagine El Greco's *Laocoön*, or Raphael's *The Small Cowper Madonna*, lost forever."

Simpson might as well have spoken in Greek. He just got a shrug from the aide who had listened to him on behalf of the president.

A computer program had organized the exodus of the rest of the residents of D.C., and for 80 percent of them the automobile, in whatever condition it was, had to do.

And so just after six in the morning, the first cars were—block by block—permitted to travel on primary roads leading to exit roads such as routes 95 and 66. By ten A.M., the first convoy of cars from the northeast section of the city between C and K and Second and Fourth streets came to a halt when an old school bus overloaded with patients of a nursing home broke an axle. Since the convoy was not on the designated primary roads by the time specified by the computer printout, it prevented others from moving at all.

At first motorists behaved as they would in normal circumstances. But two hours later, it was obvious that a planned evacuation by automobile would not work as scheduled.

"The American dream," radioed a reporter from a helicopter, "is fast becoming a nightmare vehicle. It will be a deathtrap for people who rely on automobiles. And there is no snow yet on the roads. Imagine what things below will look like when New York City is ordered to evacuate."

It was the first time a presidential aide had handed a note directly to the president and not to the chief of staff. Originating at NASA headquarters, it informed the president that there were now problems with the tinfoils placed in orbit. It had just been discovered, the note said, that the sun rays reflected by the tinfoils were overheating many of the navigation, communications, and spy satellites in the same stationary orbit. And not just United States satellites. That morning the Russian ambassador had asked to see the secretary of state, a visit many believed was related to the reflectors.

There was another problem. The mayor of New York City had requested that triage begin immediately. "With transportation at a minimum, it's either the living or the dying," he wired. There was an appeal by Cardinal Connelly and other religious leaders that the millions of people slated to be left behind not be allowed to die unattended.

"Okay, so NASA's venetian blinds are out," the president told the chief of staff, "and every member of the physics department at the University of Chicago signs a letter urging me not to allow the use of ion machines because they fear a dangerous reaction from an overly charged atmosphere." In the letter the physicists had pointed out that massive charges of ions would destabilize the electrical properties of the atmosphere at a time when glaciation-related climatic patterns were sure to cause severe instability. He grabbed the letter and waved it at the chief of staff. "Fifteen signatures: one of a Nobel laureate, no less."

The chief of staff nodded and placed the tray with a glass of milk on the desk.

The president looked at him with flat, sightless eyes. "Do you think milk is going to solve my problems?"

"No, I don't, Mr. President. But . . . it's warm."

The president drank it in one draft, noticing the blue briefing folders that the chief of staff held under his arm.

"What's the other problem?" he asked after he had replaced the glass on the tray.

The chief of staff was silent for a moment, then shifted in his chair uneasily. There had been an outbreak of influenza in Cleveland and Boston; violence on exit route 93; the citizens of Canton, Louisiana, had barricaded the entrance to the town after hearing that a ship loaded with patients evacuated from a Baltimore hospital was nearing their harbor.

And more.

"Our troops in Europe, Mr. President," he said, reluctantly. "Despite the breakup of the Warsaw Pact, they are still out there in the cold."

"I know. I know," the president said. With the corner of his mouth twisted with exasperation, he leaned back in his chair and listened to the reports from Europe.

In Germany, General W. S. Westmoreland, commander of the U.S. Third Armored Division stationed along the Lübeck-Ulsen defense line, could count on only 240 tanks. Cold temperatures and winds raging down from the Baltic Sea were congealing the oil in the engine block of the remaining 310 tanks not yet lubricated for Arctic operation because of the shortage of the special oil. Along the entire east-west border, only three armored units of the Federal Republic of Germany, two British, and five American ones had been winterized for Arctic conditions. Westmoreland knew that the thousands of jeeps, trucks, personnel carriers, communications and radar vans under his command were not expected to start up.

When he went out for an inspection tour later on the morning of August 29, snow was falling thick and the temperature was minus four degrees. Inside an M-1 Abrams tank, the best the heater could do was to raise the temperature some nine degrees.

"Did you have your hot chow?" the general asked, his voice robust and sharp. It echoed metallic inside the tank.

The tank crew gave him a lethargic nod.

"Any complaints?"

The tank commander shook his head. Vapor streamed through the woolen scarf wrapped around his mouth.

The general turned to look at the loader in back of him, who also shook his head.

"How about you?" the general said, looking up at the gunner who had quivering eyes.

"No complaints, sir," he said as he took off his gloves. "Just an observation."

"Your name?"

"Specialist second class Louis J. Johnson," he said in a pained voice.

"Go ahead, son."

Johnson, a black youth of twenty-two, put a swollen hand on the breach of the 120-millimeter gun. "Sir," he said, his teeth chattering, "this thing is so brittle that if I pull the trigger, it will kill everyone in this tank instead of whoever is out there these days."

The general reached up, patted Johnson's knee and said, "Well, Louis J., let's hope whoever is out there, as you say, realizes the same thing."

Inside One-Charlie, a concrete observation bunker six miles south of Gottingen, a medic was putting a surgical sponge over the eye of an observer.

The general put a hand on the observer's shoulder. "What happened to you, son?" the general asked.

The observer seemed unwilling to open his mouth, cold as it was. The medic answered for him. He explained that a piece of the observer's eyebrow and the viewfinder of an infrared field glass had welded like two ice cubes, the cold apparently killing the pain. "He didn't realize what had happened until he saw it dangling from the eyepiece," he said.

"Take him to the hospital," the general ordered, "and keep him in there a couple of days."

The general moved on; snow piled up, and so did his problems.

"It's a torrent of snow," Hans Stametz radioed back to his base. The director of the Swiss Federal Research Institute for Snows and Avalanches, he was looking at one of the glaciation phenomena, soft glaciers. Conditions favored the formation of these fast-moving "ice streams." He had been watching them as he flew over the Jüngfrau aboard a helicopter.

Unlike the first snow of the season, the wet and heavy variety that clings to the surface, what had fallen at the highest elevation, because of the sudden drop in temperature, was a granular snow, sugar snow, so called for its cuplike crystals. As such, it held together poorly on the smooth, treeless slopes, acting like ball bearings for the pack of snow accumulating on it.

It was also holding poorly on the southern slope of Mount Roccione (12,854 feet) overlooking Dorsano de' Monte, a tiny ski village fifty-six miles west of Cortina d'Ampezzo, scheduled to evacuate in a week.

There an additional threat to the five hundred inhabitants had developed during the night. A cornice formed by drift snow perched dangerously along the ridge line at the height of the leeward slope. It hung over Dorsano like the scroll of a huge Ionic column.

Avalanches in the Dolomites were daily occurrences, and people had learned to live with them. So just before four-thirty P.M., by order of the mayor, the bells of St. Paul's Church began to toll nine times every nine minutes. Quickly the people of Dorsano moved into the massive stone monastery high on a hill. It was a precaution, and they all felt safe there. Built like a fortress, the monastery had two anti-avalanche measures: a *schützwalder*, rows of pine trees, and a reinforced concrete wall shaped like a ship's prow that faced uphill beyond the *schützwalder*. These had broken up hundreds of avalanches.

By the time the last Dorsanese walked into the monastery, the orange and gold colors of sunset were fading, and the few billowy clouds in the sky looked like pink Japanese lanterns. Smoke rose from the monastery's chimneys. Winter was in the sight and smell of things.

When the special mass ended just before seven, only a chink of purple-blue light remained between mountains and sky, and heavy-bellied inky clouds appeared along Roccione's ridge. Dusk crept in at once, then darkness. The air thickened and blackened. Soon a stiff wind roared again, howling like a wounded moose. Shutters banged against walls. Then came the pealing, tinkling, telltale patter of frozen rain pelting windowpanes. Gusts of wind made chimneys hum. And more sugar snow fell.

Nothing extraordinary for the people of Dorsano. Life in the Alps was a succession of grandiose spectacles, and they loved it.

As big rosin-scented logs burned in the huge medieval fireplace of the refectory, people ate, talked, joked. Along the wall adjacent to the chapel, small children slept comfortably inside sleeping bags. Monks played chess with youngsters. Older citizens dozed. The abbot walked around from table to table, stopping to chat.

Ten-twenty P.M.

Standing on a table, the mayor, a bald and chip-toothed man in his fifties, was reassuring everybody that explosives would be dropped by helicopter on the cornice on Mt. Roccione to induce controlled avalanching after sunrise the next day. But even as he spoke, the overloaded cornice shifted suddenly. Slowly it began to slide down over the granular base. Virtually frictionless, it tumbled along the steep decline. Now the inside core picked up more snow and grew in size. It accelerated. A cloud of icy particles rose ahead of the rampaging ice stream. Within seconds the white juggernaut became a full avalanche.

There was a whistle, swelling to a screeching whine. Soon the leading edge of the ice stream hit the *schützwalder* about a mile from the monastery. It passed through it like a tidal wave over beach cabanas.

A rumble, then a long echoing roar . . .

The mayor faced his ultimate nightmare.

He recognized the sound of an avalanche. "Get the children upstairs," he shouted, and pulled the nearest one out of the sleeping bag.

There was a bluish flash as the ice stream plowed through the ski gondola power lines. The lights went out. Shouts came from the children. "Mama . . . !" They cried, screaming hysterically like colts surrounded by fire.

The emergency lights flickered on feebly.

"Don't panic," the mayor cried out.

At that instant, the blast wave, like a hammer of air, swished ahead of the avalanche, a blur of bluish white mass

behind. It was a frozen hurricane. The windows imploded.
Glass shattered, darting in all directions like shrapnel. A
piece pierced a monk on the neck and blood oozed out
uncontrollably.

"Everybody upstairs!"

The refectory rocked. Tables toppled, glasses smashed.
Then came the grating sound of masonry breaking apart
and the sharp creaks of wooden beams splintering. Snow
pushed through the windows, the cracked walls.

There were muffled screams, then nothing.

And the ice stream, like a river of wet plaster, moved
onto Dorsano. Within minutes, a mangled mass of bodies,
animals, automobiles, trees, and masonry floated with it like
driftwood.

The wind howled for hours—triumphantly, it seemed—
and then abated. A stillness came over the village and it was
quiet. The sun shone. Dorsano was lost in whiteness. Only
the toppled steeple of the bell tower of St. Paul's Church
was barely visible, the hands of its clock frozen at 10:25.

And now even children knew there was something wrong
with the world. In Cherbourg, France, sunlight through a
magnifier glass no longer ignited pieces of paper or burned
the skin of their hands.

25

Andrei Konlikov was perspiring, but not because of the heat in his cabin. Report after report had made it clear to him that there were no significant activities around the U.S. ships at anchor south of the Florida Keys.

Russian sonar at Cardenas, Cuba, and aboard Russian tankers passing through the Strait of Florida had not noticed any new blip patterns or profiles.

"Yet more ships are joining this . . . this anxious fleet," Konlikov said to the intelligence officer who had briefed him on the latest report from Cardenas. "Why?" he shouted, mopping his forehead and pacing the cabin like a restless inmate. He stopped in front of the porthole and looked out. He could see fishing boats heading for Cape Catoche some eighty miles to the south. He turned and repeated the same question.

The big brass marine clock on the wall struck six bells.

Konlikov walked to the officer and stood in front of him and searched his face for the meaning behind the officer's silence.

When the officer spoke, he could only offer an opinion. Obviously the ships were there for an action yet to be ordered by the president of the United States. "But," he said deferentially, "we do have reports of very heavy truck traffic to and from Cape Race." The officer paused. "Obviously whatever they are building there has something to do with the ships at anchor. The latter and Cape Race seem to be on a line connecting the south and north extremities of the current."

Konlikov shrugged. "Maybe," he said, and restated that since the stream originated in the Gulf of Mexico, any attempt at modifying its course would have to take place near there. "Anyhow, I need more conclusive evidence before going to Cape Race and reconnoitering. Whatever the Americans are planning looks global from here, and not necessarily good for us."

There were satellite photos of the area around the cape, the officer told Konlikov, but they were not recent surveys. The satellite was garbling transmission of data due to a malfunction. "I'll report immediately to the directorate. They'll figure out a way to get you what you need."

On the *Challenger* Felton was shouting, "We don't need a modifier, Dr. Lorenz, we need an exorcist. The devil is running the weather," he added, his voice deadened by an icy, dry air. "I'm postponing the next dive for a day, if we're lucky."

Though Alfi had moved up the Connecticut River valley and did not slam on the flotilla broadside, it had churned up the North Atlantic.

Ships bobbed and bucked so much that cups, glasses, and dishes slid off tables. Whiffs of latrine eddied all the way up to the bridge.

It was wet, it was cold, it snowed. An unsparing, whistling wind, filled with tiny frozen pellets, first sandblasted any object in its way, then coated it with a glassy layer of ice. Radar antennas, radio whips, and lifelines were all jacketed with it and glinted jewel bright. The horizon, washed in a whiteout, hid all visual clues to depth, distance, and bearing. It was like being inside a glass of milk.

Parkas worn by roughnecks became heavy with accumulated frozen perspiration; pants as stiff as stovepipes.

The decks were a slippery, gray, muddy mess. Drilling, too, had to be suspended.

Inside it was not much better—the mess hall was too warm, the heads were too cold, the sleeping quarters were stifling and filled with the smell of unwashed bodies. Steam hung like a temperature inversion.

And then there was the sawdust. It covered all passageways because of the condensation, sweating walls, the snow and ice people brought from the outside. It could be found on the pillows, in the changes of clothes, floating on the coffee.

That was day nineteen on the Operation Drill and Load calendar.

Of course, there had been good days, too—sunny and windless. But they were less and less frequent.

Loading resumed after twenty-four hours; day followed day, but conditions remained the same—work for four hours, rest for four, work for another four.

But that was the good part.

With fatigue came accidents. A roughneck might go the whole day without a scratch only to slip and break a leg going for a cup of hot chocolate, while another would forget to cover his nose after blowing it and find it frostbitten a minute later.

And what happened to Felton was awful.

With a temperature of minus thirty, one morning, a sudden pickup in wind speed lowered the chill factor so much that it caused his eyelids to freeze shut. Tiny slivers of ice sliced his corneas. To hear him moan was to know what real suffering was.

Cliff was depressed enough.

From a roster of fifty-four specialists ranging from divers to derrick operators, he was really down to two—those in sick bay and those on their way to it with the permanent existential scars of having been in hell.

There was also the fact that he felt he had to help, but for the success of the mission it was imperative that he stay out of the cold and keep healthy. Operation Drill and Load had an odd resemblance to life—his life, lately.

Day twenty-four.

Snow in the morning, the same cold, same sandblasting wind in the afternoon, and sooty skies.

The following day, as a translucent mist of ice particles lifted, Cliff gasped. *Jesus!*

Lead ice, a soft rubberlike coating of ice nodules, had formed around the ships.

"We have to get out of the area quickly—if we have any hope of getting out at all," Adams told him, showing Cliff a layer of thicker lead ice about a mile away. It was time to consider some options.

Adams proposed staggering drill holes, skipping every other one in order to save time. "And let's hope that the force of the stream will do the rest."

"Hope?" Cliff shouted so loud that Adams flinched. "Either we know it'll do the rest or we keep on drilling."

Adams nodded. "Fine, but at least radio the navy for icebreakers."

It stopped Cliff for a moment, aware as he was that the crisis required action, but it had to be the right action.

Six-foot waves pounded the drill ship, shoving it off the mark. He could feel the convulsive throes of the powerful outboard engines pushing it back on it. She was built to take it. Could she take the pressure ridges and rubble ice created by grinding floes?

He held his breath for a while and started giving Adams's suggestions serious thought.

Skip was dead. Tony, Fred, and the others were near death with exhaustion. He shuddered at the possibility of more fatal accidents. Just being on the open deck for a few minutes prior to going to the op room was enough for Cliff to realize that the wind-chill factor was no longer a sensation, but a paralyzing pain.

Things could get a lot worse—and they would.

After lead ice would come solid ice. That was certain.

Maybe he'd better listen to a man who had advised him well so far. And staggering was better than leaving one-third of the Hull unloaded.

"Okay, you win," Cliff said to Adams.

Adams nodded wisely at that, relieved, and unwrapped his scarf, accidentally knocking his watch cap on the floor. Cliff picked it up and brushed the sawdust off. "Would have had more sense than to have been so rough on you if I weren't so stressed. I'm sorry," he said, and handed Adams the cap.

"Forget it, but you're still a stubborn s.o.b." Adams smiled, a smile that made one forget.

So staggering went into effect.

Now crews went from the warmth of the bunk to the freezing air of the deck energized by a sense of urgency born out of fear and one's belief of being able to beat the odds.

Oddly, everything worked, and the tooler was able to spit out BD readings like a walking calculator.

Operation Drill and Load was now in its twenty-fifth day.

There was much commotion because lookouts had spotted an iceberg. Cliff went to see it from the bridge and focused the navigator's binoculars on it. Judging from its nearness to the horizon, it was four miles away, slowly bobbing its way south. A small translucent crystalline mass of glistening blues and greens, it looked like a diamond in a Tiffany setting. As predicted, this first iceberg made its appearance on time, almost to the hour.

Still looking at it, Cliff said to the navigator, who was standing to his right, "It's going to miss us."

"Yes . . . this one will. But not the others," the navigator said, and informed Cliff that the International Ice Patrol had spotted dense areas of floes ahead of the icebergs. "Lookouts on the *Charibdes* should pick 'em out the day after tomorrow . . . maybe later."

Cliff thanked him and remained standing by the large porthole, eyes now on the drill crew.

Eighteen was a linchpin hole, an important one. And the deepest. Located at the southern end of the upper section of the Hull, with holes nineteen and twenty to the south, fifteen and sixteen to the north, it was to be loaded with two nukes at the apex of a V-shaped cleavage separating two rock planes of different geological age and composition.

Adams had given hole eighteen much attention. He had spent three days pinpointing the cleavage with his Precision Acoustic Sounder and bringing the *Challenger* over it.

Even so, it would be a difficult task to accomplish. After all, the depth indicator on the drill shaft wasn't designed to be a precision instrument.

At noon the announcement Cliff was waiting for came. "BD reached. Go to it, guys!"

Another day passed, and day twenty-nine finally came.

Cliff woke up to a brilliant morning. He had slept well and the depression was gone. He dressed quickly, packed his last few things, and then picked up his duffel bag and went to look for Felton.

Outside, organized pandemonium reigned. Divers, roughnecks, and cooks were helping deck crews coil stiff ropes, washing tools, and scraping ice off wiper blades, enjoying—perversely, so it seemed—what they were doing. The deck was all cold slush and grime.

Felton. Where the hell was he? Cliff had to talk to him before he left the *Challenger* by helicopter. Running, he searched everywhere, stopping to thank the divers and the toolers, and shaking hands with anyone with a free hand to give him.

Cliff finally found Felton just inside the helicopter's crew room, sitting on an oil drum, unsuccessfully trying to put drops in his eyes.

"Wait. Roy, I'll do it for you," Cliff said, reaching for the dropper, and managed to squeeze a few drops in each eye.

They were good eyes. They had been open on the *Knorr*, too. "There, do they feel better?" he said.

"Not yet." Felton blinked, drops of medication streaking down the long, durably boyish face. "They will."

Cliff extended his hand. "Roy, thank you for everything."

Felton shrugged, pulling out a dingy handkerchief. "That's nice of you, sir." He wiped his cheeks, then looked up. "And I waited here to thank you for letting me be crew chief."

Outside on the helipad, the big helicopter's engine coughed, then roared to life.

"Well . . ." Cliff shook Felton's hand. "Call me if you ever need anything," he said, competing with the noise.

Felton looked up. "That I'll do, sir. I want you to tell me how in hell we managed to kick glaciation in the ass."

Minutes later, after the helicopter had lifted off with Cliff and Adams aboard, the P.A. system blared: *"Close all hatches. Let's get the hell out of here."*

And so they did.

26

The Sikorsky P-11 helicopter, also carrying two medical evacuees, lifted easily off the pad.

Brushing off sawdust, Cliff felt the slight sensation of going up a fast elevator and saw the flotilla disappear in a frigid world of icy waters and reflections of a cobalt blue sky.

He did not let himself think of the odds against the stream doing its job of removing the Hull with four nukes never loaded. Instead he let memories of Skip, Tony, and Felton keep him company. For a long time he recalled how they looked, spoke, laughed, worked. As individuals they were as different as their faces. Collectively they were a solid and warm humanity full of the all-American fighting spirit. That was all he was carrying back to D.C. Memories worth keeping alive.

From behind the shoulder of the pilot, he could make out the time on the clock: 11:05 A.M.

Water gave way to land, and finally a helipad.

The hug could have come from a bear, so strong did Roscoe's arms feel around Cliff's body. Even the air seemed to partake in Roscoe's excitement. A fine spinning snow, raised by the helicopter's blades, whirled cheerfully around. It also lashed Cliff's face as he listened, eyes closed, to his boss tell him that if anyone deserved the Medal of Honor, it was Cliff. "I'm proud of you." Roscoe hugged him again.

"Thank you, Roscoe. You look great," Cliff said.

"Come," Roscoe said, pointing to a big U.S. Marine helicopter a hundred feet away. "We have no time to waste."

Cliff was freezing, tired, and he didn't know where he was going. Nothing looked familiar, and Roscoe was talking on the cellular phone.

He was shaken and silenced by the sight of the convoy of motor vehicles beneath him jammed nose to tail in an endless chain. Bicycles, boxes, and bundles balanced precariously on car roofs and vans. Passenger cars toiled on slowly, exhaust fumes swirling behind them. There were cars abandoned along the road edge. At an intersection he saw a long line of people trying to board a bus and a mile down . . .

"Pam and Butch are fine," Roscoe said. They were in Bailey, Texas, and billeted in the dormitory of Denton College, where the Department of the Interior had moved. Conditions were crowded, but they had made it there. He didn't have to say more, and Cliff thanked him for all he had done for his family.

With a change of expression on Roscoe's face came the change of subject. Denucleation had been successful, Roscoe explained, but after a week of tests the Weather Bureau had to cancel plans to install the machines. A dangerous level of ions was triggering violent electrical storms—even tornadoes—over test sites.

"That leaves Marshall and NASA," Cliff said.

"Well, let's say that leaves . . . Kronin and the chief of staff."

"So politics got into modifiers, eh?" Cliff replied in a pensive tone, and shook his head, unbelieving. Nothing new in D.C., he supposed. "Now, can you tell me where we're going?" he said, but his voice was choked with disgust.

"Camp David," Roscoe answered. The quiet and relaxed atmosphere of the place was what the president needed. The cabinet and his advisers were also there. "You'll be pissin' with the big dogs, Cliff," he added, slapping him hard on the knee. "Anyhow, the president has wanted to talk to you for a long time."

"I wonder why."

Cliff could understand why an odd collection of log-sided lodges had so much attraction to presidents. From the moment he stepped down onto the helipad, Camp David gave him a sense of hermitage that appealed to him.

Long interconnecting paved pathways led to Birch, Larch, and Redwood, the guest lodges. Everywhere stood tall pine trees, wooden benches, rustic-looking gazebos, and sentry boxes.

The temperature had dropped below freezing, smoke rose from the stone chimney of Elm, and snow from the day before covered the Maryland landscape that from the 1,400-acre hilltop had an odd Currier and Ives Christmas look.

"You'll be billeted in Larch"—Roscoe pointed—"there, just behind the tennis court. Very nice."

But first there were things to be done.

Cliff was longing for a hot bath, a sawdust-less meal, and a quiet bedroom. But Roscoe sprang an unpleasant detour on him.

Roscoe took a pathway that led to a trailer camp on a rise a quarter of a mile from the lodges. It was the communications park with vans of various sizes and shapes and equipped with special hooks that allowed them to be airlifted by helicopters. There was also Kronin's van. "It's a climate-analysis center on wheels. That's where we are going," Roscoe said. "But play it cool while in there."

The door opened into a long and narrow high-tech room, mostly busy space. Noisy fax machines and teleprinters lined one wall, work counters and desks the other. A kerosene heater kept the place warm. Wimbly, Kronin's assistant, sat undisturbed in front of a color monitor.

The greetings were brief.

"So nice to see you again," Kronin said pleasantly. "I have read your daily reports. Quite a success story. Congratulations."

Cliff thanked him, and Kronin got down to business.

Removing his glasses, he leaned over very close and told Cliff that even though they were a few days behind schedule because of Alfi, Professor Marshall's jetty off Cape Race was progressing well, and that from what weather ships were reporting, mean temperatures near Cape Race had already gone up one whole degree Celsius. He looked at Cliff with a face glowing with pleasure and added, "One whole degree already."

Cliff nodded with pleasure, but Kronin scowled. "Dr. Lorenz . . ." His tone was controlled, tight. "It is very clear to me that if you succeed in cutting off the J Current from which come the waters Professor Marshall is rerouting so successfully, there will be no more flow of them."

Christ, he's beating on that dead horse again. I thought we had settled all that. Obviously, Kronin still believed in the correctness of Marshall's theory. Moreover, the way he was prefacing things told Cliff that he was in for some grim developments. He just listened, but his eyes were veined with red.

"We don't know how the stream will behave after the modification, do we?" Kronin carried on, beginning to give Cliff the rough edge of his voice. "And models are only as reliable as the information they are built on. Fallible, I mean. Of course, we have agreed to assume that the stream will behave as your model indicated. But that, however, is not sufficient reason to neutralize a modification that's already producing excellent results. Is it?"

"Nature's reactions to manipulation are unpredictable. But what I'm postulating—"

"Postulating, my foot." Kronin raised a hand. "Spare me, please," he said and paused. "Just answer my original question: Is what your model shows sufficient reason to neutralize a modification that's already working?" His tone had turned waspish.

"With proofs such as those you have given me, I'd be foolish to think otherwise."

"I thought so." Kronin extended a hand and, squinting myopically at Cliff, he said, "That's all for now, Dr. Lorenz. Thank you."

A fine welcome that was!

Outside, glaciation was rushing in with its gray colors, and two hundred yards away, the chief of staff stopped walking to read the dispatch a second time, his jaw muscles rippling.

He was a stocky and sharp-featured man dressed in the latest after-ski casuals. He had shrewd gray-blue mastiff eyes with little chips of granite; a chin that jutted arrogance. Cited by the *Wall Street Journal* for his "vulpine cunning" in corporate takeovers, he had found his real metier in Washington. Staffers eddied around him.

For a change, it hadn't snowed that day, and outside Aspen—Lodge One, as Secret Service agents called it— some of yesterday's snow was melting in the warmth of the afternoon sun. The air, wintry and calm, had the enduring smell of rosin.

After removing his boots, the chief of staff walked into Lodge One, a structure that would pass middle-class muster in Vermont.

"What is it this time?" the president asked roughly from behind his desk.

The chief of staff recoiled, then smiled and told him that he had no bad news and that he had come to inform him that Cliff was at Camp David. "The Hull is loaded," he said, "but frankly, Mr. President, that frightens me."

"If nukes can do the job, they'll save us," the president said, looking up.

The chief of staff stood with his leather-bound notebook under an arm, his mouth set in a stubborn line. "Not just nukes, Mr President. Forty-eight of them."

The president said nothing.

Cliff saw the president early that evening. It was as dark as December, but not being December, the lights along the pathways had not been turned on yet.

An aide in a beige sweater led him and Roscoe to a small paneled reception room, empty except for hard wooden chairs and a magazine rack.

"The president will see you shortly," the aide said, courteously tilting his head to the chairs.

It was Roscoe—aglow with reflected glory—who made the introductions, and not the chief of staff. All protocol. Washington was all rank even in Maryland, and Roscoe had not forgotten that. But the smile on the chief of staff could raise welts.

"You're Dr. Lorenz," the president said, shaking Cliff's hand. "The chief of naval operations has kept me informed of what you and your crews went through. Coffee or a drink?"

They sat on each side of the fireplace, and Cliff got his first close look at the president. He looked old, a bent man in his simple plaid shirt, and surprisingly humble.

Over drinks Cliff elaborated on his theory of modification, showed charts, talked about his fear of CLIMODs becoming the nuclear weapons, as he put it, of the poor countries.

"Mr. President," he concluded, "I became an oceanographer because I believed nature was to be enjoyed, not altered. At first I refused to work on the modification because of this belief and because the Gulf Stream has a mind of its own. But a mathematical model built by men known for the rigor of their scholarship makes it clear that a modification is possible with a negligible amount of radiation escaping—barring the unexpected." He paused, then went on in a lower tone. "However, should it succeed, we may be teetering on the brink of an era of weather control and of weather wars."

And then he came to the point. "My concern is that if we wait for NASA to come up with a solution to their problem with the reflectors or for Dr. Marshall's modification to really show that it works in raising temperature considerably—not just a degree or two—the extreme cold could degrade the circuitry in the firing and retrieve boxes."

Nodding, the president got up and walked to the bay window. A massive bank of altocumulus had worked its way from the northwest and now covered half the sky like one section of the Skydome's sliding roof.

Cliff went on. "My other concern is the *Dokholov*," he said, and told the president that he had heard that it was nearing the blast area. "Perhaps, Mr. President, if I could talk to the chief scientist on board, he might decide to change course."

The president turned and smiled. "I like the idea of one scientist talking to another scientist about a common problem. Let me see what I can do," he said.

With that, the president shook Cliff's hand and wished him a good night. It was now all in the hands of the president, if that was the way things worked.

Outside, by the toolshed at the end of the pathway, a staffer was filling the tank of a yellow snowplow.

It had taken less than half an hour for the specialist in the communications van to make a radio-telephone connection to the *Dokholov*.

Cliff was alone in his room when he was notified that Konlikov would be on the line momentarily.

Cliff found himself staring at the phone but not rehearsing what to say. The idea that he would be talking to another scientist like himself was reassuring. Yet there was some apprehension. But he felt that from the moment he agreed to work on the modifier, things had happened as if by divine intervention—surviving an auto crash and an underwater fight to the death, choosing the right team, going to the vaults at the right moment and getting the idea of using the nukes, and even loading the Hull practically on schedule.

Now the telephone conference seemed another link in the unbroken and fateful chain of events.

Cliff made Konlikov speak first. "We were in the same conference hall many times," Konlikov said in impeccable English, "yet we never met."

"Barcelona and perhaps San Diego." Cliff spoke slowly and clearly, as if dictating, and as they talked over the next five minutes they discovered that they had planned to attend the same marine geodesy conference in Tokyo.

"I look forward to reading your book on the purpose of the stream, or the stirrer that prevents the Atlantic from stagnating with its many countercurrents and eddies," Konlikov said.

With that came a change of tone. And of subject matter.

Cliff told Konlikov how he had asked the president to arrange for the telephone hookup so that Konlikov and those at the Kremlin would learn about the American modification. Cliff repeated almost word for word what he had told Kronin during both presentations on the modification, and it took him just as long to go into the details. "Now I can assure you that environmentally our modification will in no way affect the weather in your country. We have confirmation by virtual reality, by a trusted environmentalist, and by a mathematical model."

"I congratulate you. Brilliant." There was what sounded like a sigh coming over the line. "Nor should you fear, Dr. Lorenz, that our thermoradiators will alter things in this part of the world," he said, and took the opportunity to explain what Russian scientists were finally ready to put into effect after exhaustive testing. Power developed by fusion inside numerous small accelerators was converted into energy, then piped to recycled radar antennas strung along the Arctic Circle, and allowed to excite the air. "Much like what happens when we heat a potato in a microwave oven. It works. The only inconvenience is that while fusion takes place, there is radio interference in many bands. But we can adjust to it and live with it," Konlikov said.

It was Cliff's turn to congratulate the Russian scientist, and he did that graciously but quickly. He still had a worry on his mind. "Professor Konlikov?" There was a tentative tone in Cliff's voice.

"Yes, I'm here."

"Do you think your leaders will listen to you?" he asked. "We have the opportunity to show the world that those who live in it—not just politicians and generals—can be given the chance to decide on matters of life and death. Glaciation is a problem that we can solve with mutual trust and without the suspicion that has caused such useless military buildup during the cold war."

The line was silent for a while.

"It is a pity that we didn't have this phone call earlier," Konlikov said, and revealed to Cliff that suspicion had taken him to Florida and had forced Russian intelligence to send a photo-reconnaissance plane over Cape Race at the risk of starting a military confrontation. "Yes, Dr. Lorenz, I will communicate with the Kremlin and my colleagues at the Institute for Advanced Planning. It will be up to them."

They wished each other good luck and said good-bye.

Cliff put the phone down and smiled. Out of the fears and suspicions of the cold war, he thought, an intuitive bond was finally joining him and Konlikov. It was a start.

27

September 24, 5:13 A.M.

As the first grayness of dawn fingered the horizon, the blades of the presidential backup helicopter began to rotate. Secret Service agents ran from door to door waking up staffers.

In Cliff's bedroom the phone suddenly rang. It was the chief of staff calling from Lodge One. "Dr. Lorenz, you have a weather window between two and six this afternoon," he announced. "The cabinet has met, and the president orders you to go ahead with your modification." A pause. "You have my personal good wishes."

This was it. Cliff's heart stumbled, restarted. "Thank you," he said, and put the phone down, staring wide awake now past the fire into his own thoughts.

The phone rang again; the same voice. Ms. Wycoff was on a special line; would Cliff be brief, please.

"Cliff, good luck. It's going to work, I know. Butch and I are fine. I love you."

"You love me?" His voice cracked. "Do you know how long I've waited to hear that? I've got to go. Hug Butch for me and pray for courage. I'm no hero. *Ciao*. I love you, Pam."

He reached for the doorknob, then turned, grabbed a handful of matchbooks with the blue-and-white presidential seal, and left.

Silhouetted against a gray and sodden sky that seemed to promise little, the president and his cabinet, all in dark overcoats and caps, stood on a wooden platform at the entrance of the helipad like crows on a branch.

It was the president who spoke first. "NOAA says that the window will be the only one you'll get. Good luck, Cliff." He shook his hand. "And Godspeed."

"Thank you, Mr. President." Cliff controlled his emotion with a pause. "May I ask—"

"A young tank officer," the president interrupted, "once asked his general what the best way was to command a tank division. The general replied: 'When you are offered two alternatives, take the bolder one. It's always the better one.'"

At Andrews Air Force Base, when all the members of the special party had arrived, a bus took them to the 105th Hurricane Hunter Squadron's ready room for a briefing on the flight.

An astringent, snow-chilled air made people shiver as they walked from the bus to the ready room, but the heavy overcast of the past few days had thinned, and through breaks in the clouds dropped shafts of sun. A good sign, Cliff thought, until he heard the pilot warn everybody of the dangers of the flight.

The minimum altitude from which he and Adams could see the modification in progress was 32,000 feet. At that height, however, there were very strong winds brought by a recent shift in the Jet Stream, hence the decision to entrust the Hurricane Hunters with the mission.

Winds were not the only problem. Fast-rising columns of warm air were also being sucked up by the high winds. "The resulting turbulence will give us a rough ride," the spiky, jug-eared pilot said. "How rough? Well . . . ," he said hesitantly, "rough enough that you'll swear the rivets are coming off—and some will," he added in a condescending tone that seemed to come with the job, a dangerous one judging from the special flight suit the hurricane hunters wore. Bright orange for visibility, it featured side leg pockets bulging with canisters of shark repellant, oversized flashlights, Ranger knives, and a rescue-signal transmitter.

In the navy, the Orion was the capital aircraft for antisubmarine warfare and weather reconnaissance; the men who flew it were the "chosen" ones. Crews hunting subs had the exhilaration of finding the elusive enemy, but it was the Orion crews, with their snorting pride and arrogance, who would fly right through the eye of a hurricane. Only a few pilot/copilot teams had mastered the sequence of quick and short reactions at the "stick" that would keep the plane from corkscrewing out of control into a vortex of a hurricane.

Cliff listened and looked around seemingly at ease. After all, the underwater fight and a month on the *Challenger* had given him a sense of survival—if not downright immunity. Besides, history was being made that day, and with some luck he was going to be more than a footnote.

To avoid possible radiation, the Orion would be forced to fly high over the Hull. Even though Gallego had theorized that little of it would leak out, radiological dissipation through the air was a possibility. Loops around the Hull, therefore, were to be flown after the explosion of each firing group. These loops would allow receivers to measure levels of radiation sent to them by Geiger counters dropped by an SR-71 plane from an altitude of eighty thousand feet. Of about twenty minutes' duration, the loops were also designed to give Cliff time to observe whether the stream was no longer being sliced off by the Hull, and if there were changes in the course of the current.

Needless to say, wider loops would have exposed the plane to less radiation, but everybody knew that the weather window wasn't going to stay open forever.

The plane was a four-turboprop-engine McDonnell Douglas P-3D. Longer and wider than its prototypes, it resembled a commercial Electra. Prominent were its long, needlelike radar antenna and the dome-shaped observation windows. Ammonia, which had been used to scrub the exterior clean of oil and grease apt to collect radiation particles, still dripped from the wings.

Toothy watchdogs sat in a circle around the Orion, and stern Secret Service agents wearing tiny earphones moved restlessly about.

The cabin resembled Kronin's mobile van, with the exception of six rows of standard airline seats in the tail section. The firing console stood in a bay on the starboard side near the door to the cockpit, now open to allow heat from the cabin to keep the crew warm. Next to it was the thermosensor, an infrared image producer resembling a TV studio camera that read ocean temperatures. Orange-colored life jackets, an inflatable life raft, and boxes containing plastic jugs of water, food, and medicine stood by the exit door beyond the seats.

The voice of the tower instructing the pilot to taxi to the end of the runway put an end to all conversation, and Cliff leaned back in his seat next to an observation window that acted as an escape hatch. It was then that he remembered the *Dokholov*.

At once he got up and went to ask to the admiral what he knew about the Russian research ship.

"Still there," the admiral said. "Started to sail south, then . . . the propeller shaft hit a floe and she had to stop."

"The crew has been airlifted, of course?" Cliff asked, certain that they had.

"No helipad."

Cliff gasped, wholly surprised. "You mean we're going to leave a hundred or so men and women on ship while nuclear bombs are exploding a few miles away?"

The admiral shrugged as lights dimmed in the cockpit. The takeoff checks were complete.

The veins in Cliff's temples stood out. "You mean to say that . . ."

"I'm afraid so. We tried. They had plenty of time."

Cliff closed his eyes. His handsome features were contorted. It was too late. There was nothing he could do.

His bitterness momentarily quelled by the tremendous roar of the engines and the impact of the moment, he shouted, "We're on time," and hurried back to his seat.

The Orion vibrated and shook; bluish red smoke shot out of the turbofan engines firing like flares. It rolled down the runway as the pilot's right hand pushed the four main throttles forward. "Airborne," the pilot reported to the tower. Droplets of ammonia streaked the windows obliquely, and the landing-gear door closed, sending a thud through the plane.

At six thousand feet a layer of clouds absorbed the Orion; at ten thousand, it exploded into the clear, its long antenna piercing the sky like the beak of a giant hummingbird.

With the back of his neck on the headrest, Cliff listened to the steady, reassuring hum of the engines. There had been no delays, no change in the forecast. Events were heading in the proper direction. He turned to Gallego. "Tell me," he said to him, "what if the drift doesn't push the *Dokholov* far enough away from the blast area? From the Hull?"

"Forget it, Cliff."

"Ifraim!" Cliff raised his voice. "I've got to know."

Gallego hesitated. "All right . . . ," he began, reluctantly, "if the tidal waves do not capsize her, well . . . she might be in the path of a cloud of radiation. There's that possibility."

"Then what?" Feeling the air pressure in his ears, Cliff put the tip of his index finger in his right ear and tried to unplug it.

Gallego sighed. "I can only guess. She'll . . ." He started fidgeting with his cigarette lighter. "Well, she'll be . . . a floating something. No port will allow her to dock. Too hot." He shrugged. "I'm only guessing."

Cliff nodded defeatedly, and as the plane gained altitude, images of a spectral ship drifting with the current formed before his eyes, and he saw sailors with bald heads and open sores leaning over the overhangs like lepers.

It was eleven-fifteen A.M., and the day was now blessed with a crystalline winter sunshine. Cloudless, the sky was a deep cobalt blue. And so far the flight was smooth. Yet, the atmosphere in the cabin was hushed. In the rear of the plane, no one spoke, obviously silenced by the realization that the concerns of everyday life were now irrelevant. Quietly the petty officer, a gentle Goliath with a bass voice, moved about with a big Thermos bottle full of coffee.

In his seat, Cliff studied the specs of the firing console. Adams was seated next to him, ready to explain the block diagram of the console.

A modified version of the Special Forces' Radio-Controlled Primer UHF-2, and used to set off mine fields, it looked like a small multi-channel studio tape recorder. In reality it consisted of three rows of eighteen transmitters each, with its computer-coded frequency activated by a battle-short switch. A push button turned the console on; meters read the transmitters' output power. "It's a simple device, but it works," Adams said.

Cliff leaned into the bubble window and looked out. Quick-moving shadows of clouds skimmed over the dark blue Atlantic.

Soon he should see the lighter waters of the stream and the line of flotsam that edges its left bank. He studied the flight plan and noted the time. He figured they would be on station in twenty minutes.

Outside the window, the sky still looked clear and down below was nothing but reflections of the sun's path shimmering on the calm sea.

They were forty minutes into the flight by Cliff's watch—five minutes from the stream. In the cockpit, pilot and copilot swept the bank of instruments with their eyes while monitoring the Groton Air Route Control frequency. On top of the climb and in the clear, the Orion was on cruising power; engines held at a steady roar.

Slowly the sun patterns on the cabin's wall shifted, and a twelve-degree course correction brought the Orion over the Gulf Stream.

Somebody called out, "Icebergs."

"Floes," Cliff said. "Floes move ahead of icebergs."

• • •

Preparations began at 12:55 P.M.

All talk stopped when the petty officer, wearing a radiation dosimeter, handed out goggles.

At the console, Adams and a technician started to go through the last checklist. Cliff stood behind them, hands jammed in his jeans pockets, silent, head bent forward.

"Okay, let's check outputs," Adams said.

The technician worked a number of switches and the needle in the panel meters swung right. "Output good," he said, scanning the meter with a sweep of his eyes.

Cliff followed the checklist, biting his lower lip, hoping the divers had wired the boxes correctly.

Gently the Orion's right wing dipped, then rose to level on a thirty-degree course. It was the heading that would bring it on line parallel to the Hull and four miles from it.

An announcement. "We're on firing course."

Cliff stiffened, but he couldn't, he reasoned, look as bad as Adams, whose face—always a bloodless gray—was now shiny and candle white. And something was wrong with the way he was breathing. It seemed a great effort for him.

"The first marker should now be visible at eleven o'clock." The pilot was referring to the yellow dye that a support aircraft had dropped to mark the spot of the first shot hole.

Suddenly, from a light shade of green there appeared a well-defined V of a dark blue color on the surface of the water. Its apex, now colored in yellow, was the southern tip of the Hull.

A ready light flashed on the console.

Adams put his fingers on the first battle-short switch and removed the red cover protecting the push button. He glanced at the output meters, then turned to Cliff, who, voice taut, said, "Go ahead. It's your pigeon."

At that, Adams began counting: five . . . four . . . three . . . two . . . one. On the word *one,* he pressed the push button and closed his eyes.

Suddenly the ocean was blurred by a rippling jolt. Then came an eye-piercing burst of incredible luminescence—a flash of gold.

All at once the Atlantic glowed and boiled in thermonuclear heat.

Cliff drew back, awed by the brilliance, silenced and immobile as if watching the birth of a star. Gooseflesh pimpled his arms and legs. "I'm fascinated, horrified," he said to Gallego next to him.

Then came a deep convulsive rumble. Hydrogen molecules burned; the water fizzed with a dazzling gleam of vaporized bluish bubbles. They rose to the surface with a bright blink of glitter, transforming it into an opalescent wafer of foam.

Excited by the fusion of nuclei, nitrogen molecules in the air reacted with phosphorescent brilliance. Ice crystals glittered inside the few cumuli, making them coruscate like noctilucent clouds. The sky blazed with ocher-colored zodiacal lights, then faded into dark red, blue, and black.

And then out of the ocean came a strange thing—a black ring, a shadow of sorts. Nothing could have been more frightening. Like a bolt of lightning, it flared out, sliced the sky upward, and came hurling toward the plane. They gasped.

Gallego leaped to his feet, hands gesturing. "Stay calm," he shouted above the shouting voices. "It's only an optical illusion of the shock wave."

Just then there was a jolt. *The plane must've gotten hit,* Cliff thought, and felt it drop like an elevator out of control. Wall panels creaked, ashtrays bounced. The lights flickered.

Cliff made a desperate effort not to panic. He thought he heard a noise in the plane's underbelly. Now his heart thundered in his chest. The lights flickered again. *My God, the plane got hit.*

Approximately five seconds later—the longest five seconds Cliff would remember—he saw a greenish ball, perhaps a half mile wide, rise and spire out of the water, brighter, bigger . . . greener . . . an all-green bubble of radiation about to break. He closed his eyes for a split second and saw a ship, a spectral ship laden with ghostlike figures wandering, drifting. . . . He reopened his eyes to see Gallego blanching at the sight of a helmet-shaped bulge of water reaching a height of thirty feet or more.

"Down, down!" Gallego banged on the window. "Down, goddamn it," he added. A burst bubble meant radiation.

And the bubble rose.

Then for a split second it stood still, like a tossed tennis ball just before beginning to drop. At that moment a transparent wall of water rose around it like a gigantic swell. It was the first displacement in a compressional wave, a tidal wave.

"It's going down! It's going down," Cliff cried out.

Gallego clasped his hands. "*Gracias, Jesus.*"

Cliff threw his arms around him. "We did it, Ifraim. We did it."

As if Cliff's voice had been a signal, the others started to react. There was much back slapping, much hugging and thumbs up.

Cliff and Gallego didn't turn around. They were looking at the bubble as it started to drop, as the plane, gliding like a shadow, dropped to five thousand feet and banked to the left.

Roscoe came running to him. "Call the president," he told Cliff, "and tell him that the first nukes have gone off well."

Cliff had only to pick up the special receiver. "Mr. President, the boldest of all modification plans is working," he said, a bit hoarse from all the shouting. "I'm pleased to report to you that the first detonation of a nuclear device for practical uses has taken place as predicted."

A loud sigh came over the line. "Good planning has earned you good results, Dr. Lorenz, and may the good God keep smiling on you. Bolder is better, I must believe that now. Thank you. All America is grateful to you."

With a course correction, the Orion began the first information-gathering loop. This time it was to collect radio-relayed signals from Geiger counters dropped by the SR-71 reconnaissance plane. Similar to a holding pattern flown by planes waiting to land, it was over the Labrador Sea.

Cliff had had a hand in prearranging the loop. He had wanted the plane to fly over the advancing ice sheet, now one hundred miles north of the Hull, to see how the warm waters of the J Current were supplying moisture to the American continent.

It was not long before the plane, flying on a 345-degree course along the east coast of Newfoundland, crossed over the leading edge of the polar ice sheet.

From five thousand feet it looked like a rough slab of marble suffused with tints of blue as it met the pinkish sheen of the western sky. Pressure ridges and crushed walls of ice cast long purplish shadows over the seemingly endless surface. Crevasses, dark and deep, looked like freshly plowed furrows on a snowy field. And there were fissures, rises, and depressions of all shapes, which were the signs of expansion and motion.

There's nothing beautiful, Cliff thought, *in that inhospitable wintry world, a world of silence, of cold-glazed white that glares and burns the eye into blackness. Lord! The North Atlantic was a stilled ocean of ice.*

And then, as the Orion banked left, the J Current came into view—a shimmering path cutting through the ice resembling the wake of an icebreaker. Steam rose along the left bank of the path.

Everyone was busy looking at the supplier of moisture and Cliff, who had planned to explain things, said nothing. Nature was more eloquent than he could ever be.

It was going to be an easy data-gathering flight.

As planned, special receivers were to pick up the signals from the Geiger counters in order for Gallego to consider the level of radiation, and for Cliff to order more detonation, as planned.

But then, as it turned out, something unexpected began to take shape.

It was now just past one-thirty P.M. The weather window was still open, but heavier clouds were beginning to move over Maine.

In the communications bay, Gallego had been behaving strangely, shaking his head, as if in response to something.

Cliff, who had been looking in the direction of the communications bay for news about the *Dokholov*, realized that something was wrong. What? He went to find out.

"Cliff . . . ah," Gallego began. Bad sign. "You're not going to like what I have to say. The Geiger counters . . . not working. Frozen."

The roar of the engines grew so loud Cliff wanted to bury his head in his hands.

"Frozen," Gallego repeated, and explained that the problem was the counting mechanism inside the Geiger counters, not the radio transmitters. "Either the delicate counting mechanisms didn't survive the drop," he said, "or they are frozen." His theory was that the cold temperature had slowed down the reaction time of the hydragyrum gas inside the counters. "It's only a guess," Gallego added. "These counters worked fine at the nuclear tests in the Pacific, and not for the . . ." His voice trailed away.

Cliff was speechless, almost frozen himself. Without knowing the precise amount of radiation that might have escaped from the first detonation, they didn't dare detonate more charges.

"The best and only resource we have is time," Gallego said. "We've got to wait."

"Wait?" Cliff shouted with impatience. He was thinking of the small weather window. "How long?"

Gallego coughed apologetically, then gave him one of his scholar's shrugs. "As long as possible, I suppose," he said. He went back to listening, turning the volume of the Kenwood XR-10 receiver all the way up. Nothing, just the high-pitched tone of the carrier frequency but no intelligence, no readings. And from the Roentgen printer next to the receiver the paper spewed out without radiation traces. He looked at the console's digital clock. "At ten knots," he said, "the wind should've carried any fallout radiation over the counters five minutes ago."

The consensus was to wait no more than an hour. An announcement was made; the plane widened its loop, leaving Cliff searching for patches of silver and brown that would reveal the presence of dead fish. He saw none.

Meanwhile Roscoe, guessing Cliff needed to be alone, went to sit next to Scott. "Tell me, Professor," Roscoe asked, "what do you make of the Geiger counters?"

Scott raised his eyes and shook his head. "I don't know," he replied. "I know that chips fail." He waved his pocket calculator. "They are made of the same material and probably by the same hands as this calculator." He held it at eye level. "Twice I had to send it back to the factory. Does that answer your question?"

No one knew why—nor did they care to find out—but after thirty-two minutes of waiting, there was a burst of five high-tone clicks rising to a crescendo. One counter was working! Later they would theorize that the water of the North Atlantic, being much warmer than the air above, had raised the environmental temperature of the counters as they floated.

But Gallego wasn't smiling, and when Cliff asked him what it all meant, he answered, "Some radiation has leaked out. One hundred twenty-five rems. Modestly depressed white-cell count."

Cliff raised a finger and his voice. "Don't be pedantic, Ifraim. Is it fatal? Yes or no?"

No, it was not fatal—not immediately fatal, as Gallego put it. But at 125 rems, a long-term risk of cancer existed. "However, Cliff," Gallego said, "the radioactivity should dissipate as it travels away from the source."

"Was this the level of radiation you predicted?"

Gallego shifted his weight uneasily. "More or less. These Geigers are not perfect instruments, you know. They could be reading more than what's out there. The general wisdom is to think that they do," he answered, almost tripping over the words. "To play it safe, perhaps we'd better climb to a higher altitude," he suggested, sounding as though that was what he would do if he had the choice. "It's . . . it's all up to you."

Once again Cliff was alone with his problems. But it was actually the pilot who would determine how much time Cliff had to think things over. Four gigantic engines were guzzling 250 pounds of fuel a minute.

A burst of clicking brought Cliff back to his dilemma.

A meter cast a greenish light on the counter of the communication console. A needle swung to the right, barely entering the 100–220 zone. It was the rem indicator meter.

The remaining detonation of the Hull could now safely be viewed from a lower altitude. Without consulting with Gallego, Cliff walked to the copilot and gave him his instructions.

At once the pilot eased the controls in a tight arc, then flattened out again and headed north-northwest. Far out to port, fleecy cirrus clouds, like a herd of sheep, passed in an endless blur. The window was closing.

Kneeling in front of the window, Cliff heard the hydraulics and saw the elevator trims on the wings drop. The Orion was descending to observation altitude.

"On target," the copilot announced.

Cliff signaled the thermosensor operator to aim the unit, then focused his binoculars and waited.

Soon he saw a broad, sheared-off mass of buff-colored rock resembling the cliffs of Dover loom from under blue-green waters. "Oh, my God," he muttered, breaking into a smile. He passed the binoculars to Adams. "There," he said, pointing. Adams peered through. "Wow! Now, that's precision blasting," he shouted, sniffling. "You'd think the Hull was a wedge of cheddar cheese. How about that!"

Excited, Cliff went to see what the thermosensor printer was putting out. It translated thermal variations into digital logic, then converted them into colored visual images.

And there was no question that they were what Cliff had hoped to see. Clearly he could see a narrower band of the J Current. It was obvious that a portion of the J Current no longer flowed into the Mid-Ocean Canyon.

And then he saw Adams run to him all excited. "It worked," Adams shouted. "Yes, Cliff, it worked! The Hull's lower layer of lava has held. There's no magma flow. I see no signs of it."

"Unbelievable . . . unbelievable." They embraced. "We're lucky . . . very lucky."

Again the Orion flew on a course parallel to the Hull. Again Adams looked up at Cliff, wished him good luck, and quickly this time—as if afraid that someone might yell "hold it"—he pressed the next battle-short switch.

And more firing groups exploded, setting off a string of false sunsets. Bubble after bubble rose and disappeared as if the ocean were water boiling inside a gigantic caldron.

In a spectacular, yet frightening way, the symmetry of the flashes, the formation and disappearance of the bubbles, the ever-changing color of the sky and rippling of the waves did have a sort of grim, choreographed beauty—an infernal beauty.

And the Hull?

It, too, seemed glorious in its disappearance. The quivers and quakes were like the offensive jabs of a brave bull about to die.

"It's all over, Cliff," Adams said, slumping on the seat.

Cliff sighed gustily, nodding. Suddenly the day's reality had become a fable.

"You took a hell of a chance," Adams said with a half smile.

Cliff nodded.

Over two hours had passed since he took that chance. But many more hours would pass before he would actually believe what he had done.

It was partly overcast when the Orion began hugging the northeast coast, and the sky went through a dazzling color metamorphosis, as though showing what it could do.

Down below was Augusta. Its roads, single homes, and bridges had dissolved into a flat expansion of blue-tinted snow. Gone were the familiar weblike patterns of roads, the twinkle of taillights, the fluorescent glow of downtown. In the twilight of early evening, the only remaining landmarks were Augusta's few high-rise buildings. They stood like tombstones in a snowy seventeenth-century cemetery.

Then there was a thud through the Orion, and the landing-gear doors opened at last.

Next day, just before noon, inside the mobile van of the National Climate Analysis Center, Kronin nodded excitedly at the NOAA-9 satellite photograph. The path in the ice once created by the J Current was no longer visible.

Looking over his shoulders were the president, Roscoe, Cliff, Wimbly, Scott and Adams. Kronin stood up, reached for another photograph taken the day before, and gave both of them to the president, who compared them. "Man has finally done something about the weather," he said with a big smile.

"Yes, he has, and he isn't just part of the landscape anymore, I'm afraid," Cliff said. "He is now the landscaper, Mr. President, and something must be done about man's new and dangerous role."

EPILOGUE

The news that man could manipulate the weather—frightening for many—was big news.

Appearing simultaneously on Eurovision and the major TV networks, the president of the United States and the president of the Russian Federation revealed how they had collaborated to stop glaciation and announced that they would meet to lay the groundwork for a treaty on the remaining threat to humanity, the long-range nuclear missiles.

By June of the following year, 75 percent of the American evacuees were home. Government loans and grants helped them return to their normal routine. Losses due to the breakdown of socio-systems such as communications and transportation were in the billions, as were those due to looting.

Cliff's life began to return to normal. He read, wrote, and took long walks with Pam on the beaches of Martha's Vineyard, where they had moved after their wedding. Twice a week "the shaper of nature," as the *New York Times* called him, flew to New York to work on a ban on all types of weather modifications and to represent the United States at the conferences on an international policy for weather resources held at the United Nations.

He often thought of Fritz, whose diary and some poems Felton had found on the *Knorr*, and which Cliff was editing for publication.

Roscoe had retired from government service to become a highly paid management consultant.

Gallego was lecturing on the peaceful use of nuclear energy at the University of Chicago; Kronin had gone back to teaching at M.I.T., and Scott had become president of Virtual Reality Imaging, Inc. Adams was living on a remodeled boathouse. Charles Moran, of Sunlife, had disappeared and had probably been executed.

It was breezy on the island when a reporter for *Time* visited Cliff.

"What I've learned is that if something can be used, it will be used," Cliff said to him. "Look at the history of the nuclear bomb. It was built and dropped on Nagasaki, Hiroshima, the atolls of the Pacific, and most recently we have exploded many of them in the North Atlantic."

He frowned with alarm. "And with modifiers in the hands of every nation on earth, because they are more the product of brains than wealth, you can imagine the danger they pose." He paused. "We were lucky this time. We may not be so lucky next time we try to modify the weather."

The reporter nodded. "And in quoting you," he asked, "what one statement would you say best describes your feelings?"

Cliff considered. "That man must put an end to CLIMODs, or they may put an end to man." He squinted and looked out on the Atlantic.

There, somewhere, was the ghost of the *Dokholov*.

Nobody had wanted her. The ship had absorbed too much radiation.

As far as the crew . . . well, any attempt at rescuing them

was considered suicidal. The crew members were beyond the reach of medicine, experts had said.

So she still drifts to the winds, this twentieth-century reincarnation of the *Flying Dutchman*.

AFTERWORD

In 1972 and again in 1977, the United States, the Soviet Union, and twenty-nine other countries met in Geneva to sign an agreement banning the use of weather modifiers for military purposes.

The agreement did not include provisions for a voluntary system of on-site inspections, nor did it prohibit the use of weather modifiers for other purposes.

—— About the Author ——

Born in Italy, Ubaldo DiBenedetto, who is writing as Kyle Donner, was a U.S. Army meteorologist during the Korean War. On October 12, 1976, in Mexico City, he was awarded the José Vasconcelos Prize for literature. He is Professor of Foreign Languages at Harvard University School of Continuing Education, and lives south of Boston.

437